Edwin Pallander

Across the Zodiac

A Story of Adventure

Edwin Pallander

Across the Zodiac
A Story of Adventure

ISBN/EAN: 9783337255695

Printed in Europe, USA, Canada, Australia, Japan

Cover: Foto ©Andreas Hilbeck / pixelio.de

More available books at **www.hansebooks.com**

ACROSS THE ZODIAC

A Story of Adventure

BY

EDWIN PALLANDER

WITH A FRONTISPIECE

London

DIGBY, LONG & CO., PUBLISHERS

18 Bouverie Street, Fleet Street, E.C.

CONTENTS

ACROSS THE ZODIAC

CHAPTER I

A NOVEL SPECIES OF STAR

THE year 188— was in many ways noteworthy to astronomers.

Not to make mention of Schiaparelli's indefatigable researches on the surface geography and physical conditions of the earth's sister-planet Mars, which resulted in the publication of those fine charts destined to immortalise the Italian observer's name—not to speak of the learned labours of Secchi, and the ponderous volumes of printed matter which Monsieur Flammarion conferred as a heritage on our volatile next-door neighbours—not to dwell on the invaluable boon conferred on the noble science by the works of Sir Robert Ball on the sun, by the discoveries of Palisa among the minor planets, or by Struve's sage calculations concerning the nature of Saturn's mysterious rings—setting all these valuable offerings at the shrine of Urania aside for a moment, there was one topic which far outweighed the rest, one all absorbing question which deeply agitated the minds of learned and unlearned, of credulous amateurs and sceptical professors.

The details concerning the mysterious and puzzling apparition which seemed to defy both

A

telescopes and transit circles, before which the spectroscope was impotent and the theories of Newton, Laplace, Galileo, Kant, Kepler, Arago, bald and unconvincing, appeared simultaneously in the scientific and commercial periodicals of both hemispheres.   In fact, a lucky chance favoured astronomers both in France and America.   New York, Washington and Paris had been blessed with cloudless skies for some weeks past.   The month was June—an awkward month for accurate observations, owing to the disturbing influence of the heated summer atmosphere, but certainly propitious as far as absence of cloud was concerned.   The heavens were unveiled to the curious eyes of French and American *savants*, and a score of giant equatorials eagerly scanned the dark abyss in hopes of wresting from Nature some more of those jewelled secrets which she guards so jealously in her casket.   On the night of the 15th, one of the humbler luminaries of the *Observatoire Nationale* was engaged in making some observations on the occultation of stars behind the moon, when his attention was drawn to a new object which had entered the field of the telescope, and was deliberately travelling across the silver disc of the earth's satellite in a direction, as far as the observer could judge during his first painful five-minute scrutiny, nearly parallel to the plane of the ecliptic.

A long, narrow body, cylindrical in shape and opaque in texture, was hovering between the twin peaks of the Hersynian Mountains, proceeding gradually across the moon's surface in the direction of Mount Euler.

The astronomer rubbed his eyes and called an assistant.   An examination of the outer lenses showed that the apparition was due to no dust no the surface of the glasses.   No insect could possibly have got into the instrument, nor would any insect, of known species, crawl with such accurate and methodical regularity. The oblong shape of the disturbing visitor utterly precluded the possibility of its being a satellite of any sort, kind or description.

Celestial bodies are, in fact, always spherical. The rotating movement to which they are subjected assures obedience to this natural law. Slight differences of diameter between the poles and the equator, occasioned by centrifugal force, are all that can be counted upon. Decidedly, the theory of a new and undiscovered celestial body was untenable.

What was it then? A freak of optics? a trail of vapour? the debris of a vanished aerolite?

This last hypothesis seemed the most reasonable of the lot. Vagrant comets traversing space are as liable to accidents of this kind as express trains. A thousand influences may be at work to produce a breaking up of their constituent parts. Heat, cold, an explosion of mephitic gases, the counter-attraction of two wandering stars, the shock occasioned by the chance *rencontre* with a sister aerolite. All these things may tend to the dis-memberment of the solid shell.

To calculate the elements, the density, atomic weight and specific gravity of this body would be a lengthy and delicate operation. The eye-piece of the great equatorial was for an hour monopolised by a crowd of excited, gesticulating *savants*, pro-pounding questions, offering theories, contradicting each other and being in their turn contradicted.

Here the ruling head of the observatory stepped in. A lynx-eyed old mathematician in a frieze coat, a battered felt hat and voluminous neck-tie.

At his suggestion the place was cleared and some observations were taken.

The body was evidently a large one. Seen through the twenty-six inch equatorial, its length equalled, or seemed to equal, the diameter of the crater of Tycho. This, if it were travelling actually across the surface of the moon, would give it a length of eighty-seven kilometres or so.

On the other hand, it might be merely floating in the terrestrial atmosphere—a disenchanting fact which might bring its length down to a paltry hundred feet, or even less.

This theory, fortunately for the dignity of the apparition, was instantly rejected. The force of gravitation on the earth and for two hundred miles round it, is such that no body can keep up its position as satellite unless it moves with a speed of at least several hundred yards a second. Now, such a speed would, if the strange body were really only circling at such a moderate distance, cause it to traverse the entire lunar disc in a few minutes, or less. During an hour's careful watching, the long black line was noted to have moved regularly across the landscape, from the peaks of Mount Hersynian to a position some hundred and fifty miles south of Mount Aristarchus. Would it continue its even journey, or swerve off in a curve across the lunar Carpathians or across the Sea of Rain? No. It held steadily on its course, and defied all attempts to convict it of any irregularity.

Modern astronomers are hardly the people to allow grass to grow under their feet, and important discoveries rarely remain secret even for a few hours.

A telephone connected the Paris Observatory with the observatories of Rome, Madrid, Lisbon, Berlin and Kiev, and the news spread like wildfire. A message despatched to Greenwich resulted in disappointment. England, on whose territory the sun is never supposed to set, and in whose capital city the orb of day hardly ever rises, was enveloped in a bank of damp, drizzling cloud, which allowed not even the faintest vestige of a moon to be seen. Greenwich would clearly for once in a way not mingle its voice in the matter.

But if England was 'out of it,' America was not.

Within two hours of the first appearance of the strange phenomenon, a telegram was received from Washington, apprising the director of the French Observatory that he was not the only interested party. Owing to the difference in longitude, Washington being some five hours behind Paris in time, the moon's new satellite would, weather permitting, be at the disposition of the worthy Yankee star-gazers long after it had been chased out of existence for the Europeans by the rising sun. After all, what was to prevent the phenomenon being followed systematically through the telescopes of a hundred observatories? Nothing— if only the moon was visible.

Communication was therefore immediately opened with San Francisco, Pekin, Calcutta, Bombay, Constantinople, Cairo and Algiers. A thousand observers would set to work, and it must be a remarkably smart aerolite to slip through their fingers.

Towards 2 a.m. a new development presented itself to the Parisian *savants*. The long, black object, which was then about to cross the lunar Apennines, had increased in size.

The learned Monsieur M——, who was officiating at the eye-piece of the vast equatorial, at first refused to believe his eyes. By means of an ingeniously - designed photographic apparatus, a negative was taken and compared with a similar one, obtained at the first appearance of the strange satellite. Doubt was no longer possible. The size of the object had increased by one-fourth during the last three hours.

This immediately toppled over the idea of its being a satellite of either the moon or the earth. It must be a meteorite, and a meteorite of considerable size. Nor was that all. It was directing its course towards the earth, and would probably fall on its surface within twenty-four hours. Such occurrences are frequent in all parts of the globe, and rarely formidable.

The dense layer of atmosphere surrounding our planet is, thanks to the resistance it offers to any penetrating body, an effectual safeguard against meteors, stray comets, aerolites and star - dust generally. The enormous rates of speed with which celestial bodies of all kinds travel are well known—speeds so high as to entirely preclude the possibility of their penetrating the atmospheric couch to any depth. The friction they undergo while passing through the outer layers is sufficient, in most cases, to melt them instantaneously, and a rain of shooting stars is all that remains of the audacious wanderer. The learned Frenchmen shrugged their shoulders. Some quiet hamlet in Italy or Switzerland would have a display of fireworks gratis—that was all.

Next morning the daily papers announced a brilliant shower of meteorites near Ravenna, the observations taken in Paris and New York were compared ; 'it's all over—the fuss was for nothing,' was the general opinion.

One man, however, chose to differ. This was the head astronomer of the United States Observatory at Washington. He certainly had sense enough to keep his opinion to himself, but still— cylindrical meteorites closely resembling a torpedo boat in shape are not seen floating across the moon's disc every day. The worthy man collected his papers, his photographs, his chronometrical data, shut them securely up in his bureau, and waited.

For some months all went on serenely, and the solar system reposed, figuratively speaking, in calm and regular tranquillity. Then an incident happened which once more made the pulses of star-gazers beat in double-quick time.

This incident was none other than a second appearance of the mysterious aerolite, which crossed unceremoniously the field of an English telescope on the night of the seventeenth of August between the hours of 10 and 11 p.m.

Nor was this all.

The extraordinary apparition did not, as on the occasion of its first appearance, merely content itself with floating peacefully through the dark void of night. It shone, it threw out beams of light, leaving a long luminous trail in its wake, like the trail of a high-speed comet.

Suddenly, while the observer was attentively following its movements, the beam of light was observed to shift its position in a most erratic manner. It wavered, first up, then down, then disappeared altogether for some time. At the end of half-an-hour it again became visible. This time it was the light only, minus the luminous tail. It mounted steadily up through the dark ocean of space, and at length disappeared entirely at a point almost vertically above the head of the observer. Clearly it was no meteor. Meteors do not habitually flee the earth, they are attracted by it. What it resembled most of all was a rocket—but what manner of rocket!

The skill of modern pyrotechnists is well known, but what master of the science would undertake to construct such an aerial prodigy? The duration

of an ordinary rocket's flight is from ten to thirty
seconds. This one had flaunted its magnificence
during at least half-an-hour. Besides, how about
the shifting beam of light? Rockets do not change
the position and angle of their tail at a moment's
notice, nor, indeed, do they continue to ascend
vertically after their trail of sparks ceases to glow.

It was a meteorite, evidently, and a meteorite of
the most unaccountable peculiarities.

The American astronomers were telegraphed to.
They had seen nothing—nor indeed was it likely
that they could have seen anything. A star passing within a paltry few thousand miles of Greenwich
would be wholly invisible to the Columbians, and
the Greenwich observers had concluded, from the
speed and behaviour of the stranger, that it could
not have been navigating the heavens at a very
much greater distance.

The details of this were given to the public,
of course, in the columns of those journalistic
colossi, the *Standard*, the *Daily Telegraph* and the
Illustrated London News. It is marvellous how
indifferent the average Englishman is to the
prodigies which Nature performs around him in
the solar system. Within a week of the occurrence the whole affair was forgotten, and the very
astronomer who had sighted the phenomenon was
ready to give the lie to his own senses and declare
himself the victim of a hallucination.

All these things I remember now clearly enough,
though at the time I was too absorbed in other
matters to give much heed to them. In fact, I had
just been elected member of an expedition for exploring the unknown sources of the Brahmapootra
and the northern slopes of the Himalaya Mountains. My book on Iceland and my two volumes
of published matter respecting the recent eruption
of Krakatoa had secured this honour for me.

Yes, the 'distinguished young explorer and geologist, Henry Ralphcourt, Esq., F.R.S., A.S.T.E., etc.' had consented to confer his aid in the important matter of surveying the mysterious source of the great sister of the Ganges, and in the still more important matter (as far as the safety of the expedition was concerned) of doctoring the Tibetan Lamas into something approaching amiability. Expeditions in Tibet were usually reputed to end in only two ways. Either the explorers were unceremoniously driven out of the country backwards, or else they were equally unceremoniously massacred. The attempt was now to be made on a somewhat larger scale than heretofore—nearly a hundred persons being deputed to take part in it, out of which sixty were well-seasoned natives armed with quick-firing rifles and cutlasses, besides the usual armament of Bibles and cheap liberty silks—emblems of a great and humane civilisation, where Mahatmas were synonymous for impostors, and the star of polyandry had not yet risen.

'You see, professor,' explained my worthy friend Hatton, whose fame had been assured since his recent return from South Africa in company with two baboons, a lion-cub and an interesting collection of Orange River molluscs. 'You see it's just as well to be on the safe side. If the Bibles don't fetch 'em, I guess *that* will.'

That was a sleek, shining nickel-plated cannon, of the kind patented by the ingenious Mr Maxim, and warranted to discharge several hundred shots a minute at least—if I remember rightly.

Ned Hatton patted the shining muzzle of the instrument affectionately with his horny hand, as a man might pat the shoulder of a friend to whose prowess he expected to owe his life in the near future.

Let me endeavour to describe Ned Hatton. A

tall, magnificently bony specimen of humanity, with a complexion slightly sallowed by exposure to tropical suns, and piercing, deep-set eyes, which gave a certain expression of genius, an expression which was the making of him, from an artistic point of view, and served to convert him from a lanky, decidedly ugly son of brother Jonathan into what the French call, not incorrectly, a *beau laid.* Ned had been, as is usual with most successful explorers, thrown upon the world to shift for himself at a very early age. He had been successively, miner, gold-digger, cattle-rancher, South-sea trader, Australian sheep-farmer, and instructor in matters connected with general education to the eldest son of the King of Siam.

'The profitablest job I ever had in my life,' Ned used to remark. Then, by way of explanation, 'You see, you could swipe such a lot.'

This last was a *petite* dose of brag, for although the King of Siam was famed for the negligent way in which he was wont to leave jewelled sabres, pearl necklaces, golden spittoons, etc., lying around 'kinder promiscuous,' although guards were scarce in the royal palace and policemen unknown, Ned Hatton was the soul of honesty, and precious gems, even when left by the wayside, had no attraction for him. In addition to these virtues, he was singularly courteous, and invariably addressed me respectfully as 'professor' (my services as lecturer on geology and palaeontology at the University of Cambridge had secured honourable possession of the title for me some years before)—he had seen too much during his life not to know the value of learning and was always inclined to rather over-estimate the worth of a *savant* than otherwise. This last peculiarity, it must be confessed, was the jewel in Ned's crown, for men of great and purely practical experience are as a rule given to sneering at theoretical scientists, whom they are somewhat too prone to regard as visionary dreamers. Exceptions prove the rule. Ned Hatton was certainly a very strong exception.

Our departure for India had been fixed. We were to weigh anchor on the fifteenth of September. It was now nearly a month since anything had been heard of the curious astronomical phenomenon which had puzzled people in June and August. The question seemed buried for good, when, on a certain dark night, either the tenth or eleventh of the month, I am not sure which, an incident happened which served to bring it forward once more. Instead of being a merely telescopic curiosity, however, the phenomenon assumed seriously alarming proportions. From an inoffensive speck of black, gliding noiselessly across the vault of heaven, it became a rushing, roaring cometary demon, large enough and noisy enough to frighten half-a-dozen superstitious French villages out of their wits, and set a hundred newspapers into unscientific and unsystematic activity.

On the evening when the prodigy occurred, the steam yawl, *Fleur de Lys*, was proceeding leisurely along the coast of Brittany, some ten miles west of St Malo. The sea was enveloped in a thick mantle of fog, a fact that rendered it necessary to proceed at half speed, sounding the whistle loudly at intervals of thirty seconds or so. At ten o'clock, the new moon slightly whitened the mist with its rays. The *Fleur de Lys* seemed to be floating in a cloud of dense and luminous vapour.

Suddenly a clamour arose. The engine bells clanged furiously, and the triple-bladed screw churned the water astern into a lurid patch of snowy foam. Through the fog ahead loomed a gigantic shadow, rendered still more gigantic and awe-inspiring by the weird light of the veiled moon.

The efforts of the machinery being insufficient to stop her, the *Fleur de Lys* crashed unceremoniously into the side of the ominous-looking stranger, snapping her bowsprit off sharply, and considerably damaging her prow and figure-head. The injuries not being sufficiently grave to retard her progress, the *Fleur de Lys* reached St Malo at midnight, and the news of her *rencontre* spread like wildfire through the quiet town.

What was the vessel?

The captain of the *Fleur de Lys* could not say. She was unlike anything he had ever seen, and had appeared to him to be made of frosted silver. She had made no sign, either by bell or whistle. There seemed to be no life stirring on board of her, no lights, no watch, no helmsman.

Had the *Fleur de Lys* damaged her?

That was hardly likely. From the way in which the yawl rebounded after the shock, it looked as though she had struck a hard, impenetrable body of solid armour-plate, rather than a yielding wall of planks.

What was her length?

It was impossible to guess at her length, even remotely. The *Fleur de Lys* had drifted away almost immediately, and the stranger ship was lost in the fog before she could be attentively scrutinised.

The affair was not sufficiently remarkble, however, to prevent the honest maritime population of St Malo from sleeping soundly. Within two or three hours of his landing, even the captain of the damaged *Fleur de Lys* was snoring loudly beneath his voluminous feather bed.

Towards four in the morning everyone awoke with a start. The cloaked and hooded watchmen,

silently pacing the streets, paused to cross themselves devoutly; the sailors in the harbour sprang
to their feet, then fell on their knees, quaking with
superstitious fear.

Across the dark sky, slightly yellowed in the
east by the bars of approaching sunrise, a huge
shadow, black and terrible, was dashing with a
roar like muffled thunder. A fiery tail, some miles
in length apparently, swept along the sky in the
track of the monster, now striking the clouds, now
falling on the sea, wavering hither and thither like
a gigantic arm of fire in act of striking.

The prodigy did not last long. The speed of
the monster was such that within a minute of its
startling appearance it had disappeared among
the southern clouds, its fiery tail being visible
for some minutes later.

St Malo was not the only town favoured by this
supernatural sight. In case there might have been
any doubt as to the authenticity of the flying
demon, news was received and accounts of the
phenomenon collected from the towns of Rennes,
Vitry, Angers, Sammer, Chatellerault, Poitiers,
Lussac and Limoges, this last-named one being
also the last place where the giant meteor had
been seen.

The event caused a considerable commotion, in
the scientific world as well as the journalistic.
The consumption of ink during the following week
must have been something fabulous. Everyone
had an opinion, and everyone hastened to offer it.

In the midst of the confusing flood of nonsense
which poured in from all sides as from a bursting reservoir, the learned members of the Paris
Observatory managed to collect some really satisfactory data.

The course of the meteor had been S.S.E. Its
speed must have been considerable, as within the

space of a brief quarter-of-an-hour it had been observed at over fifty points, along a line nearly two hundred miles in length. This meant a rapidity of some eight hundred miles per hour. At that rate this noisy visitant from other worlds would take only three hours to go from London to New York, five hours to go from London to San Francisco, eight to go from Paris to Pekin, etc.

Another significant fact, eminently calculated to set *savants* at loggerheads with each other, was that the meteor, which had passed comparatively close to the town of St Malo, had gradually risen higher and higher as it proceeded southwards, till, as the citizens of Limoges reported, it had merely appeared as a strip of light far above the clouds before vanishing completely into space, which it did within sight of the principal Limousin observers, at exactly twenty-six minutes past four. Incredible as it was, the aerolitic marvel had travelled *away* from the earth instead of towards it. This is of course an unheard of thing in the annals of what, for want of a better word, we might call meteorology. Wandering celestial bodies fall on the earth because attracted by it, and for no other reason.

The newspaper controversy waxed hot and furious.

Was it a rocket, a flying machine, a shooting star, or (happy inspiration of a daring contributor) a stone hurled from the crater of some distant volcano? A column of figures followed, proving conclusively that stones *do* occasionally fly from the fiery mouths of volcanoes in action, and fly to a considerable distance, too, as Sir W. Hamilton proved by the examination of stones thrown from the crater of Sicilian Etna.

This was all very well. No doubt such an occurrence was quite within the range of possibilities. Unfortunately, there was one factor wanting to make the explanation plausible. It was an important one—the volcano.

If theorising could explain the mystery, it would not remain a mystery long. The sun of volcanic debris having abruptly set, astronomy once more came forward. A popular lecturer on cosmical phenomena suggested that a meteor *might* just skirt the terrestrial atmosphere without being attracted by our planet — if its velocity were sufficient, just as a boat may safely cross dangerous rapids if propelled at a high speed. What, demanded the *Revue des Deux Mondes* sarcastically, *was* the speed necessary to save a meteor from ignominiously alighting on our globe? About twenty thousand miles an hour was the answer.

This finished the popular lecturer. No body, of any known material, could withstand, at such a rate, the impact of our atmosphere. Even a bomb of pure platinum, the most infusible substance yet discovered, must be instantly vaporised —clearly the acrolite theory did not count for much.

Was it a flying machine, with an electrical search-light attached?

It was not probable. Such machines had never been heard of yet, and even granting that aerial locomotion was a certainty, by what mechanical means could a flying machine pretend to reach a speed of eight hundred miles per hour. Figures were not wanting to show that no known material, however great its strength, could stand a strain that must inevitably wreck engines of any known pattern. No screw could turn with such rapidity, no wings beat the air with sufficient violence—no, the aerostat theory was likewise untenable.

From among the princes of science, the formidable meteor was gradually but surely banished. Learned men are rarely apt to take an interest in cosmic phenomena which they themselves have not witnessed. The question was made the subject of furious controversy during a period of six weeks or so, then it dwindled and died a solitary death among the archives of the *Bibliotheque Nationale* and the British Museum Library.

Though neglected by the learned, it was taken up by the populace. It rapidly became the fashion. 'Meteor' hats and 'aerolite' cigar-holders were the rage. A popular publisher brought out a 'comet' edition of Balzac's novels, and spectacular dramas representing aerial disasters in all their sinister variety took transitory possession of the stage Dust and ashes are the two final states of everything mundane, and the strange freak, that had been the terror of so many Breton sailors, was in its turn forgotten, as a riddle to be solved when the sea gives up its dead, not before.

Owing to various causes, the departure of our Tibet expedition was postponed, and I just lingered long enough in Europe to witness the end of the excitement. On the twenty-third morning of December, we weighed anchor, and with a vague presentiment of future glory filling my breast, I marked the low, sandy promontory of Southampton water disappearing in the grey sea-mist. Ned Hatton, leaning with his back against the railing, indifferent alike to scenery and sentiment, whistled softly to himself.

Come sunshine, come storm, we had the sources of the Brahmapootra in our mind's eye. They were a noble goal to aim at, and quite sufficient for any man.

———

CHAPTER II

VÆ VICTIS!

IT was certainly a fine thing to be so full of hope.

Unfulfilled ambition is perhaps the most awful thing on earth—except spurned love, of which I can honestly say I know nothing, praise be to Allah. Of our entire expedition, only seven weary men dragged themselves back into Assam, across those cruel, sun-scorched mountains. Ned Hatton and myself were amongst the number.

A gallant start up the river, a swamp-ridden, fever-laden camp, a score of rascally Tibetan spies, a cold reception in Lhassa, an imaginary insult offered to the Dali Lama, a midnight massacre and a precipitate flight through forests of thorn and tangle, over glacier and snow-blocked pass, under falling rocks and withered pine branches. The scenes of our misery passed rapidly through my head in a disorderly jumble, like pictures in a phantasmagoria, or scenes in a play.

At least I might have died with the rest of our poor fellows. I, too, might have found a resting-place beneath the shadow of those glorious mountains, with their eternal canopy of snow, with their sunlit peaks dreaming in the blue, far removed from petty mortal cares and sufferings.

No such luck was mine, however. The voyage home partially restored my health, broken by typhoid and bilious fevers, into something like its normal condition. Whether it was the foggy London air, or the taint of fever that still hung about my system, or the effects of a Himalayan sunstroke, I do not know. What I *do* know, however, is that three weeks after my arrival in London

B

saw me once more prostrate—this time with brain fever.

Hot, shooting pains in the head, visions of heavenly sunset clouds, dwindling down into the cold, uninteresting patterns adorning the wallpaper, glimpses of snowy horrors, needles of ice penetrating my flesh, and feverish falls down endless rocky chasms. Then a face seemed to stare through the darkness, and the yellow glare of a lamp shone in my eyes.

' I think he'll pull through now all right. How do you feel, sir ? '

' Oh, hideously,' was the only possible answer.

Drowsiness overtook me and I slept. With the first beams of the sun my misery began again. I was truly a wretched failure. All my plans, all my hopes had come to nothing. Never in this life would I follow in the track of the mighty pioneers of geography. I was disgraced and dishonoured.

' Here, drink this,' said someone.

It was a small dose of laudanum, but it tasted sweet as nectar. Ned, dear, good honest Ned, his dark flashing eyes suffused with pity, was bending over me.

' How are you, old boy ? ' he continued. ' Have the Mahatmas ceased to haunt you ? D—d rogues all of them. Do you remember that old white-robed villain who accused me of stealing his praying-wheel ? I'd like to get my hands on him, that's all. Drink the stuff up. It'll make you go to sleep, and it's not strong enough to hurt a child. You must cultivate Morpheus for all you're worth, and mind—no more falling down precipices. I guess you're about at the bottom of Gaurisankar by this.'

I smiled feebly and fell back among the white pillows. I was too miserable to answer. One idea ever recurring to my tortured mind took visible form, looming ominously through the fog of my half-awakened senses. On the table near my bed stood a tiny black bottle. Ned gave me a compassionate glance, then turned away—to empty his pipe, I think.

The idea became overwhelming. I feebly stretched out my hand for the bottle and put it to my lips. It was corked, but I tore out the cork with my teeth, and the bitter, sweet taste of the deadly nectar made my brain swim delightfully.

A cry sounded in my ears, and the phial of poison rolled away across the floor. Ned's face was ashy.

'None of that, Hal! for God's sake none of that,' he exclaimed, with a sort of sob. 'I swear, Hal, I'll put you in a strait-jacket if you don't quit this foolery. Bite on the bullet, man! You never *used* to be a coward!'

His words awakened, even in my half-paralysed condition, a vague sense of shame. I moaned softly, and fell asleep with his reproaches ringing in my ears like a fugitive lullaby.

When I awoke the room was deserted. It was evening, and the drawn blinds of the window were coloured crimson, I suppose, by the setting sun. Despite a giddy feeling in my head, my brain was singularly clear.

'It's evident that I've had a narrow squeak' thought I. Then I recollected the attempt I had made at committing suicide, and felt rather foolish. On trying to raise myself into an upright posture, I failed dismally, from excessive weakness, and was forced to lie back ignominiously. At least I could think; and I did that pretty energetically.

'After all,' I reflected, 'London is not the only place in the world where a man can make and mar his name. I wish the deuce I could turn my back on it for good. Perhaps if I were to change my home and emigrate to the South Sea Islands, they'd think more of me there. Who knows? Perhaps I'd be considered a genius in Tahiti or Samoa. In England, I suppose, I'm destined to be a nobody. Anyway I've had the devil's own luck, and my health is wrecked for life.'

These were gloomy reflections for a young man of twenty-seven, but then I never was an optimist, and all the Schopenhauerian side of my nature came out in that darkened sick-room.

Next morning I was able to sit up in bed and drink some Liebig. Ned Hatton, pipe in mouth, lounged in a cane-chair hard by, and indulged to the fullest extent in a favourite trick of his, the solace of his meditative moods, viz., giving advice.

'You see,' he said in a patronising tone, as though he were lecturing a wayward pupil, 'you're really a darned sight too young to take on in this fashion. What have you lost by this business?'

'Money,' I replied sulkily, 'and the only chance of making a name for myself that's likely to present itself for many a long day.'

'How much did you sink in the concern?' he asked carelessly.

'Nearly two thousand,' I answered gloomily, 'the result of six years' hard work. Nelthorpe and myself blew it on guns and Bibles. What I'm going to do now, the devil only knows.'

'You'll fall to lecturing again.'

'Where?'

'At Cambridge, I suppose.'

'They've got a new man at Cambridge, a gold-medallist in every university on the face of the globe. They're not likely to kick him out in order to give me another show. He's a German, of course.'

'Hustlers — those Germans,' said Ned, reflectively, biting the horn mouthpiece of his briar.

'Yes—and devilish clever in specialising too,'
I put in. 'A German 'll stick at one little point,
for nearly a century if necessary. There's no
tiring them.'

'Why don't you specialise?'

'Nothing I'd like better—if you'll kindly give
me a hint as to what subject you intend my
taking up.'

'A geographical one—correcting the maps of
the lesser-known countries.'

I tossed about uneasily.

'Great Heavens! man, haven't I just finished
making a failure of *one* expedition?'

'That wasn't your fault.'

'Tropical climates don't agree with me.'

'Nobody wants you to have anything to do
with them.'

'Ah! so you propose an Arctic journey?'

'Not exactly that, but—'

'Oh, yes, I know,' I interrupted feverishly, 'there's
the White Sea, the Kara Sea, the coast of Nova
Zembla and the unknown continents north of
Baffin's Bay. It's a magnificent field for re-
search, and I believe the maps of those countries
err by several degrees. My dear fellow, I assure
you—'

'Let me speak,' he interrupted coldly, 'it's not
necessary for you to explore either the White
Sea, the Kara Sea, the coasts of Nova Zembla
or Greenland. There are other countries, more
within reach, that you'll find it quite worth your
while to travel over with a theodolite. Have you
ever thought of Iceland?'

'No,' I answered pettishly, 'I'm not such a fool.
The Swedish Geographical Society have marked
down every lava-flow during the last half-century
nearly.'

'On the contrary, there are certain portions—

the Vatna Joküll, for example—which have rarely been crossed. And the society you name is about to issue a new map.'

'How do you know that?'

'Because I read it in the *Standard* yesterday morning. Some fellow with a long name is deputed to survey a part of the island. He's going to cross the Vatna Joküll in particular—horses and sledges are no good it appears. He's going to do it in a balloon.'

The old fire suddenly rekindled itself in my breast.

'Good Lord!' I exclaimed, 'what wouldn't I give to be able to do it too.'

Ned Hatton smiled.

'What would you say,' he drawled, 'if the professor were to ask us both to join his party?'

'Say?' I echoed, 'why, I should say we, too, were about the luckiest fellows in the solar system.'

'Well — that's about what we are, I reckon,' answered Ned, deliberately, then— 'just cast your eye over that!'

He flung a letter on the bed. I opened it tremblingly and read as follows :—

'Professor Ralphcourt.

'SIR,—'You have possibly heard of my coming expedition to Iceland. As my right-hand man, Professor Eulenberg, has, for reasons of his own, chosen to desert me in order to accept the post of lecturer at Cambridge, I find myself forced to seek aid elsewhere. I have heard of you in connection with the Tibet expedition. You have had great misfortune, but may yet live to retrieve your luck. Your friend, Mr Hatton, furnished me with some details about you the other day, and I have come to the conclusion you are just the man we want.

If you will kindly favour me with a call at my hôtel, perhaps we shall be able to make some arrangement to our mutual advantage. I shall expect to hear from you, at least, within the next few days.—Believe me, sir, yours sincerely,

'NORDENROTHER.'

HOTEL LANGHAM, *Friday.*

'Nordenrother!' I exclaimed, 'why that's the fellow who explored the high Andes and the Cordilleras three years ago. He's a great man. Ned—I can hardly believe it's true. Luck doesn't turn in that way nowadays. No—it's my fate to remain tied to this beastly city till the end of my days, doing lecturing work at the rate of a hundred and fifty a year.'

'We'll see about that!' replied my companion, sagely.

CHAPTER III

INTO THE DESERT

NED'S wisdom, prophetic or otherwise, was rarely at fault. Within a fortnight of my recovery we were on the sea, bound for Reikjavik.

Professor Nordenrother was certainly an admirable specimen of the modern *savant*. Cool, calculating, courageous, exact as a chronometer and totally indifferent to either hunger, thirst or physical perils—he was the ideal man for a dangerous journey across the icebound northern wastes or through the torrid southern plains.

In stature he was rather tall, and, like most energetic men, inclined to leanness. A phren-

ologist, examining his head, would have been
surprised as much at the entire absence of those
bumps which betoken domestic virtues and vices
as at the extraordinary development of the sections
appertaining to calculation, reflection, foresight and
argument.   His nose (a fact which is taken by
many people to signify genius) was large and
hooked—his religion, which *selon les apparences*
ought to have been Jewish, was conspicuous, as is
the case with many clever men, by its total absence
of definite form or dogma.   Science was his God,
and—to be open-minded, there are many worse
ones.

Was this clever man familiar with Iceland?
Undoubtedly.   He had already been sent twice
there on geographical missions, once by the
Swedish and once by the German societies.   His
life had evidently been an active one, but he bore
no traces of anxiety and exertion on his face.   He
might have been any age between thirty and sixty,
but I believe his actual age was forty-two, the fact
being confided to me confidentially one day over
a tumbler of whisky and soda by the captain of
the *Fünen*—a grizzled old sea-lion who adored the
professor nearly as much as he did his own tar-
stained, weather-beaten hulk of a ship.

The whole of our scientific force really consisted
of Nordenrother, Ned Hatton and myself.   Not
that we were expected to perform the difficult
journey unaided—far from it.

A relay of fifty picked Icelanders was to meet
us at Reikjavik, and an extra dozen were sent on
in advance to Ingolfshöfdi and Husavik, the fishing
village which lies nearest the mouth of the Joküllsa
River, on the northern coast of the island.

Everything had been planned, everything foreseen.   From the professor's balloon, packed securely
in its rubber-lined case, and lashed firmly down

under a thick tarpaulin on the after-deck, to the spare shoes for the mules and the metal-soled boots for walking over hot volcanic ashes—from the beginning it was evident that business was meant.

On the morning of the 23d we sighted land—a misty, indistinct line of cloud to the north-east. The wind was blowing sharply, and I shivered under my sou'-wester. Ned, on my left, was vainly trying to smoke his pipe in the teeth of the gale.

'Well, Ned, this is rather different to our last campaign.'

'Yes, professor, we run rather more chance of being frozen than baked, I think.'

'Unless we fall into a volcano, like Empedocles,' I put in, laughing; 'there are enough of *them* about, in all conscience. We ought to be able to see the peak of Snaefell already. If it wasn't for this confounded fog we'd have a better view.'

'I wonder what our boss 'll think of it if this sort of weather continues,' said my friend, shaking the mixture of rain and spray from his frieze cape, this damp is death to philosophical instruments, and we've got enough with us to stock all the opticians in Broadway.'

I was silent. No doubt the 'boss' had prepared against this mishap. Some sailors of the *Fünen* appeared, to make preparations for landing, I suppose. Ned turned to converse with them, leaving me staring blankly out over the wilderness of green sea and misty distance. Some fishing-smacks passed us, enveloped in a shower of blinding spray. Through the fog a vague shadow loomed faintly, and the crash of billows struck my ear.

'Skagi Head,' said someone behind me. I turned and saw Professor Nordenrother. 'A volcanic promontory, hollowed by the action of the waves,' continued he. 'Iceland is a country torn by fire and water. You will find it a most interesting geological study, sir.'

'I believe you, professor. The number of active volcanoes in this small island is, I believe, computed as high as twenty or thirty.'

'Nearly a hundred, sir, if you count all the lesser-known central ones,' answered the professor 'There, that is Snaefell.'

A white summit was visible, hanging in the air above a misty base. Half-an-hour later we came in sight of Reikjavik, with its curiously-pointed roofs and gabled belfries. A few windmills were visible, their sails revolving slowly. The wind wafted odours of fish in all stages of decomposition—this was Iceland.

I have spent the greater part of to-day profitably, in examining this strange northern town, with its rows of gaily painted houses and interminable fishing nets. The women are mostly ugly enough, but their costumes are occasionally picturesque, and the long veils of muslin (faldrs) give them (from a distance) a rather graceful appearance.

There is one thing we have here — a decent hôtel. The landlord of the 'Alexandra' boasts of a billiard-room and a piano—two luxuries that I hardly expected to find in such an out-of-the-way place. Our start is fixed for to-morrow morning. I have been personally introduced to the various members of the 'picnic,' as Ned sarcastically calls it. They seem a steady, good - natured lot of fellows, though, I fear, somewhat addicted to indolence. The landlord tells me idleness flows through the veins of every genuine Icelander. This doesn't sound reassuring, but I think we'll manage to pull through nevertheless.

I shall drop writing this history in the form of a

journal. The note-book I kept my diary in has gone long since, heaven knows where—perhaps down the crater of a volcano. This being so, I must confine myself to writing my adventures in the past tense. Let me be thankful I am alive to write them at all. Six o'clock on the following morning saw us partaking amicably of whisky and water in the hotel bar-room, the genial landlord wishing us luck many times, and adding, with great candour, that he thanked his stars he was not in our shoes. His island was a fine one, to be sure, but, as far as his experience went, it was best when seen from a window or read of in the papers. Tommy Moore's opinion of Ireland—that it was a 'mighty fine country to sing about,—would, without much violence, have served to express mine host's sentiments respecting his land of ice and volcanoes.

The bulk of our luggage, tents, beds and blankets were confided to the sturdy mules. The rest—philosophical instruments mostly—thermometers, barometers, quadrants, compasses, etc.—had been carefully packed in boxes lined with indiarubber on account of the damp, and were to be transported on the shoulders of our Icelandic escort. The balloon, an important item, was divided into two packages. The car, with its accoutrements and the vast sphere of waterproof silk with its bulky and complicated network of hempen cords. Both of these articles were placed, securely corded down, in waggons of a peculiar construction, adapted for travelling along rough roads, with springs of galvanized iron and tyres of hollow indiarubber. Quite a crowd of chubby-faced islanders was assembled in the road to see us off. Reikjavik, amongst other things, possessed a university, and the portly president of the temple of learning was among the first to shake us by the hand—a process, by the way, which had to be gone through at least fifty times before we could get clear of the honest townsfolk. In the south-east a pale yellow light denoted the presence of the all-quickening sun. The atmosphere was dull and heavy, foreboding rain within twenty-four hours. Ned Hatton, hurrying about among the mules and waggons, set an example of activity and industry which the sluggish northmen utterly refused to imitate. Eight o'clock struck from the distant belfry. I turned towards the professor, who was solemnly bidding farewell to the landlord of the 'Alexandria' and his family on the hôtel steps.

'Forward!' he said.

'Forward!' echoed Ned, dealing the nearest mule a whack with the buckle end of his leather belt that made the worthy animal kick out viciously, to the eminent amusement of those enthusiastic spectators, a group of loitering Reikjavik schoolboys.

The wheels of the waggons began to revolve, and the caravan moved off amid the cheers of the onlookers.

The landscape was typical of what we were to pass through during many a long day. In the far distance, to the north, rose the snowy peaks of Snaefell. Behind us Reikjavik, with its roofs and windmills sharply defined against the cold sky, did not fail to awaken the preliminaries of home-sickness in the breasts of some of our escort. Travel, as I have already explained, is to the Icelander, of all amusements, the most inexplicable. Diminutive stone bridges led across Liliputian streams, tumbling merrily among grey blocks of lava. Occasionally a caravan of donkeys laden with dried fish and seaweed passed us with jingling bells and cracking whips. Here and there in the desolate country among the hollows and on the bleak mountain sides rose faint trails of smoke. They came from tiny springs, much valued by the

Icelanders on account of their medicinal properties, and because of the yellow patches of sulphur that surround them—a valuable source of revenue to the country, which shares the honours with eider-down, and is, moreover, far more easily collected.

For some time our march was undistinguished by any incident worth dwelling upon except when occasionally our amusement was aroused by the phlegmatic movements of some honest Icelander whose donkey had incontinently kicked his bundle off. The slowness and deliberation with which the package was picked out of the mud, the methodical dawdling necessary before it could be readjusted on the back of its unruly bearer, all served to give us much valuable insight into the character of these torpid northerners. Ned Hatton stormed at each fresh delay, I could hardly conceal my vexation, the professor alone was serene and unmoved. A beautiful sheet of water confronted us at a turn of the road. It was lake Tjörn. The volcanic rocks that fringed its sides, veined with yellow streaks of sulphur, were the resting-place of countless families of aquatic birds—seagulls, terns, wild ducks and ptarmigan. I noticed some fine specimens of grouse (*lagopus alpina*), and among the marine birds the handsome silvery gull (*larus argentatus*). Ned, the sportsman in his nature rapidly coming to the front, produced a small saloon rifle and began some ineffectual shooting. Later he exchanged the weapon for a more reasonable duck-gun, and brought down half-a-dozen golden plovers, to the delight of Herr Nordenrother, who, I believe, is a bit of a gourmand as well as a geographer. Presently we fell to conversing.

'You are a botanist professor?'

'I have studied botany as well as other subjects, sir. I have not made it a speciality. I fear there is not much to excite one's admiration here. The flora of Iceland is insignificant at best.'

A few saxifrages and ranunculuses were growing in the interstices of the rocks. I noticed also some specimens of the *Pragas octopetala* and the wild geranium—only their plants, as it was too early in the year for flowers.

We came across another interminable train of donkeys, carrying sheep s wool done up in bags of canvas. A score of women, their smiling faces bound round with coloured handkerchiefs, followed the animals, some bearing children on their shoulders, in the Scandinavian fashion, others carrying nets and fishing implements.

'Flowers,' continued the professor, as though he were lecturing before an audience of university graduates, 'are the offspring of a country. Their form, their colour, their fragrance even is determined by the nature of the soil surrounding them. To have gorgeous hues, the climate must be proportionately vigorous. Orchids and ranunculuses of the most striking loveliness expand under the ardent sun of the tropics. In our own temperate zone, the colours are more moderate and the perfumes less intense. Come as far north as this little lonely island and you meet with nothing, even in the heat of summer, but a few pale saxifrages and straggling daisies.'

'And men, professor—how about them?'

'Men, sir, are as directly the produce of a country as flowers. Their intellect, their strength, their reasoning powers are in direct relationship to their surroundings—just as much in fact as the hues and perfumes of flowers are.'

'Nevertheless, professor,' I objected mildly, 'according to your theory, the most striking human existencies ought to flourish at the equator, whereas—'

'Man's power,' interrupted Herr Nordenrother, 'lay formerly in his muscles. Its total aggregate has not diminished now, but its seat of activity has changed. It is the brain, not the arms, which must now be taken as the principal factor in man's triumphs over Nature—and the most vigorous brains certainly belong to the people of the temperate zone. No doubt this gain is accompanied by a certain loss in bodily vigour, but then, as machines largely take the place of manual labour in any advanced community, the deficiency is hardly felt.'

'Do you think then, professor, that we are really less perfect physically than formerly?' I asked.

'I am afraid I am obliged to think so,' answered the professor, smiling. 'When and where did our modern European warrior perform the prodigies related in connection with the victorious legions of Cæsar, Sennacherib, Hannibal, Scipio, Ramses, and the rest of the great shadowy existencies who were once the terror of the world? No—we have advanced mentally, but the temperate zone has been fatal to our bodily energies.'

'Then what is to be done?'

'Done? Nothing that I know of, sir, unless some kindly astronomical catastrophe changes the obliquity of the ecliptic, and furnishes humanity with a climate equally favourable to mental and bodily development.'

I nodded. The professor spoke with conviction, like a man who has, after many years' labour, succeeded in solving an important problem. Ned Hatton, gun in hand, was still banging away industriously at the birds. I looked out suspiciously over the lonely country streaked with white patches of snow and asked myself whether Herr Nordenrother had not been unwise in starting so

early in the year. Suppose the weather changed
to snow in grim earnest. We should be caught
with a vengeance. And the famous balloon?
Wasn't it a mad scheme, a crazy attempt only
worthy of some delirious enthusiast? Surely the
professor was not in earnest. We were to traverse
Iceland—very good. We were to explore the
sources of the mysterious Joküllsa—good again.
As for the balloon expedition, apparently it was a
pure piece of scientific bravado. What good
could it do us to cross the Vatna Joküll at a
height of several thousand feet? We should
neither be able to measure the height of the
mountains, the diameter of the volcanic craters, or
the width of its unknown glaciers. Crossing the
Vatna Joküll on foot in March was entirely out
of the question. Then why had we started so
early? The balloon appeared in the light of an
excellent practical joke. Where and how were
we going to inflate it? Gas was completely
unknown in Ingolfshöfdi. Perhaps Herr Nordenrother would take upon himself the duty of
generating hydrogen gas for the purpose, with
broken iron and sulphuric acid. The more I
pondered over the idea, the more unreasonable
did it appear. I therefore did the best I could
under the circumstances. I held my tongue, and
contented myself with quietly awaiting develop-
ments.

At noon we halted before a grove of withered,
frost-bitten trees. Fires were kindled, and Ned
presented us with the golden plovers — rather
tough, by the way — spitted on sticks in the
African fashion. The rest of the men apparently
nourished themselves on dried fish and brandy ;
at least, that is all they seemed to have provided.
At the end of an hour we resumed our march.
The distances had evidently been accurately timed

in advance, for at sundown we reached a collection
of scattered huts, roofed with sods of turf in the
fashion of the country. Whatever merit there
may be in the Icelandic architectural style, it
cannot be said that it is conducive to comfort—
at least, from a civilised European point of view.
In one hut, about twelve feet square, we found
three families huddled, about eighteen people in
all. Ned, declining to take shelter along with
people of such ultra-sociable habits, unfurled his
small tent and enjoyed what must have been, in
spite of his ample wraps, a rather cold slumber,
especially trying to a man whose life had hitherto
been spent under the glowing sun of the Equator.

The professor and myself, wrapped in our rough
blankets, endured the pestilential atmosphere of
the hut and the unmusical howls of a healthy Icelandic baby till daybreak. In spite of my fatigue,
I hardly slept a wink. Our journey may have been
interesting, but it had its disadvantages.

CHAPTER IV

ACROSS THE VATNA JOKULL

OUR surveying operations began on the following
day. The professor had brought with him a curious
collection of maps, large and small, old and new.
The errors, or doubtful parts, were marked in red
ink. Every hill, every water-course, every lava-
flow had its share of attention. Besides the merely
topographical part of the work, Herr Nordenrother
began a series of interesting experiments on the
electrification of the atmosphere, on the variations of
the dipping needle, and on the various astronomical
peculiarities which the sky of these latitudes

C

afforded. During these latter investigations we were once or twice favoured with magnificent auroral displays. The phenomenon produced a powerful effect on me. Never shall I forget my sensations when one evening I for the first time beheld the floating streamers of purple and gold, spanning the blue vault in the form of a gigantic arch. Ned and the professor, having witnessed the marvel before, were not particularly impressed with it. As for the Icelanders—it was for them a daily occurrence, and not worth the trouble of noticing. Strange how indifferent familiarity with any beautiful sight makes one.

On the 6th we skirted the base of fire-breathing Hecla, and our escort gave us some interesting details respecting the terrible eruption of 1878, which, however, I will not weary my readers by recounting.

The country was full of interest. Geysers, solfataras, smoking wells and gleaming tunnels of ice, filled with strange roaring noises and curling clouds of steam, served to keep our interest alive. Ned superintended the men, the professor and myself wielded the theodolite and compass. I don't think we left a square yard of the country unexplored. I am in a hurry to begin the really marvellous part of my adventures, so I must condense.

On the 18th we reached Ingolfshöfdi, a fishing village situated on the south side of a good-sized inlet. Any plans the professor might have formed for further operations were certainly for the moment nipped in the bud by a violent fall of snow. Luckily, the accommodation here was better than any we had yet found. Stone houses and roaring fires went far to mitigate the horrors of an Icelandic winter. Here, too, the professor took me through some of his plans, which for reasons of his own, perhaps in order to avoid my accusing him of folly, he had been sufficiently reticent about till then.

The Vatna Jökull is an elevated table-land, about fifty miles by eighty in extent. It is seamed by rugged valleys and overtopped by a myriad of unknown peaks, many of them volcanic. Glaciers pursue their methodical course down the mountain sides, and crevasses yawn at every step. It is a complete wilderness of volcanoes and ice, often entirely hidden under a tempest of driving snow. To cross this plateau on foot would be dangerous, without at least knowing something of the ground first. To acquire this necessary experience, Herr Nordenrother had conceived the idea af a balloon excursion. Under the influence of a gentle southerly breeze, we should be enabled to cross the Vatna Jökull easily and comfortably in four or five hours at the most. We could also note the principal mountain ranges, the craters and valleys. Photographs taken from the car would be of immense value in designing accurate maps. Ned Hatton, when the project was explained to him, shrugged his shoulders.

Whoever heard of such a thing in the annals of serious scientific exploration! Cross a country in a balloon! Let the reverend professor acknowledge at once he was going to gratify his weakness for a pleasure trip. The scientific value of the attempt would assuredly be *nil*.

'Oh, I don't know, Ned,' I objected. 'Why shouldn't one be able to observe geographical details as well from the car of a balloon as from the ground? It seems to me that if only we go high enough up, and if the day is clear—'

'Go on,' said Ned, sarcastically.

'It seems to me we'll be able to get a first class map of the region simply by taking a snap-shot with a camera.'

My practical friend refused to be convinced, however, and went off grumbling. At the end of a week, the weather cleared up and the sun appeared once more. Herr Nordenrother consulted barometer and storm-glass attentively.

' The winter was over,' he said, as he triumphantly exhibited the instruments to myself and Ned. I smiled and nodded, while my Yankee companion turned away indifferently, after shaking the barometer violently once or twice, to persuade it to go down, and so give the lie to the professor.

As it happened, our chief's weather prophecies turned out to be correct. For a week we had cloudless skies, the snow melted everywhere, and Nature resumed her spring garb. In the distant north, the snowy peaks of Oraefa, one of the largest of Icelandic volcanoes, towered ominously above its fields of ice. On the morning of the 1st of April, Herr Nordenrother announced his intention of starting.

The men were summoned, and the preparations for this strange excursion went on merrily.

As I had suspected, it was the professor's intention to inflate his balloon with hydrogen—coal gas not being available—generated by allowing sulphuric acid to act on zinc filings or broken bits of iron.

The materials were readily forthcoming. The acid, in massive stone jars, had been sent on by sea from Reikjavik together with several hundredweight of granulated iron, and a liberal allowance of galvanised piping to conduct the gas. Hydrogen is several times lighter than coal gas, an important fact, which renders a balloon of moderate size only necessary.

Barrels of wood, similar to those used for transporting dried fish, were the only available receptacles for the acid, which, however, being diluted

with five times its bulk of water, would not eat
through the wood before the end of the operation;
at least we hoped not. I was enthusiastic, the
professor methodical, Ned Hatton cynical as ever.

We worked hard all the morning, arranging the
barrels in rows—there were fifty altogether—filling
them with water from the stream, fitting them with
tubes for the introduction of the acid, and connect-
ing them together by pipes of a larger calibre.
From the last barrel a galvanised iron tube, about
thirty feet long by six inches in diameter, led to
the balloon. Finally the tops of the barrels were
flowed over with melted pitch, to prevent leakage
and loss of gas. I paused, with grimy hands, to
contemplate the distant range of snowy hills that
we were going to traverse.

'Well, sir, and what do you think of it?' asked
the professor, folding his arms and looking at me
sharply, as though to challenge my admiration of
his audacious plans.

'Well, professor,' I answered, 'I think the whole
thing seems rather vague. If an accident happens
to our balloon, we shall be prettily caught. How
do we know where the wind will carry us to?'

Herr Nordenrother smiled.

'Oh, I fancy that will not present much difficulty,'
he said musingly, 'by rising or falling, as the case
may be, we ought to be able to hit on a current of
air that will take us in the right direction. There
is a party of men ready to receive us at the other
side, with boats to descend the Jokullsa. Do you
like river trips, sir?'

I evaded the question adroitly.

'I did not know,' I remarked carelessly, 'that the
Icelandic rivers were fit for navigation. I thought
they were all cataracts and rapids.'

'So they are—in summer. But just now the
melting of the snows make them into quite for-

midable masses of water. The waterfalls, of course, will have to be avoided.'

'What instruments are we going to take, professor?'

'Two theodolites, the usual compendium of telescopes and barometers, and a small photographic camera for topographical views will be sufficient, I imagine,' answered the phlegmatic German, quietly. 'Provisions for a week will be ordinary prudence, though our trip will really only last a day and a night at the most. After all, sir, if you are afraid of a catastrophe, you need not come. There is always plenty of work here which needs attending to, and I wouldn't mind your stopping at Ingolfshöfdi—if only to keep an eye on our instruments and supplies. You can rejoin us at Husavik later in the season—by long sea if you are afraid to tempt the mountains.'

The last sentence was said with a touch of sarcasm. For fear the great man would think me a coward, I hastened to assure him of my intention of following him to the ends of the earth if necessary. Besides, I added, the few details which he had given me till now had rendered me fearful.

'You never told me you had prepared an escort to meet us at the other side of the Joküll,' I said reproachfully. 'I thought it was a case of crossing Iceland at least.'

The professor laughed and stroked his beard.

'And if it *had* been a case of crossing Iceland *without* an escort, would you have been afraid?' he asked, in a half-defiant tone.

This was a poser, and I was silent.

'I, sir,' said Herr Nordenrother, drawing himself up proudly, 'would cross the entire world, if necessary, in the interests of science. Can you, an Englishman, dare less?'

I made no answer. Ned, who was superintending the caulking of the barrels, began to whistle softly to himself.

'To-morrow evening,' said the professor, oratorically ,'we shall have crossed those mysterious table-lands, and be standing, uninjured, on the banks of the Joküllsa River.'

'It is just as well to have a leader who has confidence in himself,' thought I. 'A vacillating captain is worse than one who is prone to dare too much.'

The glorious sun was already furrowing the ocean with a broad track of gold when I awoke. I dressed hurriedly and descended the ladder, to find my friend Ned endeavouring to swallow some boiling coffee out of a tin mug.

'Well—and the balloon?' I asked jocosely.

'We've been getting it ready for the last two hours, while you were having your sleep,' was the answer. 'Here, take *this*, and look sharp, or his nibs 'll be after us.'

This was a salted herring, boiled over the turf fire, and tasting very much of smoke. Ned bolted his coffee, seized his overcoat and hurried out. The herring was very nasty, but I managed to swallow it, nevertheless. This done, I muffled myself up warmly and rushed through the door after Ned.

Our men had certainly not been idle. Under Herr Nordenrother's direction, the balloon was slowly filling, rising from the ground like a huge yellow bubble. A crowd of villagers stood grouped about in knots of three or four gazing on what to them must have been an extremely novel sight. Some of our companions were pouring acid into the barrels, others were tying and untying the leaden weights of the silk bag. I joined the latter, and proffered my assistance, which was not refused.

No one could have wished for a better day. The

wind was blowing steadily from the south, the sea was calm and the sky was of that pure pale blue colour usual in northern latitudes. Filling a balloon is at best a lengthy process, even with well-supplied gas mains at one's command. Four hours were needed to complete the work. At ten o'clock the hugh machine was ready to start, swaying to and fro in the light breeze like some aerial monster impatient to be free.

To buckle on the car and to place in it our provisions, our instruments and blankets, together with twenty small bags of sand to serve as ballast was the work of a few moments only. My heart beat nervously, and I looked with a certain awe on the impassive countenance of Herr Nordenrother, who was apparently as unmoved as though he were about to take the express train from London to Brighton instead of being on the eve of launching himself into the unknown perils of an ice-bound desert.

We took our places in the car—the professor, Ned Hatton and myself. The men crowded round to shake our hands and wish us luck.

'It is a three weeks' farewell only,' remarked the learned German. 'Have you got the maps, Mr Ralphcourt?'

'Yes, sir.'

'And the electroscope?'

'Here it is, professor,' said Ned, tapping a wooden case which he had secured to the wicker side of the car with straps.

'The blankets, provisions, water, ballast, snow-shoes—yes, that is all. Now I think we can let her go. Stand clear there, all of you!'

The ropes were cast off, and the balloon, under the influence of six thousand cubic feet of hydrogen, tore us upwards into the air at a fearful speed.

What a moment! I shall never forget it. Sensations of the most varied description chased one another through my brain without leaving any distinct impression save one of mingled fear and wonder.

We rose rapidly and without stopping to a height of twelve thousand feet. Iceland was no longer a desert island, it was simply a vast heap, drawn in white and grey. To the south, my eye roamed over the long, waving coast line, fringed with snow-white breakers, stretching away to Cape Portland, with the island of Vestmanneyjar beyond, a solitary, white wave-swept rock, the haunt of the eider and the gull. To the west rose the gaunt outlines of a huge volcanic mountain chain, overtopped by the giant Hecla. Further north, the great Icelandic desert, a waste of soda and sulphur, stretched away, bordered by a chain of lofty mountains, some of whose peaks were crowned with whitish vapour. To count the total number of volcanoes was difficult. At least fifty were in sight at once, though, of course, the number must have been considerably greater in reality. Here and there, in the valleys, appeared jets and clouds of vapour. They were the far-famed geysers, or boiling springs. Some of the streamlets falling down the broken lava chasms appeared to be in a state of ebullition, but in this I may have been mistaken. The distance was too great to observe the details with any accuracy.

We were drifting northwards at the rate of about fifteen miles an hour. If this speed kept constant, we should cross the Jöküll in six hours at the most. I shrewdly suspected, however, that the wind would drop as the day were on, nor, as events proved, was I mistaken.

At eleven-thirty a diminution of our altitude bcame apparent. The professor consulted his barometer, drew out pencil and note-book, and said,—

'Eight thousand feet only,'

'So I see professor,' I replied. 'Shall we lighten the car ?'

'I think not,' he answered. 'We can work better at a moderate altitude. I want to take some photographs. Have you the plate-holder there?'

I produced the article he named, and watched while he manipulated the apparatus, which was pointed downwards at an angle of some thirty degrees. We were passing the lofty peak of Mount Oraefa, and a picture of its rugged sides and smoke-crowned summit was easily secured. A few minutes later we were floating over the table-land itself.

Here, for some reason or other, perhaps owing to the protecting influence of the higher summits that fringed its borders, the wind dropped by degrees, till at length all motion seemed to have stopped. The car had in the meanwhile sunk nearer the earth, and we found ourselves, by one o'clock, hanging, to all appearances motionless, some five hundred feet above a chaos of steaming snow and fantastically piled rocks. I looked at Herr Nordenrother.

'The wind is held in check by the mountains,' he said. 'If we chose, we could find a stronger breeze by ascending higher. I think, nevertheless, that we shall get a better view from where we are now, don't you?'

'But we are not moving,' I urged.

'I beg your pardon. Take this telescope and examine the ground.'

I did as I was requested.

'We are moving,' I answered, 'but very slowly —not more than two or three miles an hour.'

'That is enough,' replied the professor. 'If the hydrogen shows signs of giving out, we can throw out some ballast.'

'We are crossing the crater of a volcano,' said Ned.

'Is it possible?' I exclaimed.

I put down the barometer and rushed to the edge of the car.

Only some twenty feet or so beneath us yawned a huge circular opening, some three or four hundred yards in diameter. As the car swept slowly over its rocky edge, a confused murmur was heard, echoing up from the depths beneath. Far down, I caught a glimpse of fiery red, through a fog of white vapour. Explosions and rumblings struck my ear. Clearly we had to do, not only with a volcano, but with an active one.

'If the netting was to break,' mused Ned philosophically, scanning the gloomy abyss through his opera-glass, 'I would not give a straw for my life.'

Hardly had he said these words when I experienced a fearful sensation of choking. A pale, sickly yellow mist undulated round the car—we were suffocating! we were poisoned!

Quick as thought Ned seized a sand-bag and tossed it into space. A violent upward jerk followed, and in the space of some seconds we were breathing the pure air at a height of six thousand feet. Half laughing, half choking, we congratulated ourselves on our lucky escape.

'Narrow shave that,' remarked Ned, in intervals between fits of coughing. 'We were nearly gone—moral: steer clear of volcanoes.'

'A difficult one to follow in a voyage of this kind,' I answered. 'They're strewn around here as thick as currants in a plum cake, and we have no means of directing our course.'

'Look at those clouds,' said my companion, pointing away at the far-off eastern horizon, where a low bank of grey was visible. 'Do you think that bodes stormy weather?'

'The barometer doesn't say so,' I answered
vaguely, 'better ask the professor. Look, we're
moving along splendidly now.'

The change of altitude had, as Herr Nordenrother
predicted, brought us into a stronger current of air,
and for half-an-hour we sailed briskly along. Ned
sketched, the professor took photographs, and I
occupied myself with studying closely, from the
maps, the geography of this curious region, so desolate, so vague, and so little known. At half-past
two we had again fallen to within a few hundred
feet of the plateau, and our rate of travelling diminished in proportion. At the professor's advice,
another sand-bag was thrown out, and for the second
time we rose far above the mountain tops.

These manœuvres continued till towards sunset,
when we were rewarded by one of the most glorious
sights it is possible to conceive. The red ball of
the sun was almost touching the sea-line. Above
it hung a dark mass of cloud, its wavy edge tinged
with crimson glory. A vast sheaf of luminous rays,
in form like a gigantic fan, stretched out across the
heavens, seeming to reach the farthest limits of the
atmosphere. Overhead, a wilderness of rosy clouds
were floating—I say overhead, for we were not
above the cloud-line altogether, though patches and
flakes of vapour eddied round the car, enveloping it
in a rosy mist through which the sun's disc appeared
twice its usual size, magnified by the refraction.
To the north, between the roseate cloud-continents,
the golden and lilac streamers of the aurora were
seen spanning the heavens. Beneath us a greyish
mist was collecting, in which the black mountain
tops appeared scattered like islands in a shadowy
ocean.

As I watched, a change came over the landscape.
The delicate shades of pink and pale scarlet became
deeper—the grey mists turned to purple. A vague

phosphorescent reflection, the light of the auroral
fire no doubt, played over the floating mist-forms,
the mountain summits grew blacker and more distinct as the balloon sank lower. Here an exclamation from Ned roused me from my artistic stupor.

'An eruption,' he said.

The professor let fall his note-book, which he had
been annotating by the light of a small portable
reading-lamp, and we both hurried to the other side
of the car. Ned was not mistaken. At a distance
of some five or six miles was a crater on fire.
Dense masses of smoke rolled away over the dark
country, occasionally the black mass parted to
reveal sheaves and fountains of glowing scoria.
Rocks heated to whiteness, occasionally forced their
way up through the heavy vapour, to burst like
shells in the cold sky beyond. A sluggish stream
of dark red matter flowed down the side of this
nameless mountain, which must have been some
seven or eight thousand feet in height at least.

The balloon was rapidly nearing this furnace,
whose explosions and rumblings became more
audible every moment.

'If we clear it,' muttered Ned 'we're all right, if
not—'

I shuddered. The possibility of being swallowed
up in the fire of an unknown crater was not pleasant.
We were moving steadily onwards at a speed of
nearly ten miles an hour, and the course of the
balloon was carrying us straight across the summit
of the burning mountain.

'Throw out some ballast,' ordered the professor.

Ned Hatton took up a bag, the last of our store,
and tossed it over the side. We rose immediately
to an enormous height.

'I guess that'll do it,' said my companion, con-
fidently.

For half-an-hour or more we floated among the

clouds, which partly veiled the glare of the volcano beneath us. Then, as before, we felt the car sinking. A cry escaped from the usually impassive professor.

'The wind—the wind—we are not moving!' he cried.

In fact, the position of the currents of air had changed. Instead of rising into a more rapidly moving portion of the atmosphere, we had risen into a zone of almost total tranquillity. A couple of miles still separated us from the glowing mountain, and the rapid lower current was preparing to dash us against its fiery sides.

The explosions and mutterings became more audible. At the end of a few minutes it was necessary to yell at my companions to make them understand. Even at that distance I could feel the heat and hear the hissing of the melted snow.

'If one of those rocks should strike the balloon,' I heard the professor say, 'we shall be burnt like flies!'

A roar from the volcano interrupted him. Through the heavy clouds of yellow smoke a gigantic fountain of fire shot into the sky, coruscating and flashing in diabolical beauty. A noise of falling rocks followed, and a rain of volcanic meteorites fell, with loud hissings, on either side of the car.

'Out with the instruments!' shouted Herr Nordenrother. 'We must save our lives at any cost.'

His command was followed to the letter, and the fierce heat diminished as we rose into the pure cool air.

'Should we clear the mountain? If not, our earthly existence was at an end. I confess not to have any particular leanings towards piety, but during that painful quarter-of-an-hour, I prayed more fervently than I had ever prayed till then

My devotional exercises were abruptly cut short by a vigorous curse from Ned.

'We are sinking!' he cried.

I opened my eyes in horror. Through the surrounding ocean of cloud, the fiery circle of the dread crater was beginning to glow hideously. We were falling at an angle of about forty-five degrees—straight into its mouth. My shoulder was clutched in a grip of iron.

'We must cut away the car!' yelled someone (I think it was Ned). 'Cut away the car and hang on to the ropes!'

Of the scene that followed I have no distinct recollection. Drawing my clasp-knife, I held fast to the netting with one hand, while with the other I slashed and tore furiously at the cordage that supported the car. A complex roaring filled the air. We were enveloped in a cloud of stifling, suffocating gas. Paralysed, my hair rising with cold fear, trying to hold my breath in order not to breathe that deadly vapour, I let fall my knife and held on in a half-fainting condition. All sensation seemed to have left me—fear had been driven out of my system by the certainty of approaching death.

We drifted across the lip of the crater. An ocean of molten lava was roaring some hundred feet beneath me, in waves of yellow, green and gold. Molten rocks flew hissing past me. I was swimming in fire. My cheeks were scorched, and I felt my hair frizzling up.

Suddenly, with a tearing sound, the car parted from its fastenings and was hurled into the midst of the glowing sea of lava. The balloon gave a great bound—we were saved!

At that moment a dreadful explosion rent the air. Tongues of fire shot upwards, a myriad of blazing meteors passed before my eyes. Even in that moment, so full of death-agony, I noticed a

vast belt of white light which seemed to be spanning
the dark void behind the volcanic fires. Then came
a violent shock, a feeling of being carried along
with immense speed, a confused rushing in my ears
—and oblivion.

CHAPTER V

DURA GRAVITAS

THERE is a peculiar state of torpor, induced sometimes by any very great peril or excitement in
which, the mind being still lucid enough to think,
the body is completely dead to physical sensations
of any kind. The condition is somewhat analogous
to that of a patient under the influence of chloroform or any other anæsthetic. They see without
feeling, they understand their personal hurts without that understanding awakening a sense of dread,
as it would under normal conditions.

Such was the state I found myself in on awakening from my insensibility. A sickening consciousness of being stifled, a sense of oppressive darkness
and a violent pain in the lungs were the first impressions that passed through my half-awakened brain.

Above my head, swinging in space apparently,
was a vague, dim circle of light. I believe my
reasoning faculties were slowly coming into play,
for an undefinable curiosity took possession of me.
Where was I ? What had taken place?'

Then, as the mind's awakening was about to
open the way for a spell of bodily agony, my brain
whirled and a merciful Providence again bereft me
of my senses. How long my stupor lasted, I could
have hardly divined, at the time. Hours, minutes,
days pass with equal rapidity to a man in a trance.
Slowly, slowly my brain resumed its thinking

powers, a strange light shone in my eyes, surrounding objects began to take visible form—I was awake.

The first impression was one of overwhelming surprise. I was lying, as far as I could see, in a ship's cabin—a cabin of the most luxurious type—on a couch, so soft and downy that I hardly felt it, under a ceiling, adorned with graceful paintings, shut in by walls of beautifully-panelled wood and shaded by curtains of the finest blue silk.

I started bolt upright. As I did so, I felt the couch I was lying on rock gently to and fro. Clearly it was a 'hanging berth,' similar to those in use on Atlantic liners and elsewhere. I had to do with civilised people evidently. But this was not all.

An indescribable influence was at work on me. I hardly felt the weight of my body. A slight effort which I made, to get out of bed, resulted in my rolling prone on the floor and getting severely bumped, not against the floor, but—here was the startling part of it—against the opposite wall. An irresistible force seemed to glue me against the mahogany panels. Above my head was a railing. I grasped it, and with difficulty hauled myself into a standing position. Then I noticed for the first time that my bed, curtains and all, was hanging, not horizontally, but at an angle of about sixty degrees with the floor.

Whether it was this fact, or the effect of the horrors I had been through, I cannot say, but a fit of shivering terror took possession of me. I sank helpless on my knees, still closely pressed against the wall by that mysterious unknown force, and burst into sobs of mingled nervousness and despair. Presently the suffocating feeling came back, a leaden weight crushed my chest, and, for the third time, I lost consciousness.

D

I must have remained insensible for a considerable time, for on awaking and looking about me, I found that the situation had slightly changed. My bed, which had frightened me so by its peculiar behaviour, was hanging nearly horizontally. I myself was lying at full length on the floor, where I had fallen, but the strange influence that had thrown me so violently against the hard panels was no longer at work. I felt less mystified altogether than on the two former occasions.

A mysterious twilight illumined this curious apartment, as tasteful in its interior decorations as it was mysterious in its behaviour. Above my head, by the side of what I supposed was the door, I perceived a tiny brass box, similar to an electric light switch.

Actuated by an irresistible impulse, I stretched out my hand and twisted the flat, revolving piece of ebonite that served for a handle. Instantly the twilight made way for a beautiful golden-yellow radiance.

Four pear-shaped globes of ground glass, supported on gracefully-modelled metal brackets at either side of a costly looking-glass, flooded the apartment with soft light.

'Come,' thought I, 'this is not so very mysterious after all. It is evident that I have been suffering from an attack of brain fever. Under the circumstances the worst thing I can do is to lie here. Besides, I'm making a beast of myself. I'll get up.'

Getting up was this time almost easier done than said. All weight had apparently vanished from my body. I no longer walked along the ground, I glided over its surface without my feet touching, almost. Then, before I could understand what was happening, I lost my balance, and fell backwards against the fateful wall, without, however, hurting myself in the least. My head struck the panels as lightly as though I had only fallen an inch or two instead of six feet.

At the same instant my eyes fell on one of the cabin windows—there were four in all, I think— and the feeling of horror returned. Outside there was blackness of darkness, illumined by a myriad points of silvery light. Then a revulsion swept over me. I had awakened during the night, that was all.

But no—surely *that* was not the darkness of night—those powdery atoms of light could not be the stars!

The matter was easily settled. Without moving, for fear of some new horror developing itself, I felt in my inner pocket for my watch.

It was uninjured, luckily. A chronometer divided into twenty-four hours is useful in cases like this. Mine was of this description. I opened it and looked at the dial.

Half-past one p.m.

I raised it to my ear. It was ticking merrily as ever. Then, by way of setting the question at rest for good and all, I boldly determined to go and look out of the window myself.

The mysterious influence held me back, but the stupendous curiosity that had taken possession of me made it of little account. I fell on my hands and knees and began to crawl painfully across the cabin floor.

Twice I slid back against the wall. Twice I experienced that feeling of impotent terror sometimes felt in nightmares when one is brought face to face with some dread mystery never seen by waking eyes. The third time I succeeded, by clutching hold of the furniture, in dragging myself over to the opposite side of the apartment. Then I stood up and looked out through the circular window.

Were we on the sea?

There was no sea visible.

On the earth?

There was no earth in sight—nothing but the most intense blackness strewn with those myriads of powdered jewels—they couldn't be stars. No stars, seen through our terrestrial atmosphere, were ever so steady or so invariable in brilliancy. The displacement of sheets of air, by heat or other causes, produces that intermittent wavering which we call twinkling, and which, in this case, was totally absent. Besides, there are limits to the number of visible stars even on the clearest night. Here there were certainly none. Above, beneath, stretched a universe of silvery gems, a perfect ocean of diamond-dust, with here and there a ruby, an emerald, or a sapphire.

Some inkling of the tremendous truth must have dawned on me, for my heart began to beat fearfully as I dropped, helpless and gasping for breath, on a magnificently-upholstered lounge that lay invitingly near.

The sound of a key turning in the lock attracted my attention. The door swung open and two men entered.

'Where are we?' I panted. 'For God's sake tell me where I am.'

'Calm yourself, sir. You are among friends, and in no danger whatsoever,' answered the younger man, in a soft voice.

Then he turned and said some words to his companion in a language quite unintelligible to me—I think it must have belonged to the Magyar or Slavonic branches. The words expressed a command of some kind, for the elderly man, a sturdy, sailor-like individual with grey hair and beard, turned on his heel without a word and shuffled out of the door, leaving us alone.

The young man, evidently the commander and owner of this strange vessel, bent over me, and, with a look of sympathy in his dark eyes, inquired, in very good English, how I felt.

I paused before answering. This unknown individual was one of the most beautiful men I had ever seen. In age, he might have been any-- thing between twenty-five and forty. A massive forehead, indicative of great intellect, over which curled wavy masses of silky black hair, a face, oval and perfectly chiselled as that of the Delphian Apollo, and a pair of large, poetic eyes, intensely blue and piercing, like globes of deep sapphire, went to make up a type of male loveliness, that I might perhaps have dreamed of in romance, or read of in legendary fairy tales, but never seen face to face in flesh and blood. I remember at the time it struck me that no woman ever was half so fair, and yet—with all its perfect loveliness and lofty purity, there was something wanting—. I could not say what just then, but I knew it later.

A genius, and a poet! Truly I had gone far to find such a combination. Goethe, in his most in- spired moments had never looked like that! No *Lohengrin* had ever glided on swan wings across the dreams of a great master; no *Parsifal* had up- held the sacred cup with such divine fire in his eyes. Yet there was something wanting. I felt that between us was a barrier that nothing could re- move. The stranger's beauty, after moving me to awe and admiration, left me cold and unsympathetic.

Huldebrand might have regarded thus the chilly water-nymph, *Undine*, or *Pygmalion* his *Galatea* of icy marble. It was not human, and, despite the great soul that struggled through those dark blue eyes, it—strange though it may seem—jarred on me disagreeably.

My scrutiny of this superior order of mortal

must have been somewhat long, for he repeated
his question in a tone of impatience. I put my
hand to my head with a dazed gesture.

'Oh! I'm pretty well,' I stammered ; 'but it
looks as though I had been rather ill.'

The stranger laughed musically.

'Oh! that is not surprising,' he said, with a
smile. 'And now, pray, whom have I the honour
of addressing?'

I told him, giving a history of myself and my
companions, and an account of our trip to Iceland,
which had so nearly culminated in a fearful disaster.
Then I started up, and, with anxiety in my voice,
asked for news of my companions.

'Your companion, you mean,' corrected the
stranger. 'Mr Ned Hatton is confined to his
cabin as yet, but I think he will pull through.
If there were any others, I fear they have perished.'

So the learned professor had succumbed.
Perhaps it was not surprising, taking it all in all.
Like a second Empedocles, he had found a fiery
grave. Any grief that I might have experienced
at the news of my companion's end was, however,
very much softened, not to say annihilated, by the
overwhelming curiosity I experienced respecting
my own miraculous escape.

'Where are we now?' I asked almost breathlessly.

'On board the *Astrolabe*,' answered the stranger.

'You are the owner of this vessel?' I continued,
inwardly longing to put a decisive question, but for
some reason or other fearing to do so.

'I am both owner and captain,' replied the young
man, with a proud flash of his dark blue eyes.

'We are in—Iceland?' I queried.

He shook his head and smiled.

'Iceland is a long way off I fear by now. I cannot even say that we are in Europe.'

'Where on earth are we, then?' I asked fearfully.

'In space,' answered the blue-eyed stranger, 'nearly a hundred and fifty thousand miles from the earth. If you are acquainted with the use of nautical and astronomical instruments, no doubt you will be able to verify the matter yourself soon. The calculation is not a difficult one.'

I stared. The captain's statement was not so overwhelming as it would have been had not some suspicion of the truth already crossed my mind during that brief glimpse through the window. I shrugged my shoulders slightly. Of what use was it to doubt, when the immediate future would decide whether the stranger were speaking the truth or not.

'You have been ill, I see' continued he, pointing to the floor and to the couch, where patches and stains of blood were visible, 'but it is altogether a strange matter that you are not smashed to atoms, instead of being alive and in the full enjoyment of your five senses. There is nothing bad in the universe, but that it might have been worse.'

The captain had chosen a strange moment for uttering this philosophical platitude.

'I owe you my life,' I said simply, 'and the thought that I may never be able to repay the service is more galling to me than fifty illnesses.

He bowed slightly, then continued,—

'I was travelling across Iceland at the rate of a hundred miles an hour only, when your balloon obstructed my path. You were caught up by us, and carried along for a distance of ten or twelve miles, at least, before we were able to take you on board. I fear the curious effects of gravity, which, doubtless, you must have noticed already, have given you cause for anxiety.'

I smiled and nodded faintly.

'There is really no danger,' he said apologetic-
ally, 'and you will soon be accustomed to the
peculiarities of my vessel. Fortune has favoured
me as well as you, if only for the reason that my
Icelandic crossing has secured me a learned companion—but come, you must be hungry. Our
breakfast awaits us in the saloon, if you will be
so kind as to give me your arm—perhaps you
would like some hot water first though—please
make yourself at home.'

The captain touched an electric bell. A liveried
servant appeared with a copper can. What my
new acquaintance called the 'curious effect of
gravity' was still at work. The water did not
rest at the bottom of the basin, but inclined to
one side. I had to hold on to the marble slab to
prevent myself falling backwards. As the water
touched my face I gave a cry. No wonder!
All the skin was burnt off one side of it.

'Let me give you some vaseline,' said the
captain, politely, 'it is invaluable for burns and
scaldings—there. You will find a brush and comb
in the drawer. So—you look better now. Pass
your arm through mine—you might fall otherwise.

He opened the door, and we passed out together.
I did not walk, I glided along. It seemed to me
even that a positive effort was required to keep
on the ground. Every moment I expected to find
myself soaring up ceiling-wards.

We traversed a broad, handsome passage, lit
by electric lamps placed at intervals. No doors
opened off it, but the walls were tapestried with
sombre drapery, relieved here and there by groups
of strange weapons, cutlasses, tomahawks, etc.,
arranged symmetrically, and flashing back the
electric light from their polished surfaces. Without much effort, I might have imagined myself

in the lofty corridor of some baronial castle in Normandy or Poitou.

At the end of this passage, fully a hundred feet long, I should think, by fifteen high, a curtained door led into a beautifully-furnished drawing-room.

Vast windows, curved in the oriental fashion and shaded by costly silk blinds, allowed a subdued sunlight to linger over the gorgeously-coloured draperies that decked the divans and ottomans. By a curious effect, which I sought in vain to explain, the light penetrated through the windows on one side only—the others might not have existed, for all the light they admitted.

I had to do with a man whose taste was as fantastic as it was luxurious. Colours were mingled indiscriminately, and without any attempt at harmonious arrangement. Blue china vases, adorned with golden dragons, evidently of Chinese origin, reposed on scarlet mats. A magnificent grand piano, draped in grey and gold, was covered with what appeared to be a choice collection of Burmese and Japanese idols. Near the piano, on an inlaid table of ivory and ebony, I noticed several gold crucifixes, a small marble effigy of the Virgin and a tiny green statue of the Egyptian Osiris, evidently disinterred from some tomb in far-off Thebes or Memphis. Perhaps the captain's religious beliefs were as mixed as his artistic ideas. Fixed codes were probably as strange to him as they had been to my unfortunate friend, Nordenrother. From the drawing-room we passed into what appeared to be a mingled library and workroom. Several globes stood on pedestals in the corners and the walls, where they were not occupied by book-shelves, were hidden beneath an interesting collection of planispheres and star maps. I recognised Beer and Mädler's excellent moon-charts, and

Schiaparelli's recently published maps of the planet Mars.

The captain left me no time for wonder. He opened a door and ushered me into the dining-room.

It was about twenty feet square, and as lofty as the preceding rooms, that is, about fifteen feet high. The walls were adorned with paintings, let into the panels—historical subjects mostly. Galileo before the Inquisition, Columbus landing on the Bahamas, Sebastian Cabot, Ferdinand Cortes, the Carthaginian Hanno, and a score of others, naturally unknown to me.

'These men were travellers,' explained my strange companion, 'and I am one with them— —in spirit at least.'

We took our places at the table. The glasses and plates, each bearing the name of the *Astrolabe* and its device—the winged globe of Ancient Egypt —were standing in a sort of shallow wooden rack, that enabled them to be moved without allowing them to topple over.

'Take some of this wine,' proceeded my handsome companion, handing me a graceful decanter shaped like a parrot with a beak of silver, 'and do not fill your glass too full.'

I followed his instructions. The wine, like the water a few minutes back, ran up one side of the glass, instead of remaining level, that is, parallel with the table.

'It is the attraction of our miserable planet,' put in the captain, with a smile ; 'six or seven hours more will put us out of its reach.'

I thought I had not heard correctly, and applied myself to the meal in silence. We were served by a solemn domestic, in dark blue livery, whose olive tint and black hair proclaimed his southern origin. The dishes seemed to me to consist mostly of admirably-preserved meat and vegetables. I recognised the ham of Westphalia, the diminutive sausage of Vienna, more prized than the 'tomacula' of the ancient Romans, some excellent *haricots verts*, as fresh as if they had been torn from their mother-plant but a few hours since, Jerusalem artichokes and asparagus. The captain became communicative and entertaining.

'Yes, professor,' he said, 'you must have been considerably astonished, on awaking, to find yourself on my boat. There were many curious things which you could not be expected to explain. Ah, sir, you have much to see and much to learn that will be useful to you. Humanity, like moles burrowing in the darkness of the soil, are too apt to judge of the unknown by their knowledge of the known. Their vanity at times carries them so far as to make them believe that the universe was moulded for them, that the earth, with its forests, its oceans, its coal mines, was made solely for *their* convenience, and for no other purpose— ah, professor, what a foolish thing it is to be a man!

I smiled. Certainly no one could accuse this extraordinary being of existing on the same plane with the mediæval *savants* whom he professed to despise.

'Try some of this wine, professor,' he continued, handing me a decanter. 'It is of my own growth, and I can recommend it.'

I stared incredulously.

'Is it possible that you have a vineyard on board your vessel?' I asked in an astonished tone.

The captain laughed gaily, and his blue eyes danced merrily as he replied,—

'No—I am afraid that would be difficult. But I am not wholly an outlaw, sir. From time to time I revisit my native land.'

' Then you are—'

' Roumanian—a native of Transsylvania. Bucharest is my town. They are a worthy people, in
their way, but ignorant and bigoted—not at all on
the same intellectual scale as you or I. Now, professor, if you have finished, we will begin our journey
of exploration round the boat, which, I trust, is to
be your home during many a long day. I see you
are devoured with curiosity, and curiosity is, to a
man in your present situation, of all vices the most
excusable.'

CHAPTER VI

SOME EXPLANATIONS

FROM a small lobby off the dining-room, a staircase led to the deck. We ascended, the captain
still holding me by the arm, as though to prevent
my falling. Never shall I forget my sensations
when for the first time my eyes gazed on space. I
shrank back overwhelmed and horrified. Could
any sight ever have equalled this in gloom and
grandeur?

The deck of the *Astrolabe* was a covered one, like
the second deck of on Atlantic liner. A massive
metal covering, seemingly made of polished silver,
protected it from end to end, with the exception
of two spaces at the bow and stern, which, for
purposes of observation, I suppose, were left un-
covered. One side of the platform was deluged in
sunlight, a sunlight ten times as brilliant as that of
the earth, which is necessarily enfeebled and weak-
ened by the opacity of our atmosphere—the other
side, the one turned towards space, was nothing but

a mass of blackness, palely illumined by the light of the stars.

No light, however powerful, can light up the depths of space. We, living on our little planet, surrounded by two hundred miles of azure air, are apt to argue, from the bright hues of the sky which we daily see above our heads, that space is a perpetual ocean of sunlight. Nothing could be more erroneous. What we see from the earth is merely the reflection of the sun's light on our atmosphere. Beyond that all is darkness, darker than night itself. Above me, beneath me, around me, stretched that immense void. The impression of my own insignificance was so overmastering that I could have dropped from sheer fright, had not my attention been suddenly drawn from the horrors of the void to a new object—it was the earth.

A vast, luminous disc, in size about twelve times the diameter of our moon at her full, hung suspended a little below us, clearly outlined against the inky blackness beyond. No map could have been more plain, no photograph more minute in all its details, continents, peninsulas, islands, all appeared delineated against the green oceans with startling accuracy. From the pure snows of the northern pole my eye travelled down over the vast plains of North and South America, here and there veiled by vapoury streaks of cloud, to the dread Cape Horn, the king of tempests, and the mysterious whiteness beyond, the outlying ice-floes of Graham's Land.

Half of the Pacific Ocean was enveloped in shadow. The Marquesas Islands were the last landmarks that I could discern—Europe was invisible, a yellowish patch on the eastern edge of the earth-ball was all I could see of Africa. Down the western half of South America, the snowy Andes made a connected line of white, set off by the golden sands of the burning Atacama Desert.

In the eastern half, the Selvas of the Amazon
valley and the grassy plains of Brazil made a huge
triangular green patch. It seemed to me that I
could even trace the courses of certain rivers—
the Parana, the Pilcomayo, the Paraguay and the
Uruguay, that giant fourfold sisterhood that mingle
their waters to rush together seawards down their
long estuary—the Rio de la Plata. I was rapidly
losing myself in contemplation of this spectacle,
as novel as it was glorious, when a word from the
captain of the *Astrolabe* interrupted my reverie.

'If you waste all your admiration on the earth,
professor,' he said, 'you will have none left to confer
on her beautiful satellite—the moon.'

'The moon?' I exclaimed, for I had entirely
forgotten the existence of that valuable luminary.
'I see no moon.'

'It is above your head,' answered the captain.

A revolution took place in my mind. I rushed
to the edge of the platform and craned my head
upwards.

Yes—there it was. Mountains, plains, valleys,
all complete. A shining semicircle that seemed to
cover nearly a quarter of the heavens.

'It must be uncomfortable craning your neck like
that,' remarked the captain. 'We will turn the
Astrolabe round on her axis—then you will be
able to contemplate the dead world at your leisure
in a horizontal position.'

He approached the stairway, and called down
what appeared to be a speaking tube. Then a
wonderful thing followed.

Sun, earth, stars began to revolve around our
vessel in a semicircle—at least the sun, moon and
stars did, the earth, being almost directly behind the
Astrolabe's stern, kept her position nearly. Slowly
the sun rose higher and higher, the shadow of the
upper deck crept regularly across the width of the

vessel, till we were plunged in comparative darkness—I say comparative, for the reflected light
from the moon's gigantic semicircle, illumined us
with a clear cold radiance, like an electric beacon.
We ourselves experienced not the slightest sensation from the turning movement. One might have
almost thought that the universe was revolving
round us. Clearly it was as impossible to ' fall off '
the *Astrolabe* as off the earth. The surprise which
this new aerial evolution might have caused me
was swallowed up in contemplation of the glorious
lunar landscape, which was now almost on a level
with my eyes.

One-half of the disc was, as I have said, completely enveloped in shadow. It was only by the
occultation of the shining star-dust behind that I
could guess of its existence.

On the southern border, Tycho, with its gigantic
crater and radiating valleys, appeared sharply
defined under a noonday sun, like some vast
centipede with limbs outstretched in all directions.
Beneath it, rising in regular order from the Sea of
Clouds, came the three craters, Arrachel, Alphonse
and Ptolemy, beautiful in their uniform and mathe-
matically constructed circumferences. The Sea of
Tranquillity, the Sea of Storms, and the Rainy Sea
appeared like black patches on a yellowish ground.
I noticed, too, that the mountains on the western
edge of the lunar disc were as clearly and sharply
defined as those in the centre—a fact that can only
be accounted for by the absence of an enveloping
atmosphere, which would, owing to the obliquity of
the angle, tend either to veil or refract the details.

It then struck me to ask the captain whether he
had ever set foot on the moon, and if so, whether
he had found traces of any atmosphere.

'Only in the valleys, professor,' he answered.
'Air possesses sufficient weight, as you know to

make it, like water, seek its own level. The higher summits are as devoid of breathable air as the bell glass of a receiver or the globe of an incandescent lamp. After to-morrow, when we shall be making a promenade across the Sea of Clouds—'

I started. Was it possible that we were going to land on this lonely planet, where no living creature had set foot during incalculable ages?

'You will be able to see and verify these facts yourself.'

'Ah, captain!' I cried, 'you are certainly a marvellous man. Newton and Galileo were children compared with you! What a vessel! What a journey! I confess I am devoured by curiosity respecting your extraordinary invention. What force keeps you in space? What mechanical agent propels you? How comes it that I am breathing life-giving air on board, in the midst of a void where till now life has been considered impossible? All these are prodigious mysteries. I feel myself crushed. I am in the position of a man who would fain not believe, and who does not dare to doubt.'

The captain laughed.

'There is no such great mystery about my boat,' he said simply, 'and I am sure I shall be most happy to give you as many explanations as you require, if you will kindly follow me into the smoking-room.'

I cast one last look at the beautiful dead planet, with the geography and physical conditions of which I was destined to become so familiar later on, and descended to the library. The captain drew out a silver cigarette case and placed it on the table. Then he dropped into a chair, motioned me to a seat, and began,—

'You know, professor, that all bodies floating in space are subject to the laws of gravitation. None can escape—not even the smallest. So powerful and so far-reaching is this force, that two bodies, placed in space at no matter how great a distance, on being released, instantly feel each other's influence across the void, perhaps measured by millions of miles, and, unless diverted from their course by the attraction of some more powerful body, will rush steadily towards each other in a straight line, and eventually collide at a moment which is easily and accurately determinable by the simple laws of dynamics.'

'You are also aware that the force of gravitation on the surface of any body, that is the force with which extraneous bodies are attracted towards its centre, bears a direct proportion to its mass, density and volume. Thus on the earth, objects allowed to fall from a height of, say a hundred feet, traverse, under the influence of her attraction, nearly five metres during the first second of their fall; on Mars, owing to the inferior size of the planet, this distance would be reduced to one and three-quarters metres; on the sun, largest and most powerful of all our neighbours, it would be augmented to a hundred and thirty-four metres; lastly on the moon, the distance would only amount to some eighty centimetres. These are the eternal laws of Nature, which nothing can annul or destroy—nevertheless, by exerting a little of that ingenuity of which we human atoms are so justly proud, we may be enabled, if not to destroy Nature's laws, at least to overcome their effects for a short time.'

'What?' I almost gasped, 'you have succeeded in annulling gravity?'

'I did not say so,' answered the captain somewhat coldly; 'but if you will listen to me you will

E

learn that, without exactly annihilating gravitation, I am enabled, by a very simple mechanical contrivance, to produce, for a short time at least, that inertia on the part of my vessel which might be taken by the ignorant to indicate a complete insensibility to natural laws of weight and motion.'

'I am all attention, captain.'

'In fact, professor, if I cannot exactly construct a ship to fly through space like a meteor or aerolite, I can at least design one that will remain motionless, or nearly motionless, while the planets, together with their satellites, move to and fro, above it, beneath it, or around it.'

A light broke on me all of a sudden. So we were motionless in space! The stupendous distance we had traversed amounted to nothing! It was the earth that had moved—not we ourselves!

'The peculiarities of rapidly-revolving discs,' pursued the captain, 'have been long observed and studied by men of science in both hemispheres. Their strong disinclination to change the position of their axis has been the basis of modern warfare, in a sense. Rifled cannon have, thanks to this peculiarity, brought about an important change in many national relationships, and if, thanks to the savagery inherent in man, the wise decrees of a Higher Power have been made to inflict suffering on thousands, it is only a fitting compensation that the brain of a thinker should have been permitted to bring them into action in another and more peaceful manner.'

The captain, besides being a scientist, was evidently a bit of a philosopher as well.

'Years ago,' he continued, 'while engaged in making some curious experiments with revolving metal discs in my laboratory at Bucharest, it struck me that a combination might be possible, which would not only assure the resistance of the various discs to any change in the direction and inclination of their axes, but also their resistance to any change of position in space.'

'What?' I cried, 'is such a combination possible?'

'The *Astrolabe*, sir,' answered my instructor, 'is a visible and tangible proof of its possibility. I do not say much respecting the efficiency of these arrangements, but such is the rapidity with which our earth and the solar system generally, is hurled through space, that even a very low percentage of efficiency is sufficient to enable us to travel, apparently, at a rate of from one to a hundred thousand miles an hour.'

'But, captain,' I objected, 'it is not alone the revolving discs that keep their position in space —the whole mass of our vessel is depending on them.'

'That is why the efficiency is so low,' replied the captain ; 'without being able to tell you exactly the percentage of perfection reached, I can nevertheless affirm that it is not lower than ten and not higher then twenty per cent.—counting absolute immobility as a hundred.'

I felt dazed, and buried my face in my hands My companion laughed and lit a cigarette.

'Why—then,' I faltered, 'how fast does the earth move?'

'Oh—some tens of millions of miles per hour,' answered the captain. 'You know, professor, that I am not alluding only to the annual journey round the sun.'

'Then you are referring to—'

'The motion of the entire solar system towards the constellation of Hercules—not only that, but also the vast orbit traced by the colossal unknown sun round which our sun is revolving. In fact, professor, motion is endless in the universe. Nothing is at rest—everything moves, falls, dashes through space with inconceivable velocity. There is no centre, no border, no middle, no end—it is Infinity. We revolve round the sun, it revolves round another sun, which in its turn is doing the same thing. All the forces, added and combined, make a total displacement on the part of our insignificant atom · of a world, of which the smallest percentage is an infinite number of miles per hour almost. You will understand, then, that the efficiency of my machines need not necessarily be very high.'

'It is marvellous,' I answered, 'but how do you direct your course?'

'I do not direct my course—I allow it to shape itself,' was the answer. 'Bodies are continually crossing and intercrossing each other in space. What is to prevent me stopping or diminishing the revolutions of my discs when I wish to be attracted by any planet?'

I stared. It was difficult to doubt this man, when the visible proofs were about to unfold themselves before me.

'And your air—your atmosphere,' I ventured timidly, 'how can we breathe, travelling through a vacuum?'

'Just in the same way as the earth breathes,' answered the captain, with a smile. 'We carry our atmosphere along with us.'

'But this atmosphere must be fearfully rarefied.'

'Well, and I do not pretend that it is up to the standard of terrestrial density. Your own inconvenience and suffering when you awoke this morning after a swoon of nearly thirty hours might have guided you to a knowledge of its rarefaction. Nevertheless it is dense enough to exist in. A man can accustom himself to nearly anything in the way of atmospheric variations. In Chili and in

Peru there are villages whose inhabitants live and make merry at an altitude which would suffocate an Englishman or Dutchman nearly. It is an affair of habit entirely.'

'You store air under pressure then, captain?'

'Professor, ordinary mechanical appliances permit me to compress atmospheric air into one-hundreth of its volume. My reservoirs, made, not of iron, but of aluminium, as being lighter and more suitable for my purpose, besides not being liable to rust, are placed in the centre of the vessel. As they are fully a hundred feet in length, the amount they are capable of storing at one time is enormous. The number of cubic feet must be reckoned by millions. On reaching the higher regions of space, the taps are opened, and the enclosed air diffuses itself about the *Astrolabe* like a transparent aureole. I might add that, as most gases are non-conductors of heat and cold, this protecting envelope does much to mitigate the low temperature of space, which, as doubtless you are aware, is twenty or thirty degrees below zero in reality.'

'Bravo, captain! But does not this air tend to dissipate itself in space?'

'Certainly not—no more than the terrestrial atmosphere. The attraction of the *Astrolabe* keeps it in place. If I were to approach too near any of the planets or their satellites, the case might be terribly different. This difficulty, however, is got over by my taking care to absorb my own atmosphere directly the approach of any large body, planet, meteor, or comet is signalled. The pumps are started, and the air is pumped back into the reservoirs, where it is quite safe. The doors are closed, and we live a simple life below deck till the danger is past.'

'Nothing could be more simple,' said I. 'It is the principle of a snail retiring into his shell on a grand scale. But does not the air tend to become exhausted?'

'And what if it does? Caustic potash to absorb the carbonic acid, and a supply of compressed oxygen gas to rekindle its life-giving properties, are all that is necessary.'

'I have no more arguments left,' I said rising, 'there is nothing for me to do but to confess myself vanquished in an encounter with a superior mind. The nature of this marvellous craft, its machinery, its fittings, its interior decorations, all excite my curiosity and imagination. Were I to presume to ask you for a sight of the mysterious engine-room whence its movements are directed, would you refuse me?'

'Certainly not, professor,' replied the captain; 'learned men need have no secrets from each other. If you will step this way, we will examine the mechanical fittings of the *Astrolabe*.'

We passed through the splendid drawing-room and along the lofty corridor. The captain tapped the walls at either side.

'My air reservoirs are placed behind these partitions,' he said. 'The centre of a vessel is the best place for them.'

'And the engines—the famous revolving discs?' I asked curiously.

'They are placed in the bow and stern, and along the keel,' answered my companion. 'Even now, under your feet there are a hundred large spinning tops revolving at between two and three thousand revolutions per minute. I might add, that most of them act independently of one another, thus ensuring safety in case of accident.'

'What astonishes me, sir,' I said, 'is that with such a tremendous expenditure of energy, there should be absolutely no vibration.'

'Ah, professor,' replied the captain, ironically,

'you have evidently not digested the theory of gravitation, or else you have digested it very imperfectly. What is it that causes an engine, say a two-thousand horse-power one, to shake a vessel?'

'Its weight—its momentum.'

'You mean its weight pure and simple. What has momentum to do with it? Now, on the *Astrolabe*, the weight of my discs, which on the earth would be considerable, amounts to practically nothing. Light pinions of steel, working in agate sockets, offer practically no frictional resistance whatever. As for the air—they work in *vacuo*.'

I stared. The captain's explanations were each more striking than the last. Science evidently offered few insoluble problems to this strange being.

At the end of the corridor a curtain of thick chintz admitted us to the habitable part of the *Astrolabe*. Doors opened on the right and left. A manservant with mop and broom was engaged in busily tidying the cabin in which I had passed such an eventful night.

'I have put your friend next door to you,' explained the captain. 'Would you like to pay him a visit? Let us go softly—he may be still asleep.'

Poor Ned! So occupied had I been with my own reflections and impressions, that no thought of my faithful comrade had crossed my mind till then. I experienced a feeling of shame as my handsome companion pushed the door open.

The room was something similar to mine. The same curtains of gathered silk veiling the portholes, the same basin-stand of red marble, the same swinging couch with blue curtains—everywhere the same lavish magnificence.

Ned was sleeping peacefully, like a child, his right arm hanging negligently over the side of the couch, his head resting on his left, which was bandaged carefully, as though he had received a wound.

'A mere skin-deep affair,' said the captain softly, in answer to a questioning look of mine. 'You both had a narrow shave for it. I can really hardly understand how you are alive now. Had our speed been greater than it was, we would have gone clean through your balloon instead of carrying it along with us—now come and leave your friend to his slumbers.'

We left the apartment and continued our exploration of the *Astrolabe*. A beautifully-fitted bathroom attracted my attention. The polished taps and pipes of aluminium stood out in bold relief against the slabs of variegated stone which lined the walls.

'We use our water over and over again,' explained the captain. 'It is distilled and redistilled, thus rendering it unnecessary to carry more than a certain quantity. Otherwise the consumption would be enormous.'

'Certainly,' I said, 'but does not the coal you burn take up space as well as water?'

'Coal? What do we need coal for?'

'For distilling the water of course.'

'Our water, once used, is conducted by a series of copper pipes into a small boiler. Here the solar heat, which on the *Astrolabe* is considerable, owing to the thinness of our atmosphere, is brought to play on it by a system of mirrors and reflectors. The heat thus distributed over the surface of the boiler is sufficient to vaporise a cubic foot of water in less than a minute. It is a very economical system—here is the engine-room.'

A large quadrangular apartment, open at the top, was revealed. The engines, of the six-cylinder type, and strongly built, were placed to work vertically, like those of a screw steamer. At present they were motionless. Not a sound was audible save the faint whirring of the discs beneath the floor. Surprise and wonder were again taking possession of me.

'We use neither steam nor gas,' said my companion, indicating the massive cylinders with a wave of his hand, 'they would not be sufficiently powerful. Pyroxyline is the agent employed. Mixed with ordinary cotton, to prevent its bursting the shell by a too rapid combustion, it gives a power which nothing else can equal. Those levers over there serve to connect the discs with the engine, when it is necessary to set them in motion. A simple multiplying gear of cogged wheels assures rapidity. A high rate of speed being once attained, the discs are disconnected by a stroke of the lever, the air is exhausted from the tunnel in which they work—we are off.'

'And how long do the discs continue to revolve without bringing the engines to bear on them again?' I asked.

'About a year and a half,' answered the captain —'quite that. Owing to the absence of both air and gravity. Were it possible to completely exhaust all air, and to do away with the infinitesimal friction of the pinions, they would revolve for ever!'

'Ah, captain! your wonderful contrivances inspire me as much with pity for the humanity that ignores them, as with admiration for the genius of the man that called them into existence.'

My companion smiled bitterly.

'Perhaps if I were to give my discoveries to the world,' he said, in a low tone, his blue eyes growing large and vague, like those of a man in a reverie, 'I should run some risk of ill-treatment in recompense for my trouble. Who knows? Galileo was not the only man that suffered for possessing too much knowledge. Wisdom is at times a dangerous possession, and never more so than when it aims at the enlightenment and elevation of a foolish humanity.'

CHAPTER VII

A FEW DAYS ON THE MOON

NED HATTON awoke late in the afternoon. Never shall I forget the surprise of my worthy friend when he found where he was, and whither he was going. A deluge of questions poured from his lips, most of which I was able to answer but imperfectly. What was the captain's name, his nationality, his age? When did he calculate returning to earth? What was our exact whereabouts? Could one get anything to drink on board? This last request was not so difficult to gratify. I rung the bell and called the steward, whom Ned immediately began to pump. It was no use. The man was a diplomatist, and though he spoke French perfectly, as also did Ned, he would give us no information on any subject relating to the captain's name or origin.

At least he could tell us where we were.

As far as he knew, we were seventy thousand miles from the moon—he had heard the chief engineer say so about an hour ago.

Ned whistled lugubriously, and laughed.

'I'll believe it when I see it,' he said. 'Now get me something to drink please, for I'm dying of thirst.'

The steward bowed, vanished and returned with a bottle of some wine, resembling claret, which he handed to us on a salver.

'By Jove!' exclaimed Ned, whom the sight of a bottle evidently moved to greater enthusiasm than any amount of scientific prodigies, 'these people are uncommonly civil. What a pity we don't even know the captain's name.'

This last remark was understood by the discreet servant, who gracefully drew a visiting-card from his pocket, which he handed us with another low bow. I read :—

CAPTAIN CHLAMYL,

Commander of the 'Astrolabe.'

'Chlamyl—Chlamyl,' repeated Ned, tossing off a glass of wine and replacing the glass carelessly on the table, whence it bounded merrily, rolling away across the floor like a conjuring trick, 'Chlamyl— what an outlandish name. Here, let's get up and dress—good Lord! Hold me up! What the devil's the matter with me?'

Truly poor Ned must have been strangely confused. Aided by the impassive steward, I picked him up and tried to explain matters. It was useless. Evidently he thought we were playing a practical joke on him.

'Look here, Ned,' I said at length, when we had propped him up on the bed and persuaded him to keep quiet for a minute or two, 'do you see this penknife?'

Ned, with a grunt, admitted that he *did* see it. What's more, it belonged to him. Didn't I remember having borrowed it to sharpen a pencil about a week ago? Why the devil didn't I, etc., etc.

'Look, Ned—now, I'm going to let it fall.'

And the penknife sailed away gently at an angle of some forty-five degrees.

Ned shook his head.

'I believe I'm drunk,' said he. 'The cap.'s claret is infernally strong.'

'Why, you pig-headed old silly!' I burst out, getting exasperated, 'if you don't believe me, look out of the window. It's just over your head.'

He did as he was told and turned to me with his eyes starting out of his head.

'Good G—d, man! Look! Just look!' he said hoarsely.

'I know, I know. I've been admiring the spectacle for the last half-hour myself. Give yourself a wash and brush up, and we'll go on deck—hurry your stumps a bit. The captain 'll be curious to see you.'

Ned had the sense to do as he was told. Several times he was in danger of coming a cropper, but he persisted manfully, and at last succeeded in making himself look presentable.

We passed down the corridor, through the drawing-room, library and dining-room, Ned stopping several times on the way to testify his admiration for some beautiful work of art or handsome piece of furniture. On deck we found the captain, seated in a cane chair, smoking a cigarette. He rose and greeted us affably.

'Well, professor—so you have found your friend. I trust Mr Hatton has not suffered too much from the novel forces at work around him, or, at least, that the marvels which he will witness on board this vessel may compensate, in some measure, for any inconvenience he may have had to put up with.'

Ned grasped the captain's hand.

'It is wonderful!' he said simply.

The moon's disc had grown enormously since the morning, and no wonder, for we had traversed a matter of thirty thousand miles in the last four hours. I pointed out to the astonished Ned the various geographical landmarks known to astronomers—the crater of Tycho, the Sea of Dreams, the lunar Apennines, the mysterious region between the Ocean of Vapour and the Sea of Tranquillity, supposed by some learned men, notably by the celebrated M. Flammarion, to be covered with a growth of lunar vegetables. Ned was in ecstasies. Captain Chlamyl corrected my remarks, or refuted them as the case might be—always in a tone of studied and perfect amiability.

It then possessed my genial companion to ask the captain whether or no the moon was inhabited.

'Life is not wholly extinct yet,' replied the commander, 'but you will not find the last remnants of a dying fauna particularly interesting. Snakes burrow in the sand and tortoises creep along the edge of the marshy pools.'

'Then there is water there?' I asked.

'Only in very small quantities,' answered the captain, 'no large amount could exist in such a rarefied atmosphere. Perhaps you have already noticed the low temperature at which water boils on the *Astrolabe*. It is in a normal state of evaporation.'

'Then how do you manage about the cooking?' asked Ned, whose mind was essentially practical.

'The food is enclosed in boiler-like metal cylinders, surrounded with a network of platinum wire, through which flows a powerful current of electricity. The small amount of water present in the preserved meats is thus evaporated and the food is cooked in its own vapour.'

'But about the moon,' I continued, 'have you found on its surface any traces of intellectual man?'

'Traces there certainly are, professor, but the last survivors of the Selenite race must have perished over a hundred thousand years ago. The feeble atmosphere of the planet alone preserves the more venerable ruins from decay. To-morrow at 9 a.m., if all goes well, we will make our landing, and you will see things for yourself. Are you fond of music, professor?'

'I adore it, captain.'

'Then let us go down to the drawing-room. I fear Mr Hatton is beginning to feel cold, and I should not like him to mar his lunar trip by a preliminary attack of influenza. Do you like Wagner? I will play you the prelude of *Parsifal.*'

A few minutes later we were seated among the silken cushions of the divans, under the soft electric light. Captain Chlamyl took his seat at the piano, and the ethereal harmonies of that wonderful prelude floated round us, like a parting message from the world we had left behind.

At 11 p.m. I retired to rest, closing the curtains of my windows carefully, to shut out the sunlight, which, owing to some new revolution of the *Astrolabe* on its axis, was tracing dazzling circles on the opposite wall. My slumber for several hours was deep and unbroken. Towards 4 a.m. I was awakened by an unaccustomed noise—a rythmic pant that seemed to shake the vessel. We were evidently drawing near the moon, and Captain Chlamyl was taking the precautionary measure of absorbing his atmosphere, storing it at high pressure in the vast reservoirs of aluminium, to prevent the danger of its being attracted away by the lunar mass. I fell asleep again with the fugitive sing-song lullaby of the engines ringing in my ears—then I awoke with a start. Ned was standing over me, a broad smile on his good-humoured face.

'Wake up, Hal—they're waiting breakfast for

you. The captain says he wants you particularly to make haste, as it'll take some time to get our diving-dresses on and we're to start before sunrise.'

' Diving-dresses?' I said confusedly. Then with a glance at the clock, which indicated a quarter past 8 a.m. 'Do you mean to say the sun isn't up yet?'

'No; it doesn't rise here till three in the afternoon. Look slippy!'

I dressed in a hurry and rejoined Ned in the dining-room, where he was having a *tête-à-tête* breakfast with the captain.

'Ha, professor!' said the latter heartily, 'better late than never. I was beginning to despair of seeing you. Take some of this macaroni—it's excellent. You see we're obliged to keep the electric light going, on account of its being still dark in these latitudes. Nevertheless, the sight is a fine one. We are crossing the Sea of Sleep. That peak to the north is Mount Macrobus, the one at the other side, far south, is Mount Taruntius.'

Through the polished glass of the window I beheld a glorious sight.

Beneath us, at a distance of some five or six miles, lay an interminable stretch of landscape deluged in silvery light, which at first I took for moonlight. A moment's thought, however, revealed my error. The moon illumined by the moon! What a paradox! No—the flood of light came from our own distant planet, which I perceived hanging above, nearly in the zenith, a disc of pale yellow, mottled with green and blue. Under the keel of our vessel, the gaunt mountains seemed to glide away like spectres, vast crescent-shaped shadows, thrown from the circular craters, assumed curiously-distorted forms under the varying perspectives which the *Astrolabe's* rapid speed was continually changing. There were few halftones, which require atmospheric reflection to produce them. Nothing but light and shade, pale yellow and silver alternating with black. My heart began to beat excitedly and my hands closed nervously.

'Come, come professor, your macaroni will get cold, and as we have far to walk, you must fortify yourself.'

That brought me out of my trance. I was in a state of absolute ebullition. There were a million things I would like to have said, a million questions I would have liked to ask, but they tripped over one another, and none came as far as my lips. I did the next best thing—I held my tongue and devoured my breakfast with avidity.

The meal was finished in profound silence. Captain Chlamyl, rising, contemplated the flying landscape for some moments in silence.

'We shall be at the base of Mount Archimedes in about half-an-hour,' he said ; 'it will be the starting point of our excursion. I think, professor, we had better go and put on our diving-dresses. Although I propose a lunar promenade, I cannot create air for us to breathe on the way.'

'I thought you said there were animals on the moon, captain,' I ventured to put in ; 'how do *they* manage ? I suppose they require air as well as ourselves.'

'Quite so, sir—but considerably less. Besides they crawl mostly on the surface of the ground, where perhaps the vital fluid is denser. Anyhow we shall only need our diving-dresses for a short while, till we get into the lower regions. I am going to take you down a volcano, professor, so prepare for something out of the ordinary !'

We proceeded to a room in the crew's quarter, where half-a-dozen men in flannel jackets and corduroy trousers were sitting breakfasting at a long wooden table. On our entering, they rose respectfully.

The captain motioned to them to continue their meal, and gave some orders in the Magyar dialect. Presently two or three diving-dresses were brought in. There were one or two peculiarities about their construction which puzzled me, and I examined them with interest.

'You see, professor,' said the captain, 'there are many ways of supplying a diver with air. First, there is the usual way of sending a continual stream down to his nostrils by means of a pump. This, however, attaches him to his vessel, without permitting him to move about freely to any great distance. A better system is to carry a knapsack of compressed air with one and use it as required. The idea has already been made use of, and for all practical purposes on our world, it is certainly good enough. Unfortunately, however, it would not do for me. Setting aside the large expenditure of my precious atmosphere, the weight of a heavy metal reservoir would be a great disadvantage—not on the moon it is true, but on other planets where the power of gravity is more intense. The only remaining alternative, therefore, is to keep purifying the air as fast as I consume it, thus enabling me to consume it over again and again, as long as I please. The system possesses few disadvantages, and is certainly the most profitable for me, both in regard to economy and lightness of the necessary apparatus.

Here, professor, is a portable cylinder of aluminium, constructed to fit on the shoulders, like a knapsack or wallet. The breath from your lungs is made to pass first through a vessel containing a saturated solution of caustic potash. Deprived thus of its poisonous elements, it ascends into the upper part of the cylinder, where it mingles with

F

an infinitesimal quantity of oxygen from a tiny reservoir. Thus equipped, you are ready for a promenade of at least four hours in atmospheres of any kind, under all manner of strange suns.'

The captain's explanations now ceased to surprise me. I had already had so many proofs of his ingenuity and inventive genuis, that I did not even trouble to express any surprise. Ned Hatton, for whom these mechanical marvels possessed the charm of novelty, stared open-mouthed.

We encased ourselves rapidly in these splendid dresses, which, I noticed resembled the pattern universally adopted by the French Government, with four lenticular openings, one in front of the eyes, one above, and two at the sides. I drew my first breath somewhat nervously. The air was good and pure—Captain Chlamyl's invention was certainly a great success. Through the glass of his helmet, I saw Ned's eyes laughing at me—the situation was evidently to his taste.

A sinking movement, followed by a slight shock, told me that the *Astrolabe* had reached *terra firma*. A double door, contrived so as to close in an airtight manner, conducted us to a ladder—a minute later I was standing on the surface of the moon.

He who would paint in words even a common terrestrial landscape, a landscape perhaps visible to him every day for a week, a month or a year, as the case may be, yet ofttimes runs considerable danger of shipwreck, but he who would daringly attempt to describe, not a mere earthly scene, but a view supernatural in its awful beauty—the view of a dead world sleeping in the black void of space—may well consider his steps and measure the chance of failure.

Imagine, then, a vast moonlit plain, airless, lifeless, desolate, stretching away to westward for nearly a hundred miles in a straight line, bordered by a

chain of lofty needle - shaped hills of bare rock,
standing clear, erect and distinct against the blackness of night, dreaming in an eternal vigil over the
deathly plain beneath, with its burnt-out fumaroles and ghostly crevasses, seamed with twisted
flows of stony lava—grey, yellow and ruby red—their
peaks of gneiss or granite assuming here and there
the most fantastic shapes—domes, pinnacles, cups
or pyramids—in apparent defiance of all the known
laws of equilibrium—they were the lunar Apennines, that giant range of gaunt peaks beside which
their earthly representatives sink into tamest insignificance.

On the eastern border of this vast plain, which
terrestrial astronomers have, not too poetically or
too aptly either, named the Sea of Putrefaction,
almost above our heads, as it were, towered the
gigantic crater of Archimedes, looking like the
frowning wall of some giant fortress, equalling Mont
Blanc in height and far surpassing it in width of
base and wild ruggedness. To the north, at a
distance of some fifty miles or so, rose two lofty
volcanoes, one behind the other — Aristillus and
Autolycus. Although I had many times contemplated them through the eye-piece of a telescope, I grieve to say that I failed utterly to
recognise them, till Captain Chlamyl came to my
aid by pointing them out to me on a scleno-
graphical chart which he extracted from the
pocket of his dress for the purpose.

Our party consisted of four men only, the
captain, myself, Ned, and one of the *Astrolabe's*
men, a short, thick-set, muscular-looking individual
whom I had noticed cleaning the main crank of
the engine on the previous day. Our route was
evidently well-known to the captain, for he stepped
out briskly in the direction of the huge volcano,
whose top, though nearly three miles off, yet

seemed, so colourless and transparent were the lunar solitudes, to be almost within reach of one's hand. Presently the *Astrolabe*, with its rows of luminous port-holes, was lost to view among the myriads of small craters and volcanic monticules that dotted the plain on either side.

Some of these burnt-out seats of Plutonian energy were several hundred yards in diameter, others were no bigger than the basin of an Icelandic geyser. Sometimes, by way of shortening our path, we passed through the broken-down lip of these fantastic circles, that I could not help likening in my mind to the ruins of a Roman amphitheatre, and scrambled over the precipitous wall at the other side ; not a very difficult task, for the feeble attraction of this lonely satellite made climbing operations of any kind five times easier than they would have been on the earth. The soil was mostly composed of a soft, friable sand, unfavourable to walking exercise, and, I believe, thickly impregnated with alkaline particles, like the desert plains of western America, so dreaded by travellers in that region.

The walk was conducted in an absolute silence, for it was well-nigh impossible to communicate our thoughts to one another, except by touching our copper helmets together—an inconvenient expedient at best. Not even our footsteps echoed on the ground. Sound needs an atmosphere to propagate it, and here an eighty-one ton gun would hardly have made more noise than a baby derringer. An hour's silent tramp brought us to the edge of a precipice—nearly a mile in width and fathomless, for all I could see. The scene here was one of unparalleled grandeur. Above us towered the great mountain, its yellow tops seeming to kiss the stars, at our feet yawned the hideous abyss, streaked in places with veins of red granite

and green serpentine, leading down to a world of
shadows beneath—a veritable Inferno, grander
than that of Dante, at the sight of which many a
sleeper might wish to wake, and many a waking
man might deem himself dreaming.

Captain Chlamyl, after following the edge of
this crevasse for about ten minutes, commenced to
descend it boldly. Casting one final look at the
sleeping plain, with our far-off earth hanging
above it in the tranquil zenith, I screwed up my
courage and plunged after my companions into
the gloom.

Walking here became comparatively easy.
Owing to the difference in gravitation, we slipped
and slid over abysses which on our own world
would have presented insuperable difficulty, or
have been quite impossible to traverse. The de-
scent, winding and zigzagging in an irregular
manner, occupied about an hour. Long before
this time we were enveloped in total darkness. I
was groping my way along rather helplessly, when
suddenly a light shone in my eyes. It came from
an incandescent lamp affixed to the captain's
helmet. His companion, the engineer of the previous day, bore a similar light. Thus aided, we
saw our way without difficulty.

The precipice, torn in the soil by some terrible
volcanic convulsion, I suppose, must have been
about a mile deep. We proceeded carefully along
its sandy bottom, which I fancy must once have
been the bed of a river, and which I noticed was
even then crossed here and there by patches and
bands of marshy soil—till under some overhanging
rocks a dark tunnel opened before us. I shuddered.
The scene was becoming positively terrifying. At
either side of the path, which was sloping downwards in a gentle incline, the rocky walls, veined
with streaks of shining mica or volcanic obsidian,

reflected the light of our electric lamps in rivulets of soft fire. Stalactites hung from the roof of this tunnel, and several times I saw streams of moisture trickling down its walls. Captain Chlamyl plunged still lower. We must be nearing the heart of the volcano, extinct, no doubt, for some hundreds of centuries. Ned Hatton, whose diving-costume but ill concealed his natural lankiness of figure, kept passing to and fro between me and the captain's light in a most aggravating manner. Once or twice (must I attribute it to a sort of nervousness?) I heard rumblings and mutterings, and the disquieting thought of an eruption crossed my mind. Finally we stopped abruptly.

The captain, proceeding to divest himself of his diving-dress, motioned me to do the same.

A vast portal, hewn out of the living rock, and resembling, in form, the pylon of an Egyptian temple, yawned before us.

CHAPTER VIII

A BURIED NATION

FOR a moment I felt astonished, then the explanation suggested itself to me of its own accord.

We were nearly two miles beneath the surface of the moon—any atmosphere that there was must perforce linger in the depths on account of its weight alone. Thus, in this dark tunnel, we were once more surrounded by life-giving air.

'Place your dresses and helmets on this rock,' remarked the captain, indicating a table-like formation of granite, 'we shall not need them for some hours, torches will be sufficient to light our way.'

The air in this place was dull and singularly warm. Captain Chlamyl's companion produced several long sticks of some resinous substance, which, on being lit, burned with a clear bright flame.

'Now forward into the City of the Dead,' said the commander.

My heart thrilled strangely. Were we going really to explore a hidden lunar town, buried in the bowels of these wild mountains? Captain Chlamyl had stopped under the vast gateway, which must have been fully a hundred feet high. The red torchlight played fitfully over the obliquely-slanting walls of hewn stone that formed its two sides. Gigantic characters appeared, cut deeply in the stone like hieroglyphics, though they more resembled the cuneiform writing of the Euphrates than the Pharaonic inscriptions of the Nile. Ned grasped my arm convulsively. Neither of us spoke, the scene was too impressive. Presently the captain's voice broke the spell.

'Some hundred thousand years ago,' he said, 'the active life on the moon's surface was drawing to its close. Water and air, those indispensable requisites of all animated existence, were beginning to fail. A certain quantity of them became lost every year, combining chemically with the rocks, or otherwise receding from the surface. Soon there remained but a few marshy pools where once there had been seas, and the rarefied air, many degrees below zero in temperature, failed to supply the lungs with the necessary amount of oxygen.

Under the circumstances a natural emigration towards the deeper regions took place, and this great city, which I have named Selenopolis, for want of a better name, was the result of that emigration. As each step in the history of a planet may, and generally does mean a period reckoned by thousands of years, this town appears to have flourished for an age far exceeding that of Thebes or Alexandria. Tentative explorations on the frozen upper plains, accomplished perhaps by means of contrivances no less scientific than those of my own invention, became rarer and rarer. A high degree of civilisation had no doubt been attained, but all its knowledge and power was unable to save a doomed race from extinction. By degrees the needful water began to recede farther and farther into the heart of the dying world. Countless wells, bored doubtless amid inconceivable sufferings and at the expenditure of almost limitless engineering skill (as you will see for yourself) resulted only in prolonging the misery of these buried unfortunates, who thus dwindled from a nation as great as any which our earth can boast of, to a few solitary groups of starving nomads, wandering among the dark aisles, sightless, homeless, hopeless, seeking, perhaps vainly, the offal that was to prolong the mockery of existence, craving for death, yet clinging to life with the tenacity of a poisoned slave, who hugs the cup that is crushing his heart —even faith had left them, for faith needs moral support of some kind, and from which of these sombre abysses were they to draw a knowledge of the Creator's beauty and wisdom? Finally the end came. Who can tell who the last survivor was—perhaps an aged man, perhaps a new-born babe, clinging to the breast of a dead mother. Ah, professor, that is the final scene in the history of a planet, the last act in the drama of human existence.'

Then suddenly rousing himself,—

'Let us be off,' he said abruptly.

We passed on. A broad street of stone, flat and level as the pavement of a Paris boulevard, shone under the light of the torches. Above our heads was intense blackness—the cavern must have been at least a hundred and fifty feet high, if not more. Shadows loomed at the side of the road. They were the ruins of lunar buildings, yellow and crumbling with age. At first I thought they were built of stones united with mortar or super-imposed in the Egyptian fashion. I soon discovered my mistake. There was no attempt at building, the houses were hewn bodily out of the solid rock, resembling in their rough simplicity a series of caverns rather than an agglomeration of human dwellings.

They were windowless for the most part, for of what use would windows have been in that deep gloom? and their walls were in some places covered with cuneiform writing. I asked Captain Chamyl whether he had ever discovered the key to this strange alphabet.

'No, professor,' he replied, 'and I cannot say that I have been very energetic in searching for it. From an antiquarian's point of view it would no doubt present many curiosities, but I am not an antiquarian, and as a scientist merely, I do not believe the translation of these documents, which probably are purely historical, would furnish us with any new facts respecting the laws of Nature.'

'And why not, captain?'

'Because, sir, the moon was a far shorter-lived planet than our earth—its size alone would vouch for that. Discoveries in science are slow, and I fear the poor Selenites had hardly time to arrive at any great perfection. They may have reached the period at which we now are on the earth, but they certainly went no further. This writing is a visible proof of that fact.'

I looked at the captain curiously, and fell to examining the inscriptions. The regularly-traced lines crossed and inter-crossed one another, forming many geometrical combinations, which Ned said reminded him of a Chinese puzzle. The more I looked, the less certain I was of finding a solution of the captain's statement.

'He means,' vouchsafed Ned, giving me a dig in the ribs with his elbow, 'that no very civilised people would use that kind of barbaric writing.'

'More than that, Master Hatton,' answered the captain, smiling. 'I mean that no highly civilised people would write at all!'

'You astonish me, sir!' I said simply.

'Why so, professor? The art of writing, that is the art of expressing one's ideas by certain pre-arranged combinations of signs, is an extremely slow, unpractical and tedious one. The rate at which an ordinary individual writes is rarely more than sixty or seventy words a minute. This excessive and wearisome slowness of the pen has given rise, in the nineteenth century, to a system of shorthand, which enables experts to record thought at over double that rate. The invention of the phonograph has quadrupled the speed nearly, and the peculiar wonders of mesmerism, which may in course of time permit us to impress on others thoughts which are passing through our brains without rendering it necessary to formulate them in words, will do away with slow and elementary writing altogether in course of time—if only the world lives long enough.'

To this, as to the captain's other statements, it was impossible to invent an answer. We continued our examination of these Selenite dwellings, the doors of which, hewn squarely out of the light rock, were some of them nearly ten feet high, and broad in proportion, thus seeming to endorse the theory of certain astronomers, who, arguing from the standpoint of gravity, maintain that the dwellers on the moon surpassed those of the earth in physical stature.

In the open space outside, resembling a public square, were several wells, enclosed in the remnants of ruined circular walls. Captain Chlamyl pointed to them and looked at me without speaking. Presently a gigantic building confronted us, its vast pillars looming through the darkness like spectres.

'A palace,' said Ned to me.

It was indeed a dwelling worthy of a king. Steps of lava, forty in number, and rather exceeding the height of our steps on the earth, led up to a row of Titanic columns, twenty feet broad at the base and at least two hundred feet high. The torchlight failed to reach their tops, but our sturdy engineer produced a roll of magnesium wire, and in an instant the whole building, with the silent square in front of it, was enveloped in blinding white radiance. The imposing edifice was evidently some public building—perhaps a cathedral. The stone had decayed in places, leaving unsymmetrical gaps and holes. In some of the chinks I perceived lichens growing—dull, colourless plants, not differing much from their earthly representatives. An exclamation from Ned attracted me.

'A statue!' he said.

The figure of a man was visible, standing erect in the centre of this vast temple, his arms crossed on his breast.

Come now! thought I, we are on the moon, not on the earth, and this figure looks singularly human!

The statue was about thirty feet high. It had the head of a monkey, and was dressed in a gown not unlike the Roman toga. To my surprise, I noticed that the ears were totally absent—at its feet was a circular ball, about five feet in diameter.

'A geographer!' suggested Ned.

'An astronomer,' corrected Captain Chlamyl, 'that globe represents the earth!'

We examined this lunar model of our native planet with interest. North and South America Africa and Australia, were drawn with great clearness. Europe was less distinct, and the smaller details were lost in the traces of decay that were visible everywhere over the surface of the stone. Time pressed, however—our supply of torches was not too large, and we had a long way to go back. We passed through endless arcades formed by countless columns of lava or granite, up and down, in and out—there seemed to be no end to this vast place, nor indeed, after the first shock of surprise, was it very interesting.

'We were born too late, professor,' then said the captain. 'Had we arrived here some five or six thousand years earlier, when the world was young and Thebes was still an affair of the future, we might possibly have found something curious—as matters stand now, everything has been long ago consigned to the sarcophagus of antiquity. Nothing can resist the encroachments of age, not even in a dry cavern like this. Not a single human bone, not a solitary bar of iron could survive—stop! listen a moment! Do you hear anything?'

We halted and stood motionless, our ears on the alert. The torches sputtered and crackled, dropping their burning sparks on the hard pavement. Captain Chlamyl's finely Grecian profile appeared cut out against the darkness behind as he peered, with a shade of anxiety on his face, far away into the gathering gloom.

At first I could distinguish nothing, then after a few moments' listening—a faint rustling sound,

like the falling of dried leaves, became audible
above the hissing of the torches. I was about to
go on, when the commander of the *Astrolabe*
stopped me.

'Stay where you are,' he said. 'There may be
danger in proceeding. Let me see—have any of
you got weapons with you?'

I thrilled with horror. The captain was not a
man to speak without a reason. His whole appearance had changed. The calm look of abstraction
on his face had given place to a certain expression
of uneasiness. Yet what could molest us in the
heart of a dead world?

'Perhaps the volcano—' began Ned.

'Oh, bother the volcano!' answered the captain,
irritably. 'Do you think you could manage to fit
between those columns over there?'

A row of square stone pillars, about eighteen
inches apart, rose at some little distance. We
directed our steps towards them, the captain leading
the way I hazarded another question.

'Is it a danger you are acquainted with, captain?'

'What does it matter?' he answered nervously,
trying the edge of his long dagger against the palm
of his hand. 'Yes—no, it has dogged my steps more
than once already, but I never had a fair sight of it
—get back and keep quiet!'

We stepped back between the protecting
columns, holding our torches well above our heads,
and, for my part, I felt decidedly frightened. What
could this mysterious peril be that the captain had
such a profound dread of? A hideous creeping of
my spine made my teeth chatter nervously as I
pondered over the chances of my being attacked
from the back—but no, not far behind me there
was a solid wall of stone that nothing could pierce.
I was safe there at least. Our four torches

illumined about fifty yards of pavement in front
of us, after that all was grisly shadow. I strained
my eyes into the darkness, and a host of vague and
unreasonable fancies began to crowd on my brain.

It was not an eruption that Captain Chlamyl
dreaded, not a flood or an avalanche—no, it was
something of more material form. A man? An
animal of some kind?

I shuddered as I pictured to myself a Cyclops
with one burning eye in the centre of his forehead,
and a huge club of bronze to pound us with. Could
it be a hyena? Troops of them usually prowled
about deserted cities, especially when it was dark.
No, it must be some more than ordinarily horrible
monster, to provoke such nervous dread in the
breast of our usually impassive captain. Visions
of supernatural horrors, ghouls, ell-women, vampires,
were-wolves, crowded into my mind all at once,
and I peered fearfully out into the darkness, while
a conviction that we were running a near chance
of meeting with some horrible death or other forced
itself gradually upon me.

For some minutes nothing was heard. All that
struck my ear was the crackling of our torches and
the panting breathing of Ned, who was next me,
separated by the column of stone, which was about
four feet thick. Then again upon the stillness
rose that dreadful creeping sound, like a rustling
among dead leaves—a sound as if something were
being dragged forcibly along the rocky floor, sweeping and scraping the stone in its passage.

Nearer it came and nearer. Presently my
horrified eyes could dimly perceive a vast phosphorescent object moving slowly along about a
hundred yards away. A confused sound of hissing struck my ear, and I pressed back against the
wall behind, while I mentally cursed the hour
that brought me on this extraordinary journey,

and shivered all over like a child in a darkened room.

The phosphorescent object approached, winding about in a most mysterious fashion. Seventy yards—sixty yards—fifty yards—oh, heavens!

Before us, rolling its huge length along the smooth floor, its curved back, white as milk, glistening and shining palely in the light of the torches, was the most gigantic serpent I had ever beheld!

It was nearly a hundred feet long. Its huge head, in the form of an isosceles triangle, swayed to and fro as the monster paused to look at us. I heard Ned utter an exclamation of horror, and the blood froze in my veins as I contemplated the possibility of one or all of our number falling a prey to this terrible creature, who certainly would have swallowed a man as easily as a shark would swallow a haunch of bacon—and we were unarmed!

Of what use would a pitiful revolver, or a tiny steel dagger, be against this beast, whose scaly armour, for all we knew, might be bullet-proof?

The vast head, still swaying gently backwards and forwards like a cobra about to strike, advanced nearer, and, in the shadow behind, I saw the huge folds of its body roll after it in wavy undulating rings, the tough, horny scales scraping heavily against the pavement, thus producing that ominous noise that had sounded at a distance like the falling of dried leaves. I then noticed a thing that I had not suspected—the monster was blind!

Its triangular head, some four feet across at the base of the neck, was absolutely devoid of eyes. Six long feelers, white and phosphorescent as the rest of the body, waved in the air like the tentacles of a sea-anemone. A forked tongue, nearly a yard in length and split into three equal prongs, shot occasionally from between its closed jaws. Though blind, to all appearances, it seemed aware of the

presence of light, and shifted its head slowly up
and down to drink in this new impression, which
was in some way acting on or caressing its deadened
optic nerves.   A momentary sense of pity shot
through me as I contemplated the sightless monster,
but a sudden advance of its horrible head dispelled
the kindly emotion, which gave place to repulsion
and sickening fear.   The space between the pillars
was not sufficiently large to admit its head, unless
it chose to turn it sideways, and even then, I
calculated breathlessly, the great jaws would not
be able to open more than a few inches.   Thus,
unless it were able to damage me with its tongue,
I was comparatively safe.   The moral terror was
all I had to fear.   I tried to shut my eyes—in vain.
A dreadful fascination made me open them again.

The head came nearer by degrees, contemplating
us from a height of about fifteen feet, its pale,
flesh-coloured tentacles waving like serpents.   A
strong odour of musk filled the air, and for a
moment I wondered whether or not it was poisonous.
The triangular head, one of the characteristic points
about venomous serpents, seemed to confirm this
belief, and I shuddered as I thought of the agonising death that awaited me if the monster succeeded
in touching me with its fangs.   Presently, half
paralysed with terror, I saw the great head sink
lower—lower yet, till it was within a few yards of
my face.   The triangular jaws advanced, and the
triple tongue shot out in the direction of my torch.
I pressed back against the wall, my spine creeping
with accumulation of horror.   The white tentacles
gently touched the pillars on either side—they
seemed to be armed at their ends with curved claws,
like the pincers of a lobster—

'Throw down the torch!' said a voice, which,
even in my extremity of terror, I recognised as
that of the captain.

I did more. I hurled the blazing stick of resin full in the monster's face.

A horrible rattling, like the noise of artillery, filled the air, echoing and vibrating down the dark aisles of the deserted square. It was followed by the loud bang of a revolver, and the white coils writhed in gigantic rings, rolling hither and thither in knots. A crashing of fallen stones and the sting of dust in my eyes obscured everything for a moment—somebody grabbed my shoulder.

'Run for it!' shouted Ned.

And we *did* run. Most of the torches had been thrown down—one was still alight, the captain's. With its flickering trail of sparks to guide us, we hurried and stumbled along, that terrible rattle still ringing in our ears, like a ghostly death-knell. Twenty times I fell, severely bruising my face and arms, and each time I fancied I felt the long, white fangs imbedded in my flesh. What a chase! How is it possible to adequately describe the horrors of that flight through the darkness? Once, every joint in our bodies half dislocated, we stopped to take breath. But out of the gloom behind us came that dreadful rustling, telling of the foe on our track. We pressed on, and stopped no more till we reached the gate of the town, more dead than alive.

The march across those frozen plains was accomplished in silence, for no sound could pierce the massive helmets of copper. Once Ned, stopping me by a gesture, pointed prophetically towards the eastern horizon.

Through a gap in the bleak sand hills a bright trail of golden light was visible—I understood.

The sunlight was creeping gradually over the darkened surface of this vanished world, and soon the lunar day, equal to fourteen earthly ones, would

G

dawn over this silent plain. I nodded my head, and through the thick glass of his helmet, I could see Ned's black eyes sparkling. The adventure had certainly not displeased my worthy companion, who, as explorer and trader, had faced many dangers, quite as great, on our own inhabited planet. As for me, I own I felt considerably shaken. Once or twice I even looked back across the white waste of sand and lava, to assure myself that the monster was no longer following us.

Hallo! Where was the captain?

He had vanished behind one of the crescent-shaped fumaroles. Ned was staring (open-mouthed, I suppose) at the illuminated mountains in the east, the engineer was engaged in apparently examining the ground at his feet, as a prospecting silver miner reconnoitres the rocks before preparing to sink his shaft.

'Ned, you fool! do you want to lose yourself? Come on!'

I could not make him appreciate these remarks, but I uttered them to myself, nevertheless, as I stepped up to where my thoughtless companion stood, wrapt in silent meditation.

A rapid gesture from the engineer attracted the attention of both of us.

He was staring at some marks in the sand—footmarks?

We bent down to make sure.

Yes. Large, unmistakable footprints—hob-nailed boots with square toes, similar to the ones we were then wearing.

Perhaps they were our own? No, they led eastward, away across the level plain in a regular track, as far as the eye could see. I felt puzzled. The engineer stood like a statue, pointing downwards with hand outstretched. The vague, distant sunlight, striking through the circular glass plates,

lit up his pale face, which was convulsed with
horror. I started. What was the matter?

The dark eyes were rigidly fixed on the ground,
the lips were bloodless, the teeth set. Never had
I seen such a curious expression on the face of a
man. Agony, fear and fury were mingled in one
diabolical contortion of the muscles. There must
be some history behind this. For the moment, so
intense was my curiosity, that I would have torn
off helmet and dress, regardless of consequences,
to deluge the man with questions, to seek a solution of this strange mystery.

A light, clear as a ray from Aldebaran, shone
between two far-off crests of rock—the captain was
signalling to us.

Footprints, mystery, all were forgotten. To be
abandoned in this dreary world would be an awful
fate. We ran across the shifting sand in the direction of the light . . .

An hour later we reached and boarded the
Astrolabe—just as the first rays of sunlight were
striking on the silent crater of Mount Archimedes.

I X

COMETS AND METEORS

DURING a great part of the following day I remained a prisoner in my cabin, the contusions
and wounds on my arms and legs being much too
serious to make moving about a pleasure. Ned
Hatton, his arm in a sling and his face covered
with scratches, came in once or twice to talk to me.

What we had passed through was certainly a
grisly experience, but not sufficient to entirely

stop our lunar excursions, if Captain Chlamyl did not hurry us away too soon.

Towards nightfall I began to feel hot and uncomfortable. Attributing my sensations to the general feverishness occasioned by my unusual nervous excitement on the previous afternoon, I paid no attention to the matter, and soon drifted off into dreamland.

At three in the morning I awoke in what felt like a Turkish bath. Perspiration burst from every pore, the air was heavy and stifling, the very blankets felt as though they were made of hot iron. I lit the electric lamps, dragged myself painfully to the door and opened it.

The vessel could not by any chance be on fire? thought I.

Ned, his face still bandaged, his long nightdress flapping ungracefully round his thin legs, looked comically at me from the door of his cabin.

'What a fearful heat!' he said.

'Something's gone wrong somewhere,' I growled. 'I wish our captain would be a little more careful, while *we* are on board at least. There must be ten thousand fires alight under the keel!'

'Not a bit of it,' replied Ned, 'it's merely the sun! You never saw such a glare! Just come and look out here a minute.'

'Oh!' I said simply, 'of course!'

What had happened was not so difficult to explain after all. The long lunar day, equal to fourteen of our terrestrial ones, had dawned. There being no atmosphere worth speaking of to break the vigour of the solar rays, the intense cold of space had instantaneously given place to a temperature fully equal to that of boiling water. We were being cooked by the sun, that was all!

'What on earth is to be done?' I asked tremulously, after half blinding myself by attempting to

gaze on the dazzling landscape without, through
Ned's port-hole.

'Grin and bear it,' was the unconsoling answer,
'unless our confounded captain possesses some
dodge for cooling off.'

This did not seem unlikely—the ingenuity of
Captain Chlamyl was no doubt quite equal to
contriving some method (compressed air would
have been the simplest) for lowering the tempera-
of his boat to suit external variations. Whether
this was so or not, he certainly took no steps for
our comfort—the corridor, between the reservoirs
of air, was coolest, and thither we dragged our
mattresses, to await the day or hour when we
should leave this intolerably uncomfortable and
inhospitable satellite.

A clanging of bells awakened me. The curtains
parted and a figure in a long red dressing-gown
appeared—it was the captain himself.

'We are going to start,' he said.

'Thank heaven!' I ejaculated fervently ; 'it was
time !'

A few minutes later the panting rhythm of the
engines was heard — an ascensional movement
began to be felt.

'We're off!' murmured Ned, 'now let's go and
get something to eat.'

It was not poetical, but it was sound common
sense. For some hours we glided noiselessly across
the moon's surface, at a speed somewhere between
a hundred and five hundred miles an hour. Finally,
at ten thirty, the 'translation' movement carried us
away obliquely into the dark regions of space, and
our life on board reassumed its usual regularity. The
speed of our wonderful vessel increased in an enormous ratio as the distance between her keel and the
moon's centre augmented, and the efficiency of her
machines rose in consequence. I was nevertheless

considerably surprised when, at 4 p.m., Captain
Chlamyl appeared in the drawing-room and—

'We have traversed nearly a hundred thousand
miles,' he said, 'and I am going to let out our
atmosphere.'

I had been engaged in the examination of some
first-rate lunar photographs, presumably taken by
the captain on some former visit, but at this remark,
delivered in the commander's usual tone of indifference, I put down the album.

'Your rate of travelling is as variable as it is
marvellous, captain,' I said, 'but I am puzzled to
know how you manage to measure your distances
with anything resembling accuracy.'

'That presents no difficulty, sir,' replied the commander. 'The variations in gravity, as we approach
or recede from any planetary body, would alone
suffice to give me tolerably accurate results, were
it not for the fact that the disturbing influences of
other such bodies step in and serve to mar the
calculation.'

'Precisely, captain, that is exactly what I was
driving at. Every star in space exercises some influence on this floating vessel. Therefore a calculation—'

'Which I have no intention of wasting time over,'
burst in the captain, laughing. 'No, professor, we
have not all of us got the patience of a Leverrier,
and even if we had, the time necessary for such
work would run into days, weeks even—and these
I would not be disposed to give. I employ more
direct means.'

'I am at a loss to understand you, captain.'

'If you will kindly step this way, professor,
matters will soon explain themselves.'

A small metal staircase conducted us from the
crew's quarters to a sort of oval deck-cabin. It was
fitted up as a scientific laboratory apparently, for

the walls and shelves were crowded with a medley
of instruments, some of them already familiar to
me, others of which I could not possibly guess the
use. Five oblong panels of toughened glass permitted a clear view in every direction. The yellow
disc of the moon occupied an enormous angle on
the port side, behind us was the earth, of which
both poles were nearly equally visible. I concluded,
therefore, that the *Astrolabe* must be travelling
nearly parallel to the plane of our earth's ecliptic,
nor was I mistaken.

' Here, sir,' said Captain Chlamyl, indicating what
appeared to be a small telescope, with a manometer
dial affixed to it above the eye-piece, ' here is the
contrivance which I use to measure our distance—
not from any body in space, but from some known
centre—the sun, for instance. If I know my distance from the great planet which rules our system,
the remaining calculations are easy enough. You
understand the laws of radiation, do you not ? '

' I fancy so, captain.'

' Then you will easily comprehend this instrument. It is a simple telescope, which, instead of an
eye-piece, is furnished with an electric thermopile.
The solar heat, concentrated on the cells, generates
a current of electricity absolutely proportionate, in
a fixed ratio, to our distance from the orb of day.
This dial which you see is merely a galvanometer,
registering the strength of current with tolerable
accuracy. A table of figures suffices to indicate
the number of thousand miles for whatever degree
the needle swings through—that is all.'

A loud hissing interrupted my eulogies. A
whitish vapour floated round the *Astrolabe*, enveloping it from stem to stern in a mantle of
steam, which presently grew more transparent, as
the liberated air dispersed round us in space.

' You can go out on deck now,' said the captain,

'but I should advise you to fetch a wrap of some kind, as the newly-expanded air will be freezingly cold.'

I did as I was recommended, and found that the commander was right, the deck of the *Astrolabe* was more like an ice-house than anything else.

'Look, professor,' said my friend Ned, who was hanging over the port railing, meditatively smoking a Turkish cigarette and studying lunar geography, 'look over there a minute, will you. Is that a star, or what?'

A thin trail of light, condensed at one end into a burning focus, was visible against the ebony blackness, standing out clearly among the stars that make up the constellation of Andromeda.

'A comet!' I said.

This was a curiosity to be more carefully studied. Descending to the saloon, I pocketed a telescope and returned to examine this celestial stranger.

Whence had it come? Whither was it going?

It was impossible to say. Its speed, however, must have been prodigious, for it managed to double its size within an hour, and its gigantic tail stretched over an angle of fully ten degrees.

'What would happen if that thing should happen to cross our path, professor?' asked Ned, carelessly.

We had abandoned the deck on account of the cold, and were sitting on a luxurious sofa before the port window of the saloon. His question set me thinking. Undoubtedly this was the forerunner of countless other wandering stars that the *Astrolabe* was sooner or later bound to come across.

From a scientific point of view these erratic bodies were, no doubt, highly interesting; from a physical point of view they might be decidedly dangerous. Indeed, our short experience on the moon was quite sufficient to show me that Captain Chlamyl was not the man to fight shy of danger in any form. No doubt he had a wholesome respect for it—most people have that, especially clever ones—but as to whether he would go out of his way on its account, as to whether he would think fit to abandon one of his marvellous journeys just on account of running the risk of being smashed—*that* I could only look on as highly problematical.

'Why, Ned,' I replied, 'there are many things that could happen if we by any chance crossed the orbit of that flying devil. One thing is, that we should certainly have the satisfaction of ending our days gloriously and mysteriously, as well as expeditiously and painlessly.'

'Would it be painless?' queried Ned, doubtfully. 'Mightn't we get scorched a bit first? That'd hurt, I guess.'

'Much more likely to get suffocated,' I answered, 'suffocated and burnt up at the same time. Depends on what sort of an atmosphere the brute has round him. If it's composed of pure carbonic acid gas, or of sulphuretted hydrogen—'

'Do you think the captain ought to be warned?' asked Ned, indolently. 'Suppose he hasn't noticed it!'

'That's hardly likely,' said I. 'The watch on deck'll let him know soon enough, if he hasn't seen it already. By Jove! it *is* coming along at a pace!'

The comet had nearly doubled its size again during our dialogue. Two tails of intense whiteness stretched away behind the glowing head, which shone with a cold lustre, like blue-fire. Even through the thick glass and through the soundless void of space, I fancied I could hear it hissing and rushing. Long streamers of red and orange now and again broke loose from the main body, and circled about it in rings of fire, compelled, no doubt, by the attraction.

' It is the birth of Saturn over again,' I said.

' It'll be the death of *us* if it comes much nearer,' was Ned's reply.

At that moment the door opened and Captain Chlamyl entered. In his hand was a rolled-up map.

' Ha! professor,' he said, ' so you are admiring our visitor? Take a good look at him, for neither you or I will ever set eyes on him again.'

I glanced out of the window at the glowing green focus with its scarlet and yellow rings.

' So it is a parabolic comet, captain?' I said.

' Yes, sir, to judge from its speed, which we have managed to measure pretty well. Bodies can only travel at a certain speed round fixed orbits. Anything beyond this certain speed, which has been estimated at about twenty-five miles a second, hurls the body, whether it be star, comet or meteor, clean out into boundless immensity, where it goes on burning and hissing, till in the course of time it burns or hisses itself quite away. Now look at that one! How far should you say it was off?'

I considered. The blueish light was shining with marvellous intensity, almost rivalling the sun itself.

' About fifty miles,' I said.

' A hundred,' said Ned.

' About two thousand,' was the captain's reply.

' Is it possible!' I exclaimed. ' Why it looks as if one could touch it with one's hand. What diameter do you suppose it has?'

' Oh, I should think it is about three times the size of London.'

Ned whistled with the air of an unbeliever.

' To estimate distance in space with the naked eye is nearly impossible,' continued the captain; ' mistakes are certain to occur. Does it not look as if it were racing us?'

The glowing mass was apparently moving along in a parallel line with the *Astrolabe*, but at a much higher speed. Its action, indeed, resembled that of a racer, but a racer by the side of whom we little atoms had not even a chance. Already, having passed us, it was diminishing in size.

' In a few hours it will be almost invisible,' said Captain Chlamyl, ' but we have not done with it yet; we have still the tail to face.'

' Are we in no danger, captain ? '

' No, sir—at least I think not. The only really serious thing that could happen, would be if any of the million aerolites that follow in its track should come near enough to steal our atmosphere, or perhaps to poison it—then—'

The captain shrugged his shoulders significantly. No doubt, accustomed as he was to continually gazing at eternity in various forms, the prospect of abruptly being absorbed in the fiery centre of some unknown cometary mass had no terrors for him. But for me it was otherwise, and I gazed out after the vanishing comet with feelings better imagined than described.

' After all,' I reflected, ' space is large and we are small. It will be a pity if there is not sufficient room for us to wander about without knocking up against a star.'

Never had prophecy been more correct. We certainly had *not* seen the last of our green comet. During the next three days at least, meteors and aerolites swarmed past the *Astrolabe* at varying speeds and distances. As they were only dull masses of cold stone for the most part, it was not easy to distinguish them. Sometimes they glowed in balls of fire, at other times they simply resembled a cloud of yellow dust, obscuring the farther stars.

As I had suspected myself, we ran some danger,

not from the actual masses of aerolitic stone, but from the larger spheres of noxious gas that some-times surrounded them. A very small proportion of carbonic acid, mingled with a breathable atmos-phere, is sufficient to turn it into poison of the deadliest kind, and I could not help thinking it imprudent of our captain to run this risk, when he might have obviated it in so simple a manner.

Some idea of the kind certainly seemed to strike the commander of the *Astrolabe* simultaneously with myself, for on the night of the 15th I heard the pumps working, and in the morning the doors leading to the deck were hermetically sealed, thus making our customary daily exercise impossible.

To ask the captain for explanations was difficult, to say the least of it. We only saw him at meals—that is, he consumed most of his time in the observatory on deck. When a man's entire mind is given to the solving of some more than ordinarily intricate problem in mathematics or astronomy, to get a straight answer out of him is next to im-possible. Captain Chlamyl's attitude during the next three or four days was one of 'divine abstrac-tion,' and to 'pump' him on any fixed subject was quite out of the question. Not that we had any-thing to complain of. On the contrary, we were delicately and carefully looked after. The food, always good, reached, during these days of confine-ment, the level of a first-class European hotel. It was as though our captain endeavoured to make up in hospitality what he lacked in personal attention.

The time, on the whole, did not pass slowly. A copious library was always at our disposal. The books of the *Astrolabe* were carelessly selected and equally carelessly arranged. The uniform and harmonious binding, of black and gold, was given to every member of the captain's shelves. Walter Scott vegetated by the side of Humboldt and

Arago—Victor Hugo reposed alongside of Schopen-
hauer—Thackeray, Ball, Swift and Huygens fra-
ternised amicably in rows—it was a veritable
pandemonium of learning.

I studied astronomy and physics. Ned perused
the novels. When we were tired of reading, we
struggled somehow over the keys of the grand
piano, and improvised sundry inharmonious ducts
from our common theatrical reminiscences. Had
Captain Chlamyl heard us, he would, I fancy, not
have been edified, but his astronomical labours
occupied him completely, and he never came near
the saloon, nor did he offer to interfere in any way.

This complete insensibility to our attempted
frivolity—this indifference to our doings and continued scientific abstraction on the part of our
commander, became galling in the extreme.

The views taken by Ned and myself of the case
were different. My worthy companion, having
tired of his literary pursuits, fell to grumbling.

Life in a hotel was all right for a bit, he said—it
was all very well now and again, but to remain shut
up under deck for a week or more, without even
being permitted the pleasure of a walk, was quite
another matter.

' If he'd even tell us when he was going to take
us back to the earth, and how,' insisted Ned, lolling
back among the silken cushions with the amber
stem of a gorgeously-decorated ' Hookah ' between
his lips, ' it would be all right. The mischief is,
not only that we don't know where we are bound
for, but also that we seem to have no certain means
of getting back again ; if what you tell me about
that " translation " movement is right, we have really
no chance of getting back at all ! The universe
only goes one way, I suppose, and we are letting it
slip farther away every day ! '

Ned's remarks, delivered in a sleepy soliloquy

over the benumbing bowl of nicotine, were, in spite of their drowsy innocence, sufficiently true to be startling. My smart Yankee companion was one of those people who, while capable of great exertions when external influences call their latent energies into existence, relapse nevertheless into dreamy indolence when their surroundings are vague and uncertain.

This was certainly not my case. The unknown has a vast attraction for some natures, mine amongst others, and this continued uncertainty served to excite me to a high pitch of nervousness. These prolonged studies of the captain must mean something, I thought. Either he was not sure of his route or else some danger was looming. Impatiently I scrutinised the heavens hour by hour through the polished glass panels of the saloon. For want of something better to do, I fell to lecturing Ned on astronomy. My knowledge of the noble science being, unlike that of our captain, of a limited nature, I was forced to draw on Newcomb's admirably written book for references and figures. Ned, reclining at full length on the sofa, with *Tom Jones* in one hand and the stem of the inevitable water-pipe between his lips, nodded drowsy assent, though to this day I am certain he understood not one word of what I was saying. As, even with the enormous speed of our vessel, it remained practically immovable with regard to the distant stars—so vast was the intervening space that the Creator had chosen to place between them and us—I was able to make frequent and excellent use of the various magnificent telescopes which formed part of the captain's scientific accoutrement.

Day after day, hour after hour, I perused the marvellous universe like an open book and took childish interest in pointing out its beauties to Ned, who listened complacently, more for friendship's

sake than for the sake of any genuine astronomical
enthusiasm.

Far off, in the abyss, among a wilderness of
sprinkled jewellery, glowed those unknown suns
those strange systems, shining with a light different
to that of our sun—worlds floating in waves of red,
green, blue and orange. Seated at the panel, with
a book on my knee, and a telescope close to my eye,
I lost myself in admiration of this unending abyss,
where all was life and colour, where there was
neither great nor small, neither up nor down,
neither east, west, south or north. Ned, when he
was not grumbling, became enthusiastic. Together
we admired the far-off gems of the Almighty's
jewel-casket,—the constellation of Perseus, with its
ruby and sapphire suns, that of Andromeda, shining
in topazine and emerald, the pure white diamond-
sapphire combination of the Ram, etc.

On the morning of the 20th, the precautions
taken by Captain Chlamyl were explained. I was
sitting in the saloon, attentively studying the visible
universe with the aid of a splendid planisphere,
corrected and annotated by the captain himself,
when Ned, who was gazing abstractedly out of the
window on the starboard side, uttered a hoarse
exclamation.

'What is it?' I said, turning abruptly.

'Look!' was the only answer.

I threw down my chart and hurried to the
window.

'It is a gigantic meteor!' I exclaimed.

'Rather!' answered Ned, 'and passing precious
close to us too! I suppose that's why we've not
been allowed up on deck this long while.'

The meteor, a cold and inert miniature of our own
planet, was certainly big enough to steal twenty
atmospheres. At its real distance there was no
guessing. Perhaps it was ten miles off, perhaps a

thousand. It filled up nearly a quarter of the visible heavens, and was travelling the same road as the *Astrolabe*, slightly faster however—its size astonished me.

'I have never heard of such a body existing hereabouts,' I said. 'We surely cannot be more than a few million miles from the earth. Mars himself is the nearest planet, and he's full fifty million miles off at this time of year.'

'What size do you suppose that ball is?' queried Ned, irreverently.

'I don't know,' I answered. 'There's no forming any theories about distance here. I should say it's at least a few miles in diameter, and there seem to be plants growing on it.'

A greenish efflorescence of some kind covered the vast globe in places. This could only be due to some kind of vegetation—lichen or moss probably. It was a wonderful sight, the great sphere hanging immobile in space, three-quarters illumined by the sun, one quarter in shadow.

'Do you think there is any air there?' asked Ned, curiously.

'I don't know,' I answered, 'but it is easy to find out.'

I got the telescope and attentively examined the distant stars as, one by one, they were eclipsed by the floating body of the meteorite. Then I handed the glass to Ned.

'Look at Sirius over there,' I said, 'and tell me if you notice anything queer in his appearance just before our travelling companion cuts his light off.'

Ned did as he was desired. For a few moments he was silent, his eye glued to the brass ring. Then he said,—

'I see the light blinking and wavering—sometimes it goes out altogether.'

'That is the refraction, friend Ned, and proves

that the wandering body over there has an atmosphere possibly denser than that of the *Astrolabe*.
It may even be inhabited, for all we know.'

'By what, in the name of all that's holy?'

'By small creatures—insects, perhaps, or miscro-
scopic beings, pure and simple—foraminifera, infusoria, algæ. There must be many worlds inhabited
by no loftier creatures. It is the planet that moulds
its own inhabitants, not the inhabitants who choose
their planet!'

CHAPTER X

A LONELY WORLD

THE rest of the day passed without incident, and
without our setting eyes on Captain Chlamyl.
The presence of this solitary meteor evidently
occupied him completely. Of the rest of the crew
we never saw anything, though sociable Ned made
several attempts to strike up an intimacy with
some of them, notably with the herculean individual
who had accompanied us down the crevasse of
Mount Archimedes, and who, on board, seemed to
divide his time between cleaning the engine and
polishing the ancient armour that depended from
the walls of the corridor. This man was apparently
of French extraction, and lucid in his comprehen-
sion of one's wishes. He was also quick and
active—never seeming to be idle for one moment
if there was any possibility of finding work. To
draw him out on the subject of Captain Chlamyl
and his plans was quite out of the question. Some
vague dread seemed to stop his tongue whenever
he was about to say anything. Ned's questions
he bore with ill-concealed uneasiness — always
escaping from them when ever he got the chance,

and occasionally actually shunning the good-
natured American when ever he suspected the
latter of any designs on his secrecy.

The rest of Captain Chlamyl's crew behaved
much in the same way. Of their respective nation-
alities we could guess nothing, but I think they
were either Roumanians or Russians. Being
ignorant of both languages, I could not even accost
them, and this providential fact probably saved me
from many a humiliating failure to draw them out.
Every manœuvre was noiselessly and expeditiously
carried out on board. The captain rarely spoke
to his men. Signs were used more than anything
else, and even these were occasionally so vague
that it must have been an admirably-trained crew
to be able to interpret them.

One thing was certain—they were absolutely and
completely subservient to the captain. Never was
discipline more clearly portrayed than in the rapid,
almost nervous, manner with which his lightest
orders were executed. Towards Ned and myself
the men were certainly deferential and courteous,
but their attitude towards the commander was not
merely one of civility or respect—it was fear—
abject, grovelling fear—and I own the sight of this
was distasteful to me. Ned Hatton, on whom the
reticence of these worthy men acted as an incentive
to grumbling, said,—

'Why, anyone would take them to be a company
of criminals undergoing the penalty of silence!'

Argument and theory was no good, however.
We were forced to content ourselves with observ-
ing and wondering. Besides, just at this time we
had other things to think about. A new and
fantastic adventure claimed our attention.

It was on the night after we had observed the
phenomenon described in the last chapter that
Ned made a desperate attempt to draw the attentive

French steward, who looked after his and my cabin, into conversation.

He might just as well have saved himself the trouble. Not a solitary answer did he get out of the man. Disappointed and sulky, he came in to complain to me.

I was sitting on the edge of my bed, in scanty costume, conning over my notes and finishing the remnant of one of Captain Chlamyl's excellent cigars, when my friend entered and threw himself moodily into a chair.

'What's the matter, my boy?' I said.

'Oh, nothing. These people are getting tiresome, that's all. Such a set of bores! One can't get a word out of them. How long do you suppose this journey 'll last?'

'You'r not sick of it already, friend Ned?'

'No, not yet. But I *will* be sick of it in a very short time, if something doesn't happen—Hallo! you've forgotten to close your blinds. That cursed sun is making mischief with my eyes.'

'I didn't know is was at that side of the vessel!' said I as I complied.

'You never know where it is on board this ship,' grumbled Ned. 'We turn and twist about in a disgraceful way. I suppose there's nothing to be done, is there?'

'What would you like to do?'

'Plan a mutiny and take possession of this craft. We could lock up the captain and awe the crew into subjection. Such things have been done before. I've often read about it, haven't you?'

I burst out laughing.

'You intolerable idiot!' I said. 'What on earth could have put such nonsense into your head? Ned, much sight-seeing is evidently driving you crazy. And suppose you *did* succeed in getting hold of this vessel, what would you do with it?'

'Find my way either back to the earth or back to some other inhabited planet—and stay there,' was the answer.

'I am afraid we have hardly the necessary knowledge,' I answered. 'Once deprived of the captain's skill and experience, we'd go to wrack and ruin in a very short time. Suppose you hook it and let me get to bed. I'm as sleepy as an owl.'

Ned withdrew, still grumbling to himself, and I turned in.

Despite my sleepiness, I awoke several times. On the first occasion, for want of something better to do, I stretched out my hand to the blind-cord and pulled up the blind—total darkness. Evidently the *Astrolabe* had turned on its axis while I had been asleep, and his solar majesty was now lighting the port side of the ship.

I fell asleep again and dreamt I was falling through space at a dizzy speed, towards a point that never seemed to come any nearer, and as I fell I grew older. My face became wrinkled, my hair became grey, my back bent itself into a bow, yet I could not die. Sometimes I overtook a flying comet, and rode on it through millions of miles. Then it burnt itself out, and I was left alone again in the great void. But the end came nearer. The distant star (I think it was Andromeda's emerald sun) grew bigger and bigger. Attended by strings of meteors, I was rushing towards the vortex of destruction. A great joy took possession of me as I contemplated the end of my wanderings. Then the green fires roared, and I awoke deluged in sunlight.

The luminous circle traced by the port-hole was creeping slowly down the wall opposite, pricking out the edges of the china and marble on the basin-stand in lines and dots of yellow fire. The *Astrolabe* was still revolving. I waited till the circular disc, elongated and converted into an oval by the angle, touched the centre of the scarlet carpet. Then I rose on my elbow and looked out of the window.

I uttered a cry of surprise. The boundless abyss of space was gone. Under the keel of the *Astrolabe* stretched an acre or two of solid ground, sandy and yellowish in colour, covered here and there by patches of moss—we seemed to be on the rounded summit of a mountain, a mountain which commanded a view of the stellar universe—we must have landed on some planet while I was sleeping.

I sprang out of bed and dressed in a hurry. In the dining-room I found Captain Chlamyl and Ned breakfasting quietly as though nothing un-usual had occurred.

'Where are we?' was the first question I asked.

'On the back of a wandering star, professor,' was the answer. 'A mere mass of rock floating lazily round the sun in a fixed orbit; to the earth an invisible nothing, to us a resting-place in the midst of immensity. If you wish to explore this tiny oasis, you can do so after breakfast. There is a lot to be learnt, even from these unknown and useless star-fragments. It has a slight atmos-phere, so you will not need your diving-dresses.'

'But this atmosphere must be horribly rarefied, captain,' I said.

'It is not very dense, sir, in point of fact,' answered the commander, 'and what is more, the actual surface of the globe is covered to a depth of two feet or so with a layer of almost pure car-bonic acid gas—so take care not to sit or lie down, as in the event of your doing so you will run a great risk of being abruptly smothered, like a dog in the *Grotto del Cane* at Naples.'

'What is the diameter of this sphere, captain?'

'About one mile, sir; so you will be able to walk round it easily enough. Master Hatton, this will be a capital lesson in physical geography for you, I fancy. The body is an exact miniature of the earth, except for the fact that it is absolutely cold from circumference to centre, which our earth is not.'

'Then there cannot be any life on it,' said Ned, dogmatically.

The captain smiled.

'Why not, Master Hatton?' he asked.

'Why?' echoed honest Ned, his face flushing up as he perceived he had let himself in for a poser. 'why, because dead bodies can't support life, can they?'

'And pray, sir, what would you define as a "dead body"?'

'A cold one,' replied Ned, who was beginning to get warm.

'Indeed, sir? And yet the icebergs of the North Pole teem with myriads of interesting animalculæ. To be cold does not necessarily mean an extinction of life. The most charming flowers bloom on the icy summits of the Andes.'

'But there is air there,' objected Ned. 'I mean when a body is cold without possessing an atmosphere.'

'The depths of the ocean, Master Hatton, are almost glacial in temperature, nor is there any air there worth speaking of, yet divers draw some of the earth's most precious delicacies from these dark regions, and I fancy if you were to visit them in a closed bell, the way I have often done, you would not accuse them of lacking animated life. Come, sir, take another glass of this claret, and let yourself be instructed by a man who has long studied the question. Believe me, professor, the word "dead" is one which does not apply to the universe, however well it may suit certain well-meaning but misguided wise men on that far-away little speck that is our home. If I were to affirm that there is not a solitary block of matter in the whole void of space that has not, at certain periods of its history, if not at *all* periods of it, traces of animated life on it, I would run a great risk of being laughed at—yet so it is.

'After all, what is death, professor? Your body decays, and in decaying becomes the birthplace of a million of busy animalculæ, who in their turn vanish to be absorbed by the roots and filaments of plants, to become roses, violets, yew-trees—thus we have life springing out of death, and the cold corpse which drew those tears from you has blossomed again into graceful life — no, to the intelligent thinker there is no such thing as death. It is a chemical change, that is all. In face of this truth, the theory of uninhabited worlds falls flat. So endless is Nature's invention, so fertile and ingenious are her expedients, so manifold and infinitely varied are the forms under which she produces life, that I cannot imagine any substance existing, from the coldest ice to the hottest vapour, that does not contain, in some form or other, those mysterious and invisible germs which are the foundation of all animated Nature.'

The captain's eyes glowed enthusiastically. He was transfigured. His attitude and expression were inspired, and I caught a glimpse of a singular past in the life of this man, so far removed from his fellow-men, so isolated on his pinnacle of genius. Certainly, no prophet, unheeded and unhonoured on his own native planet, had ever been blessed with so splendid an opportunity for confirming his views, with such wonderful confidences on the part of that Nature which it had been his life's pleasure to study.

Breakfast finished, we clad ourselves in our overcoats and sallied forth to explore this diminutive world. As we were standing in the ante-room preparatory to setting out, I received a curious shock. Some order was given by the captain, to which one of the men responded, as usual, with silent alacrity.

'You see, Mr Hatton,' said the commander, turning to us with a smile, while his blue eyes gleamed maliciously, 'a mutiny is the last thing my crew would dream of. Despot as I am, my slumbers are calmer than those of the most dearly-loved earthly king. One of your mediæval satirists compared the Holy Roman Empire to a " chaos upheld by Providence." Of us might be said, with equal truth, that we are order itself upheld in chaos.'

Ned Hatton murmured something, I don't know what, and our eyes met. Then we descended the ladder and stood together with the captain on the surface of this unknown world.

As I have already said, the ground sloped away in a gently - rounded incline, like the top of a mountain. In spite of the light envelope of oxygen, the air was fearfully cold—the sun glaring above us at the zenith, being apparently unable to communicate much heat to this cold remnant of some broken-up world. The soil, of yellowish clay, with here and there a splinter of blackish basaltic rock, was covered with a thick growth of untidily-matted algæ, whose vigorous development I was unable to explain till a sudden occurrence enlightened me.

We were walking along slowly, turning from time to time to look back at the shining decks of the *Astrolabe*, which were disappearing from view behind the rounded circle, when my lungs experienced a choking feeling, as though a warm aromatic fluid were being forced down into them. At the same moment my feet began to sink in the soft soil. Captain Chlamyl, seizing me firmly by the shoulders, dragged me aside.

'Look where you're walking!' he said severely; 'you nearly went head foremost into a mud-volcano!'

I gazed round me. Ned was coughing and laughing by turns. At my feet was a stretch of black soil, sparkling and bubbling under the light of the sun. It was a spring of poisonous gas—of carbonic acid, similar to the ones in Java, only on a far smaller scale.

'There is some chemical operation going on under the surface, perhaps near the centre of this globe,' explained Captain Chlamyl, 'which gives rise to these bubbles of gas. Most of it goes to feed the plants, the rest hangs about over the surface of the soil, especially over the lower parts.'

'How long do you suppose, captain, is it since this planet was in a state of fusion?'

'Some thousands of years only,' answered the captain; 'small bodies take a very short time to cool. What's Master Ned looking at?'

'Hallo!' exclaimed the individual addressed, 'the sun's going to set!'

I turned abruptly, and witnessed a curious sight.

The glowing disc was sinking towards the horizon with a regular motion like clockwork. Ned's shadow lengthened yard by yard, till it vanished, so to speak, 'over the edge' into space. There was hardly any sunset worth speaking of in that rarefied atmosphere. I could hardly notice any change in the colour of the burning disc as it approached the irregular line of hillocks that bounded our view.

. Slowly it sank. The shadow crept rapidly up from our feet to our waists, then I saw it run up Ned's tall form, the reflection and diffusion being so insignificant that he appeared to vanish away into nothing, like a ghost. For a second or so his head, vividly illumined, hung between earth and heaven, the way I have sometimes seen the peak of Chimborazo hanging some hours before the dawn, then it vanished and we were left in total darkness, only set off and toned down by the feeble glimmering of the stars.

Captain Chlamyl pointed westward with his finger. A large star of a greenish colour was rapidly sinking—it was the earth. Venus and Mercury, perhaps on account of their being too near the sun, were invisible. In the zenith, Mars was riding majestically, a glorious red star, larger than the first magnitude, attended by his two satellites, one of which was distinctly visible from where we stood.

'It is a perfect procession!' said Ned. 'The worlds are defiling before our eyes like regiments at a review.'

The idea was tinged with a humorous conceit, but really it was excusable, so orderly and brilliant was the panorama of floating planets.

'Let us go on,' then said the captain; 'we shall catch up the sun in a minute or two.'

We stumbled on, picking our steps carefully to avoid falling into some deadly pool. After about ten minutes walking, a brilliant gleam of light illumined the curved distance before us, pricking out the hillocks in strong relief, then the sun's disc emerged, and it was day. The night had lasted twelve minutes!

An idea struck Ned.

'Let us visit the North Pole,' said he.

The project presented no difficulty. We were

nearly at the equator then. Whereas the whole circumference only measured some three miles or so, a walk of three-quarters of a mile was all that awaited us.

On our way we passed another spring of gas, similar to the first, and I noticed streaks of what I took to be burnt ashes among the lichen.

'Is it possible,' I said to the captain, 'that savages sometimes come here to light a fire, or that volcanic phenomena still go on from time to time. Look at those mosses! They are completely charred!'

'A body floating through space,' explained the captain, 'is sure to attract many fragments of planetary matter in its course. The number of meteors that annually fall on the earth amounts to nearly a million. Owing to the much feebler action of gravity, the number that fall on this small globe would of course be considerably less. However, if you consider the very slight shield of air that protects it from the shocks of these aerial projectiles, you cannot be surprised at finding traces of their destructive work. A very moderate-sized body falling on the surface of this world from an infinite distance would be sufficient to kindle an enormous amount of heat.'

'The sun doesn't seem to be hurrying himself about setting,' remarked Ned, to whom the glowing orb of day seemed to be especially interesting.

Here a curious vagary was executed by the object in question. Instead of completely disappearing and leaving us in darkness, it merely dipped beneath the horizon for a minute or two, then reappeared, skimming lightly along the surface of the planet, and, in fact, as I told Ned, reproducing the phenomenon visible on our own world in certain latitudes—the north of Sweden, for instance.

We stood at the pole. Owing to the obliquity
of the rays, the icy cold was slightly increased.
Our breath, as it left our mouths, actually froze,
changing into snow as it fell. I was rapidly passing from wonder to stupefaction. The whole thing
was so strange; Captain Chlamyl alone, being
probably *blasé* in such marvels, expressed no
surprise whatever.

'This planet inclines at an angle of five degrees
with the plane of the ecliptic,' was all he said; then
'Let us return—this cold cannot be healthy, even
to such people as we are.'

I laughed. It was kind of the captain to include
Ned and myself in the same category with himself,
and I said so.

'What name would you like to give this planet,
sir?' continued the commander of the *Astrolabe*.
'It is not recognised by our poor earthly people,
but then it has its interest for all that. It has its
orbit, its life, its chemical laboratory. If you will
take the trouble to examine some of those dull-
looking mosses under the microscope, I have no
doubt you will find them teeming with infusoria—
a name is all that is required.'

'Your own name, captain,' I suggested.

'Sir, my name has already been bestowed on fifty
stars of different dimensions. I can therefore
afford to be generous. Let us call it Hattonia,
after your worthy friend Ned.'

The new owner of this world bowed politely, and
the captain proceeded.

'In fact, Mr Ned, a satellite is all that is needed
to make your new possession perfect in its little
way. You shall give it one yourself.

'I, sir?' exclaimed Ned, astonished.

'Certainly, Master Hatton. Take up that piece
of rock yonder and fling it away from you
horizontally with all your force.'

Ned did as he was bid. Lightly picking up a mass of volcanic tufa, which on the earth would have weighed at least a ton, but which here only amounted to a couple of ounces, he flung it away at an angle of thirty degrees with the ground.

It soared up to a height of a hundred feet, growing smaller and smaller as its distance increased. Then it seemed to fall gracefully, vanishing quickly behind the horizon. We waited anxiously.

At the end of five minutes or so it reappeared, winging its way over our heads like a large bird, to disappear again behind the western hills. I clapped my hands. Ned raised a shout of triumph.

'Had you used a little more strength, Master Hatton,' remarked the commander, coldly, 'you would never have seen your piece of stone again. It would have completely disappeared in space, instead of continuing to circle round your new possession, as it will do—to all eternity. Now let us go on board.'

How was it that the amazing comedy did not end there? Why should jealous Fate have kept an accident in store for us at the last?

As we advanced, the silvery form of the *Astrolabe* seemed to dive up from the ground. Overhead the sun was blazingly hot. Ned, into whom the spirit of reckless devilment had entered all of a sudden, amused himself by skipping over the ground in long, flying jumps of twenty or thirty feet. On our nearing the *Astrolabe* an idea struck him.

'See me jump over the ship!' he exclaimed.

Before we could stop him, he had taken a spring, and was sailing up into the sky like a rocket.

The danger he was running had struck Captain Chlamyl and myself at the same moment, for as my unfortunate friend left the ground we made a frantic grab at his boots, missing them ignominiously and bumping our heads together in the most undignified fashion.

'Ned! Ned!' I called, horror-struck. His voice, upraised in a wailing cry of fear, reached me faintly.

'Help! Help!'

'The fool!' exclaimed Captain Chlamyl in such a contemptuous tone that I could have struck him furiously, had not respect for his genius stayed my hand. As it was, I seized him angrily by the collar.

'You must save him!' I shouted.

The captain shrugged his shoulders.

'No power on earth can save him!' he said coldly, 'unless he falls again of his own accord.

A mist gathered in my brain, and I stared, sick with grief, upwards into the blackness, where the form of my friend was growing smaller and smaller each moment. Then, without warning, the sun sank and left us in darkness. Ned, hanging in the void, lingered for some instants in sunlight, then he, too, vanished, and the sound was only broken by the rushing of the newly-created satellite, as it whizzed past through the thin air.

'Ned!' I called ; 'Ned !'

A bright light shone about me. It came from a large electric lamp on the deck of the *Astrolabe*. Captain Chlamyl and some sailors were standing on either side of the lantern, examining my poor friend through their opera-glasses, and talking volubly in their Slavonic dialect. Presently the captain said something in French.

'He's coming down, professor!'

I started up. Yes, it was true. Ned was descending slowly, revolving on his own axis, so to speak, as he grew larger and larger. Breathlessly I counted the seconds and minutes. Over our heads he floated, twirling like a top. He made no sound, and the rapidity of his evolutions prevented us from distinguishing his features.

He struck the upper deck of the *Astrolabe* with his foot, and fell over sideways, stiff and stark like a man in a trance. I gave a spring, catching him by the hair and executing a wild aerial pirouette before we both whirled down on the ground together. His lips were blue, his cheeks hollow and contracted. The mouth opened and shut feebly, without making any sound.

'Ned!' I cried; 'Ned! don't you know me?'

There was no answer, only the same inarticulate muttering and gasping.

'Take him in,' commanded the captain.

We bore the poor fellow gently into the saloon and laid him on one of the sofas. A faint colour became gradually visible in his pale cheeks.

'He'll pull through,' said the captain, 'but he has had a narrow shave. A few minutes longer, and he would have been dead.'

I shuddered.

'You mean he would have vanished into space, captain?' I said.

'I mean that he would have been suffocated.'

'Suffocated?' I exclaimed.

'Yes, suffocated, professor,' was the quiet answer. 'One can make aerial trips easily enough on this planet, but one cannot always be sure of finding air to breathe. Your friend jumped beyond the limits of the atmosphere—that is all! Let us take him into the kitchen, and get him warm. He looks sadly frozen. I think he will be more careful next time.'

CHAPTER XI

THE MIST OF LIFE

ON the following day Ned was as right as ever. The pride he had momentarily felt in his newly-acquired territory vanished before the disgust its peculiarities caused him. We made several more excursions on its surface, but without discovering anything new. Captain Chlamyl, for reasons of his own, kept hanging on day after day without making an attempt to quit this barren place. Once, being in a communicative mood, he pointed out to me our position on the planisphere of stars.

'Why, we are nearly on the orbit of Mars,' I said wonderingly.

'Yes, but considerably beneath it,' replied the captain. 'Even in periods of opposition, which only occur once every fifteen years or so, there is still a distance of twenty million miles. Would you like to visit Mars, professor?'

'Captain, how can you doubt it?'

'Unfortunately, sir, the voyage is unfeasible just at present, as Mars is too far distant to exert any effective influence on us, and its distance increases every day. Incident to liven our voyage will not be wanting, however. Have you begun your microscopic investigation into the nature of *Hattonia's* inhabitants?'

'I have discovered three species of *salpæ*, captain —curious little atoms that quite seem to bear out your theory. When are we going to leave this island?'

'In a few days, professor; I wish the rotation of this planet on its orbit to get me into the proper position for visiting some of the more distant worlds —Saturn for instance. Here is an excellent map of the ringed star. You can amuse yourself study-ing at your leisure—if my pianoforte-playing does not disturb you.'

This last was ironical, for the captain's piano-forte performance was quite on a level with his other attainments. He usually played Wagner,

and once or twice expressed to me his admiration
of the Titanic German master.

' He penetrated beyond the confines of the visible
world, sir, and such daring must always command
my respect,' the captain used to remark. 'What
could be a finer expression of chaos that the opening of the third act of *Siegfried*?'

After half-an-hour's music, he rose from the piano
and left the room. The glittering, shimmering
harmonies of the magic fire scene were still ringing in my ears, when Ned Hatton opened the door
and looked in.

' Is he gone?'

' Yes. What have you got to say? More
grumbles?'

' If you please, Hal, don't be so confoundedly
cool with me. I don't like it, especially under the
present circumstances, when we're both sailing at
imminent risk of smashing into eternity—when I
can't even raise my voice above a whisper for fear
of being heard. Did you ever see anything like
that captain? I believe he listens at our doors, or
else sets some of his d—d crew to do so.'

' Nonsense, Ned. He's much too honourable.'

' Honourable?—I tell you I'm sure of it. Did
you hear that remark he made about mutiny
yesterday morning? I swear I believe he goes
in for eavesdropping.'

' It was a coincidence, my dear fellow, nothing
more. Don't get into a stew about nothing. We're
all right ; so is the captain.'

Ned rose, and clenched his fist suggestively.

' If I ever catch one of these fellows spying on
me,' he said, I'll—'

Here the curtains parted and the captain himself
appeared.

' Ah, professor,' he began amiably, ' I propose a
curious expedition for this afternoon. We will

I

go and take some instantaneous photographs of Hattonia. Are you a photographer? Perhaps Mr Ned would like to operate himself?'

We assured the captain that nothing would please us better, and went in to luncheon, Ned looking rather guilty and allowing his eyes to drop before the steady gaze of the commander.

Two days later the *Astrolabe* shook herself free from her fetters, and left the planet, plunging boldly out into the dark belt that separates the orbit of Mars from those of the minor planets. Each morning, on entering the saloon, I consulted the charts, on which Captain Chlamyl never failed to mark the route traversed. Since our starting from Iceland on the 5th of April, we had traversed nearly sixty million leagues, and this distance was destined to increase in an enormous ratio as each day brought us farther from the central sun that retarded our movements.

It was on the afternoon of the 4th of May that I first beheld some of these small stars— Medusa, Flora and Arian, inclining at degrees varying from one to six with the ecliptic. Then Victoria (called after the English queen), Vesta and Clio. As we advanced, the visible number increased, sometimes as many as ten being sighted simultaneously from the windows by either Ned or myself.

On the morning of the 10th, we started across the gap separating Andromache from Ismene and Hilda, which is the last of the series.

A strange prodigy awaited us here. Calling me up into the steersman's cabin, Captain Chlamyl pointed at a white speck that loomed vaguely across the bows of the *Astrolabe*.

'Do you see anything there?' he said.

'I see a globe of nebulous something or other,' I answered.

'It is a sphere of cold gaseous matter, contracted at the centre into a burning heat,' explained the captain; 'it is the lemur of a future world, the unformed mass of vapour that will one day become a seat of life and motion—we are going to cross it.'

'To cross it?' I exclaimed.

'Yes, sir, or to traverse it, if the expression pleases you better.'

'But I thought, sir, that these nimbi of vapour were in a high state of incandescence.'

'Not necessarily, professor. It is the contraction of the vaporous mass that imparts heat to it, and, owing to the ordinary laws of mechanics, the centre of any mass is always the part that becomes heated first.'

'Will it not be dangerous for the *Astrolabe*, sir, to pass near this burning focus?'

'Perhaps so, professor, but we shall manage carefully so as not to come too near. It will be an interesting sight for me as well as for you. I do not remember ever having met with such a nebula before.'

'You are not going to traverse it with your atmosphere exposed to the attraction, captain?'

'No, sir. I should never see an atom of it again. It would be absorbed by the glowing focus. I shall give orders to start the pumps.'

He pressed a button, and a well-known panting sound announced that the gaseous halo surrounding our vessel was being taken into the reservoirs. I gave a final look at the whitish cloud of vapour through a large binocular telescope, noting streaks and dashes of peculiar colour, due, I suppose, to chemical substances held in suspension—then I rejoined Ned in the saloon.

'Well, what's up now?' queried the latter; 'has the cap. been exhibiting any more of his confounded instruments?'

' No, friend Ned, but something's going to happen that'll amuse you. We're going to cross the nebula of an unformed world ! '

Ned ejaculated, ' Oh Moses ! ' and hurried to the window.

' It's no use,' I said, ' you can't see it from there. It's right across our bows, and we won't reach it for some hours yet.'

' How far is it off ? '

' About a hundred thousand miles or so. But what is that to the *Astrolabe ?* You know she goes at a pace that would shame any express-train, even one driven by a Yankee engineer. I think we may prepare for something wonderful.'

' I think we may prepare for something uncommonly nasty in the disaster line,' answered Ned, grimly (since his accident he had grown nervous), ' when mortals like ourselves go where God never intended they *should* go, they must expect to get smashed.'

Ned's prophecy was ominous enough, and at a later date I recalled it.

Captain Chlamyl, whether from cautiousness or from some other reason, slackened his speed some moments later, and it was not till towards 3 p.m., that we struck the mass of shifting vapour, which stretched above and below us like a vast wall of fog.

The *Astrolabe* continued to slacken speed, till at last, to judge by the motion of the shifting sheets of vapour, we were only moving at the rate of some fifty miles an hour. The force of translation, combined, perhaps, with the gravitation of this vaporous body itself, was pulling us forward, while the attraction of the distant sun was dragging us back. Captain Chlamyl, accustomed, no doubt, to cope with the various forces at work around him in space, managed his apparatus with the greatest nicety, and cautiously threaded his way through the gathering streaks and layers of mist, which undulated round the *Astrolabe*, rising and falling like the ocean after a storm. The most fantastic shapes appeared. Here a vast circular whirlpool yawned, there a cataract of dark vapour shot downwards, cleaving the various strata apart with a roaring noise, and spreading out as it reached the denser layer into a huge aigrette of feathery plumes.

This medium was only transparent to a certain extent. After the first few minutes we entirely lost the light of the sun, whose globe shone redly through these wavering clouds, shimmering with heat like the air above an oven. A dull twilight only remained, through which we could still note the vapour-fountains shooting and eddying. An indescribable awe, not unmingled with cowardice, took possession of me. Glancing at the opposite windows, I saw that they were completely yellowed by a layer of fine dust. Ned looked at me fixedly. The gloom here suddenly vanished, and we seemed floating in a sea of white glory. The light from our lantern gave relief to these shifting masses, dividing them into summits of purest alabaster and chasms of black shadow. It was a cloudy panorama rolling away before our eyes.

At first I was surprised at this rapid movement, but then I recollected that the rotation of this nucleus on its axis would cause the layers of vapour to continually keep shifting their position with regard to the *Astrolabe*, which was proceeding, apparently, in a straight line, impelled by the *translation* movement of the universe.

Several questions here presented themselves.

Firstly: Would not the continuous impact of these dusty clouds cause the vessel to veer from its even course, thus tending, perhaps, to drag it

across the very centre of this unformed world—
into an abyss of fire from which there could be no
possible escape ?

Secondly : Might not the revolving gaseous
masses grow denser and denser as we approached
the centre, till at last they reached the consistence
of fluidity, and we should be miserably drowned, if
not boiled, in a tumultuous sea of liquid rock ?

I tried to explain these theories and fears to Ned,
but I gave it up almost immediately, for Ned's
fancies are never of the pleasantest, and the
stupendous sights we were witnessing through the
panels filled him with uneasiness.

For an hour or so we admired the novel spectacle.
Some of these streaks of gas were evidently composed of metallic substances, to judge from their
varying and brilliant colours, and a spectroscopic
investigation (difficult enough to conduct, however)
would here have been highly interesting.

The fine yellow dust, coating the port window,
drifted in through the chinks and crannies of this
hermetically-sealed vessel ; even the solid walls of
aluminium, carefully riveted though they were,
proved insufficient to keep it out. It settled on the
pages of Ned's book, on the polished ebony of the
piano ; it imparted to one's hands that peculiarly
dusty feeling which is usually felt at the termination
of a long voyage by rail on a hot summer's day.
Our lungs did not suffer much. Instead of feeling
suffocated, I experienced a strange sensation of
delight, mingled with excitement. At first it was
merely a genial sort of warmth, a sense of cosy
comfort, that spread itself through my being, but
soon it gave way to a feeling of elation and buoy-
ancy, similar to that induced by champagne or some
other kind of wine—was I getting drunk? I looked
at Ned. Clearly he was undergoing the same experience as I, for his eyes were glowing strangely,

and his cheeks were flushed. He whistled a lively tune, beating time stupidly with his hands and feet. Presently:

'By George!' he said, 'if this continues we won't be able to see at all!'

It had grown darker without, and the light of our brilliant lantern was now nearly unable to pierce the gloomy sheets of matter, that seemed, in corroboration of my own fearful prognostications, to have grown denser as we gradually approached the burning centre. The temperature increased too. Looking at the thermometer, upheld in the tiny hand of a delicate silver statue, I saw, through the increasing stupor of my brain, the mercury marking eighty-two degrees. Ned, rising suddenly, tossed off his jacket, still whistling, and motioned me to do the same.

A vague rumbling became apparent. Dark streaks of reddish cloud shot across the gloom with a rending noise like a million rockets simultaneously fired. My stupidity increased, and I wondered drunkenly (the way one is apt to wonder in such cases) whether there was a superabundance of oxygen in the air we were breathing. One can get tipsy on oxygen as on champagne, and it might be that that was at the bottom of my strange delirium. Ned, making horrible grimaces, was shouting furiously at me from his sofa, only a few yards off, but my ears were deafened by the roaring without and the buzzing in my brain—I couldn't hear a word he was saying.

Helpless, motionless, I witnessed everything passively, my eyes wide open, my senses dulled into sleepy contentment. A lurid flame crossed the windows. Even in my state of fearless impotence, I felt my cheeks pale, and I saw Ned, who had ceased to jabber, staring fearfully with open mouth and eyes protruding.

A great sphere, a perfect sheet of flame, glowing in several colours, mottled in patches of green and blue, streaked with lines and fissures of brightest light, which drowned entirely the power of our poor little lantern, was revealed by the parting of two black, cloudy masses. Triangular tongues of fire, not unlike the corona of the sun during an eclipse, pierced the surrounding envelope of sooty black, to fall back in cascades and rivulets of jewels. The *Astrolabe's* position changed slightly. I felt it turning horribly—the end was surely near. A strange madness possessed me. Through the misty void of my brain a myriad of strange shapes appeared. Life crowded on me—life in all its most uncouth and hideous forms—life as it is given to the mammoth worlds of space, as it glows in the depths of unknown abysses, under the wide sea, among the heavy clouds that crown the tops of fire-breathing mountains. Goblins, spectres, hamadryads, tritons flashing on shell-cars across curving green waves, satyrs with eagle claws and yellow, pointed teeth, winged gryphons, their large, cold eyes shifting restlessly under the thick lids, their triangular scales glittering with a metallic lustre. . . .

In the heavens behind vast shadows appeared, stretching to the remotest zenith, like columns of transparent porphyry, seen in the light of a phantom sun—a rainbow palace where Nature brooded smiling over her endless handiwork.

Garlands of glowing unknown flowers hung in festoons around those tall pillars. Their petals curved strangely, dropping tears on the mother-of-pearl steps, tears that changed to blossoms as they fell to be trodden under foot by the passing shapes and spring again into thousandfold life — they were living, these jewelled chalices, with their twining tendrils and drooping blossoms ; their wide, wild eyes sought the light, expanding and contracting in rings of scarlet and blue. Between the columns with tranquil heads caressed by the waving flowers, Sphinxes brooded calmly, motionless and unmoved amid the effervescence of activity around them. Over the pearly steps, rippling with sea-water, glided a host of strange beings, some beautiful, some hideous, all of them wonderful.

Basilisks, chimeras, iguanodons, vampires, stryges with the hearts of fishes, and serpent-women, their long, needle-shaped teeth glistening with accumulated venom ; hippogriffs, winged steeds that pace the air, armed with shining claws and adorned with flowing white manes ; unicorns, flying serpents, dragons, from whose mouths pale flames issued ; elves, fairies, gnomes, sprites, all the panorama of life was unveiled before me.

And it was unending. From the serene depths of the sky above me to the glittering slabs of pearl at my feet, with their thick layer of floating blossoms and perfumed flower-dust, all was living, breathing animation.

I saw the troops of gryphons and other flying monsters form winged processions across the purple sunset, losing themselves at the uttermost ends of space, beyond the farthest pole, among the golden streamers of the northern light. I saw the breath of the thousand flowers rise in vapour, bearing with it a million germs of existence, each of them capable of fertilizing a world. The stones shone, the stars blinked, there was nothing dead anywhere, the very columns seemed to move, to pulsate under the force that vibrated from within.

Crushed, overwhelmed, my head on fire, my senses staggering before this infinite display of Nature's might, I sank down among those twining myriads of petals, enveloped in a rosy mist that seemed to be carrying me down the last path of oblivion.

CHAPTER XII

THE RINGED WORLD

'IT appears I've been hideously ill,' I remarked as somebody tried to force some aromatic liquid or others down my throat with a table-spoon—it was Ned. I was in my own cabin, and the impassive French steward was smiling coldly over Ned's shoulder.

'You've been conducting yourself like a raving lunatic,' was the answer ; 'we've had to hold you down to prevent you killing yourself. I've been a little that way myself, so have all the crew. There was something in the air of that cursed star that knocked us all over. We've got clear of it at last, thank heaven !'

I groaned, and tossed about painfully. There were pains and aches all over me. Ned was looking as pale as a ghost—so was the steward. We had evidently been through an ordeal—

'Where are we now ?' I queried. Going back to the earth ?'

Ned uttered an oath.

'No, by G—'he exclaimed. 'The captain, for want of something better to do, took me up into his laboratory and gave me a long jaw about that patent way he has of measuring distances. It's very ingenious, but when he told me we were a hundred and forty million leagues from the sun, I guess I didn't express much enthusiasm. That'll do, you can go, monsieur.'

This to the French steward, who withdrew noise-lessly.

'Now, my dear Hal,' began Ned, sinking his voice into a whisper, ' what the devil *are* we to do? One more experience like this'll be the death of us. Instead of thinking about returning, Captain Chlamyl is plunging deeper and deeper into space. My own opinion is that he'll never come back. He's talking about visiting Saturn.'

'Nonsense!' I said incredulously, 'the distance is too great! Why, we'll never get there. Let's see, there's nearly a matter of four hundred million miles to be traversed still, before we cross its orbit.'

'Not to speak of the significant fact that it's not at all so certain that we won't be smashed up when we get there,' put in Ned. 'I think we had better frame a remonstrance.'

'Frame one by all means, my boy—if you can get the captain to listen to you. But I fear your objections won't amount to much.'

Ned put his idea into practice. That afternoon he accosted the captain in the saloon.

'We are going to cross the orbit of Saturn, sir?'

'I believe so, Mr Hatton,' answered the commander, smiling; 'but that will not be for some time yet, so calm your fears.'

'When are you going to take us back to earth, captain?'

'I do not know, sir—probably this time next year.'

'But, captain, we are prisoners on board this vessel, we're in a perfect dungeon—a dungeon which any moment may be smashed to atoms. Even though the rest of your crew consent to be thus incarcerated, do you think it is quite fair?'

'Mr Hatton,' interposed the commander, leaning with one elbow on the piano, his legs crossed indolently, 'was it for my own pleasure that I carried you off?'

'I do not say so, sir.'

'Do you not owe your life to me?'

'I cannot deny it, captain.'

'Then be silent. You are gaining an experience which many mortals would give their lives to gain, you are seeing sights that no man, save yourself, has ever looked upon. Be content to contemplate Nature's marvels for a short while yet. Even though I wished to take you back to earth, I should not be able to do so—at present. Perhaps you, who no doubt consider yourself quite able to manage this vessel (here Ned crimsoned violently) have some method to suggest—come now, Mr Hatton, if you were master of the *Astrolabe*, how would you bring her back to earth?'

The captain smiled maliciously. Ned, divided between a fear of saying something foolish, and the certainty of looking a fool if he remained silent, shuffled about. Presently,—

'I should stop the engines and allow the earth's attraction to draw us back,' he said boldly.

'Indeed?' answered the captain sarcastically, 'Then, Mr Hatton, I think, for your own safety at least, it is just as well that I am at the helm. If the engines were to be stopped just now, we would fall into the sun, and perish miserably.'

Ned stared incredulously, put his hands in his pockets and strolled over to the panel.

A tiny green star, of the second magnitude, was visible against the ebony blackness of space. Captain Chlamyl pointed to it.

'Do you think that far-off speck is capable of exerting much influence over us here?' he said.

Ned looked vacantly at me.

'Then how on earth are we going to get back?' he said.

'That is my affair,' responded the captain, laughing. 'In the meanwhile, let us wait and hope.—How do you feel now, professor?'

'Much better, Captain. I seem to have been literally out of my mind while we were crossing that nebula. What do you suppose could have been the cause of our sufferings?'

'Well, sir, we entered an electrical focus of life, so to speak. What you absorbed into your lungs were probably the germs of a million unborn existences. We were all affected in much the same way. My crew had a hard time of it, poor fellows, but we pulled through somehow, and I think we shall keep clear of such phenomena in future. It will only be prudence.'

June 5th.—An uneventful month has passed away. Diary-writing becomes a terrible bore when one has nothing to record. We are slowly drifting into an existence of shell-fish inactivity, which anything but agrees with Ned Hatton.

The distances in space are so enormous that it hardly seems reasonable for any human being to contemplate traversing them. From the last of the minor planets, it will take us fully five months to reach the orbit of Saturn—I think we shall be dead first.

That is, no. Our life, hitherto monotonous enough, has suddenly become enlivened by a series of curious incidents, which have certainly given us something to think about.

To begin with, we have succeeded in communicating with the crew, that is, with the impassive and discreet French steward who supplies us with hot water in the mornings.

One night last week, Ned rapped me up at a late hour, and,—

'The captain's ill,' said he.

'Ill?' I answered, vaguely imagining that some disaster was looming.

'Yes. Got the mumps, or the blues, or something,' was the reply, 'and he wants you to prescribe for him.'

'Does he?' said I. 'Well, I'll do what I can.'

The steward conducted me to the captain's cabin,

which was almost enveloped in darkness. Blue screens veiled the glowing lamps, and the thick panels of aluminium protecting the windows had been closed.

Captain Chlamyl lay on the couch, his face looking rather paler than usual, his eyes shining excitedly.

'I don't know what's the matter with me,' he groaned. 'My head is splitting, and I am feeling fearfully sick.'

'You're nervous and excited,' I said, feeling his pulse; 'perhaps a little feverish. What have you been doing with yourself all day?'

'Oh! nothing,' he answered vaguely; 'only working out the elements of some cometary bodies in the laboratory. What is the specific gravity of sulphuretted hydrogen? Do you know, professor?'

'You'd better take some quinine,' I answered, peremptorily, speaking like a doctor to an unruly patient, 'it'll set you up in no time. Have you got a medicine chest?'

'There's one behind you. Please be careful not to break any of the bottles. It would be difficult to replace them. Did you notice the shower of aerolites yesterday morning? I fancy they were carrying volumes of gas along with them — at least, our atmosphere has been slightly vitiated. How many grains are you going to give me?'

'Thirty,' I answered; 'that will be enough for the present. Why!—'

I stopped, transfixed. The French steward was standing behind me with a curious expression on his face — an expression of eager anticipation, mingled with a singular fear of some kind. He was listening, his hands clenched, his eyes protruding, his whole pose indicative of strange excitement. He was not attending to me. He did not even seem to notice my presence.

I turned to the captain. His blue eyes were nearly closed. As I looked at him I got a shock. It somehow seemed to me that he was scrutinising me through the half-closed lids.

A confused noise of hammering and smashing arose, echoing along the corridor. In the midst of the crash of a breaking door, Ned's voice was heard, shouting my name. The steward's face became livid. Captain Chlamyl half raised himself on his elbow.

I dashed from the room. Ned, his eyes staring, the blood running from a cut on his cheek, was staggering along the passage, holding his hand to his chest.

'I'm being suffocated!' he gasped. 'Hold me up, do! Dash it! I've smashed my hand up!'

His fingers and knuckles were hideously bruised. Across the carpet lay the fragments of a stout, wooden door.

'What's the matter?' I queried stupidly.

'The matter?' spluttered Ned angrily. 'You go and have a look in there, and you'll see what's the matter. Don't go too near, though, or you'll get killed!'

I propped him up against the wall and approached the entrance to his cabin, in the interior of which the lamps were still brightly burning. I had not proceeded two steps before a well-known sensation of warmth in my lungs sent a shiver of fear through me. Ned, behind me, coughed and raved.

'Why, it's deadly poison!' I exclaimed.

'Carbonic acid — at least!' vouchsafed Ned. 'How do you think it could have happened? I was sitting quite still, reading that book you recommended, when I felt the stuff going down into my lungs, and making me giddy. A pipe must have broken somewhere, I think.'

At this juncture several of the men put in an

appearance. I tried to explain matters to them, but they paid no attention to me. Ned dragged me along by the arm.

'Come out of this!' he said. 'I believe we'll be murdered before this journey's over. Where's the captain? God! how my hand smarts. Just ask that Johnny for some water, will you?'

We got a basin and bathed his broken wrists, bandaging them with cotton and vaseline, and installing him on an arm-chair in the drawing-room. On leaving the room my eyes met those of the impassive steward. It was only a glance, but it served to keep me awake for the best part of the night.

Just before retiring I made an attempt to see the captain, but his door was locked, and I concluded that he was asleep.

The door of Ned's cabin was replaced by a heavy curtain. Ned himself, extended at full length on the swinging bed, with both hands under his head, looked at me curiously.

'It seems that danger lurks inside the *Astrolabe* as well as outside,' he said softly. 'After all, it's only a question of time, if they really mean murder.'

I started.

'What nonsense!' I exclaimed, 'Captain Chlamyl's far too honourable to harbour any such vile thoughts about us. What a fearful slander, Ned! Remember he's our host!'

Ned laughed bitterly.

'Do you call it hospitality to lock one's guests into their cabin and turn a tap of poisonous gas on them?' he queried.

I shivered uncomfortably. Ned's face was paler than usual. He was evidently in grim earnest.

'Did anyone—lock the door?' I stammered.

'Of course,' answered Ned, quietly, 'else why did I have to break it in order to get out?'

He undid his coat and felt nervously about in his inner pockets.

'I've got my revolver here,' he said calmly; 'do you think they'll try an attack on me at night?, The door's gone now, so I can't keep them out.'

He clenched his hands nervously and looked round him with an expression of despair.

'Hal,' he said, with a sort of sob, 'I can't stand this! It's awful to be killed like a rat in a trap. I wish the devil that volcano had entirely swallowed us up—I do really. What chance have we here? None. How many men are there on board do you think?'

'I don't know,' I answered gloomily. 'There may be a dozen, there may be two dozen. It's quite impossible to even vaguely estimate the number. The locking of the door is what staggers me. Did you know it was being locked?'

'No. I never noticed anything till I felt a burning in my lungs.'

'How did the stuff get in?' I queried. 'Are there any signs of broken pipes anywhere?'

We fell to examining the walls inch by inch. First the walls, then the ceiling, then the floor, which was thickly carpeted with phormium. There was no trace of any orifice through which the deadly fluid could have been introduced.

'Perhaps it came through the electric light fittings,' suggested Ned, 'or perhaps a pipe opens under the carpet. There is no knowing what these talented assassins may be up to. I intend to sleep with my revolver under my pillow all night, and the first fellow who puts in an appearance—let him look out, that's all! For the present, I intend to pull up that carpet!"

I tried in vain to dissuade him. He fell on his knees and began tearing up the matting, which was fastened down by rows of flat-headed brass nails.

K

A thick flooring of aluminium, crossed in places by lines of copper bolts, separated us from the lower portions of the vessel, where the revolving discs were humming monotonously. Not a hole, not a crevice was anywhere visible. We nailed down the matting again, and gazed at each other hopelessly. Ned, his hands running absent-mindedly through his untidy hair, allowed his eyes to wander over the gorgeous fittings of the apartment which had so nearly become his tomb, over the polished panels of the wall, over the swinging couch with its blue silken curtains and the wash-hand-stand with its flagons and tumblers of iridescent glass. At the bottom of the pink china basin, shaped like the shell of a tridacna, an aluminium plug with a chain attached allowed the water to run off. Ned's eyes flashed to life.

'Where does that pipe lead to?' he said.

'It leads to a copper reservoir,' I answered, recollecting Captain Chlamyl's explanations of the methods he employed to economise water on board the *Astrolabe*, 'where it is re-distilled and sent back to be used over again—'

A step was heard in the passage. Ned flew to the door and drew aside the curtains violently. The French steward was extinguishing the electric lamps one by one before retiring to rest. Presently his task came to an end. He vanished. Ned let the curtains fall softly, and returned to the charge, fingering his revolver nervously meanwhile.

'Suppose they use that pipe to convey carbonic acid into my cabin,' he suggested, speaking in a mysterious undertone, 'if I put in the aluminium plug, it'll be all right, won't it?'

'Certainly,' I replied in a confident tone, though really my heart was in my boots — certainly, unless—'

'Unless what?'

'Unless they take the stuff from a high-pressure reservoir, in which case your plug 'll be blown out like a bullet from a gun.'

'That'll make a noise, I reckon,' said Ned. 'Anyway, here goes.' And he rammed the plug down the pipe, taking the additional precaution to fill the basin with water above it.

'Now they're fixed—for the present,' he said, rubbing his hands. 'As for that captain, I'll settle accounts with him to-morrow. Good-night, old man. If I'm wiped out while I'm asleep, you'll think of me sometimes—'

'Oh, come, come, Ned, this'll never do,' I said patronizingly, slapping my friend on the shoulder in a miserable attempt at gaiety. 'What reason should these fellows have for wanting to get rid of you? Don't be silly!'

Ned mused.

'It was all on account of my confounded jabbering the other night,' he said. 'What a fool I was to be so loose-tongued! Or perhaps they want to economise provisions—anyway I wouldn't trust that captain of yours the length of my little finger.'

The object of our mistrust received me civilly the following morning on deck. His condition was slightly improved, but his eyes still shone feverishly and his cheeks were flushed. At first he hardly noticed me.

'Captain,' I said, bending over his chair, 'captain, do you feel better this morning?'

'Ah, is that you, professor?' he said, starting. 'How did you sleep? I'm still very weak—but I think that dose of yours did me good. What was that I heard about Mr Hatton?'

I related Ned's strange misadventure. I added—

'The poor fellow's perfectly miserable. He's

perfectly persuaded in his own mind that some of the crew are making an attack on his life.'

I paused, to watch the effect of my words. Captain Chlamyl slightly raised his eyebrows and laughed.

'You must cure him of that,' he said carelessly. 'It is not pleasant to travel in company with a lunatic. As for yourself, professor, you know me too well to believe me capable of harbouring such nonsensical designs against anyone. The contemplation of Nature's grand works is apt to engender pity, perhaps love, for humanity, but certainly not hate. That is Saturn over there.'

I followed his gaze. The ringed world was hanging above us on the port side, clearly distinguishable from among the masses of stars. I examined it with interest through the captain's powerful binocular.

Three of its satellites were visible, the other five being apparently hidden behind the body of the planet or behind the semi-transparent rings. The globe itself was slightly eclipsed, owing to the position of the sun. Round the equator the annular shadow traced a dark band. I observed that the poles were clearer and whiter in colour than the rest of the globe, thus arguing the presence of snow or ice, as in the case of our earth.

'I thought the atmosphere of Saturn was so dense as to preclude all possibility of the poles becoming visible;' I remarked to the captain, 'certain French *savants* used to compare its density with that of water.'

'Certainly, sir,' answered the captain, 'but its density varies considerably with the latitude. The attraction of its rings plays a considerable part in tending to heap up vast gaseous masses near the equator and produce an ebb-tide, so to speak, in the neighbourhood of the poles, where the cloudy envelope is in consequence thinned down to reasonable terrestrial proportions.'

'To breathe this atmosphere is impossible, captain?'

'Quite impossible, sir. Not only would its density and pressure be inconvenient, but it is also rich, too rich, in oxygen gas to be inhaled with security. You would be drunk with the first mouthful. Contrary to our terrestrial plants, however, the Saturnian flora thrive in such an atmosphere, whose life-giving qualities are farthermore increased by the enormous volume of water-vapour which is held in suspension. Under the circumstances, it will be necessary to make use of our diving-dresses—but reassure yourself. We are a long way off as yet, and who knows whether we are destined to reach it—ah, there is Mr Hatton. We have been talking about you, sir.'

Ned appeared, enveloped in a rich coat of sables, his teeth chattering with cold. He looked, first at me, then at the captain, without speaking. The latter began affably,—

'I was sorry to hear, Mr Hatton, that you had been seriously inconvenienced last night by an escape of gas in your room. The crew are a good set of fellows, but careless sometimes, and accidents naturally happen occasionally. The gases generated by the combustion of pyroxyline in the engines are stored in a strong reservoir previous to being subjected to a chemical operation which deprives them of their poisonous qualities. Owing to some stupidity or other on the part of my engineers, a portion escaped and filtered into your room somehow. It was an unfortunate accident, sir, and I trust you will accept an apology for what, if your account is a true one, might have terminated in a very serious disaster.'

Ned Hatton bowed froggily without replying.

During the whole of the next day, the ship's carpenter was busily occupied in replacing the door that Ned had broken. Our captain's mysterious malady became aggravated towards evening, and he vanished into his cabin to court the God of Slumber while the *Astrolabe* held on her tranquil way across the void that separates the orbits of the minor planets from that of Saturn.

Lying on one of the canopies in the saloon, I was lazily pursuing one of M. Flammarion's interesting frescoes, thinking the while what the French *savant* would have said had a genii transported him from his quiet study in Paris on board the marvellous vessel that had been my prison for nearly two months and a half, when the steward suddenly entered and commenced to dust the ornaments on the piano.

Something curious about the action struck me. It seemed so very unusual for the tidying of a room to take place at midnight, farthermore, as dust was an unknown article on the *Astrolabe*, there could really be no necessity for this mania of cleanliness. Several times he paused to look at me, turning away his eyes when he found he was being noticed. A sudden impulse took possession of me. I addressed him in French.

'How is the captain?' I said softly.

The dark eyes gleamed.

'*Il dort*,' replied the steward, in an undertone. My heart gave a bound. Here at last was a chance of getting to the bottom of this mystery.

'I have been wishing to talk to you for some time past,' I continued, 'but neither myself nor my friend could get a word out of you. Is silence the rule on board this vessel?'

'*Ah, mon Dieu, monsieur!*' (with a shrug of his shoulders) 'what would you have? When the very walls have ears!'

'Do you mean to tell me the captain can hear us conversing together?'

'Yes, *monsieur*—and he sometimes makes good use of his knowledge.'

Another flash of the black eyes. A strange thrill went through me. Evidently I had to deal with a new and strange order of pirate in Captain Chlamyl—a despotic commander whom it was life and death to disobey. Ned's suspicions were being hideously confirmed.

'Come into our cabin,' I said, speaking in a half-whisper; 'we will be safer there perhaps.'

The man hesitated.

'We are not safe anywhere here,' he said.

'Still—Ned wants to see you,' I insisted. 'You may be able to tell us a good many things we want to know. You say the captain's asleep.'

'He is asleep—just now, *monsieur*; but if he should wake and find me in there with you—'

The eyes grew significant. But I had gone too far to recede. Every scruple vanished before the overwhelming interests at stake. 'Only one moment,' I pleaded—'just one.'

Half a minute later we were seated together in Ned's cabin. The following conversation ensued, conducted in whispers.

'Who is the captain of this vessel, and where does he come from?'

'I do not know—he is a pirate and an outlaw.'

'How long have you been on board the *Astrolabe?*'

'Two years at least.'

'Against your will?'

'*Ma foi!* *monsieur*—what am I to do? Where am I to go? There is no world for us any more. We cannot even see the earth.'

'How many men are there on board?'

'Twenty-two, counting the captain. They are a

crew of thieves and convicts, whom he saved from
the mines of Siberia, I think. It is difficult to
converse with them, for they do not speak my
language, and I do not know a word of theirs.'

'What did you say just now about the captain
being able to hear what goes on everywhere in the
vessel? How is this possible? Are their spies on
board?'

'No, *monsieur*; but I think there must be a telephone inside the wall.' He tapped the partition
significantly. I looked at Ned.

It was quite what I should have expected from a
man of Captain Chlamyl's inventive genius, yet the
diabolical ingenuity of the idea fairly paralysed me.

'We'll soon fix that,' said Ned, quietly. Now go
on—tell us some more. Do you think there is a plan
on foot to murder us?'

'I hardly know, *monsieur*—the captain is so dark
and mysterious in his plans. However, be sure I
will help you to the best of my ability. The event
of the night before last was so strange. I knew
something was the matter by the way in which the
captain behaved towards me. I believe he already
suspects me of corresponding with you. Does
monsieur understand how the vessel is worked?'

'I don't,' answered Ned, promptly. 'Do you?'
he said, turning to me.

'I'm afraid not,' I answered. 'There are many
things about her which I don't understand. The
captain has kept a good deal from me. As for
steering my way through space—that's quite out of
the question.'

'Because if *monsieur* could have done it,' pursued
the steward, musingly, 'we might have killed the
captain and taken the vessel. It would be very
easy. Had any of us understood the management
of the machines we might have done it long ago—
who knows?'

This was said in the calmest voice, as though the speaker were discussing an abstract question in philosophy. Ned's eyes met mine. We had evidently fallen in with a singularly conscienceless set of pirates. From the captain downwards, ideas of right and wrong seemed to be most shaky on the *Astrolabe*. The ringing of the distant bell, perhaps in the engine-room, caused the Frenchman to spring up. Ned clutched him by the arm.

'We are allies!' he whispered.

'Yes, for life or death!' murmured the other, tearing himself loose and vanishing through the doorway.

Such was the brief interview which served to reveal so much to us. Ned, experienced adventurer as he was himself, had only been too correct in his conjectures. We were no longer the honoured guests of Captain Chlamyl, but merely human playthings, to be picked up, crushed, and cast aside whenever it suited him.

For the moment I could see no especial reason why the captain should wish to take our life. We had only been three months with him, and the *Astrolabe*, if what he had told me was true, was equipped for a two years' cruise. If at the end of that time we did not either succeed in returning to earth, or in at least landing on some inhabitable planet, we should be forced to put some of the horrible expedients of shipwrecked mariners into practice.

'They'll make us draw lots and eat each other,' suggested Ned.

'You mean if we are alive to draw anything,' I said. 'You may be sure Captain Chalmyl and his reservoir of carbonic acid will have put all the superfluous members of this ship's company painlessly out of existence long before that.'

Expostulation or resistance was clearly out of

the question. Any attempt at baulking the captain's plans openly would only bring immediate destruction on us both. Terrible, indeed, if the commander kept a telephone in each room to acquaint him with any mutinous designs that his crew might be harbouring and a reservoir of poison wherewith to suffocate the offender in his sleep.

Ned continually fretted and watched, always sleeping with his revolver under his pillow, always pottering about his cabin tapping the panels, unscrewing the electric light fixtures, in hopes of discovering some new murderous contrivance of the captain's, or in hopes of finding the whereabouts of the mysterious tell-tale apparatus that reported our conversations to the commander.

But here, too, the genius of Captain Chlamyl came to light. Search as he would, Ned could find nothing. It was impossible to open the panels, besides, except by sheer force, and as I pointed out to the angry Ned, no telephone, placed behind solid boards of wood, could possibly be of any great efficiency, unless the captain had invented a new species of telephonic instrument, which, it must be acknowledged, was within the bounds of possibility.

It was under these circumstances and amid these doubts and curiosities, that our life on board again began to resume its tranquil monotony. Day by day, week by week, the majestic sun grew smaller, Saturn, its eight moons distinctly visible, as regularly augmented in size, till on the 15th of July the rings could be seen by the naked eye, separated into their four distinct bands. It then struck me to interrogate Captain Chlamyl on the nature of this strange corona, and his observations, based as they were on actual knowledge and experience, proved incalculably interesting to me.

'They are an agglomeration of small bodies, rotating round each other and on their own axes,' he said. 'The rapid rotation of the great planet, while yet in a vaporous condition, may have tended to separate them from the main body. Thus they whirl year after year.'

'Each on its own independent orbit?' I asked.

'Certainly, professor,' replied the captain. 'There is no body in the whole universe which does not move in an orbit of its own. Order is the rule in Nature.'

'Nevertheless, captain,' I argued, 'it puzzles me to know how such a vast number of tiny worlds can crowd into a comparatively narrow space, each travelling at a vertiginous speed, without jostling each other in their passage.'

'And who said they did so?'

'You inferred as much, sir. If this were not the case, the rings of Saturn would soon cease to exist.'

'And who ever supposed them likely to exist for ever? Within even the last hundred years, astronomers have recorded a marked diminution in the breadth and density of these annular ornaments of his Saturnian majesty. Who knows? Perhaps a few thousand years more will see the end of them. The number that fall annually along the equator, attracted by the gravitation, is enormous. The motion of these bodies through the dense atmosphere, suddenly checked, turns into heat by the shock, and a ring of smouldering volcanoes burns in a zone of fire round the middle spaces of the great world. Vapours exhaled from thousands of active craters serve in a great measure to compose the heavy, cloudy envelope that has hitherto veiled the surface of this planet from the curious eyes of our terrestrial astronomers — ah, professor, you are going to visit a land of marvels, a misshapen land that has no name, where Pluto and Neptune still strive for the mastery, as they did in earliest ages on our own little earth.

History, sir, usually repeats itself in the universe, and we can judge of what took place on our earth by what we see taking place on the newer and more recent planets. It is to argue by analogy, that is all.'

'What surprises me, captain,' I said, contemplating the extraordinary personage who spoke carelessly about inspecting and examining the planets as though he were a general reviewing a few regiments, 'what surprises me, is not so much this marvellous journey we are making now, as that you should have been here before to gather all these facts.'

'Why should I not have visited Saturn before, professor?'

'Because,' I answered, feeling that at last I had a statement to make which the captain would not be able to dispose of so easily, 'because the Saturnian year is equal to nearly thirty of ours, owing to the immense size of the planet's orbit round the central sun—this would make it only possible for you to hit it off, so to speak, once every thirty years. I believe the translation movement only acts one way, and for this reason—'

'And why need I necessarily use the translation movement, professor? Do you think there is no other way of crossing space than by staying still and allowing the planets to reel around me?'

'I do not see any other way, sir.'

'Ah, professor,' replied the captain, ironically, 'decidedly you never would have made a great mechanical genius. Come, be content to study and observe. There is much you have yet to learn, and let us hope Fate will be kind enough to throw enlightenment in your way some day.'

CHAPTER XIII

ACROSS THE DARK SEA

ON the morning of the 10th of August, we had traversed nearly six hundred million miles since our departure from Iceland. As our distance from Saturn diminished, various interesting phenomena presented themselves.

On the 15th a shower of meteors crossed our path. The ringed planet, nearly ahead of us, equalled in size an apple, held at arm's length. The attraction of this gigantic mass was even now beginning to be felt, and the crowd of meteors were hurrying in the same direction as we ourselves—at a far more rapid pace, however, for they had come from an infinite distance, whereas we had only the comparatively limited movement of translation to help us forward.

Some of these bodies were nearly a hundred yards in diameter, and surrounded by haloes of various gases, others were mere fragments of rock. Ned and I observed them attentively through the panels of the saloon. Our curiosity was perhaps not unmingled with a certain awe, for had one of these erratic blocks of stone struck the *Astrolabe*, our chances of salvation would have been small indeed. Each planet, gravitating in whatever direction it pleases—round the sun, or round anything else—is a focus from which nothing smaller than itself can escape. The number of aerolites that thus strike the earth each year is estimated at several hundred thousand. Saturn, being nearly seven times the diameter of our modest globe, would attract at least twenty times as many of these wandering fragments. For several days we travelled in the midst of this *cortège* of meteors.

Once or twice Captain Chlamyl, for prudence sake, was even forced to absorb his atmosphere, for fear of it being stolen. We were confined to the saloon, and Ned recommenced his grumbling.

On the 25th the space around us was again open, and our walks on the platform again became possible. Captain Chlamyl, elated possibly by the prospect of again setting foot on the wondrous ringed planet, excelled himself in amiability and politeness. Seated together, either in the laboratory or in the saloon, we conned over together the marvellous book of the universe through the binocular telescopes, and lost ourselves in speculations respecting the farther worlds of space, which, even to the mighty *Astrolabe*, must ever remain unapproachable.

The more I thought of it, the more I became convinced that Ned's extraordinary accident had been the result of chance, the bursting of an iron boiler-plate or the leakage of a joint. It seemed absolutely and completely impossible that the blue-eyed captain could be a common criminal and murderer—of the French steward we saw nothing. Perhaps, Ned suggested, the commander had suspected our intimacy and forcibly put a stop to it, perhaps (this was the more likely solution) he had nothing particular to communicate. September opened in a singular manner. Rudely aroused from a troubled slumber on the night of the 10th, I found Ned bending over me, whispering something into my ear.

I gave him a startled glance, hurried into my slippers, and together on tip-toe we felt our way to my companion's cabin. Against the couch rested a heavily-framed mirror which Ned had evidently finished taking down from its usual place over the basin-stand. A dark cavity was visible in the panelling. Certain small square boxes attracted my attention, from the tops of which wires radiated in different directions.

'They are microphones of an ordinary type,' whispered Ned, 'and sensitive enough to record the noise of growing grass!'

I stared. It was perfectly true. An examination of the ingenious contrivances left no doubt of the purpose for which they were destined. Ensconced in what I should have thought a decidedly unfavourable position, behind the vast looking-glass, the instruments were nevertheless sensitive enough to convey every word of conversation, criminal or otherwise, to the ears of the listening captain.

This put another colour on our life. The graceful blue-eyed *savant* at once made place for the designing pirate. I attentively studied the microphones, which were constructed of carbon rods arranged radially round a common centre, and connected with an induction coil of the Rhumkorff pattern. Ned flourished a steel pincers triumphantly.

'I'll soon fix the hash of these scamps!' he muttered between his teeth. With a few rapid snaps he severed three of the wires. Then he lifted the heavy glass back into its place and readjusted the bolts.

'We'll be able to talk in peace now, I guess,' he remarked coolly. 'Did you ever see such an accomplished pirate before?'

I said nothing. The affair was certainly significant. With Captain Chlamyl's science, with his endless imagination and resource, we were as much in his power as a fluttering canary is in the power of a cruel schoolboy. Whatever the intentions of the commander were when he instituted these clever spying arrangements, they certainly did not argue well for our safety or independence while on the *Astrolabe*. It is possible that at any other time Ned's discovery would have been inaugurative of a settled and determined hatred between ourselves and the captain, but just then we were too occupied and excited to pay much heed to these evidences of meditated treachery.

During the night of the 25th, I awoke with a vague feeling that some disaster was impending. As I staggered out of bed to light the lamp, my limbs refused their office, and I fell prostrate against the wall. A few moments' reflection and a rapid glance through the circular window, however, convinced me that my muscular intoxication was the result of outward circumstances rather than brain disturbance. We were drawing near Saturn. The huge globe, with its gorgeous panoply of rings, might be several million miles off yet, but it filled fully a quarter of the heavens, and we seemed actually to be touching the outer circumference of the ring, which appeared like a nebula of fine dust, stretching away beneath us in an endless line, like a path of luminous fire.

I was hurrying on my clothes with a view to proceeding on deck, when a well-known panting noise arrested me. The atmosphere was being taken in. I must content myself with contemplating these wonders through the glass panels.

Exclamations and noises resounded from the next cabin. Ned was awake and alive to the situation. Together we dragged ourselves forward into the saloon.

The *Astrolabe* had veered about. The vast planet was now beneath us, and its attraction was becoming more pronounced every hour. As we sank lower and lower, the ring, which at first had worn the appearance of a narrow band, broadened out into a sea of rapidly-moving meteorites, whirling and tossing and changing in the light of the sun under the influence of a motion that seemed perpetual.

It was then 2 a.m. At four we sank majestically past the outlying borders of the great ring, which may have been anywhere between five hundred and five thousand miles distant from our port side.

The revolving stars, rivalling the sand of the sea in quantity, produced the most singular effects of eclipse on each other, and a continual sparkling radiance, like sunlight reflected from the surface of dancing water, shone from the lower and denser portions of the ring, illumining the polished sides and panels of the *Astrolabe* with a soft light, resembling moonlight.

Electrical phenomena, something in the nature of an Arctic aurora, occasionally crowned the poles of some of these spinning satellites, and the monotonous whiteness was varied by streamers and runners of purple and blue. At five, the motion of the *Astrolabe*, which had been slackening during the last hour, seemed to be checked by some invisible obstacle.

I understood. We had struck the Saturnian atmosphere, and the brilliancy of the ring was being slowly quenched in a sea of floating vapours, which grew denser and denser as we sank lower. The attraction, too, became more pronounced, and, speaking for myself, I experienced a feeling of deadly faintness, as though I were being crushed down by an unknown weight.

'How much worse is this going to get?' asked Ned, stretching himself out at full length on the divan and holding his head between his hands. 'A little more'll finish me. I seem to be made of cast-iron. Hadn't we better ring the bell for lights?'

In fact, the saloon was growing darker and darker as the clouds gathered about the sides of the *Astrolabe*. Even the electric search-light, which just then flashed into existence, was unable to wholly dispel the gloom. The vapours wore a yellowish aspect, and seemed to me to be composed of salts of iron.

At five, lurid flashes and sheets of lightning appeared, striking through the gloomy abyss like tongues of fire. Distant explosions struck my ear, and I strained my eyes out into the inky mists, while my heart beat violently.

'Confound it,' exclaimed Ned, clutching my hand, 'we are entering the infernal regions, I believe!'

I could not be surprised at the remark. Even the brilliant light on deck failed to pierce the blackness, which was almost solid in its intensity.

Suddenly I uttered a cry. The *Astrolabe*, striking violently against some hard body, trembled from stem to stern. Strange noises, resembling the splashing of water, re-echoed everywhere, and the panes of glass quivered beneath the impact of some liquid mass. Ned groaned feebly. We were in a pitiable state of terror.

Then came the sound of an opening door, and the saloon flashed into brilliant light. What a scene of disorder! The chairs and sofas were overturned, the ornaments on the piano were broken, many of them. Captain Chlamyl, entering brusquely, was violently overthrown—the ship rocked horribly.

'We have landed!' exclaimed the commander, picking himself up and passing his hand across his forehead.

I was lying prostrate on the sofa, my head splitting with a strange giddiness.

'Are we on the ground?' I managed to articulate.

'No, sir—on the sea,' was the answer.

The rocking motion continued steadily. I staggered to my feet.

'Can we go on deck?' I asked.

'Yes, professor—the atmosphere is breathable, in this region at least.'

We dragged ourselves through the dining-room and up the iron stairs. A fearful sensation, to which, however, I soon became accustomed, made my lungs contract painfully. I felt like a diver buried in a hundred feet of water. A cold sting in my face roused me. The deck was rippling with moisture.

Yes, it was the sea. A sunless void of salt waves, overhung by a heaven of shifting black clouds, torn into ribbons by tempestuous winds and feebly lighted by a far-off scarlet glow that shone along the horizon like a diabolical mirage— the chaos of an unformed world. This was Saturn! My sensations for the moment are hard to describe. Nearly a dozen sailors of the *Astrolabe* were collected, examining the position of the vessel. Our twin lamps of some fifty-thousand candle-power apiece, revealed every detail within a radius of one mile ; beyond that, all was lost in darkness.

From the midst of the long aureole of fire that burned on the southern horizon, vast lurid flames were shooting upwards to the zenith, growing dimmer and dimmer as they vanished among the sooty clouds. Then the darkness vanished for a moment, giving way to an intense white moonlight. Ned, looking upwards, his face colourless with excitement, burst into a cry of mingled surprise and admiration.

'The ring!' he exclaimed.

A vast arch of fire spanned the sky, visible for a moment between two moving columns of vapour. In that brief moment, I thought I discerned, stretching away to the westward, a jagged line of rocks, fringed with a belt of snowy surf.

'It is the equatorial sea!' said a voice near me. I turned and perceived the captain.

'The sea that stretches for several thousand miles on either side of the equator,' he resumed. 'We are going to cross it!'

'To cross it?' I cried.

'Yes, sir, why not. The soundings are about to be taken. I imagine there is not much danger.'

Before I could express the surprise which this proposition of the captain's had awakened in me, one of the men, whom I took to be the first lieutenant, had appeared with a sounding line of steel wire, similar to those used on the Atlantic previous to the laying of Cyrus Field's cable.

Dropped over the port side, the line ran out smoothly to about five thousand feet. Then it stopped.

'We may proceed, I think,' said the captain, turning and addressing the men in his strange language.

'Is it possible that the *Astrolabe* sails over water as well as through the air?' I exclaimed wonderingly.

'Certainly, professor. The power of my engines is communicated to a propeller situated beneath the stern, and from it we get a speed of nearly fifteen miles an hour. Will you go down, or stay on deck?'

Under the circumstances, devoured as I was by curiosity, I preferred the latter course. A dazzlingly white circle of foam, clearly marked on the green water astern, proclaimed that the engines had been set in motion, and the *Astrolabe* slid rapidly forward over the dark waves of the Saturnian ocean.

As the force of gravitation on this immense planet is one-third stronger than the force of gravitation on the earth, these masses of sea-water were naturally calmer and more glassy than the waves of our own immense seas. At times the *Astrolabe* rocked fearfully, however, and the mysterious waters seemed to swirl and foam under the influence of some submarine disturbance. Pillars of steam occasionally swept across the decks, laden with suffocating volcanic gases, making us hurry towards the stairway with the premonitory symptoms of asphyxia convulsing our lungs.

Towards six in the evening we had traversed a distance of nearly a hundred and fifty miles, and the light on the horizon was beginning to broaden horribly into a sea of fiery flame.

An overpowering sense of drowsiness took possession of me, due, I suppose, to the great pressure of the atmospheric strata and the increased weight of my own body. I tumbled downstairs somehow, and, lying down on my couch, fell into a dreamy sleep.

A shock awoke me.

I was lying on the floor of my cabin, bruised and bleeding from several cuts about the head. Voices were answering each other in the interior of the vessel, which was rising and falling in a frightful manner. As I struggled to my feet I fell helplessly back. The *Astrolabe* seemed to fairly stand on end.

The door swung open, and Ned's face, pale as that of a man who has been suffering from a prolonged attack of sea-sickness, peered at me through the dim light. I lit the electric lamps.

' What on earth has happened ? ' I moaned.

' A volcanic crater, an entire mountain, has risen from the bottom of the sea and nearly swamped us,' was the answer. ' We're all right now but we've had a narrow shave for it.'

Ned had not exaggerated. The saloon, and, indeed, the whole of the ship was filled with a thin choking vapour, of a yellowish colour. Through the panels appeared a vast crater, belching forth torrents of steam and smoke, above an ocean of troubled white foam.

'What awful foolishness!' I heard Ned mutter. 'We may be consigned to eternity any minute.'

The remark was not devoid of humour. When one has traversed four hundred million miles of space to reach the planet Saturn, the possibility of getting wiped out by a tidal wave is funny in the extreme. In the situation where we found ourselves, however, the suggestion had too much grim earnest about it to rouse any merriment. Drops of cold sweat stood on my forehead, and my hair stiffened with cowardly fear.

Presently the rocking and pitching movement grew calmer. 'Let us try to get on deck,' suggested the American. 'Perhaps there we will be able to see something.'

On the staircase we met the captain.

'The doors are closed,' said he.

'Is there danger outside, then?'

'Yes, sir. We are crossing a poisonous zone of chlorine and other gases, produced by submarine springs.'

'Is it possible?' I exclaimed.

A strange sight met our gaze through the saloon windows. For a mile round the *Astrolabe*, clearly visible in the white glare of our lamps, the ocean was in a state of violent commotion. Jets and fountains of spray rose and fell in a myriad snowy hillocks that sparkled prismatically under the double action of the electric beams that fell from the deck of our vessel and the hellish glare from the line of volcanoes that shut in the distant horizon. The breath of countless subterranean laboratories was exhaled thus at the surface of the sea, which produced the appearance of water boiling in a copper. I then understood the captain's manœuvre. To emerge on deck under the circumstances would mean instant destruction. Nothing could escape with life from the midst of this fetid sea of death. A sudden idea struck me.

'Are any of the gases combustible?' I asked.

'Probably not,' answered the captain, 'else we should be sailing in an ocean of fire, and, I might add, sailing under considerable difficulty. Let us be thankful for small mercies and take events as they present themselves. Be sure we have not seen much yet. There are many marvels in store for us.'

The engines, keeping up their regular pulsation, soon carried us beyond this troubled region into calmer waters. Excitement drove away sleep, and I ceaselessly scanned this marvellous sea, wondering what new horror the morning would bring, and whether Captain Chlamyl's wonderful vessel would surmount future obstacles as easily as she had those that had already presented themselves.

In spite of all my efforts, however, Nature asserted itself, and I slept, with the ceaseless wash of the waves over the glass panels ringing in my ears like a far-off lullaby.

I was awakened by the French steward, who tapped me gently on the shoulder, and,—

'Your breakfast is served,' said he.

Glancing at the chronometer, I saw it was nearly midday. A strange light illumined the windows of the saloon. Without pausing to inquire its origin, I hurried into the dining-room.

CHAPTER XIV

THE GIRDLE OF FIRE

NED and the captain were seated at the table, waited on by two of the *Astrolabe's* stewards, a grizzly veteran with piercing grey eyes and a young man of twenty-five or thereabouts, whom I had already noticed several times plying his office between the crew's quarters and the kitchen. As I took my seat, a dull shock caused the vessel to tremble all over. The captain rose and gave some hurried instructions to the younger servant. A bell began to ring somewhere near the engine-room, and two massive panels of aluminium slid noiselessly across the windows.

'We have to be careful occasionally,' remarked the commander, with a pleasant nod to me. 'If those glasses were broken, we would find some difficulty in replacing them.'

A gentle see-saw motion was felt. I listened vainly for the beating of the screw, however. It was clear we had ceased to move. Not a sound was heard, save the occasional splash of a wave mingled with far-off thunder.

'We are no longer moving, captain?'

'No, sir. While you were sleeping we made another hundred miles at least. We have touched the north side of the great continent that girdles the Saturnian equator, and which, as I told you before, is the seat of volcanic energy in its wildest and most outrageous forms. After breakfast we will take a promenade—for the present I beg you will do justice to the meal, for our cook has to-day put his best foot foremost. What do you take these to be?'

Broiled fish of a brilliant scarlet colour, covered

with hard scales in the fashion of a lobster, and ornamented with formidable dorsal spines, sharp as needles, were handed round on a napkin.

'Can they be Saturnian fish?' I exclaimed.

'You have guessed right, professor. We did not give ourselves the trouble to fish for them, however. The nets of the *Astrolabe* are held in place by iron rods on either side of the bows, extending right and left like the triggers of a Whitehead torpedo. A lever on deck raises them to the surface, to enable the fish to be taken out. Some curious specimens came to light this morning, which I have no doubt the cook will be proud to show you if you are really interested in the fauna of these distant worlds. In the meantime, breakfast like a man who will probably not dine till late. Do you prefer red or white wine?'

The meal was excellent. I observed that Ned had not as yet completely vanquished his mistrust of the commander, and that he took care only to taste those dishes that the latter had already partaken of.

'Will it be necessary to put on our diving-dresses captain?' I asked.

'No, sir. The air is breathable in these parts; at least near the ground and on the sea-level. The fact that we can dispense with our heavy dresses is an enormous advantage, as, owing to the increased power of gravity, walking would become almost impossible if, in addition to the natural weight of our bodies, we were forced to encumber ourselves with heavy helmets and leaden-soled shoes.'

'What I am surprised at, captain, is that we are not already inconvenienced by this terrible force. I believe Saturn's diameter equals seven times the diameter of our earth. From that a power—'

'Calm yourself, professor. If we are not crushed down by this mighty attraction, it is because there is another equally potent force that is tending to repulse us from the surface of Saturn, and whirl us off into space. Have you ever seen water fly from a mop that is being trundled rapidly?'

'But, captain,' I answered, 'at this rate, if Saturn were to turn a little faster, we would possess no weight at all! The centrifugal energy would exactly counterbalance the natural attraction.'

'I cannot deny it, professor.'

'May I ask if you have ever, in space, met with planets, in which this was the case?'

'No, sir; but it does not follow that there do not exist such worlds. But, as a general rule, the force of rotation only partially counterbalances the attraction of gravity—and that for a very good reason.'

Why so, captain?' asked Ned.

'Because if a planet were to revolve too rapidly on its axis, it would very soon cease to exist. Its component rocks would simply fly apart and lose themselves in space. Shall we go now?'

In the dressing-room we exchanged our comfortable slippers for thick boots soled with thin sheet-copper. Captain Chlamyl, attired in a coat of seal-skins, with a cap and gloves to match, put a weapon into my hand. It was a single-barrelled rifle of the repeating kind, long since patented in England and elsewhere.

'What? Is Saturn inhabited then?' I asked.

'Enough to render it only prudent to arm ourselves,' answered the captain. 'Do you understand how that acts?'

'Perfectly, sir. I am ready to start and devoured by curiosity.'

'Our lamps!' exclaimed Ned, struck by an idea.

'We shall not need them, Master Hatton,' was the commander's reply, and Ned had to content himself with buttoning his coat in silence.

Our party was a large one—seven including the

captain. Among the men I recognised the French steward and the tall man who had accompanied us in our grisly lunar picnic.

Instead of making our exit by a small side door, we mounted on deck. A scene of the most unparalleled grandeur confronted us.

'Right and left, as far as the eye could reach was a perfect chain of fire-crowned mountains, burning in jets and cascades of scarlet, green and blue, sending up columns and spirals of black smoke, across which, as they intermingled, pale lightnings played incessantly. Nor was this all. High up, above the drifting vapours, the sky seemed to be in flame. Lambent streamers, of a pale golden colour, wavered and undulated in a broad arch over this continent of fire, throwing a soft twilight over the farthest limits of the dark sea. The inflammable gases, lighter than the surrounding atmosphere, rose of their own accord into higher regions, igniting in their passage across the boiling lava-flows and curving upwards to join the flaming sea above. Sometimes the clouds parted, and a clear white light shone through, mingling weirdly with the lurid red of the smouldering volcanoes. It came from the great ring, spanning the sky like a Titanic arch of moonlight. As for the boasted eight moons themselves, they might just as well have been absent, for all that was seen of them under the thick curtain that hung like a pall over everything. The sea, flecked in places by patches and puffs of steam, undulated peacefully round the *Astrolabe*.

We were anchored in what appeared to be a shallow bay, shut in by two protruding peninsulas, formed by glowing lava-streams. The hissing and roaring was indescribable. Everywhere fire and water were in conflict. At times masses of incandescent rock, hurled aloft by one of the hundred craters, fell with a roar like thunder into the sea, which boiled furiously at the contact—rings of white steam, similiar to those produced by an expert smoker with a tobacco-pipe, floated away to condense on the colder rocks, and run back oceanwards in gleaming cascades and rivulets.

A boat was fastened alongside, into which we descended. Four men sat at the oars, and we flew along over the glassy water, which I noticed was boiling in several places. The air under these circumstances could hardly be cool. It was intolerably hot owing not so much to the proximity of the spouting lava-streams as to the glare from the burning sky above. We rapidly neared the shore of this dreadful continent, which I could see was overgrown here and there by some kinds of trees—firs and larches for the most part. Cone-bearing plants flourish in places where no other varieties can exist, and the carbonic gases from the volcanoes aided rather than checked their growth. It was two in the afternoon when we set foot on solid ground. The men drew up the boat, and deeming our wraps unnecessary, we left them behind, only taking our weapons and belts.

For half-an-hour we toiled up a gentle slope, composed almost entirely of old lava-flows, and seamed with a million fissures. Surprises greeted us at every turn. Geysers of salt water, larger than the Icelandic ones, roared into the air, breaking and foaming into rainbow-crossed sheets of spray. On reaching the summit of the incline, an exclamation from Ned made me start.

A curious and wonderful sight greeted us. Disporting themselves harmlessly in a shallow arm of the sea were a score of strange animals, with long necks and pointed heads. The red light gleamed along their wet scales as they dived and plunged about, rolling among the pink foam like giant porpoises.

'We've struck a shoal of antediluvian dragons!'
cried Ned.

'Very nearly. They are plesiosauruses.'

The sight was one that would have convulsed
a naturalist with delight. Instinctively I wondered
what my revered old professor at the university
would not have given to be able to share my
impressions for a few moments. I was lost in
admiration at the symmetrical beauty of these
creatures, equally adapted for swimming under
the water or on its surface, their smooth, undulating necks, curved like a swan's, writhed to
and fro like serpents. It seemed to me that I
could even distinguish the double row of gleaming teeth and the flashing green eyes, armed with
thick lenses of horn to protect them from the
pressure of the watery strata when diving after
their prey.

Some of the party were warming themselves
on the slippery rocks. Graceful when swimming,
these creatures were awkward enough when they
tried to waddle over solid ground, aided only by
their short stumpy fins, shaped something like
the flippers of a seal. Hoarse cries escaped them,
cries resembling the bark of a sea-lion, only louder,
and at times they made a hissing sound, beating
the sea furiously with fins and tail. Ned, his
human instincts beginning to assert themselves,
fingered his gun impatiently. Captain Chlamyl
noticed the movement and checked him.

'They are very happy like that,' he said simply.
'It would be a pity to disturb them. Your weapon
is for defence, not offence, Master Hatton.'

We continued our walk. A low copse of strange
trees confronted us, their branches standing out
gaunt and black against the glare behind. In
height they were about a hundred feet, broader
at the top than at the bottom, which was only a

long trunk, covered with diamond-shaped scales like those on a pine-apple. In the centre of this coppice, which the lava had spared till now, was a small clearing.

'Hallo, what's that?' queried Ned.

A curious jagged object lay on the ground at some distance, like a gigantic bat, with wings out-stretched. One of the men took up a stone and threw it.

A horrible cry burst on the stillness, and a great shadow rose from the ground, beating the air with its giant wings, and soaring high above the trees.

'It is a flying dragon!' I cried.

The monster resembled a lizard in shape, or better still, a crocodile. Its long head, armed with a formidable row of teeth, resembled that of a large bird rather than of a reptile. It flew anxiously round in circles, uttering fearful cries, like the shrieking of a pencil across a slate, or the creaking of a carriage-wheel. Presently the cause of its anxiety was explained.

'We frightened it from its nest!' said the captain.

The nest was merely a hollow scooped out in the warm sand. Three greenish eggs, in size larger than those of an ostrich, lay at the bottom. At a word from the commander, one of them was transferred to the wallet, to enrich the museum on board. Leaving the other two intact, we continued our way, slipping and sliding down banks of sand, composed almost wholly of shell-dust and fossil remains.

Here, while rooting among the stones with my fingers, I was severely stung by a venomous insect of the scorpion type, and suffered great pain for some moments. The offender himself was popped into a bottle with some bichloride of mercury. He will not sting any more strangers in a hurry.

The colour effects from the burning craters were positively marvellous. The ordinary flame-tint is a yellowish-golden one. The admixture of certain chemical substances, however, causes this to vary considerably. From a mountain some two thousand feet in height, dominating the sea in cloud-capped solemnity, a stream of ruby-coloured lava escaped, creeping slowly down the rugged sides, half-hidden under a vapoury curtain, and changing to a deeper shade as it cooled. Curious phenomena, too, were produced by the varied nature of the soil over which the flowing streams passed. An orange flood, veined with lemon-coloured fissures, heaped itself up against some obstructing rock, containing, I suppose, nitrate of baryta, or some similar substance. The resisting wall, under the influence of the terrific heat, melted like wax, and a bright green glare attested the effect of the new combination. Too awestruck to speak, we contemplated this fearful display of celestial fireworks in silence. The profuseness and number of the fiery streams was such that it was difficult to know what part of the strange land was quite safe to tread. Behind, before, stretched a shining network of liquid fire. The imprudence of our venture became more apparent each moment. Gusts of hot wind carried with them deadly sulphur fumes, that compelled us to hide our faces in our mufflers, like firemen facing the horrors of a burning house. Captain Chlamyl, keeping his eyes fixed on the distant summit of a wooded hill, plodded steadily on.

A hissing sound on the right attracted us. It was caused by a gigantic column of thin vapour that appeared to rise and almost touch the sky. Before I could reflect on this strange phenomenon, which must have been simply an intermittent form of gas-geyser, I uttered a cry, and sprang back.

The pillar of vapour was transformed into a pillar of flame, which spread out far above our heads into a gigantic flower of fire! The heat was so intense that we had to put up our arms in a feeble attempt to shield our faces. Evidently the gas was inflammable, and after having risen to a prodigious height, had caught fire in the higher strata. Strange rumblings shook the ground on which we stood, and the solid rocks quivered under the force of the jet. Then, almost instantaneously, the flow of gas was checked, and the pillar collapsed, its last remnants floating away overhead in globes and tongues of rolling light. So great had been the glare, that I experienced a disgreeable sensation in my eyes similar to that felt when one has been gazing at the sun.

An inspection of the ground revealed a circular pit, ending in a funnel resembling those of the true Icelandic water-geysers. Not only gas, but also stones and sand were thrown out of this curious volcanic vent, as the surrounding ground proved. The fear of a new and sudden explosion prohibited us from making more thorough investigations. Ned, following the custom of the Icelanders, threw stones down the funnel by way of inducing an eruption. His efforts were vain, however, and we were forced to leave, disappointed.

About a mile farther on, a low hill, fringed with gaunt trees, permitted a view over the surrounding land and sea. On our way thither, several flying dragons were noticed, flapping their way heavily across the smoke, probably searching for food. Twice we halted from sheer weariness and exhaustion, but the indomitable captain kept forcing us on. The *Astrolabe*, looking, with its twin lights, almost stranger than even the phenomena around us, disappeared by degrees, a mere speck on the black water. Above, among the shifting seas of cloud, the crest of a lofty volcano thundered furiously.

'We are treading on the home of an unborn humanity,' said Ned, and he was right.

Here, among these wild islands and bays, under the very shadow of these flaming hills, would hereafter spring up a busy civilisation—a million years hence, perhaps. Harbours would line these dreary coasts, towns would flourish, nations would fall. Perhaps that lonely copse of trees was the site of a future citadel, or of some barbarian garden, rivalling those of Babylon or Thebes in uppish magnificence. Perhaps intelligent iron-clad vessels of war would beat those sombre waters with their noisy screws, or sow destruction from their armoured sides. Perhaps—and at the thought I shuddered strangely — the forerunners of an industrious humanity were even now haunting the dark averns, lonely cave-dwellers, at war with Nature and with each other, dragging out a cruel existence in this savage, primeval world, which, in course of time, they were destined to subdue and conquer.

So clearly marked did this idea become, that once, as we crossed the mouth of a gloomy cave, down the sides of which mysterious murmurs were echoing, I interrogated that encyclopædia of knowledge—the captain—on the subject.

'Humanity, like other forms of life,' he answered, 'only comes into existence on a planet when natural circumstances are favourable to its creation and maintenance. This world is hardly yet sufficiently quiet to permit frail men and women to drag their lives out on its surface. Look at our own experiences! Had it not been for the hermetical sealing of the *Astrolabe's* doors, we would none of us have survived last night. Within the last half-hour we have risked being suffocated fully fifty times, and our excursion is not over yet. Even the animals,

M

huge and muscular as they are, must have a hard
time of it between fire and water— Look there!'

We had reached the crest of the hill. Between
the stem of the lofty firs, a curious sight met our
gaze.

At the end of a spit of sand, overgrown here and
there by circular patches of lichen, stood some huge
animals. There was no difficulty in recognising
them. They were mammoth elephants. Accustomed only to view them in feeble illustration
on paper, I was fairly stagggered on beholding
them in nature. Never had I seen such strange
beasts.

In height they surpassed that of the loftiest
Indian elephant. Vast masses of brownish hair
covered their backs, hanging vertically along their
vast shoulders in matted clumps, from which the
huge tusks, curved like the blade of a scythe,
emerged, white and gleaming. The eyes, covered
by the thick hair, were totally invisible. Captain
Chlamyl, after admiring them for a few moments,
turned to Ned.

'Well, Master Hatton, what do you say to
bringing down one of these gigantic beasts? They
are excellent eating, as doubtless you know?'

Ned grinned and looked at me. When had he
ever feasted on a mammoth before?

I reassured him however. What the captain was
alluding to was the adventure of some Siberian
prisoners, who, while working at the salt mines, had
come across the body of a frozen mammoth imbedded in the ice. The flesh was quite good,
although over twenty thousand years old, and a
numerous party of these unfortunate exiles had
borne testimony to its nutritive qualities. We had
dwelt too long on the marvellous *Astrolabe* to be
any longer surprised at such a trifle as a mammoth-
hunt. The animals were four in number—a bull,

two cows and a calf. The latter member of the party measuring some fifteen feet in height at the shoulder—a promising baby. They were occupied in quietly cropping the scanty lichen, pausing every now and then to utter a kind of subdued sigh or snort, like that of a restive horse. Presently, as we watched them, the younger one, forsaking his parents, came ambling down to the beach, and commenced pumping up sea-water in his trunk and throwing it over his back, screaming hoarsely with pleasure meanwhile. A jagged end of rock was in his way. He curled his trunk round it, and, with a sudden effort, wrenched it bodily out of the sand. In its place appeared a jet of steam, hissing fiercely into the air, enveloping the mammoth's hairy head in a halo of white vapour.

The bang of a rifle woke the slumbering echoes round us. Ned was on his knees, and the red light gleamed along the long steel barrel of his weapon. Our baby elephant paused for a moment in his trumpeting, scrutinised us disdainfully, and then continued his steam-bath as if nothing had occurred.

' I've missed him ! ' exclaimed Ned.

One of the *Astrolabe's* men, resting his gun on the serrated edge of a rock, took a long aim. As the second bullet struck him, the vast creature seemed to realise his danger, and, raising his trunk aloft, uttered a scream of fear.

This changed the scene. The cry was answered by a loud roar from the male beast standing some three hundred yards off, and we saw the gleaming tusks swerve slowly round as the monster came slowly forward to rescue his offspring. Even at that distance we could hear the measured tramp of those great feet, crushing the pebbles at every step —what if he should think of attacking us ? I looked uneasily round, gauging our chances of escape.

A loud roar from the volcano made the earth

tremble. A gigantic bunch of fiery meteors shot into the air, disappearing for some moments among the clouds, then falling round us with a crashing sound. The sea was flecked with snowy patches, and I saw the stem of a great fir on the hill near by snap off short. One of the falling rocks struck the ground some fifteen yards off, hurling a shower of dust and gravel in our faces. It was awful. Even the mammoth himself was surprised, for he stopped and contemplated us with raised trunk, looking more like an animated hillock than a living animal. At the same moment a horrible shrieking arose, and from their nests among the firs, a whole colony of winged dragons sped away, flapping across the red light like enormous bats, and clattering their long jaws like storks. One of these poor creatures, struck in the wing, fell fluttering down in front of us, beating the sand with its mutilated member, from which the blood was flowing.

A momentary sense of pity seized our captain. Stepping up to where the poor dragon lay, its triple rows of white teeth working convulsively in the wet sand, he took aim and fired. The flapping of the agonised wings diminished and the green eyes closed.

I had just time to notice the completion of this humanitarian act, when a shriek from the men, and a dreadful sound like the braying of a thousand trumpets, made me almost jump out of my skin. A gigantic shadow towered above me, looming up like the wall of some mighty fortress. Instinctively I threw myself to one side, and as I did so, a huge brown arm seemed to sweep through the air within a foot or two of my head.

'Run for it!' yelled someone, and I bolted, scudding along the sand for dear life, as though there were ten million devils flying in my wake. At the same time a volley resounded. I heard the whistling of bullets, and turning, I saw the mammoth standing up to his knees in water, brandishing his huge trunk as though he were trying to reach some object that had escaped him.

Could it be that the animal was blind? Eyes are only useful, and, in fact, only possible where there is constant employment to keep them in order. In this murky twilight, lit only by the intermittent glare of the lava, the sight of any animated being would of necessity be decidedly feeble. The elephant advanced still further into the sea, beating the waves into froth with his trunk, and roaring hoarsely. Above, on the moss-grown incline, stood the two cows, contemplating us in mingled fear and curiosity. The calf, wounded in the leg, I think, dragged himself feebly up to where they stood and commenced pouring out his woes in a series of shrill cries.

The men of the *Astrolabe*, kneeling in a row like trained riflemen at a review, were about to pour a second volley on the unfortunate father, when suddenly the scene changed. A wonderful thing happened. At some distance out the ocean seemed to boil, a vast head and neck appeared, overtopping the waves, swaying to and fro like a giant serpent about to strike. Its huge body, in form like an egg, and shining like that of a seal, floated between wind and water—it was a plesiosaurus.

Never had I imagined these creatures could be so vast. The family we had seen bathing on the rocks had not given me any impression of huge bulk—probably because of the distance that had separated us.

A complex sound of whistling and roaring arose, and, while the sea flew up in columns of foam, the two monsters closed in combat. What a scene! How can I attempt to describe it?

Pale, trembling, nervously pressing myself up into a rocky cavity which opened conveniently near, I shivered all over as I watched that terrible struggle. They were an almost evenly-matched pair, in point of size, but the plesiosaurus had a triple row of teeth against the mammoth's bare trunk and almost useless tusks—useless against such a soft, pliant body as that of his antagonist—besides this, the plesiosaurus was amphibian, and could exist, for a short time at least, beneath water. It was a mighty combat, and terrible to see.

At first, the mammoth, twining his iron proboscis round the other's supple, swan-like throat, tried, to judge from his exertions, to wrench the plesiosaurus's head off. The tough bones and sinews resisted long enough, however, to enable the latter to bury his threefold rows of teeth in the elephant's trunk.

With a yell of fury the latter undid his grip and strove to wound his enemy with his right tusk. He succeeded partially, for a fearful gaping cavity made its appearance in the side of the amphibian, dying the sea scarlet with a crimson flood, that ebbed and pulsated with every beat of the giant heart within.

Forsaking his hold on the elephant's trunk, the sea-monster succeeded in biting his antagonist on the leg, and the latter sank down groaning, lying on his side, half-covered with the swaying purple waves—then the end came.

A rushing sound of slipping pebbles and a hiss of angry foam announced that the ground was slipping from under the mammoth's useless limbs. Bit by bit, inch by inch, he was being dragged under the waves.

Once, indeed, his vast head, covered with blood, rose through the ring of scarlet foam to hurl a dying challenge at the pitiless sky, then he sank back, and the waves grew calmer as the plesiosaurus dragged him deeper and deeper into the depths of his ocean home. Captain Chlamyl, as calm as though he had been assisting at a performance of one of Wagner's operas, examined the sea for some time through his binocular telescope, then, turning to the men, gave some directions about cutting up the carcase of the calf, whom his two parents, terrified probably at the death of their lord, had incontinently left to his fate.

It took nearly twenty bullets to give the young mammoth his quietus. The tusks, harder in structure even than those of our terrestrial mammals, had to be chopped out with a hatchet, and each of them proved a heavy weight for two men. The rest of the flesh was subdivided into pieces of fifteen or twenty pounds each, destined to be salted on the *Astrolabe* for future use.

'What do you say to dining here, gentlemen?' remarked the captain, surveying the vast framework of ribs that lay on the strand like the decayed remnant of an ivory vessel.

'I am quite agreeable, captain,' I answered.

'There is one delicacy I can offer you, sir, which not even the pantry of the *Astrolabe* can muster.'

'What is that, captain?'

'It is clear, professor, that you have never travelled in equatorial Africa. Elephant's feet are there considered in the same light as we are accustomed to consider caviar or plover's eggs. We shall need no fire to roast them, the ground is hot enough already.'

What he said was true. A few inches only below the soil the layers of grey ashes and marine deposit of shells were in a high state of incandescence. A hole dug with a shovel revealed a smoking cavity, from which sparks and thin spirals of steam issued.

The gigantic foot, enveloped in seaweed and aromatic lichen, was laid at the bottom and covered over with sand.

An hour later we sat down to a strange collation. I think I still see the scene—the overhanging mountain crest with its crown of yellow and red, the silent party of men, and, between the rounded sandhills, a glimpse of the dark-green, foam-flecked sea, with its covering of clouds and its shadowy islets half-buried in white spray.

Hardly were we seated when the deep black over-head, varied by blue flashes, parted abruptly, allow-ing a clear white moonlight to filter through. The wonderful ring spanned the heavens above the burning streamers of gas. It was too beautiful! Never had such a prodigy been seen by mortal eye. Who knows? Perhaps we were destined never to return to earth alive with our glorious impressions—perhaps—

Here my reflections were cut short by an un-expected marvel.

Far in the depths of the sky above us appeared a burning light. So bright was it, so intense, that it stood out against the silvery ring like the sun against a summer heaven. Each rock, each gaunt fir tree was illumined with an electric lustre. The sand revealed its smallest particles, the crests of the waves were tipped with a diamond sheen. Even at that distance a sensation of heat became apparent, increasing as the light grew brighter.

We rose to our feet. I saw Ned's face, shown off in brilliant relief against a background of jagged trees and wavy bands of smoke, directed upwards, his eyes half-closed, as though they were unable to face the glare.

A fearful sense of scorching heat struck us, like the breath of a simoom, only ten times worse. For an instant the thought struck me that a dreadful catastrophe was about to happen—we were lost!

A roaring filled my ears. I closed my eyes.

When I opened them it was to find myself lying on my back, bruised and half-paralysed, with my head against a stone. The sky overhead was streaked with scarlet. During one moment at least the solid earth had been shaken to its foundations.

A vast fountain of fire spouted from the bowels of some distant mountain, rising and rising till it spread out over the whole sky like a huge umbrella. A myriad streamers of scarlet bent earthwards, and a swarm of rocks, mingled with fine cinders, came crashing down, breaking into flashes of fire as they struck the hard cliffs with a noise like thunder.

'Forward!' shouted the captain, and we stumbled along, pell-mell, in an agony of fear, while the preliminary warnings of a hurricane began to moan across the land, bending the tall trees in two, and snapping their mighty stems like matches.

'The sea! the sea!' screamed someone, as a great green wave came rushing up along the heated rocks, glowing and fermenting in that diabolical light. For an instant I beheld the waters closing over me in the form of an arch, through which the flow of the celestial fire shone palely, like a ray from a distant green star, then came a dreadful shock, and I was struggling for dear life in a lukewarm flood that eddied and boiled round me like an army of demons.

'Help!' I cried. 'Help! Help!'

Through the murky light, obscured by a fog of almost luminous vapour, I distinguished the outline of a rock on which the forms of some men were visible. I struck out, swimming despairingly, as a man swims who is fighting for dear life against the liquid element. My boots weighed me down. It was with the utmost effort that I could manage to keep afloat, even in that bitter salt water. The flood gurgled in my ears, penetrating through my nostrils, down into my lungs, making me cough convulsively—lights flashed before my eyes. I was sinking; I was drowning.

Then a violent pain in my leg roused me to life. I had struck against a hard, resisting object. A hand clutched me by the collar and drew me forcibly up the rock, round which a broad sea eddied and swirled furiously. The sky was full of meteors. A whirlwind was lashing the waves into fury. Screams came from among the trees, some of which were being invaded and carried away by the rushing water. Gigantic winged monsters were faintly seen as they blundered past, between the wind and the flame, forsaking their shattered nests.

'Courage! We shall have to swim for it!' said a voice close to my ear. It was that of the French steward, who had been my providential deliverer. His words stirred me into something like approaching energy. Our solitary companion, one of the *Astrolabe's* engineers, had already dived from the rock, every moment more closely invaded by the sea, and was swimming off in the direction of a vaporous wall, which marked the termination of a superheated stream of volcanic matter. To see the land was impossible. To linger on the rock meant death. Disencumbering myself of my heavy boots, I plunged in.

The water was warm, and it grew warmer as we approached the curtain of hissing steam, to which the farther lava-flows imparted a rosy-golden colour. Great bubbles of gas rose every now and then to the surface, and our lungs began to ache fearfully. On several occasions my feet became entangled in floating masses of kelp and sea-wrack—twice at least I gave myself up for lost.

Should we be boiled alive?

It seemed likely, for the warmth of the water increased rapidly as we proceeded, and the thick steam prevented us from seeing each other.

No, we struck the land. A hot, soft strip of volcanic mud mingled with sulphur, over the surface of which danced lambent blue flames.

'Hallo!' shouted a voice somewhere on the left; it was Ned's. Three men, the captain and two engineers were standing by him, safe and sound, wringing their dripping clothes. One only was missing, a fair-haired young athlete who filled the office of steward on board.

Delay, however, was impossible. Death seemed to be floating in the very air we breathed.

'We must be off!' said the captain.

Half a mile out to sea, the electric lamps of the *Astrolabe* were dancing up and down on the waves like twin will-o'-the-wisps. A fiery streak shot from her bows, breaking into balls and spirals of green. It was a rocket.

As we neared the rising ground, Ned uttered a cry of horror. During our absence the lava-streams had closed in a compact network of fire, cutting off all chance of returning; the road itself was in flames. I recognised the very rocks on which we had trodden, as they melted or crumbled away slowly to mingle with the glowing flood undermining their bases. On the small hillock, some hundred yards away, the copse of fir trees was burning. I looked at the captain. If signs went for anything, our frightful situation only formed part of his day's amusement.

'It looks as though we were blocked in,' was all he said. Then, in a brusquer voice, 'You are a good swimmer, professor?'

I had just emerged from one unpleasantly realistic battle with the waves, and felt hardly inclined for another. Nevertheless it was a case of life or death.

'It will only be a matter of a few hundred yards or so,' continued the commander, 'but there is no time to be lost—come. We must swim out a little way to circumvent this lava-stream, and land again at the point yonder.'

Choking, breathless, we forced our way across the hot soil, through the dense curtain of vapour that concealed the sea. Then one of our number slipped, stepping into a pool up to his knee. He screamed wildly and scrambled out, falling prone at our feet with expressions of pain and despair. At the same time a gust of fetid wind swept the cloudy curtain aside, revealing the heaving masses of dark water beyond. I uttered a cry. The sea was boiling.

We were thus shut in between hostile fire and water. Ned, still cool and collected, suggested signalling to the *Astrolabe*. Blue lights and rockets to the number of a dozen or so had been entrusted to—whom?

Whom, of course, but the fair-haired steward who had been swept out of existence by the great wave only a quarter-of-an-hour back. Captain Chlamyl clenched his hands nervously. The men betrayed signs of uneasiness. I was simply paralysed with cold fear.

We hurried back to our post on the rising ground, where the sulphur fumes were less active, and surveyed the situation.

'Those lava-flows do not seem very wide,' mused Ned, almost to himself. 'One might try to jump a couple of them, don't you think?'

The captain seemed to assent. A shiver passed through me. I looked at the blinding, bubbling streams of fire, half-hidden by lurid smoke-wreaths, and, as I looked, I hastily made up my mind to be boiled alive in the ocean rather than to risk falling into one of them.

Ned's horrible proposal seemed to be reasonable enough, however. Out of the many streams of incandescent matter, only one had reached the sea —the one nearest to us, which measured, as far as I could see, some fifteen feet in width at its narrowest part. Fifteen feet! At college I had jumped twenty-four, but what a difference!

Half-a-dozen tired men, most of them middle-aged, fresh from a fatiguing struggle with the inhospitable elements, sick at heart and head, short of breath, half-suffocated in fact, their normal strength reduced to one half at least. What slender chance of success was ours!

For a moment we stood still, hesitating, then an exclamation from the captain made my heart jump.

'Look!' he exclaimed, pointing up the mountain.

I followed his gaze, and thrilled with horror. A glowing torrent, nearly half-a-mile in width, was sweeping down on us, the trees and mosses burning furiously in its passage. Delay was no longer possible. I turned sick.

The lava-flow was, as I have said, about fifteen feet wide at its narrowest part. On the near side a broad, flat rock facilitated the 'take off;' on the far side was a similar rock.

Ned, to whom the affair apparently did not present any unusual difficulty, threw aside his wallet in a business-like manner, clenched his fists winked at me in a rather ghastly fashion, and started off.

Bravo! For an instant we caught sight of his gaunt form, suspended in the air above those hellish fires, then he vanished among the smoke, and we heard him hallooing on the other side. He was over.

The captain followed, then the four men, one after the other. It was my turn. A loud roaring resounded on the right, the new flow was descending rapidly. A bubbling in the sand at my feet attracted my attention, and I began choking convulsively. Ned's yells reached me feebly, and I thought I could distinguish the captain's voice upraised in encouragement.

Now for it! Never shall I forget that horrible moment. Away I went, scudding along in the heavy sand as fast as my tired limbs would allow. I reached the rock. A million fires scorched my cheeks. Then the wild jump, and the sickening moment of suspension over that hissing cauldron. I rolled over and over on the hard stones, barking my shins and burning my hands fearfully among the loose ashes. I was safe. It was not so awful, after all.

Half-an-hour afterwards we reached the *Astrolabe's* boat. Securely moored to a projecting rock, it had suffered little damage from the rapid influx of the tide, though it was full to the gunwale with sea-water, in which a promising family of small fish were disporting themselves.

As we stepped on board, a terrible thing took place on the land we had quitted. The conflict of fire and water began in real earnest. Imagine a stream of molten lava, over a mile wide, pouring into the cold sea in a steady torrent. Hell seemed to be unloosed, and a vast world of vapour curled in rose-tinted majesty towards the remotest zenith. Captain Chlamyl, his teeth set fixedly, looked darkly out over the boiling chaos that had swallowed one of his comrades, and, for a moment at least, his eyes filled with tears.

CHAPTER XV

A STRANGE BURIAL

September 28th.—All day long the *Astrolabe* has held steadily northwards at a rate of from ten to fourteen knots an hour. The awful fate that has overtaken our poor steward did not, I grieve to say, prevent me from sleeping with unusual soundness last night. Alas for the heartlessness of human nature! When one has glutted oneself with marvels and horrors during a day and a half, one cannot be expected to have much feeling left to bestow on a mere human atom.

Captain Chlamyl, unwilling to leave the gloomy spot without making a last attempt to rescue the missing man, ordered out the pinnace, and had the coast-line minutely explored, but without success. Our other sufferer, the one who fell into the pool of boiling sea-water, is in a bad state, and everyone seems anxious on his behalf.

When I rose this morning, we had already started, and the long aluminium hull was trembling beneath the impulse of the screw, making the glasses and plates on the dining-room table jingle musically.

After breakfast we witnessed an interesting spectacle, the drawing-in of the vast nets with their finny burden. I examined each specimen carefully, classifying and naming them to the best of my ability.

Above and around us all was darkness, even the distant light from the girdle of volcanoes was disappearing, so thick was the fog.

'Captain Chlamyl must be a fatalist,' remarked Ned sarcastically, shaking out his pipe into the black waters over the lee taffrail, 'to navigate at full speed in such a devil of a sea.'

The decks of the *Astrolabe* were illumined by a double row of incandescent lamps, nestling in circular reflectors of silvered metal. Ahead of her bows, the powerful search-light strove in vain to pierce the darkness, which a falling shower of fine ashes rendered positively opaque. Four of our men, in sou'-westers of indiarubber, were emptying the nets, tossing the fish, one by one, into buckets, and lowering them down the companion-way to be salted. The haul was enormous. Fully half a ton of food was taken on board.

To enumerate half the specimens that were submitted to my inspection would be a labour of weeks.

The eyed pteraclis (*Pteraclis ocellatus*), at once recognisable by the enormous size of its fins, which are, in fact, larger than the body to which they belong, attracted my attention. It was almost a shame to doom the beautiful creature, glittering in a gorgeous array of gold and silver scales, to the unpoetical frying-pan. Several gobies, resembling vaguely the British ones, only larger, were taken, together with an unusually formidable specimen of the spiny fishing-frog (*Lophius piscatorius*), a voracious animal, to whom no kind of bait comes amiss.

And then the monsters? Creatures without a name, Saturnian wonders with six fins, with triple tails and double sets of eyes. Long grey serpents, whose tails, rapidly revolving, imitated to a nicety the action of a screw-propeller. Electrical ones, in form like a Whitehead torpedo, whose heads, shaped like the tail of a gigantic fire-fly, threw out an intense white light, equal to that produced by a carcel burner. Cuttle-fish with twenty arms, double-headed lampreys (Siamese twins Ned called them), rays, clad in scaly armour, like those strange terrestrial mammals, the armadillo and the South American manis—truly Nature has the same representatives everywhere.

For more than an hour the unloading of the nets continued. Then the men vanished silently, leaving Ned and myself alone.

That tranquil individual, leaning indolently against the railing, his face begrimed with a layer of ashes, shot a piercing glance at me from under his black eyebrows.

'You have something to say?' I ventured.

'I had a conversation with the Frenchy again last night.'

'Indeed? That was clever of you. How did you manage it?'

'Captain Chlamyl was one of the party who manned the pinnace to search for poor Heinemann, the steward. His death makes a vacancy on board which may materially alter the benevolent captain's intentions with regard to ourselves. There are now less mouths to feed.'

Ned smiled grimly. I was indignant.

'Perfect bosh!' I exclaimed. 'I don't believe for a minute the captain would intentionally get rid of anyone on such a pretext.'

'Don't you, Hal? Well—no more do I. That is, I don't *believe* anything, but I *know* a good deal.'

'S-s-s-sh! Talk softly. Telephones dog us at every step here. What did the fellow tell you?'

'He told me (curse that spray!) that the amiable captain was in the habit of occasionally getting rid of any man whom he was tired of, or whose services he could dispense with, by the simple process of abandoning him during his sleep on some planet—uninhabited or otherwise. It sounds like bunkum, but from what I've seen, I judge there's a pretty good ballast of sense in the story.'

I passed my hand across my forehead. The affair was certainly more than ordinarily curious, besides being somewhat terrifying. Abandoned in space! What a singularly awful prospect!

N

'In case you should want what the lawyers call a " precedent,"' continued my inflexible companion, coolly arranging the hood of his overcoat to shelter him from the flying jets of foam, and crossing his legs comfortably, 'one was certainly furnished by those singular footprints we struck while crossing the Sea of Putrefaction, or whatever the devil the name of that place is on the moon. Do you remember the antics our muscular friend went through?'

Remember them! They had haunted me in my sleep for weeks afterwards. The expression was a hollow mockery. Through a long vista of pale terrors, of shadowy nightmares, I caught a glimpse of some terrible, sickening crime—some piece of devilish heartlessness—some drama of misery and anguish, that those dreary plains had witnessed— abandoned! In my mind's eye I saw the haggard face, the wild, hopeless eyes of the condemned wretch, plodding vaguely onwards across that inhospitable desert, onwards towards the light that glimmered in the east, onwards to his death among the sandhills and burnt-out craters of a dead world.

'Impossible, Ned! It's too horrible!'

'Is it? It may be horrible, viewed from a merely human point of view, but seen through the eyes and brain of our demon commander, it is merely a picturesque incident, hardly worthy of a second thought. Hal, you have no idea how utterly feelingless the continual contemplation of these sublime things can make a man. No truly great genius ever has a heart.'

At other times the sentiment would have provoked a smile. Now, alas! I had no smiles left; nothing but cowardly fear—fear that was none the less intense from the fact that hand in hand with it went a certain fatal admiration for the giant intellect that had planned the dreadful tragedy.

'To a philosopher like the captain, Hal, all things

are possible,' pursued Ned. 'Right and wrong are merely relative terms, neither of them really exists!'

I leant against the taffrail and strained my eyes out into the darkness, while my heart grew cold within me.

Yes. I knew it. I knew that splendid heartlessness, that cynical disregard for the sufferings of others that conscious greatness breeds in the mind of a man, that cool method of discussing cause and effect that a study of Nature's grand phenomena induces. No—we were not on the same plane as the captain. We were to him as the dust of the universe is to the roaring sun, to the flaming comet that, marking its own path across the void, drags a million existences to death in its fiery embrace. For a moment (may I be forgiven if the thought was blasphemous) I realised what it must be to be the Almighty Architect Himself. To be able to contemplate misery unmoved! to be so wise that evil and good, like greatness and smallness, height, depth and breadth, darkness and light, were nothing but expressions—thoughts formulated by the brain to distinguish the different states of matter, nothing more—it was the magnificent indifference of an intellect that looked forward to the end of all things, where we—finite minds and small —neglected the ulterior designs of Fate to fret and worry over our transitory grievances.

Ned, practical as ever, brought me out of my reverie by remarking,—

'So you see, Hall, we've nothing to hope from the captain.'

'What do you propose doing?'

'Well—I don't know exactly. We're a fearfully helpless set, all of us, and quite in that fellow's power. If he were to take it into his head, for instance, to drop us overboard to-night—'

I shuddered. The idea was not inviting.

'What was the name of the poor chap they left on the moon?' I asked.

'Andersen—Jacob Andersen—a Swede,' replied Ned. 'I got that from the Frenchy. It appears he did something to anger the captain one day, while the *Astrolabe* was circling round the earth at a distance of some fifty thousand miles. He threw a letter overboard—shot it overboard out of a gun, in fact—in the vague hope that it might reach our planet and communicate some facts respecting his whereabouts. Our commander has strong reasons, it seems, for wishing to preserve an incognito, and resents any attempt made by his crew to reveal it to their friends on earth. So you see it is really not in the captain's interest to let us loose again among civilised people—in fact—'

'For God's sake, Ned!' I broke in angrily, 'don't go on talking in that strain. It unsettles one. I don't believe a word you're saying. I don't *want* to believe anything so hideous. Give us a rest, man!'

Ned merely smiled.

'The time will come when you yourself will have to face the bitter truth, Hal—but, till then, I'll drop it if you like. Let's go down. What's that over there?'

A ruddy glow shone through the fog ahead, far above our heads. Presently the wind tore the ashes apart, and a sheaf of fire became visible, suspended in mid-air, like some ghostly torch.

'A volcano,' suggested Ned, carelessly. 'I'm sick of them! Let's go down.'

I assented. Even the sight of an eruption was beginning to lose its charm for me. Besides, I was too agitated by what my companion had disclosed to feel much interest. I followed Ned down the ladder.

In the smoking-room we met the captain him-

self, pale and emaciated-looking, from his prolonged
vigil on the previous night, no doubt.

'One of your men is ill, I hear,' I suggested. 'If
I can be of any use—of course, I shall be happy.
Medicine was one of my studies at the university.'

'No, no!' answered the captain, vaguely, making
a rapid gesture as though to ward off some un-
imagined evil. 'It is only a surface burn—a mere
singeing of the skin, nothing more. What is it to
you? Leave me!'

There was nothing more to be said. I bowed,
and withdrew silently.

September 29th—October 8th.—Since our start,
ten days ago, we have made nearly four thousand
miles, and to-day we have, for the first time on
Saturn's surface, beheld the sun. The sun, but
how pale and poor in comparison to the same
planet seen from our own world!—a large star,
nothing more.

On the platform this morning I met Ned.

'Where are we?' I asked.

The screw was still beating the waters astern
into an endless track of white. Overhead, the
inky mists had parted, revealing a sky of palest
green, across whose outer limits the expanse of
rings formed a shadowy arch. Right and left, out
of the dark, sea-water, rose pinnacles and crests of
rock, some tipped with snow, and furrowed with
miniature glaciers of ice. Columns of steam here
and there attested Plutonian agency, while an
occasional foaming on the waters—patches of
floating ashes or scoria, combined with certain
undefinable, trembling feelings in our hull, told
of the forces at work in the dark caverns beneath
these primæval seas.

'Where are we?' echoed Ned. 'That's what I
wouldn't mind knowing myself. We've struck

another continent during the night, and are at
present navigating on the surface of a river.'

'A river?' I exclaimed.

'Yes; a river some thirty miles wide, I should
think,' was the answer. 'Look there—you can see
the opposite bank.'

I took the opera-glass. Ned was not mistaken.
A faint, yellow line of sandy cliffs stretched southwards along the horizon.

'It may be an inland sea,' I suggested.

'Not by a long shot! The water's fresh—or
nearly so. By the way—you know that poor
fellow who burnt himself? He's dead! Died
during the night. The captain's not in a particularly good humour in consequence. Look! what's
that?'

A gigantic head, shaped like that of a horse, rose
above the water. Two green eyes, shining like a
cat's, were contemplating us; behind, a long white
eddy traced a line like the wake of a screw-propeller.

'A sea-serpent!' I exclaimed.

It was really and truly a serpent. Fins of vast
power were attached to the long body, beating the
green waves furiously as the monster glided noiselessly along. To classify this wonderful creature
was difficult, as no naturalist had ever yet set eyes
on it, except in theory. In my own mind, I decided
that it belonged to the order of large amphibious
snakes, of which the anaconda and the boa are our
earthly representatives.

For more than half-an-hour the wonderful
creature accompanied us, swimming at an easy
distance, in a regular parallel line, and diving at
intervals, to reappear on the other side of the
Astrolabe, having passed beneath the keel like a
flash of lightning. Once I thought it was making
up its mind to board our vessel, and I uneasily
eyed the cabin door—but no. Its intentions were

pacific, and the formidable beat of our screw, no doubt, showed that we were not to be trifled with. Finally, towards ten-thirty, it dived out of sight and disappeared. Overhead, in the sky, appeared a curious sight. Four luminous crescents were riding across the green void in silent beauty—two near the zenith and one on either horizon.

'What a gorgeous affair it must be when the whole eight moons are visible,' soliloquised Ned, through his teeth.

Such a conjunction of circumstances, however, was unlikely, if not impossible. I surveyed the wild scene in silence, while a cold breeze from the land made my teeth chatter. The farther we proceeded, the colder it seemed to get. At twelve a huge bank of fog lifted, disclosing a belt of white ice-covered mountains, some of whose tops were smoking. At the same time the speed of the *Astrolabe* diminished—it was going to stop.

'I vote we go and put on our overcoats,' said Ned. 'I ll bet a dollar there's some excursion or other looming.'

At breakfast I broached the subject to the captain. ·

'We are going on shore, sir?' I said, in as careless a voice as I could muster.

He nodded without replying. In spite of the instinctive fear with which this strange being inspired me, my heart went out to him as I noted his sunken cheeks and tired eyes. Respect for a man is a wonderful thing. Here were we, a company of weak, human beings, cut off from all intercourse with our kind by some hundreds of millions of miles—devoid, even, as far as I could see, of the bare means of retracing our steps. And yet, such, I suppose, was our confidence in that man, that, instead of being overwhelmed by naturally terrible reflections respecting our own future, we were tranquilly committing ourselves to his care like children, existing calmly and quietly under circumstances, of which the bare recollection would be paralysing—an excursion on Saturn! I had already been through one, and was not experiencing any particular desire to attempt a second. A word from the commander made me change my resolve, however.

'If you and Mr Hatton are afraid,' he suggested quietly, 'of course we will excuse you.'

Ned coloured violently. The sarcasm settled the affair. It is better to die fifty times over than to be laughed at by such a man. We would go, and perish if need be. Look which way I would, annihilation seemed to be our fate anyway. It might just as well come one way as another.

The trembling of the screw stopped short, and we heard the anchor-chains rattling—two hundred feet of water at least, to judge from the time it took them to strike a bottom.

Our party was numerous enough—nine men in all. Four of these carried on their shoulders an oblong box, swathed in grey canvas. It was a coffin, containing, no doubt, the body of our poor steward, who had died during the night.

I was strangely impressed by the scene. Right and left rose a wilderness of gaunt snow mountains, half hidden beneath thick layers of cloud for the most part. Overhead, crossed in places by trails of dark vapour, stretched the gigantic ring, silvery at the zenith, but deepening in colour as it neared the horizon, owing to the refraction of the atmospheric strata. A cold grey twilight reigned everywhere on the surface of this embryo world, a twilight vaguer and more mysterious than moonlight, yet permitting every detail, far and near, to be seen with the utmost distinctness.

The *Astrolabe*, motionless on the dark green

water, seemed to be floating in space once more, so calm were the reaches of the river, undisturbed, as far as we could see, by a single living creature.

The cold was intense, but our jackets of sealskin moderated it enormously.

Gradually, as we receded farther and farther into the interior of this cloudy continent, a new and indefinable feeling began to oppress me. At first I paid no heed, believing it to result from my over-strung imagination, but presently an exclamation from Ned, who was lagging behind, developed the imaginary feeling into a real grievance.

'Phew!' gasped my companion, 'I'm glued to the ground. I can't move worth a cent!'

The expression was not unnatural. My legs seemed robbed of their locomotive power. A fearful weight was crushing me down, causing the blood to leave my head and tingle unpleasantly about the region of my feet. I felt as though a thousand needles were sticking into my limbs, and, resigning myself to the inexplicable influence, I sank down, breathless, on a convenient rock and gasped like a fish out of water.

Several of our men, muscular giants though they were, evinced a disposition to follow my example. The captain, standing magnificently upright in his armour of skins, smiled faintly.

'Undo the crutches,' he said, turning to one of his companions, 'lame men need assistance.'

This sounded suspiciously like humbug, but, as it turned out, there was meaning in the captain's madness. One of the sailors proffered me a pair of stout wooden crutches. I essayed them doubtingly, and found myself able to walk easily once more.

'Gravity is resuming her rights,' explained the commander. 'We are no longer under the ring!'

He pointed to the sky as he spoke. Light burst in on me all of a sudden.

The powerful attraction of Saturn is nearly equal to twice that of the earth. Hence, our weight became doubled on all parts of the planet which were not situated directly under the vast equatorial rings, whose counter-attraction modified and annulled the crushing force that was now weighing us down. Had we been at the poles instead of where we were (some thousands of miles south of the Saturnian Tropic of Cancer) we would probably have been unable to move a step, crutches or no crutches.

The men, no doubt accustomed to hard physical toil in all its sinister forms, struggled on manfully, relieving each other at intervals in the arduous task of bearing the heavy coffin, which here weighed nearly half as much again at it would have weighed on our own planet.

A formidable mountain, of which, thanks to the heavy cloud-masses, only the summit was visible, obstructed our path, blocking up the entire eastern horizon. Glaciers of blue, hummocky ice traced regular lines down its precipitous sides, which every now and again were broken and shattered, disclosing rugged fissures and precipices, seamed with veins of glittering minerals and snowy bands of frozen water. Silent columns of steam curled up here and there, and black circular openings in the ice-flows marked the presence of subterranean springs.

The grey twilight imparted a ghastly look of desolation to the place, which seemed totally uninhabited and destitute of animal life. It was a glacial world—dead, cold, deserted.

Once or twice, nestling in crevices above the floating stream-jets, I noticed some of the most elementary forms of life—foraminiferæ, eozoons, yellow funguses that seemed endowed with a strange sensitiveness, cockle-shells, limpets of gigantic size

(some measuring two feet in diameter nearly).
For a moment it struck me as peculiar that we had
come so far without seeing anything more marvellous. Who, to gaze on this silent landscape, would
believe it to be a glimpse of the far-off planet
whose light contributed towards the adornment of
the summer nights on his own little world?

Suddenly, as though a mirage had seized its
image and held it fast, the lofty summit with its
vapoury crest appeared doubled, photographed, so
to speak, on the ground at our feet. I rubbed my
eyes.

A glassy river lay before us. Never had water
appeared so smooth before. At the same moment
a singular odour assailed my nostrils. The men
had halted, uncertain as to how they were to
proceed. Every detail, each projecting rock, each
cloud, the ring itself, were mirrored with startling
fidelity. The river seemed about a hundred yards
in width, though, owing to the difficulty of judging
distances over water, it may have been wider. Its
shores were lined with a peculiar greyish kind of
rock, familiar to me from my mineralogical studies.
A strange idea struck me. I bent down and
touched the water with my finger.

'It is oil!' I cried, 'petroleum oil!.'

'Yes,' answered the captain, 'and uncommonly
good petroleum at that. The spring that produces
the combustible must not be far off!'

Here certainly was something worth looking at.

'It would make the fortune of those California
millionaires over again,' soliloquised Ned. 'We
could literally flood the market with petroleum
if we could only import it.'

Such a consummation was not, however, to be
thought of. There was certainly enough of it.
For miles right and left, the river of oil stretched
away. There was no perceptible current though,

and it more resembled an elongated lake than a
river. Examples of similar formations on our
native globe were not wanting, though they were
mostly on a far smaller scale. The naptha lakes
of Mesopotamia and the pitchy deposits of the
island of Trinidad were not very unlike after all, and
again it struck me what an enormous difference
there was between the abstract ravings of visionary
enthusiasts like Bernardin de Saint-Pierre or Edgar
Poe and the actual living reality.

They, viewing a host of planets through the
medium of an imaginative brain, had conceived
rivers of liquid diamonds, cascades of jewels, sylphs,
demons, mermaids, trees bearing gold and silver fruit,
animals that sung in harmony like trained choristers,
and a host of other unnatural impossibilities. But
for the singular aspect presented by the green sky,
with its pale rings, its four moons and its wonder-
fully-coloured layers of mist, I might have believed
myself to have been crossing the interior of Iceland.
The earth was totally invisible—nor, if it had been
visible, would it have been very imposing. A tiny
speck of emerald on a ground of aquamarine, nothing
more. Instinctively I wondered whether this was
all—whether, after, all, some new prodigy would not
suddeuly unfold itself before our startled eyes. I
wondered uneasily whether it would come in the
form of a cosmic phenomenon or a novel problem
in natural history. We had faced a giant serpent on
the moon, we had wrestled with mammoths, flying
dragons and long-necked saurians. What was going
to appear next?

I was soon to know.

A vast plateau of smooth white snow unfolded
itself before us. At a sign from the captain, the
coffin was set down and preparations for the burial
were begun.

I think I can still see the scene, enacted in that

mysterious, diffused light, that permitted no shadows to be thrown by any object. As the body was lowered into the crypt, several of the men fell·on their knees. Captain Chlamyl, myself and Ned remained standing. From across that desolate waste came a strange sound, floating on the wind like a wail of human pain.

My blood froze. I touched the commander on the arm. He was staring intently out over the plains towards where the ring disappeared behind a bank of heavy red clouds.

'Captain !'

He did not seem to hear. The clods of sand and snow fell heavily on the coffin lid. Some of the men rose to their feet to gaze uneasily about them. There it was again ! That low, wailing sound, that echoed far and wide like the cry of a wounded animal.

Across the golden crescents spanning the sky, black specks came floating, growing larger and larger, like gigantic bats, flapping up and down, rising and falling, darting to and fro in unsymmetrical lines.

Now one of them crossed a bright belt of green light where the largest moon shone between two clouds, and I thought that its wings were shaped like those of a dragon.

'Have you your revolvers, gentlemen ?' said the captain, turning abruptly.

We were all of us armed, but we felt uneasy nevertheless.

'What awful brutes !' exclaimed Ned.

As he spoke, a fearful howling arose, and I could see a legion of yellow eyes gleaming horribly under those dark wings.

'They are flying wolves !' said somebody (I think it was Ned), and at the same moment a revolver-shot made the distant masses of poised ice and snow rattle down on the hard plateau with a sound like the firing of far-off artillery.

'To the boat!' shouted the captain, as a great shadow fell with a dull thud at my feet, snapping and snarling like a demon, its pointed yellow teeth closing like a steel-trap within an inch of my foot.

The terrible chase had begun. It was not a chase, properly speaking, for what chance had we struggling men, embarrassed with heavy crutches for the most part, against these winged furies, more awful than those that haunted legendary Orestes.

I gave myself up for lost, hardly daring to look behind me. The wounded wolf, struggling help-lessly on the snow, was pounced upon by his companions, and during some moments a fearful carnage ensued. The ground was a mass of beat-ing wings and snapping teeth. Another group settled on the newly-made grave, tearing up the soft snow with their paws, scattering it over and around themselves in a white cloud.

Were they going to abandon us?

The hope was soon quelled. We had hardly proceeded a bow-shot from the place when we heard the hungry band once more on our track.

On they came, their long fulvous bodies be-dabbled in places with hideous streaks of red, their eyes shining like demon stars through the murky light. One great monster flew at our hindermost man, his crutch was wrenched from his grasp and over he rolled, burying his face in the snow to avoid the impact of those dreadful claws and shrieking to us for help in the jabbering dialect of fear.

Three shots rang out. The vast wings beat the air unevenly, and the brute fell, screaming shrilly, like a dog crushed by the wheel of a cart.

Our unfortunate follower picked himself up. Ned offered his arm to help him. I had just time to see this much when a violent shock overthrew

me, and I felt sharp teeth penetrating my flesh.
A horrible growling sounded in my ears and I was
shaken as a rat is shaken in the teeth of a cat.

'Help!' I called feebly. 'Help!'

A strange drowsiness was robbing me of my
senses. I think for a moment I must have fainted.

Then the heavy load rolled off my chest, and I
caught sight of two great eyes closing glassily in
the death agonies.

Four wolves lay dead. The rest, to the number
of some twenty or thereabouts, were flying uneasily
round us in circles, as though uncertain how to
commence an attack.

We struggled on, sinking up to our knees in the
snow, shouting encouragements to one another.
Once a great grey brute, whose fur was falling off
in patches like that of a mangy dog, succeeded
in overthrowing the captain. Ned, dropping his
crutches, coolly stepped up to where the animal was
worrying its prey, and grasping one of the wings
in his left hand, sent a bullet crashing into the
brain. The captain rose, blood streaming from his
face where one of the claws had struck him, and—
as though not willing to be behindhand in politeness, even at such a moment—inclined his head
froggily in the direction of the American, who was
replacing his revolver.

The impromptu bow nearly cost him his life, for
a second wolf was upon us like a flash, and had it
not been for a peculiarly lucky shot of mine, at
least one of us would have paid the penalty.

The horrors of that pursuit still remain indelibly
fixed in my memory. Three times I thought we
were lost. Most of the crutches were gone, but
fear lent strength, and in spite of the crushing
weight, we hurried on courageously.

As we reached the petroleum river, another wolf
fell. Ah! that crossing! With those slippery

rocks to stand upon, those nauseating fumes dimming our senses, and that shrieking army of demons at our back.

The captain was the first to reach the shore, and in the intervals between my stumbling jumps, I saw him standing, revolver in hand, his eyes fixed on the snarling pack who were tearing their dying comrade to pieces on the opposite bank.

I glanced round. The winged monsters were massed together in a dark-brown cluster, rising and falling like bats, striking at each other with their mailed claws, and shrieking discordantly in a dozen keys.

Presently the noise diminished. With a bound the foremost wolf sprang into the air and sniffed about him, a hideous mass of clotted blood.

Ah—he saw us !

In a second the whole diabolical band were flapping rapidly across the oily surface on our track. I saw the captain bend down and discharge his revolver—seemingly at the water.

A lambent blue flame flashed into life, oscillating and wavering, growing and expanding, racing off in every direction, pulsating and flowing in pyramids of yellow fire, seething round the black rocks and bounding upwards to the sky, a hell of savage flame more terrible than that of the imaginary Inferno!

In the scene that followed I had time to bestow admiration on the ingenuity of our commander. I myself would have been the last person to think of firing the lake. It was an inspiration, and it saved our lives.

The wolves were baffled. For a short moment we beheld those gaunt wings flapping above the roaring fire, then they beat a retreat, and through the dazzling curtain we could hear their shrill cries as we toiled homewards down the ice-bound fields to where the *Astrolabe* lay cradled on the dark bosom of the river, a haven of rest in an unshapen world of ice and fire.

————

CHAPTER XVI

IN TOW OF A COMET

ON the night of the 4th of October we quitted Saturn. I was sleeping at the time, unfortunately, and was thus prevented from once more enjoying the magnificent passage of the rings. My coffee was brought me by the French steward, who said, as he drew aside the curtains of the window,—

'Monsieur—there is no more land.'

'No land! I said.

'No land, no sea, no anything. Will monsieur look?'

I raised myself into a sitting posture, and glanced eagerly through the circular aperture.

Yes—we were back again in space. But the jump had been made with singular rapidity and ease, for I noticed none of those indescribable disorders in my system that had tortured me during that long night—the first I ever passed on Captain Chlamyl's vessel.

'Where is Saturn?' I queried.

'Beneath us, monsieur,' was the answer.

Ah! that explained it. Gravity was acting in the correct way,—from below, instead of at an angle.

'And the captain, my friend?'

'He is in bed, sir—with a swelled face; his wound has broken out again.'

'Aha! that accounts for your singular communicativeness. Where are we bound for?'

'For the sun, monsieur. I heard the engineer

O

talking about it yesterday—but we have not started yet.'

'What *I* want to know,' I muttered between my teeth, 'is how in the name of the devil we're going to get back anyhow. The translation-movement only acts one way, and if we have to wait till Saturn gets on the other side of the sun—'

I don't think the steward understood me, for he went on tidying the wash-things in an unconcerned manner. A barking sound in the next cabin roused me. It was Ned's new pet—a baby wolf with wings of soft velvet, and feathers (not fur) of hazel-brown. Presently Ned himself appeared, arrayed in a flaming dressing-gown with the baby in his arms. The little animal dug its claws into the red wool and, putting up its pointed snout, adorned with long bat-like ears, strove to lick its master's face.

'He's quite like a dog!' said the proud possessor, 'and twice as beautiful. Here—I'll put him into bed with you.'

'If you do anything of the sort, I'll murder you,' I answered, but before I could even make preparations for carrying out the awful threat, my trusty friend had flung the animal down on the quilt, where it amused itself making frantic dives at my toes, no doubt mistaking them for rats (as Ned calmly hinted.)

It was decidedly pretty, though its claws *were* sharp. Imagine a cross between a dog and an owl—a quadruped clothed in silken feathers, with bright orange eyes, long ears, and a pair of bat's wings of russet velvet. In my classifying zeal I named it *Lupus Chlamyli*—and really, the name was as good as any other.

'That reminds me,' began Ned, after he had wasted a good five minutes teasing and caressing master 'Jip' (of all the extraordinary names to give an extraordinary animal, this was surely the most so)—'that reminds me. Do you know the latest ?'

I shrugged my shoulders. Ned has a habit, when he is in a good humour, of asking questions for the purpose of 'scoring' one off, and I did not feel in the mood for such nonsense just then.

'Seriously,' continued my interrogator, 'has Monsieur Johnny Crapaud' (with a toss of his head in the direction of the steward) 'told you what we're kicking round here for ? We haven't advanced a yard since morning !'

'What do you mean ? Aren't we moving ?'

'Moving ? We're swaying about in a see-saw fashion several thousand miles above the north pole of Saturn. Does that tell you much ? It's a beautiful sight, but if we have to pay for it with our lives it'll be rather an expensive one.'

Ned's words roused me quickly enough. I dressed and hastened into the saloon. Underneath the keel of the *Astrolabe* a huge, white circle completely filled space. On one side, the ring made a foggy crescent, hardly opaque enough to obscure the larger stars, while on our own level and above us, six moons were floating silently, in various stages of eclipse, some of them casting a vague light over the dark half of the giant planet beneath, two of them being accompanied (so far as we could see) by revolving satellites of their own; the sun, ahead of the *Astrolabe's* bows, was shining like a large star, of a peculiar reddish colour, owing, I suppose, to some streaks or bands of ethereal substance that lay between us and him. Beyond—all was blackness of darkness. The earth was totally invisible.

All day long we admired the marvellous spectacle. Captain Chlamyl never came to offer any explanations, and the doors leading on deck re-

mained hermetically sealed — the near proximity
of the planet not permitting the liberation of our
atmosphere.

'What do you bet the captain's up a tree?'
inquired Ned.

To say the least of it, our manœuvres were
peculiar.   We did not seem to be stirring.
Independent and motionless in space, we watched
the circular layers of cloud sweep majestically
round as Saturn moved on his axis.   Occasionally
a shaft of white smoke pierced the envelope for
a moment, presenting the appearance of a solar
protuberance and indicating probably the seat of
some cosmic or volcanic phenomenon on a large
scale.   Not a sound came to us; the *Astrolabe*
was cradled in the most profound silence.

October 6th-8th.—No change.   Everyone seems
asleep on board.   How are we going to get back?

October 9th.—Captain Chlamyl appeared at
breakfast this morning.   I was just engaged in
swallowing down some boiling coffee, and rose
to receive him as he entered.   Ned, who was
hand-feeding his pet animal, did the same.

'Be seated, sir,' he began; 'I have much to tell
you.   I hope you have not been boring yourself
too much lately.   Unfortunately, my illness—'

I interrupted him with an assurance that we
had been enormously interested in the phases of
Saturn's moons, and had found the study extremely interesting.

The commander seemed pleased.

'Well, take your last look at them,' he said,
'for I fear you will not see them again for many
a long day.'

'Are we leaving Saturn then, captain?' I asked,
in a voice from which I had made a miserably
unsuccessful attempt to banish the desperate
curiosity.   Ned, at the other side of the table,

was allowing Jip to lick his hand quietly, not offering to caress the animal, staring fixedly at the table-cloth and fingering his fork nervously.

'We start in two hours, sir.'

I suppose my ignorance must have been written on my face, for the captain proceeded with his explanations easily and naturally, without waiting for me to pump him.

'You know, professor, that all bodies traversing space are bound to obey the laws of natural attraction.'

I nodded. Was the captain going to repeat his lecture on gravitation *verbatim ?* If so, I must grin and bear it politely.

'My system of mechanism,' pursued the captain, 'enables me to overcome and nullify the force for the time being. Were the engines of the *Astrolabe* stopped, professor, we should be as amenable to the laws of gravitation as the humblest mass of unintellectual stone.'

'Well, captain?' I asked, not knowing what he was driving at.

'Well, sir. Does it not strike you that this peculiar power enables me to practically choose my own way through space? By starting my engines or by stopping them, as the case may be, I can be attracted by any body I please.'

'Quite so, captain. But permit me to say that if the engines were stopped now—'

'Well, what, professor?'

'You would fall back on Saturn.'

'Unless there is another body in sight whose attraction is more powerful, sir.'

'And is there such a body?'

'Perhaps there is, professor. Anyhow, you understand my principles.'

'But, sir,' I burst out, in a pitiable state of bewilderment, 'what good can it do to you to be attracted by some minor planet or other? At this distance from the sun, our journey round the ecliptic must necessarily be of some fifteen years duration at least, hence—'

'Who spoke of being attracted by a minor planet, professor? If I only wanted to travel round the ecliptic, I might just as well have stopped on Saturn, instead of having traversed nearly two hundred thousand miles during the last twenty-four hours—'

I started. Then Ned rushed to the window and drew aside the curtains.

Yes, there, beneath us, in the void, the huge planet was hanging in its golden girdle, quite as far off as the captain had said. Evidently the *Astrolabe* had shifted while I slept—but with what prodigious speed! Greased lightning—that favourite Yankee simile—was nothing to it!

I resumed my seat. The captain, nothing daunted, was attacking a boiled egg systematically. Ned, lost in contemplation of the ringed globe outside, stood still, his nose almost pasted against the glass, while Jip, whining impatiently, dug his sharp claws into the cloth of his master's trousers, and endeavoured to flap his brown wings.

The steward entered with a smoking dish of boiled vegetables—peas, I think. For a moment the captain ate in silence, then,—

'We are not going round the ecliptic, sir, but diametrically across it!'

'Oh, certainly!' I answered, in a tone from which all the energy in human nature could not banish the sarcasm, 'certainly, captain — you're going to take a short cut, I see! And, might I ask, what complaisant body is going to do the attracting? Who is going to play the *rôle* of locomotive?'

'An incandescent body of hydrogen gas, sir, some two hundred and fifty miles in diameter, with a solid nucleus formed by the aggregation of hard, metallic particles.'

' A comet !' I cried.

' A vagrant wanderer through the realms of space, sir, whose roving course, inclining at an angle of fifteen degrees with Saturn's ecliptic, will carry him to the sun—perhaps round it—at a rate varying from a hundred to two hundred thousand miles an hour!'

Ned's face, stiffly set in a spasm of dogged wonder, confronted me from the other side of the cloth.

Here was the impossible with a vengeance! If Captain Chlamyl had intended to astonish me, he certainly succeeded. To be towed by a comet! Even on board the *Astrolabe* the idea partook of the supernatural. And yet—it was possible! Actually and truly possible!

For some moments nothing was said. Then I ventured another question.

' And this comet, sir?'

' Is hanging far above our heads in the void, professor. The movement of translation is carrying us across its tail. You can see it from the observatory—come!'

He rose and led the way. As we left the dining-room, Ned's eyes shot a glance of mingled amusement and weariness at me. The Yankee shoulders were hoisted in a contemptuous shrug. Ned is a difficult man to convince, though he *has* traversed several hundred millon miles of space to get experience.

The observatory was not as dark as usual. A curious starlight filtered in through the thick panes, gleaming along the polished metal bars of the electrical instruments, and making the white manometer-faces shine with a ghostly light.

Above us, space seemed on fire.

Blue and white streamers, like those of a lengthened aurora, spanned the blackness like a luminous canopy. The fore-runners of the giant tail must even then have been sighted, for, as I looked, a score of flaming meteors hurried past, scaring me nearly to death and almost making the entire hull of the *Astrolabe* quiver, though they must have been a wonderful distance away.

'They are going to Saturn!' said the captain, and a moment's reflection showed me the truth of this statement. Beneath our keel, the ringed planet was demanding toll of every passing wanderer, and no doubt much of this monster's aureole would go to weighten the strange world we had quitted, compelled by the terrible strength of his attraction.

'How is it that the main body is not itself diverted from its course and drawn downwards, sir?' I asked, releasing the spring that held the curtain of the bow-window, and lifting my hand to my eyes as a torrent of blue light flooded the apartment.

'Its momentum is too great for that, sir. Each trip past a large planet may diminish it in bulk slightly, but, at the rate of its present flight, nothing short of the sun itself could arrest its motion—see, even now we are changing our position!'

The planet under our keel had swept away to the right by several degrees. For several hours I watched these thrilling changes, sometimes from the saloon, sometimes from the observatory, while Ned alternately professed open disbelief and uneasily gnawed his tawny moustache over the thumbed pages of *Nicholas Nickleby*.

Towards 4 p.m. (how ridiculously vain all estimates of time seemed on the *Astrolabe*), the gorgeousness of the. spectacle roused even my torpid companion.

We were entering the domain of this blue flying

demon. Glowing balls of green and yellow, twirling rapidly on their axes, descended majestically past the windows on the left, while, on the right, Saturn with his eight moons clomb higher and higher. We were turning completely head over heels, and though I had often before witnessed the feat, it nevertheless filled me with interest.

Higher and higher mounted Saturn, brighter and yet brighter grew the blueish sheen on the left, till the whole saloon was drowned in waves of ebbing, pulsating colour, that crushed and paled the brilliant hues of the Oriental ottomans and Turkish hangings. A distinct feeling of heat became apparent, and I wondered, for the fiftieth time since my setting foot on Captain Chlamyl's vessel, whether we were going to meet a death by fire, a death more strange than any to be met with among cold lunar volcanoes or Saturnian lava-belts—utter annihilation in that seething, streaming blue furnace and an endless peregrination across sunless voids round and round the central sun in an ellipse of wavy flame. What a future! The Apocalypse was nothing to it!

Towards 5 p.m., the *Astrolabe* had accomplished a complete revolution on her keel. Saturn was above and the comet beneath us. Glued to the crystal panels, we eagerly watched every manœuvre, our tired eyes shaded by spectacles of smoked glass, expressly provided by Captain Chlamyl for the safer contemplation of these dazzling cosmic marvels. As the twenty-four hour clock chimed 6 p.m., or its equivalent, I felt the vessel sinking more rapidly. A greyish dust was gradually beginning to cover the outside of the panes, dimming the blue glare and making observation more difficult.

Something was going to happen. Voices were answering each other across the long corridor, and the engine-bells clanged twice.

'They're starting!' said Ned.

He was right. The moment for annulling the attraction of this dangerous mass had arrived. A well-known trembling feeling told me that the discs had begun to revolve. We were not to be drawn into the vortex without a protest.

Here the door opened and Captain Chlamyl entered.

'Well, sir, and what do you think of it?' he said.

I pointed to the darkened windows. We were sailing blindly—almost.

'Come into the observatory.'

I followed him. The bow-window, deluged with light, probably, was closely veiled, but the side-windows, coated with some substance that prevented dust from adhering to them, permitted a clear view in all directions.

Let me attempt to describe the scene.

We were floating in the midst of a perfect ocean of flying fires, separated by strips and layers of golden dust, which, ahead of our bows, paled and thickened into a blinding mass of azure, crossed at intervals by dark bands. The number of revolving bodies seemed endless, and the distant star-jewellery became almost invisible in the patches of black between the glowing foci.

For a moment I shuddered, thinking of the consequences if one of these beautiful globes should strike the *Astrolabe*; but they were hundreds of miles off, and there could be no immediate danger.

I glanced at the manometer. Its slender needle was trembling at two thousand. The speed of the discs had increased, and the *Astrolabe*, retained by that inexplicable force, invented and controlled by Captain Chlamyl, slid slowly back towards the darker regions, while the hydrogen world held steadily on its way, burning and fretting in halos and coronas of shifting fire. The long journey had begun. Four hundred million miles lay before us—at the end of which lay—what?

- - -

CHAPTER XVII

SOME REVELATIONS

October 15*th*.—The coolness and accuracy of the captain's genius is an ever-increasing wonder to me. Unwilling to navigate in the neighbourhood of so mighty a fellow-traveller, he has allowed the *Astrolabe* to fall back nearly ten thousand miles. We still move forward with a terrible velocity however, for the momentum imparted by our strange traction-engine lasts practically for ever, in space. Saturn might stop us, but his influence gets weaker hour by hour. We are plunging forward in the wake of the blue comet at a speed which will carry us across the earth's orbit in less than four months —plunging with helmless keel and immovable engines. Our walks on deck are renewed, and life goes on regularly as before.

November 1*st*.—Still chasing in the wake of our beautiful guide. Idleness is traditionally supposed to breed mischief, and from teaching Jip tricks, poor Ned has once more unpleasantly veered round to gloomy broodings on the variable and unpromising nature of our destiny.

Not but what he may justly have some reason for it. Captain Chlamyl's manner, always lofty and somewhat condescending, has lately undergone a change for the worse.

From a genial, hospitable commander, he has degenerated into a grumbling cynic, silent and morose for the most part.

' He's thinking over the inconveniences that are awaiting him in a future world,' said Ned, leaning

against the taffrail and absent-mindedly picking
his teeth with the end of a steel pen.

'That's hard, my boy,' I answered. 'Most of us
haven't got so particularly clean a record that we
can crow over the captain. Remember the Basuto
you knifed, and that Tibetan praying-man whose
head you split open that night on the river.'

'That was in self-defence, Hal,' quoth Ned, looking at me fixedly. 'Our lives were given us to
defend. It's a darned sight better to kill a fellow
then and there, than to be butchered and left to
the vultures. As for this pirate—'

'Sh-h-h! Not so fast!'

'Why not? He nearly had me yesterday, the
murdering blackguard!'

'For the Lord's sake—' I began, then my words
died in my throat as Ned pulled his left hand—a
bandaged bundle of lint and blood-stained flannel
—out from under his jacket, and commenced to
unwrap the poultices with the air of a man who
intends to back his words.

'Great Scott, Ned! Where and how did you
get that?'

It was a hideous wound. Three of the fingers
were crushed into an almost shapeless mass by
some heavy instrument, the flesh was completely
stripped off the thumb, disclosing a scraped white
piece of bone, half covered by a layer of torn blue
muscle. I nearly jumped out of my skin.

'Poor old man! My dear old boy, why ever
didn't you tell me? Oh, Ned, tie it up, do! It
may mortify.'

'No danger!' was the grim answer. 'It'll take
more than that to kill me. Wounds don't mortify
in this atmosphere. I suppose you'll be pestering
me with questions about what happened for the
next half hour, so I'd better serve up the affair in
the form of a narrative. Do you think you could

light this cigarette for me.   I've only got one hand.
Pah! it makes me sick to think of touching a grain
of that fellow's tobacco or a drop of his liquor—
there, thanks.   I hope to God there isn't a telephone under the deck.   Perhaps we'd better not sit
down.   We'll dish his charitable intentions better
so.   Where do you think I was yesterday afternoon,
between four and six?'

'How the deuce am I to know?   Reading
Dickens in the saloon.'

'I was drinking whisky and soda in the captain's cabin.'

'The devil!'

'Yes, and he was making up to me for all he
was worth.   You never heard such civility.
Finally,—"One of my engineers is ill," says he,
"and I've had to work the affair by myself all
night.   That's why I'm feeling so sleepy.   Have
another drink?"

'"No thankye, cap," said I, for the liquor was
beginning to mount to my head.

'He rung a bell, and we both lay back in our
chairs, him looking at me from under his dark
eyelashes and myself trying to appear at my ease,
studying the patterns on the ground-glass ceiling
till my brain got giddy.

'Devil an answer did he get to his ring, although
he kept his finger pressed on the button for nearly
a minute, and I could hear the clanging of the big
bell all down the corridor.   Then,—

'"I'm afraid they're busy in the engine-room,"
said he, "we'll have to go and dig them out by
ourselves."

'With that he rose, and I followed him down
the passage, through the heavy blue curtains.

'"Throw away your cigar," he said, as we opened
the door of the engine-room, "there's too much
gun-cotton about for smoking to be safe.'

' I did as I was told. Half-a-dozen chaps in blue-and-white blouses were crowding round the near crank of the big engines. One fellow was standing, with an oil-can in his hand, on the crank itself, while the others were passing him up bits of waste and such like, for him to clean the steel with.

' I saw our friend the Frenchy standing on one side cleaning his oily fingers with a piece of cotton and looking rather pale. The man who was standing on the crank stepped off on to the plates, shooting a quick glance at me as he did so.

' Underneath each of the big cranks there's a large cavity, to give 'em room for working in. The captain said something in his confounded Roumanian dialect, and one of the men got slap down, lowering himself by his hands and knees into that devil's hole, and trying to clean the nuts on the under side of the shaft, or something, I couldn't clearly see what. As I turned my back on the captain and walked along, examining the cranks and fittings, I caught the eye of the Frenchy, and there was warning in it, a kind of a sneaking expression of fear and cowardice mixed. The beggar had something to tell me, but daren't let on before the captain.

' At any other time I'd have felt uncomfortable, but five or six whiskys and sodas are enough to upset any fellow, and I took no more notice of our friend's mysterious glances than if we were sailing for a trip on a two-hundred-ton pleasure yacht in the Mediterranean, instead of being cooped up with a set of murdering pirates a few million leagues beyond the ken of the Lick telescope.'

' Ned, I *can't* believe it, I simply *can't*,' was all I could say, despairingly.

' Can't you, though,' answered my companion, looking out fiercely over the lee taffrail, his

angular features tinted with diabolical blue from
the distant fires, 'can't you, though? Listen to
what happened.

'I was examining the dynamo that feeds the
lamps in the saloon, and whistling softly to myself,
when the captain orders the Frenchy out to wash
dishes in the scullery, I think, and begins talking
earnestly with the men. The man underneath
the crank came up, tired and panting. Then the
captain sends another down to take his place, and
starts explaining in his usual cool style,—

'"There's a new oil-cup going to be fixed on
under there," says he. "We're drilling a hole in the
steel shaft to screw it tight, and they're working
at it from underneath."

'"Why not turn the crank round and try it from
on top?" says I.

'"There isn't anywhere to rest the brace except
on the iron floor underneath," he replied. "Steel's
very hard to drill."

'I looked down between the railing and the
crank and saw a fellow in a blue blouse, turning
away at something down there in the dark, while
another black-whiskered devil hung over the
opposite guard rail, pretending to give him light
with a bull's eye lantern. Then he comes up
sweating like a nigger and the captain makes the
black-whiskered chap relieve him. After half-an-
hour of this game,—

'"I wish you'd take a turn at it," he says, laying
his white hand on my shoulder in a fatherly
fashion, "the poor fellows are dead beat."

'And sure enough they were, sitting in a row on
the long bench, gasping like dredged salmon. It's
odd how ideas take one. For the life of me I
couldn't resist that infernal politeness. The fact
that these muscular pirates were so soon exhausted
might have started my suspicions, but I put it

down to the rarefied air, and in a second I was slithering down into that black pit, straining my eyes to see the work, for it was darker than a wolf's mouth, besides being slippery with oil.

'All the weight seemed to have left my body. I suppose I was in the very centre of gravity of the *Astrolabe*, for my feet actually refused to touch the steel plates, and for a few seconds I floated about ridiculously, grabbing the crank with my hands and besmearing myself with oil as I did so.

'I got my bearings quick enough, and managed to get a grip on the handle of the brace. Then a surprise awaited me.

'There was no trace of a hole in the shaft. The huge polished roller was as devoid of anything resembling the impression made by a drill as my arm. The brace was merely propped against one of the heavy collars. Not even the commencement of a boring was visible.

'I had just time to notice all this when a deep hissing began above my head and the light of the lantern vanished suddenly. I felt the handle of the brace swing upwards, nearly striking my face in its passage. There are moments in life when one's thoughts go quicker than lightning. I tell you it was touch and go. I've seen a great hooded cobra preparing to strike at my naked foot as I was getting out of bed, but the jump I executed in the Laswaree bungalow on that grilling September morning in '79 wasn't to be compared with the spring I gave when that brute of a captain started the engine on me. In half a second I was up, the gravity helping me, and hoisting myself over the rail for dear life. As I did so the big crank came thundering round and—there!'

He held out his bandaged hand. I felt my heart go down to zero.

'You should have heard the screech they gave when I jumped out!' continued Ned. 'For a moment I didn't notice the injury to my left hand, and with my right I lit out at that black-whiskered devil's face, sending him sprawling over backwards among the dynamos. Captain Chlamyl was wonderfully apologetic. I never saw a man take on so. His politeness was only to be equalled by the bungling way in which the murderous trick was contrived. Dash it all! if *I* wanted to kill a fellow, I flatter myself I'd manage affairs better. What do you suppose he can mean by all this?'

To say the least of it, Ned was justified in allowing himself to be puzzled a little by Captain Chlamyl's mysterious and bungling accidents. First the strange escape of poisonous gas, then the engine-room disaster—failures, both. Genius and profound scientist as the captain was, it certainly was strange that he should make such childish and uncertain experiments. If he really wanted to kill us, where was the difficulty? Every mouthful we swallowed on board his vessel could, with a little ingenuity, be made a vehicle for the conveyance of some deadly poison or other. What was to hinder our being murdered during our sleep any night? Even if the worst came to the worst, could he not simply order his crew to make away with us? His authority was that of the most perfectly absolute monarch. No law, human or even divine, fettered him, for all we could see. Truly these horrible adventures were inexplicable. Ned, unconsciously, put his finger on what, to my present way of thinking, is perhaps the nearest solution of the puzzle.

'Perhaps he wants to pretend to himself in killing us, that we were stricken down by the hand of God.'

'How do you mean? If he wants to murder us,

he wants to murder us. If we die, he's guilty. Isn't that clear ? '

' No, my dear man. It's wonderful how easily salved some people's consciences are. A little carelessness here and there, a little hint thrown out to one of these rascally servants, perhaps a moment's forgetfulness—and the thing's done. I'll bet you anything you like, the captain's persuaded himself by this that poor Andersen, or whatever his name was, got abandoned on the moon purely by accident. I tell you I'm beginning to see through the beggar. Besides, I got a lot of information out of the Frenchy last night. It appears the captain wept a perfect Niagara of tears when he discovered Andersen was missing.'

' Nonsense ! ' I said incredulously.

' Yes, and he refused food for a few days. He carried on like a lunatic, they say.'

Ned allowed himself to sink down on one of the skylights of frosted glass, through which the electric lights on the corridor were shining palely. Far away across the starboard taffrail a tongue of blue fire went rolling away, curling and revolving as it progressed till it assumed the shape of a perfect globe. The sun itself, drowned in the unnatural light, was totally invisible. Through the glass panels, I caught sight of the tall helmsman, bending over his instruments in the observatory and tapping the glass faces of the manometers as one taps a weather-glass, to free the needle. We had, during the last few hours, been steadily drawing nearer and nearer the glowing focus, whose heat, as I stepped from behind the protecting partition of aluminium, shone on one's face like the glare from an open furnace door.

The man in the observatory stooped forward and touched a button. Presently a rhythmic quiver told me that the engines were starting. The whole ship trembled. We experienced that disagreeable feeling that one undergoes in a railway train when the brakes are put on too suddenly. I held on to the railing to steady myself, and looked at Ned.

'There's only one thing for it, Hal,' he began, his voice sinking into a kind of inward whisper, 'we must supplant the captain.'

'Supplant him!' I exclaimed. 'What on earth—'

'Seize the vessel, I mean,' continued Ned, still in that same inward voice, that hardly seemed to proceed from his lungs at all, so soft and noiseless it was. I must confess Ned's proposition sent a thrill of fear through me. At heart I believe I am an arrant coward. The idea of seriously opposing this puissant individual and his crew of trained desperadoes was anything but pleasing.

'Half the men are on our side,' continued Ned, gloating over his scheme, while I racked my brains for some plausible reason for backing out of it. 'We are navigating nearly parallel to the ecliptic, and must infallibly reach the earth in course of time—'

'Unless we are waylaid by Jupiter or Mars,' I put in.

'No danger,' said Ned quietly. 'Both will be far enough off when we pass their orbits. I examined the charts yesterday. Besides, Captain Chlamyl doesn't intend landing on either planet—confound him!'

'Why—what do you know about his intentions?' I queried, beginning to feel surprised.

'I got it from the Frenchy, who in turn got it from the engineer. The captain's already once landed on Mars, and was hunted out of the country by the inhabitants.'

'Stuff!'

'Yes—there seems to have been some danger of his being set up as a god and worshipped. The prospect didn't please the Martian wiseacres, whose experience, considerably more complete than ours, has taught them to mistrust all religious creeds. Science tried to explain him, and science failing, they kicked him out of the blooming planet. As for Jupiter, landing on him's utterly out of the question. Firstly, he's in a state of perpetual boil ; secondly, his atmosphere's heavy enough to crush one flat ; thirdly, the force of gravitation is so confoundedly strong, that it would be impossible for any of us to walk a step on his surface. It would be the crutch-experience of Saturn over again, only ten times worse. That is why I say the captain will avoid both Jupiter and Mars. Now do you begin to see light ? '

' Yes, I do, I answered, ' and I think you're an extremely ingenious reasoner. Now for the plan of campaign. It seems to me that if the captain is neither going to land on Jupiter or on Mars, he must be going to the earth, therefore—'

' Therefore a fight is unnecessary ? Is that what you're trying to get at ? I tell you, Hal, we'll have to fight for our lives if we wish to preserve them. Going back to the earth, indeed ! What if the captain should choose to visit some of the inner planets —Mercury for instance ? We'll be scorched alive.'

' Captain Chlamyl won't do anything so silly.'

' Won't he, though ? He did once, about two years back. They cooled the ship's interior with compressed air, while the very glass on the panels was getting ready to melt. The crew were kept at work day and night for several months. The captain went slap round the sun in tow of another and bigger comet than the one that's pulling us along just now. When they were nearly round, the compressed-air machine broke down and three men died. The rest came within an ace of it. The fellow who did the steering, or whatever it's equivalent is, in the observatory on deck, was roasted

—roasted alive! A daisy time they must have had of it!'

I shrugged my shoulders impatiently. Ned has an awkward way of clinching an argument by piling on the horrors till you're smothered under them. The unlikelihood of the contemplated trip might at any other time have made me cynical. Now, however, seeing what we had already been through, *was* it so very unlikely after all? A sensation of deadly cold crept along my limbs as I thought of being roasted alive, shut up in this aluminium cage like a rat in a steel trap. As I thought, the manhood returned to me. Ned renewed his entreaties.

'What do you want me to do?' I said, half-yielding.

'Ensure our reaching the earth, by stopping the engines at the right time.'

'But the engines aren't moving—at least they may not be moving when we cross the earth's orbit,' I said, feeling rather muddled.

'If they aren't moving, then well and good,' was the reply. 'That'll mean that the captain's going to land. We'll have got rid of our traction-comet by that time. The engineer says the captain is going to cut himself loose, so to speak, directly we get across Jupiter's orbit, which is all he is afraid of— the attraction of Jupiter I mean.'

'But then—how will we get along?'

'By our own impetus. Motion in space is perpetual when nothing tends to stop it. We'll go on for ever and ever, Amen, till we butt up against the sun, and then the captain's trips'll come to an end quick enough. How long'll we take to reach the earth? You ought to know—a mathematical man.'

I drew out my note-book.

'I can only give it to you very roughly,' I said, 'as

neither our exact whereabouts nor the precise rate
at which our strange locomotive is travelling are
known to me—say eighty thousand miles an hour.
He can't be going faster than that. The captain said
something about four months to me yesterday—'

'Did he?' exclaimed Ned, eagerly.

'Don't be too exuberant. I fancy his estimate
was low. Let's see—taking the approximate distance as four hundred millions of miles—'

'Great Cæsar!' ejaculated Ned.

'Yes—that makes—three and six are nine—we
can't possibly do it under six months, at the very
least.'

Ned's face fell.

'Half a year more of this beastly pirate's society,'
he muttered. 'Hal—if you go back on me, I swear
I'll murder you in cold blood—you, the captain and
myself. I swear to God I will.'

'I won't fail you, friend Ned.'

'And mind, if another of these careless "hand of
God" attempts on my life takes place, I shall fight
the captain man to man. Either I kill him or he
kills me. I believe he's found out about our dishing
the telephone wire.'

'No?' I said horrified.

'Yes, the French chap hinted as much. So hereafter we'll have to be doubly careful. Do you think
you could manage to steal a chart?'

'No—besides it's unnecessary. We can consult
the ones in the library *ad lib*. Of course, if you
bungle this affair, we'll all get killed, simply.'

'Never fear. I'll make a good job of it. Six
months more Hal, just think! Six months!'

We passed the evening reading and strumming
the piano. Captain Chlamyl never appeared.

'He is at work,' said the steward, 'and will see
nobody.'

CHAPTER XVIII

A MUTINY AND ITS END

DECEMBER and January passed in soulless monotony. Diary-writing, under the circumstances, becomes an insupportable nuisance, and I have shirked my pen regularly lately, worse luck. There is absolutely nothing to record. Not a star, not a comet (save our blue guide), not a meteor to enliven our dullness. I wished at times that a catastrophe might happen, if only to break up the unemotional jelly-fish life on board.

But no—the machinery of the *Astrolabe* withstood all strains, and the complex movements necessitated by Captain Chlamyl's navigatory policy were performed with the most scrupulous and dull regularity.

On the 5th of February we crossed the orbit of Jupiter, and for the first time since my embarkation on our daring vessel, I was able to contemplate at my ease this wonderful world, a vast field of battle for fire and water, torn by interior convulsions and perpetually shrouded in its opaque layers of dark mist which the light of its four satellites vainly strives to pierce. Three of these latter were plainly visible with the naked eye from the deck on the morning of the 6th.

Europa, Ganymede and Io, the last-named moon gravitating at four hundred and thirty thousand leagues from the central planet, could be clearly distinguished. The fourth, Callisto, was hidden behind the great circular disc, which every moment was carrying farther away from us, away into the abysses of space, on its orbit, five times the size of ours, through the perpetual springtime of its long year, nearly equal to twelve of our terrestrial ones.

Ned, unpoetical as usual, scanning the beautiful planet through his opera-glass, likened it to half a Dutch cheese suspended by some invisible agency against a background of pepper and salt.

'It's a cheese that ruled the destiny of monarchs once,' I replied, 'and the victims offered to it on the sacrificial altars of our pagan nations must be reckoned by millions. Since its discovery in the year 3250 by Shi-Hung, the pig-tailed Chinese sage, it has had much to answer for.'

'Were the Chinese the only nation that knew of its existence?' queried Ned.

'No, my boy. The Babylonians and Chaldeans reckoned it among the known bodies of Heaven, and I fancy it has been observed many thousands of times from the temple-tops of Sardanapalus or Sennacherib.

'Anyway, it's Jupiter,' assented Ned, 'and that's always a step in advance,'

'Are you in a particular hurry to get home, my friend?'

'Yes, more than that. I'm in a particular hurry to know what's going to become of us. This uncertainty is killing me by inches. The captain's become uncommonly civil lately. I don't half like it.'

'*Timeo Danaos et dona ferentes,*' I suggested.

'Bother your classical quotations. It's no joke for me, I assure you. The captain's as dark as ever about his plans. I tried to pump him the other day and failed hideously.'

'If we stick to our fair, blue-eyed guide, we can't help being carried somewhere in the direction of the earth,' I said consolingly.

'Yes, but that's just what we're not going to do,' answered Ned. 'The captain's going to cut himself loose as soon as we are safely out of Jupiter's range. What he's going to do then, God only knows.'

I was silent. We were the playthings of a power mightier than ourselves, and had only to submit to its decrees.

Five days later, on the afternoon of the 11th, the threatened event took place. I was reading a novel on deck, when the clanging of the engine-bells attracted my attention. Ned appeared, an expression of discontent on his face, and turning to the blue focus at our bows took off his sealskin cap with mock reverence. Through the port-holes and skylights the crew contemplated the scene. It was as if everyone wished to take away a last recollection of the burning mass that had piloted us so safely through nearly two hundred million miles of darkness.

The comet was hurrying off sunwards, and we were hurrying—where?

To the sun also, to judge by our movements.

Cutting the *Astrolabe* loose seemed to have been a mere matter of form, for during the next fortnight, impelled by our impetus, which in space was all-powerful, we stormed along in the wake of those blue fires, as though we were still under the influence of their attraction. I felt puzzled. Ned's mistrust of the captain increased every hour.

The 1st of March brought a change. A whim of some kind seized the captain. During the night of the 28th the pumps were heard working, and on trying the door of the central stairway on the following morning, I found it closed. There must be danger without in the shape of some new vagrant body, to account for this sudden taking in of our atmosphere.

'It's a meteor,' suggested Ned, as we gazed intently out through the port panel at a large star, apparently falling down on us from above.

'Neither meteor nor comet, gentlemen,' said a

voice behind us, 'but a planet gravitating on its own separate orbit—Hilda.'

I turned and saw the captain.

'Hilda!' I exclaimed.

The minor planets revolving between Mars and Jupiter had entirely vanished from my memory. So we were once more to cross that dangerous belt of tiny worlds. Involuntarily I thought of our last narrow escape in the mist of life, and I began to wonder dimly whether the half-wished-for catastrophe was indeed looming.

'And the earth, captain?' queried Ned, compressing his lips tightly, as though in anticipation of some dreaded revelation that would widen the breach between himself and the commander.

'When are we going to see our native planet again?'

'All in good time, Master Hatton,' answered the captain, smiling. 'We have plenty of time before us yet to return to our miserable world in. I imagine we are not in any particular difficulty with regard to food. Have you anything to complain of on that score?'

'No, captain,' replied Ned, hurriedly, crimsoning involuntarily, but determined to have it out with the commander now or never, 'no, captain, it's not that—but—'

'But what, Master Hatton?' inquired the captain, coldly. 'Explain yourself, please.'

Ned looked at me curiously, and continued in a hard voice, speaking half to himself and half to us,—

'Since we have taken up our abode on your vessel, sir, our lives have been placed in jeopardy more than once. Three of your men have actually been killed. The strange escape of carbonic acid gas in my room, eight months back, the equally strange accident to my hand, while working at a supposed defect in your engines.'

'Purely coincidences, Master Hatton.'

'I do not say they were anything else, sir. Nevertheless we have narrowly escaped annihilation on many other occasions. The perilous crossing of the mist of life, the tidal wave of Saturn, the flying wolves. The fact that we enjoy no supernatural immunity from death is proved by the fact that within the last six months you have lost—I may say sacrificed—two of your crew.'

'Sir, this is simple insolence.'

'Added to this the fearful passage round the sun of two years back, and the abandonment of poor Jacob Andersen on the moon.'

The blow had fallen. The captain's face was ashy white. For a moment I thought he was going to strike Ned. Then, with an effort, he controlled himself, and, avoiding a direct answer to my companion's observations, continued in a calm voice,—

'And which do you consider preferable, sir, to die a glorious death in some daring adventure, or to die like an ox in a stall and fatten some overfilled graveyard on that poor little planet over there?'

'That is not the question, captain. I deny that any man has the right to control the destinies of others the way you do. Personally I would, perhaps, as soon die in a cataclysm as any other way, but I am a free man, and wish to be my own master. This journey through space is interesting, but it must come to an end, and soon.'

'Who says so, Master Hatton?'

'I say so, captain,' replied Ned, drawing himself up stiffly.

They were a finely-matched pair when all was said, and in a pugilistic encounter I should have been embarrassed to know which one to back.

The captain's lip curled contemptuously, and a vague idea of danger made me shiver unpleasantly. Certainly, in intellectual force, Ned's opponent had the best of it, for without his vast knowledge to help us, what could we do?

'Perhaps, Master Hatton,' continued the captain, ironically, 'now that you have so accurately mapped out the future campaign of my vessel yourself, it would interest you to know what she is actually going to do?'

Ned remained silent.

'We have gone far,' resumed the captain, 'but, I repeat it, we shall go farther yet—we shall penetrate into a world of terrors where no man has ever dreamed of penetrating, where the ocean boils incessantly, where the very air carries death with it, where winged beings, clothed in fire-proof armour, flap their way across lakes of molten gold—we shall go to Mercury!'

I uttered an exclamation. Ned clenched his fists.

'The *Astrolabe* herself will be melted!' I burst out.

The captain shrugged his shoulders.

'It is the will of a madman!' exclaimed Ned. 'It shall not be! We shall go back to the earth!'

Captain Chlamyl made a step forward. With a rapid gesture he touched the head of a tiny brazen figure standing alone on an agate-topped table. In the corridor a deep-toned bell clanged noisily. Several men appeared.

'Seize that man!' said the captain in French, indicating Ned.

The crew hesitated. A light burst in on me. They were divided between their own mutinous feelings and their fear of this tall, blue-eyed genuis, whose will had been law till then. Presently the end came.

A muscular, brutal-looking fellow, with bushy, overhanging eyebrows, made a dash at the American, in whose right hand gleamed the long barrel of a nickel-plated revolver, the very one that he had carried on that fateful morning nearly a year ago when we had boarded Nordenrother's balloon at Ingolfshöfdi. There was a loud report, and through the smoke I saw the man fall forward on his face, crashing down dead amidst the Dresden china cupids and Chinese idols.

Again Ned's revolver rose. This time it was levelled at the captain. In a second, and before I well knew what I was doing, I was on my knees, striving to drag those deadly barrels from the grasp of my desperate companion.

'Stop!' I shouted. 'For God's sake, stop, Ned! I can't bear it. You'll kill me!'

The revolver, still hot and smoking, was pressed against my cheek. There was a fearful explosion, a sting like the cut of a whip, and I felt the blood running from the gash that the bullet had made.

I rolled, half-swooning, across the carpet, and Ned, considerably shaken himself, I think, fell like a log across me, nearly knocking all the breath out of my body as he did so. One of the men caught me by the arm and jerked me violently on to my feet. Holding my hand to my gashed cheek, I looked around me in a dazed fashion.

'What a chicken-livered young skunk you are, Hal!' exclaimed Ned, in a voice which I hardly recognised, so distorted was it by rage or fear, or both.

The captain had vanished. Half-a-dozen of the crew were pressing round my companion, grasping his hands and covering them with kisses, rather in the style of Oriental devotees in some sacred ceremony. I fairly broke down.

'Don't kill him!' I sobbed, rocking to and fro on the blood-stained sofa, and holding my pocket-handkerchief to my mutilated ear. 'I won't have it!'

The saloon was crowded in a moment. A score of men, hatred and impotent fury written on their ugly countenances, were all talking at once. A herculean negro, whose arms had been scorched white in some terrible accident (perhaps the awful passage round the sun), brandished a huge steel lever, wrenched from some part of the engine, with ferocious gestures. Some of the others carried knives and cutlasses, while a tall, bony New Zealander, with a bushy head of black hair and silver rings depending from his ears, flourished a heavy stick, weighted at one end with a hexagonal iron nut. The scene that followed was sickening beyond description. These wretches, savages as they were, fell to hacking at the body of the dead man. They gashed his cheeks with knives and spat in his face. It was a perfect hell let loose in a peaceful vessel.

Half-fainting from loss of blood, the whole thing passed like a dream before my eyes. I saw Ned speaking to me, but could not understand what he was saying.

The door by which the captain had vanished was securely fastened, but a blow from an axe tore it from its hinges, and three of the fiends, headed by the great negro engineer, tore through the aperture and down the long corridor. Suddenly, and without warning, the electric globes that lighted us went out, leaving only a pale starlight, that gleamed hideously over the gashed face of the dead steward and over the shattered fragments of china that covered the floor. At the same moment I heard someone battering at the fastenings of the metal door leading to the deck, and a continuous roaring sound told me that the imprisoned atmosphere was being liberated.

Pale, staggering under the load of horrors, half out of my mind, I stumbled to the door, grasping the torn curtains to steady myself. One solitary lamp was burning in the passage-way, and by its light I beheld a group of men struggling together in front of the captain's door, swaying to and fro, throttling each other, trampling each other under foot.

Then came a fearful shock, that made the entire vessel tremble from stem to stern like an aspen leaf. A terrible glare of yellow light, bright as a lightning flash, shone about me, and I remember nothing more.

CHAPTER XIV

WANT OF AIR

A FEARFUL pain in the lungs and a myriad of stars passing before my eyes in glittering disorder were the first signs of returning animation.

I was still on the *Astrolabe*, that was certain. Even through the darkness, intensified by my failing senses, I could perceive the circular rings of blue light that formed the windows of the cabin.

Where was Captain Chlamyl? Had he succumbed before those desperate men? And Ned. Was he alive?

I struggled to get out of bed. In doing so, I staggered and fell. On putting my hand to my head I found it bandaged and dressed scientifically. Ned, I knew, was an accomplished surgeon. I suppose I must thank him for this, as, indeed, I had to thank him for the wound in the first place.

A cold nose was pressed against my hand as I lay helpless on the floor.

'Hallo, Jip! We must'nt despair, old boy. Let's see where we are.'

I scrambled up to the window.

Still in the zone of the minor planets evidently, for several of them were visible, moving slowly past the vessel at distances which it was quite impossible, even vaguely, to estimate.

And what had happened?

I dropped helplessly back into the swinging bunk, trying to collect and classify my recollections.

There had been a shock, accompanied by a bright glare of light. Could someone have fired on me from behind? Perhaps there had been an explosion. But no—in that case the *Astrolabe* would have been completely wrecked, and I would be lying, what was left of me, on the surface of one of those tiny planets whose movements I had just now been watching.

That the *Astrolabe* had actually struck against some wandering body was likewise inadmissible. No, Ned or some of his newly-acquired friends were the only people who could enlighten me. I held my breath and listened. Not a sound was heard on board. Presently vague waves of music came to my ears from the direction of the saloon. I thrilled strangely as I recognised the opening bars of the *Lohengrin* prelude. Captain Chlamyl was alive then!

A feeling of wild joy took possession of me. Again I struggled to my feet and fell against the door, drumming feebly on the woodwork with my weak fists, and shouting hoarsely for help.

The music ceased. Steps echoed along the passage. The door swung open and Captain Chlamyl entered.

He lifted me in his arms and bore me back to bed.

'Compose yourself,' he said kindly, 'and don't try to talk. You are badly wounded about the face, and very feeble.'

'What on earth has taken place?' I groaned. 'The men did not kill you after all? I believe it was really a dream.'

'It was a dream that is destined to be followed up by a sufficiently awful waking adventure,' was the reply. 'Three of the mutineers have already lost their lives—and, personally speaking, I am not sorry. We will be better without them.'

'And Ned?' I queried.

'Mr Hatton is under lock and key in his cabin. I think he has received a lesson that will make him shun mutinies for a long time to come.'

'There has been an explosion of pyroxyline?' I suggested.

'No, sir; of hydrogen gas.'

'On board the *Astrolabe*?'

'No, professor. Luckily not. But even as it is, our lives are certainly in a position of extreme danger.'

'I am all attention, captain,' I said.

The startling events of which I had lately been a witness had driven all fear out of my system, and the idea that we might be in danger did not shock me as unpleasantly as it would have done a week back.

'When certain bodies of incandescent gas are combined in certain proportions with atmospheric air (the captain spoke as calmly as though he were delivering a lecture on chemistry at a German university), they immediately explode, more or less violently. This is what has happened in the case of the *Astrolabe*. A glowing body of hydrogen, that is a solid nucleus of rock with a hydrogen aureole surrounding it, swept past the bows of our vessel at a moderate speed. Those unfortunates had liberated the atmosphere, which prudence had bidden me confine three days back, and the door leading to the deck was actually open.

'Our supply of air, or nine-tenths of it at least, violently attracted towards the passing meteor, combined with it in explosive proportions, and a

Q

fearful shock followed as a matter of course, which smashed the windows of the observatory, and caused the entire vessel to revolve through an angle of sixty degrees on her keel.

'Providentially enough, the rush of air from the lower parts of the *Astrolabe* served to violently close the iron door, thus saving the lives of all who were below at the time. The three who were on deck died almost instantaneously. Now do you understand why we are in danger?'

A cold sweat covered my forehead. The captain had exaggerated nothing, evidently. A slow death by suffocation threatened us—suffocation all the more horrible on account of its being so prolonged.

'What do you propose to do, captain?' I asked hoarsely.

'What I am doing now,' he answered moodily. 'Manufacture oxygen by chemical means and absorb the carbonic acid by means of caustic potash. It is as good a way of dying as any other.'

'Why should we not live, captain—if your supply of potash is large enough.'

'That is just where the shoe pinches, professor. Most of my store was confined in zinc-lined barrels on deck, aft of the steersman's cabin. The explosion swept away eight out of ten. There is enough manganese to last a year—converted into oxygen.'

Again a sense of horror overpowered me. So our end had come, after all—and what an end! It was to be the black hole of Calcutta over again, without even the poor consolation of posing as martyrs before a sympathetic posterity. Here truly was a worthy end to Ned's carefully-contrived plots. He had striven against imprisonment to win, instead of liberty, a slow and agonising death.

But in the meantime we must not brood over our terrible position. We must be awake and doing.

Stirred into activity by the wildness of the

prospect, I tore myself from the grasp of sickness, and donning my sealskin jacket, set feverishly to work for the common safety.

Our impoverished atmosphere was not unbearable as yet. A few columns of compressed oxygen, liberated that evening by Captain Chlamyl, restored our spirits for the moment, and again set the sluggish blood bounding through our veins.

The potash, dissolved in water up to saturation point, was poured into long shallow vessels of copper, and disposed about the ship underneath the floor to receive the foul gas which gravity attracted downwards.

Ned, leaden-eyed and shaken, assisted dumbly at all these operations. He uttered no complaint, nor did he express any regret. I think he must have felt ashamed of himself somewhat, and he certainly worked like a trooper.

On the morning of the 7th, Captain Chlamyl announced that we had come to the end of our small below-deck store of potash. The prospect of having to succour the remaining last two barrels puzzled me momentarily, but it did not perplex the captain. One of the men, a round-faced Swede of rather repulsive appearance, donned his diving-dress (similar in construction to those which we had worn on the moon), and made his exit on deck in the following simple manner,—

Taking up his position in the hall, at the foot of the iron ladder, he allowed the inner doors to be hermetically closed on him. Then, opening the metal panels leading to the deck, he rolled the two half-charred barrels down the ladder, and returned to the crew's quarters uninjured, to receive their applause and congratulations.

With what eagerness we tore away at the iron rings and singed planks that guarded the vital treasures! One of the barrels was totally sound, and its contents were in excellent condition. On opening the other, a surprise awaited us. The entire mass of potash, thanks to some inexplicable chemical operation which had probably taken place at the very moment of the explosion, was crystallised into solid hexagonal blocks, of a deep amethyst colour, and hard as flint. We surveyed the beautiful sparkling mass of gems with feelings difficult to describe. Were the chemical properties of the salt altered?

Captain Chlamyl, enclosing some of the purple crystals in a thin glass beaker of water, plunged a tube into the liquid and blew softly through it. The test was crucial. No change was visible either in the colour or density of the mixture. The captain, moved to exasperation in spite of his phlegmatic disposition, threw the tube away, and pronounced the stuff useless.

So we had only one barrel left. Ned, practical as ever, sat down on its edge, and drawing forth a pencil, commenced ciphering something on a bit of paper. Silence took possession of us. No one dared speak, the same thought made everyone tremble. I hardly ventured to meet the captain's gaze. Our practical experience had taught us that nearly six pounds of the chemical were required daily to keep us from suffocation. There were a hundred and twenty pounds in the barrel.

'That gives us twenty days, captain,' said Ned, softly, letting his pencil drop and staring before him with wild eyes.

Twenty days! And millions of miles of space before us!

How many *had* we actually before us? The truth was brought home to me in startling fashion on the following morning, when, assuming indifference, I asked the captain, casually, where we were.

' I do not know,' was the answer.

I thought I had not heard aright, and my face must have betrayed my thoughts, for Captain Chlamyl proceeded in a slightly irritated tone,—

' I do not know, professor—I do not know where we are. The explosion utterly wrecked our observatory, which contained the thermo-piles necessary for calculating our distance from the sun. You yourself know as much about it as I do. There is the chart. Several excellent telescopes are at your disposal. See what you can make of it.'

With that he disappeared, leaving me more than ever dumbfounded. According to the most ordinary calculations, we must be still among the minor planets. No—we were rapidly leaving them far behind. I pored over those maddening circles and triangles till my brain throbbed and my head felt ready to split.

And the sun?

' The sun is under our keel,' replied Ned.

' No?' I exclaimed incredulously.

It was a fact, however. We had accomplished a quarter revolution since the morning. These diabolical evolutions were terrifying to the last degree. Captain Chlamyl, a prey to the most profound melancholy, rarely appeared during the next few days. When he *did* appear, it was touching to see the way his rough crew idolised him— the man whom but a bare fortnight back they had vainly sought to kill. They bowed and cringed before him, they vied with one another in feeble proofs of loyalty and devotion. There was something very miserable about it all, and I, for one, felt uncommonly sick.

On the night of the 15th, it became evident that the means hitherto adopted for getting rid of the carbonic acid gas generated by our breathing were insufficient. The air seemed to bite into one's lungs. My brain recled. Several times in the course of the day, I stumbled, once hurting myself severely against the corner of the heavy staircase. In the evening I was distracted by a violent headache. Ned, coughing incessantly, swallowed large draughts of cold water to alleviate the burning pain in his chest, an example which I followed for a time with success.

Captain Chlamyl, pale but composed, appeared towards one in the morning,

'Well, professor, what do you think?' he said. ·

'Think, captain?' I answered. 'I think our term is coming to an end.'

The commander stood for a few moments in silence, gloomily scanning the hopeless darkness without through the oblong panel; presently,—

'Perhaps if we were to continually shake the vessels of potash, the carbonic acid would be absorbed more quickly,' he said.

'Let us try it, sir,' was all I could answer.

A new labour thus appeared to increase our misery. Day and night, for three whole days, we relieved each other, keeping the shallow pans in perpetual motion, shaking them as a photographer shakes his developing dish. At the end of that period, the captain's ingenuity served to connect the various pans with the small donkey-engine that worked the search-light dynamo. Chains, moving freely over pulleys of gun-metal, communicated an even vibratory motion, which was regularly kept up and distributed. That night we were allowed to rest our aching arms, and whether from weariness, or thanks to the superabundance of oxygen in the thin air, I certainly slept soundly.

On the 21st, we made a desperate effort to discover our whereabouts. Captain Chlamyl's inventive genius never seemed to desert him Dis-

carding his ordinary method of ascertaining our
distance from the sun, viz., by registering the
electrical current generated in a thermo-pile, he
applied another, not less ingenious device. A
photographic camera was produced and pointed
downwards, through a window of thick glass, at
the distant orb of day. The rapidity with which
the solar rays acted on a certain standard sensi-
tised surface being already known to him from
previous experiment, he tried computing our distance by measuring the length of exposure necessary to obtain a picture of the solar disc through
plates of ruby glass, graduated in density.

The results were curious.

Impelled by the ever-increasing power of gravitation, we were rushing towards the sun at a terrific
speed—a speed not less than three million leagues
a day! But stop—was it gravitation pure and
simple?

I shook my head confusedly, as Ned angrily
produced a bulky volume from one of the library
shelves and tried to prove, with its aid, that no body,
even falling from the remotest parts of space, could
ever attain even half that speed. Motion in space,
when once started, continues eternally—and the
precise amount of impetus which the hydrogen
comet had imparted to the *Astrolabe* was, of course,
an entire mystery. Added to this, there was the
formidable explosion that had robbed us of our
atmosphere. Could it have increased our speed by
any chance? A million cubic feet of explosive
gas, expanding suddenly within a short distance
of a solid body, weighing (in spite of all ingenious
aluminium devices) little less than a thousand tons,
would, if that body were on the earth, unquestion-
ably shatter it into a thousand fragments, the
damage done to any body by an explosive being
always directly proportionate to the resistance

which that body offers, in other words, to its
moment of inertia. In space the affair was different. A ship like the *Astrolabe*, which on the
earth would have equalled a small iron-clad in
weight, now weighed but a few pounds, hence,
instead of being shattered by an explosion which
could have blown up half Paris, it was merely propelled harmlessly into space—helped on its way—
as Ned concisely explained.

Perhaps this was the solution of the mystery,
perhaps it was only one more brain-puzzling
problem sent by Fate to distract our last miserable hours. Be that as it might, our sufferings
soon become very real.

Haggard as corpses, the perspiration pouring
down their thin faces, the crew lay helpless and
inert as logs of wood. Even the desire for life was
being slowly driven out of them. Towards evening, on the 25th, a sense of warmth and comfort
crept over me. Ned, sitting at the foot of the sofa
on the carpet, his back resting against the broad
velvet curtains, distorted his face into a hideous
grin of delight. I understood.

We were being smothered in oxygen.

Some independent spirit on board had flooded
the vessel with the inebriating gas, and, while apparently giving us relief, he was slowly giving us
death.

For hours, through that long night, we dragged
on a feelingless existence. The *Astrolabe*, turning
slowly on her keel, permitted the white sunlight to
stream in over the ceiling. The electric lights were
extinguished, but the clocks were still going, and,
with drunken eyes, I saw that it was six in the
morning—our last morning alive!

The ceiling was ablaze with fire, and the lofty
saloon seemed to expand into gigantic proportions.
Once Ned tried to raise himself. I think I see him

still, with bloodshot eyes and trembling hands, feverishly clutching a tall chair back, and staring hopelessly out into the sunny void. It was a last effort. He fell with a cry across me, gibbering inarticulate words with icy-blue lips and sightless gaze.

Through the phantom realms of my imagination, I saw the yellow radiance vanish—die out as a lamp dies—and it seemed to me that its place was taken by a rosy glow, that vibrated and palpitated around me like a warm mist. I tried to rouse myself, to turn, to gaze out of the panel, but my limbs stiffened like cooling metal, and, while still striving to live and breathe, I fell into a dreamless slumber.

CHAPTER XX

THE FLOWER KINGDOM

BANG! Crash! Bump! Was I being murdered?

'Hold on! He'll do all right. Wake up, Hal, old boy!'

'Leave me alone!' I murmured, in return to the voice that buzzed through my head like the droning of a distant telephone.

Someone caught hold of my arms, and someone else grabbed me by the legs. I felt myself being carried up a steep incline, and air—yes, vital air—was pouring into my lungs.

My eyes opened of their own accord. I was on the deck of the *Astrolabe*, with several men standing round me.

'Where are we?' I said feebly, sitting up and rubbing my aching eyes.

'Look!' said someone near me (it was the captain). I followed his advice, and this is what I saw.

We were reposing peacefully at the bottom of what appeared to be an immense valley, shut in by mountains and cliffs of the most fantastic hue. Never had Nature displayed such lavish colours before the eyes of startled man. The blinding rays of blue, purple and gold, seemed to strike the sky itself, which was of a bright rose colour, overhead, softening down at the horizon to a deep greyish purple, through which the sun's disc (Was it the sun?) shone like a mirror of polished sapphire. Not a cloud, not a streak of vapour was visible in this strange heaven, and the layers of light softened off into each other in a way which no painter, however skilful, could have adequately rendered. From the lofty crests above us, covered in places with white patches of what appeared to be snow, a perfect deluge of fantastic vegetation poured down into the depths, cascades of scarlet creepers, fields of white and blue grass, mottled like Dresden china plates, trees with orange tops that blossomed out like opening roses, swaying gently to and fro in the warm breeze, their slender stems hidden under bushels of light, purple passion flowers (if I may be allowed to institute a comparison with earthly flowers), magnolias, lotuses, water-lilies of uncouth size, golden-leaved ferns, scarlet-blossomed groves of hibiscus—all the panoply of a luxuriant tropical vegetation was outspread before our eyes.

'We're in Cashmere,' said Ned.

I started.

Back on the earth? It was too good to be true!

Then came the return shock.

Roses there might be in Cashmere, also magnolia and hibiscus blossoms, but orange trees and a blue sun—never.

'Then, where the deuce are we?' exclaimed Ned, with something very like disappointment in his tone.

Captain Chlamyl laughed slightly.

'Oh, in Cashmere if you like, Master Hatton,' he said ironically, 'only I think you will find it difficult to reconcile yourself to the loss of our moon.'

I rushed to the other side of the deck. From the depths of the sombre valley came a sound of roaring water, and a pyramidal cone of fine steam rose nearly five hundred feet into the air. My eyes roamed impatiently over the sky in all directions. A large star of the first magnitude, of a pale greenish colour, shone resplendently near the eastern horizon, but no moon was visible. I uttered a cry.

'We are on Venus!' I exclaimed.

Ned was speechless. Poor fellow! Even the magnificent spectacle thus unfolded before his eyes hardly consoled him for the breakage of his magnificent soap-bubble, in whose shining sides he had seen his native planet mirrored once more.

Yes, we were on Venus, and that splendid green star over there, hanging like a beacon-light above the conical mountain crest, was our mother earth.

'Now, professor, if you are not too utterly dumbfounded, we will go to luncheon,' said the captain, smiling, 'and you, Master Hatton, if you will do me the honour.'

Ned bowed, looking rather foolish. To be thus addressed by the man against whom he had headed an all-but-successful mutiny but a short time back was sufficiently embarrassing indeed.

As we turned away from the glorious sight, a repulsive spectacle met our gaze. The three dead bodies of the wretched mutineers whom suffocation had so suddenly overtaken lay prone on the deck before us. The explosion had charred their features till they resembled long black statues of burnt wood, in which the eyeballs appeared as small white bulbs of gelatine. The terrible journey through airless space had crushed them as flat as a pancake, and the burnt remains of clothing flapped idly over their thin bodies. The most hideous Egyptian mummy could not be as hideous. It was death—but death robbed of its grandeur and poetry, deprived of its majesty, of all that sentiment could have lingered over. It was monstrous, misshapen, frightful—and to think that this might be our fate!

'Mark my words, the captain's brooding over some mischief or other,' whispered Ned, as he carefully passed a large tooth-comb through his scant hair, preparatory to rejoining the commander in the dining-room. 'I hate him when he gets so civil. You know what it meant last time.'

'Oh, give us a rest!' I answered wearily. The miraculous manner in which we had escaped death had restored my confidence in Captain Chlamyl, and I mentally resolved not to listen to any more of my companion's grumbles—a resolution which I intend to abide by, whatever befalls.

The captain was radiant. I was burning to question him concerning his wonderful conflict with the elements. How had he steered the vessel when we were dying for lack of air? How had he effected his landing? What had served to hasten the speed of the *Astrolabe?* What supernatural power had guided his reason during that awful night? He left me no time. This strange being was apparently as familiar with the planet Venus as with his own earth.

As he sat there, glass in hand, smiling into our awed faces, enchanting us with his strange stories, we felt as though we were really and truly in the presence of a God—a genie of the universe.

Presently the enchantment vanished to give place to reality.

'We are going for a walk, captain?' I said.

'It is not a walk which I have to propose, professor, it is an excursion. I warn you it will be tiring. You are accustomed to mountaineering?'

The captain's question was a singular one. I had crossed hundreds of miles of the Himalayan pine forests, I had roughed it in Iceland with Professor Nordenrother, I had, on divers occasions, tempted Providence on the snowy Alpine slopes, and an old trusty alpenstock, long since used for firewood by the unromantic porter of Magdalen College, bore the magical names 'Matterhorn' and 'Eiger' engraved on its smooth sides in honourable testimony to my prowess. These adventures, however, took place during my 'training' days. Whether I should be able to perform like athletic feats after being cooped up in the *Astrolabe* during a period of four months remained to be seen.

The preparations for this singular picnic astonished me. The atmosphere of Venus being already breathable, we could dispense with our diving-dresses, but other articles of attire, which the peculiar thermometric conditions of the planet rendered necessary, were duly forthcoming. All the paraphernalia of sub-tropical exploring parties had been prepared. Suits of white twill, white umbrellas and smoked glasses gave us the appearance of genuine tourists equipped for visiting the pyramid of Cheops or the mosque of Sultan Hassan. Guide-books were all that was wanting. Instead of a *Baedeker* we had the captain, and, frankly, it was as good a substitute as anyone could wish. We were a moderate-sized party— only four in all. Ned, myself, the captain and the tall steersman, who also officiated as engineer on occasion. The two latter were armed to the teeth. Ned had his revolver; but of this the captain either knew—or cared to know—nothing. I was absolutely unarmed, save for a tiny Swedish knife purchased at Reikjavik more than a year since.

I remarked as much to the captain.

'You will not need a weapon,' he said, and I was forced to be content.

The *Astrolabe* was stranded (if I may use the expression) on the summit of a precipitous hill some two thousand feet high, overlooking a deep valley down which a torrent foamed, more violent and rapid than the Swiss ones, fed by the melting snows of the far-off mountain chain, whose peaks were coloured a wonderful blue by the last rays of the dying sun.

The beauty of this valley, surely as lovely as any in the rose-carpeted gorges of Cashmere or Persia, simply set words at defiance.

Strange creepers and mosses, imitating in their variegated colouring the living flowers of the deep sea, covered the ground. We crushed these delicate marvels by hundreds at every step. Some of them seemed to be sensitive, for they turned and twisted like living things, coiling round our feet, embarrassing us at every turn, enfolding us in an embrace, rather terrifying than charming, for we did not know what strange poisons might not lurk under those fair chalices, poisons for which the utmost earthly medical skill might be of no avail. Night overtook us before we reached the valley. Overhead the azure peaks vanished into thin air, leaving only a vague starlight to guide our steps. As I stumbled along, forcing my way through the tangled mass of shrubs, whose aromatic perfume became intenser as we descended lower, I saw a bright light shining among the pendant bells of giant convulvuli. The captain had lit his electric lamp, an example which was speedily followed by his companion. A dark tunnel of overhanging trees opened before us, ending, as far as we could see,

in an open plateau, feebly lit by the diffused starlight.

A sting of fluid in my face made me start. Ned
uttered a cry.

'It's raining!'

Overhead the dark, thick leaves formed a perfectly impenetrable covering, water - tight as a
galvanised iron roof.

'It must come from the trees,' said I.

As I spoke a second deluge of drops fell. We
were enveloped in a shower-bath of thin spray,
warm and aromatic like a mist of chloroform. I
felt my brain growing curiously stupid.

'Run for it if you value your life!' shouted
someone in front, and I saw myself scudding
away through that deadly spray, while the gaunt
branches on either side writhed horribly, like a
nest of serpents.

In less time than it takes to tell, we were standing in the open air, panting like stranded fish.
Behind us those ghostly trees kept up an incessant rustling.

'They are the vampire-trees of the equator,' said
the captain. 'Had we stopped a moment longer, we
would have been eaten alive—look!'

The electric lamps threw a clear light back into
the foggy mist, which sprung in a myriad tiny
fountains from the long sickle-shaped leaves.
Presently the shower ceased and a curious
thing happened, that sent a shiver of fear
through us.

Slowly, slowly, like living arms outstretched to
grasp their prey, the long spiny branches, twisting
and sliding like the tentacles of a mammoth jelly-
fish, descended across the path we had traversed,
in the moist soil of which our footsteps were still
visible. Crossing and intercrossing like threads in
a weaving-mill, they swept the soil with an even

swaying movement, reminding one of the action of a scythe in the hands of an experienced reaper. These fearful arms were endowed with human senses—they lingered over our footprints, turning the earth over with their long spikes, kneading it as though they craved, from the dull clay, the satisfaction of a giant hunger. Then they rose again slowly, while a shudder passed across the darkness of the forest, a shudder that seemed half groan, half howl, a cry of wild-beast fury that struck terror to our hearts, so mournful and weird was it.

'The forest is bewitched,' said Ned, and really one might be excused for believing it.

The adventure was significant. The danger of wandering over the surface of this unknown planet was indeed very clear. Death lurked at every corner. What if Captain Chlamyl had led us to the bottom of these sombre crypts to hand us over to a wild and terrible end ? Viewed from a common-sense point of view, it did not seem so improbable. I cursed myself for my folly in ever consenting to join the party, and cursed myself doubly for not having stolen or borrowed a weapon of some kind before leaving the *Astrolabe*. Ned had his revolver, but that was insufficient for two people. As for my baby knife, it was not worth counting at all.

As we paused on the rocky edge of the plateau to admire the dark prospect, over which light clouds were beginning to gather, like ghostly veils of thin silk, shrouding the lower parts of the hills and creeping noiselessly through the tall stems of the white-blossomed palms, like smoke from the funnel of a railway engine, a faint cry was wafted to our ears, and against the dark blue strip of light that still lingered over the western hills a tiny speck came floating, like a belated bird. Whom had we to deal with? Some new species of enemy? We held a hurried consultation. I saw Ned's hand dive abruptly into his pocket, and I knew he was fingering his revolver.

The cry was repeated. This time it conveyed a meaning.

'It is Jip!' exclaimed Ned, as the faithful animal fell with a rush at his master's feet, barking with joy and flapping his russet wings at imminent danger of breaking someone's leg. He was a demonstrative dog, and, in spite of his fierce Saturnian parentage, unusually tractable and docile.

'Forward!' repeated the captain.

An hour's patient trudging brought us to the very edge of the valley. A broad meadow, carpeted with scarlet lichens, which yielded to the pressure of the foot like a thick Brussels carpet, stretched away as far as the river, whose roaring could be distinctly heard across the intervening band of trees. Every now and then a damp cloud of spray, blown by the wind, was wafted refreshingly to our faces. There was a great waterfall not far off, evidently. That must wait till to-morrow. In the meantime we must rest.

An exclamation from the captain attracted our attention. Ned, turning to look, uttered a wild hurrah.

Right and left, conspicuous under the electric light, grew gigantic flowers, in form resembling roses, but with a fainter perfume. The leaves, oblong, with serrated edges, were each as big as a small table, while the blossoms must have surpassed in size those of the famous *Victoria Regia*, in which a child might have lain cradled comfortably.

'Look at Jip!' said Ned, 'he's making himself at home.'

The intelligent animal had flapped his way into

the very centre of one of the huge pink blossoms, and was apparently preparing to curl himself down to sleep.

'One must sometimes learn wisdom in strange temples,' said the captain. 'Let us follow your pet's example, Master Hatton.'

'I am quite agreeable, sir,' replied that worthy, scrambling up into one of the roses, which bent slightly under his weight. 'We shall be as well off here as an Odalisque on a Persian divan.'

I followed suit, and in scaling the slanting leaves, nearly ran myself through the body with one of the thorns—a formidable spear over a yard in length and as thick as a man's wrist. Anything more delightful than that perfumed couch, it would be impossible to conceive. The smooth leaves, tinted as delicately as a sea-shell, yielded to the shape of the body, while the soft, yellow centre, covered with a velvety down, like that on a butterfly's wing, made an ideal pillow.

For a moment the disagreeable thought of asphyxia passed through my mind; but the perfume was so faint that my fears vanished and I composed myself down to slumber.

Above me the universe of stars appeared in an irregular circle, bounded by the semi-transparent leaves of the flower. Then fatigue overpowered me and I floated away into balmy sleep. I awoke with a start, a thousand fires burning in my veins, a thousand poisoned lances sticking into my body. I was choking. I was suffocating. I tried to scream, but a lithe hand had closed around my throat, making articulation impossible.

As I struggled frantically to tear myself loose, I became aware that the soft leaves of the flower had closed during my slumbers, wrapping me in complete darkness—a helpless prisoner, to be slowly devoured by those treacherous tendrils.

Cries came to my ears, and a dull light shone through the thick red wall. I felt the great blossom swaying to and fro. Then something seemed to crack underneath and I rolled over and over, half-smothered in oily rose leaves.

The fall disengaged my throat, and I shouted despairingly again for help. The long, tearing sound was heard, the leaves parted, and Ned's form appeared.

'Gently, Hal, old boy. Be quiet. Don't struggle or you'll hurt yourself. Wait till I cut these confounded prickles.'

He ran the knife swiftly along my sides and limbs, and I rose painfully, shaking myself clear of those murderous filaments, and, though striving to maintain an outward appearance of indifference, inwardly cursing the chance that had brought me to this singularly man-eating planet, where the plants fed on us, instead of we on them.

The captain and engineer were shaking themselves and laughing. Ned's face wore an ugly scowl. Above, the eastern sky was rose-tinted with the first glimmering of dawn. The sun's rays, striking against the upper layers of the atmosphere, slightly denser in its consistency than that of the earth, flooded the whole dim plain with a ruddy glow by reflection.

'It seems that we have got into a more than usually inhospitable world, sir,' then observed the commander. 'Once before I visited it, but these man-devouring roses are entirely new to me. It certainly behoves us to be careful, Master Hatton. A lily is making overtures to you from the back. Perhaps if you were to speak kindly to it—'

The captain's joke threw a new and humorous light on the subject. The flower in question, a lovely sky-blue water-lily, growing on the solid ground at the end of a long stalk, was inclining

familiarly over in Ned's direction, its petals opening
and contracting in the fashion of a jelly-fish. Ned,
into whom experience had instilled a good deal of
prudence, put out his hand and gingerly stroked
the velvety leaves. The inner chalice, of a bright
orange colour, vibrated curiously, and a long
humming sound—one might almost interpret it
as an expression of pleasure—came from the
beautiful flower.

'By Jove!' exclaimed Ned, 'it's purring like a
cat ; I believe the beggar can really talk! Did you
ever see anything like it?'

'If we are thinking of going ahead, professor,'
remarked Captain Chlamyl, shouldering his gun in
a business-like manner and nodding in the direction
of the lofty mountains that rose on the other side
of the valley, 'we had better be off. When once
the sun is up, it will be too hot for walking.'

The captain was right. We had no time to lose.
I hastily dusted the remaining rose fibres from my
coat and trousers, and hurried after the two men.
Ned, with some reluctance, said adieu to his pet
flower, which acknowledged his departure by a
prolonged scream of pain, 'like the cry of an ill-
used child,' Ned afterwards said. If some of
the minor flowers were affectionate, others were
certainly not so—at least their affection was of a
more awful kind. The tall, yellow-topped trees,
like waving polyps of the ocean, grew together on
an elevated knoll, dreaming in solitary beauty over
this magical plain.

'I wonder whether they can talk, too?' soliloquised Ned, picking up a stone and throwing it
adroitly right into the heart of one of the flaming
yellow crowns. Oh, what a yell broke on the
solitude! The yell of an infuriated lion whose
prey has been snatched from his famished jaws.
Down bent the graceful head, disclosing a fiery

centre, convulsively working in a fit of fury—down, lower yet—swaying over the ground like an angry serpent. Though we were a good fifty yards away, we started back horrified. And then the other monsters awoke, shaking their plumed heads and laughing in a hideous chorus of roaring, that set the echoes of the valley to work and swept over the dim land like clashing waves—it was a perfect Hell let loose. The laughter, which was ready on my lips, died suddenly, and I felt myself growing livid with uncanny fear. Ned looked awestruck, and the impassive captain even seemed to share some of our feelings.

'Look at the ground!' whispered Ned, hoarsely, as the frantic yelling died away in ferocious, tiger-like growls. 'Look at the ground! I believe it's strewn with bones!'

I literally froze as I looked. He was undoubtedly right. The soil around the base of these terrible vegetables (what a mockery the word seemed) was whitened with the ossified remains of—what?

Were there living animals here whom the trees preyed on? It looked likely. I could even distinguish, here and there, the fragments of what appeared to be a skull, a shattered spinal column, a bony claw, a snowy array of ribs upturned to the sky like the skeleton of a wrecked ship. What strange existencies had here breathed their last, strangled to death by those deathly plumes, bruised and pounded by the iron mandibles that lay concealed in the centre of those gorgeous chalices? Even the visionary wiseacres of a past age, who planned the story of the dreaded upas, had never exceeded this in their fabled descriptions.

An exclamation from Ned brought me to my senses.

'Where's Jip?'

In the excitement of discovery, he had entirely

forgotten his faithful pet. We rushed back to the place where we had passed the night. Among the giant flowers, one, a tall rose, nearly six feet in diameter, swayed its haughty petals to and fro at the end of a massive green stalk fifteen feet in height and covered with iron thorns.

'It has grown during the night,' said Ned, raising his axe.

Presently, the head fell with a crash, and we waded knee-deep in pink rose petals, tearing and cutting away like destructive angels. An overpowering odour of musk and chlorophyll impregnated everything. At every stroke our axes sank deep in oily chalices that would have made the fortune of a million Bond Street perfumers.

As Ned's weapon cleft the inner leaves of the flower, I uttered a cry.

Our suspicions were confirmed. An almost indistinguishable mass lay in the heart of the rose, half-covered by a network of slender, yellow filaments. It was Jip.

The murderous tendrils had grown through him while he slept, deadened by the aroma of the huge blossom. Life must have been long extinct, death by asphyxia having preceded death by strangulation. A faint murmuring arose from the flowers around us, and I felt my foot seized by some unseen creeper.

'Let us be off!' I cried, tearing myself loose, while a cold shiver of fear passed down my spine. Jip's fate might be our fate, and the prospect was not an enviable one.

We soon rejoined the rest of our party, who were standing at some distance on a knoll, reconnoitring this singular landscape.

Half-a-mile farther on, a roaring curtain of spray rose vertically upwards, like the breath from a volcano's smouldering mouth. Beyond, through the mists of the morning, loomed the forms of gaunt mountains, their crests of snow slightly tipped by the first rays of sunlight—not a warm, yellow light such as we are accustomed to, but a cold, greenish-blue colour, like luminous sea-water.

Presently, the sun rose—what a sun! Separated from us by only twenty-six million leagues of space, the boiling orb appeared nearly double the size of our earthly luminary, and our thick, white parasols hardly granted an efficient protection against its consuming fires. As we advanced, the roaring became louder. Then, as we reached the edge of the great valley, a sight was unveiled to our startled eyes, more terrible, in its grandeur and loneliness, than even the awful plains of Saturn, beside which the lunar solitudes, the chasm of Mount Archimedes sank into perfect insignificance.

Half a league farther on, an entire ocean of water seemed to be falling from the sky.

Above, where the thick mists hung in opaque layers, the forerunners of the cataract (equal in size to nearly twenty Niagaras) were visible, descending evenly in a gigantic wall of water that must have been quite a hundred miles broad, and so deep that it ended, some thousands of feet below us, in total blackness, darker and more opaque than the night that hangs above the legendary Styx.

The solar rays, acting on this shifting mass, produced here and there magnificent rainbows, which the peculiar chemical properties of the atmosphere tinted with blueish-violet. The noise was dreadful —we did not shout, we roared at each other.

On our right, a steep slope, carpeted with uncouth vegetation, led down into the heart of this dreadful abyss. Captain Chlamyl, axe in hand, plunged boldly along, hewing at the entangled mass of creepers that showered their intoxicating pollen around us as we proceeded.

It was a positive sin to hurt these wondrous flowers. We trod under our feet priceless collections of orchids, of ranunculuses, of spiræas with golden blossoms—algæ set with emerald eyes, like gigantic beasts of prey, that hummed and buzzed like angry bees, threatening with scarlet spines and wicked, venomous-looking tendrils.

A whirling sound overhead attracted our attention, clear and distinct as the noise of an electric bell above the thunder of the cataract.

'Dragon-flies!' exclaimed Ned.

Yes, dragon-flies. But dragon-flies fully a yard in length, with bullet-proof cuirasses of iridescent metal, and elongated trunks like those of miniature elephants. We halted, uncertain how to proceed. Indeed, if these beautiful creatures were gifted with weapons of offence in keeping with their imperial loveliness, they might prove awkward antagonists for us puny mortals.

Apparently, however, their intentions were peaceable. Circling round us, enveloping us with rings of flashing colour, like a swarm of kingfishers, squeaking like bats, the light playing miraculously over their diaphanous wings, they seemed rather to crave our companionship than to resent our intrusion into their world.

For an hour the swarm accompanied us, humming past overhead and around like animated Eolian harps. We never ceased to go into ecstasies over the beauty of their forms and the grace of their movements. At the end of this period, too brief, it seemed to me, these graceful creatures vanished suddenly. A dark crypt, wide and deep, lay before us, and the roaring of hidden whirlpools came gloomily to our ears.

Captain Chlamyl, undaunted as ever, strode forward into the tunnel (for it was nothing else), and we followed, albeit with some misgivings. A damp, clammy atmosphere pervaded the place, and indeed, as we proceeded, I was more and more reminded of a boyish experience of mine, when, on a certain summer's day, I had traversed a dark railway tunnel on foot, in company with an equally adventurous youth. The Irish mail dashed past us when we were half-way through, and the horror of that roaring, black fiend lingers in my memory till to-day. In the present instance, our electric lamps shone palely over the walls of this natural passageway, which in places might have measured fifty feet in height at least.

The roaring sound filled everything with its thunder, and soon the solid walls seemed to fairly quake under the impact of some terrible force that was rending the bowels of this strange planet. My heart began to beat fearfully. Ned's face was ashy.

Then, from the depths of the chasm, came an answering gleam of light, shifting and varying, like the reflection from a watery mass—it was the river.

It looked about a mile in width, though in reality it must have been far wider. It was probably only one of the many channels that allowed the escape of the mighty Niagara that we had seen falling from the sky. Far above our heads, a thin blueish-green stripe allowed a ghostly light to penetrate this singular canyon, larger and vaster than the Colorado ones, and crossed at intervals by slender rocky bridges, natural archways, whose existence must have dated from the first primæval cataclysm, unless they had fallen from above in recent times, as Ned fantastically pointed out.

The river was the most terrible sight of all. Such boiling, eddying waves, such yawning black cauldrons had never been seen before. Edgar Poe's Moskoe-Strom must have been a fool to it.

Our captain, a prey to no emotion whatever,

pointed up this horrid valley with his alpenstock, and we followed mechanically, clambering awkwardly over the polished rocks, that the force of the water had piled in picturesque heaps, forcing them out against the steep sides of its bed, as a glacier forces a moraine.

A mile further on the roaring diminished, and a calm sheet of dark water lay before us, swelling and surging mysteriously in the spectral twilight.

Captain Chlamyl pointed to the steep wall, which seemed to be composed of some brownish stone, resembling—what shall I say ? Iron ?

We were treading on heaps of hard, reddish sand. The captain, producing his compass, consulted it. The needle, oscillating strangely, veered round a full revolution, without taking up any settled position. Ned, stooping, examined a handful of the reddish sand.

' It is iron-mould !' he cried. ' Those rocks are composed of cast-iron ! '

I shivered strangely. The idea of miles upon miles of solid iron is not to be digested without difficulty. Yet here was the visible proof.

The strangest forms were assumed by these ponderous metallic masses. Either under the influence of the water, or through some other agency whose mode of working lay at present hidden, the ramparts were carved, fretted and chiselled into miniature towns, with battlements, spires and pinnacles. Here a fort, with bastions and rugged escarpments, in Titanic mockery at our tiny earthly ones, frowned darkly, as though forbidding access to the slender minarets beyond. Above all rose the dizzy walls of metal, relieved here and there by streaky white waterfalls that had worn deep ruts in the perishable iron. Indeed, as Ned remarked,—

' The whole thing'll eat itself away in course of time.'

'It will combine with the water to form oxide of iron,' I answered ; 'but as to the time necessary for the decomposition of this entire valley—it will be enormous, to say the least of it.'

'Especially if this entire planet is composed of iron to its base !' remarked Ned.

A sense of wonder overpowered me. The supposition, though fantastic enough in all conscience, had nothing absolutely impossible about it. In that case it would simply be a battle between iron and water, the resisting power of one against the chemical subtlety of the other.

'And in some millions of years,' added the captain, 'this beautiful world will roll, a cold, dead ball of rust, through infinite space !'

The picture thus conjured up threw me into a reverie, from which I was roused by Ned saying,—

'Hang philosophy ! I know I'm as hungry as a hunter !'

Go-ahead as ever, my worthy friend had certainly anticipated the wishes of the entire party. The sandwiches were spread out on a table-shaped stone, and we feasted in that terrible place quite as heartily as though we had been dining in the oak-panelled saloon of the *Astrolabe*. A curious sense of drowsiness seized me before we had finished our lunch. Could I attribute it to the presence of these metallic masses ? Since when had inhaled iron-dust been soporific ?

'I feel uncommonly inclined to sleep, captain,' I remarked, as the commander, having consulted his watch, was about to make some new proposition.

'Well, professor,' was the reply, 'I do not see why you should not indulge your fancy. We are in need of a little rest, and the air up there (pointing to the summit of the cliffs) will be too hot for breathing just now. Let us wait for the evening to set in before we start.'

In fact, nothing could be more prudent. Ned, producing a voluminous rug, spread it out on the flat ground, and invited me to share it with him. Captain Chlamyl and the robust sailor followed our example, and in a few moments we drifted off into dreamland.

A dull, rumbling explosion, a whip-like sting of cold water in my face, and a violent pain at the heart, sudden and intense as a death-agony, brought me to my feet with a bound.

'Ned!' I shouted. 'Ned!'

'Here you are, Hal! My lamp's out—help!'

The last exclamation was cut short by a gasp and a splash. Ned had fallen into the water.

'Look out there!' we heard him shouting. 'Don't come this way! I can get out by myself. Oh, will nobody light a lamp?'

A bright light shone about us. Following Ned's directions, the captain had set his electrical apparatus going, and the face of my poor friend appeared, peering over a rock, which he strove to clutch with his hands. Beyond all was blackness of darkness.

I rushed to aid him. What was happening. Had we slept on into the night? Was a thunderstorm breaking loose?

From the deep bowels of the earth beneath us came a hoarse rumble, like the premonitory symptoms of an earthquake. Then in the darkness a huge mound of water seemed to rise from its liquid bed, slowly, slowly, hissing and bubbling, We had just time to run for our lives to the higher ground, when it burst like an avalanche, and the waves came leaping over the black rocks, drenching us to the skin and covering us with clots of thick yellow foam, like the scum on a stagnant mill-pond.

At the same moment a torrent of white light burst forth overhead. Jagged lightning shot with an awful crashing sound across the ravine, illuming the night as with a sheet of trembling flame.

'It is an electric storm!' said someone in my ear, and the voice (I think it must have been the captain's) was directly smothered under a tempest of crashing thunder, that shook the solid iron cliffs to their bases and deafened one's ears like the firing of eighty-one-ton guns close at hand.

We were between the plates of a vast battery. The cliffs above us, surcharged with electricity, hurled lightnings at each other, and the deep river between them boiled furiously at each volley. We were literally covered with a canopy of blue flame, under which each rock, each spot of iron-stained lichen, each ring of foam dotting the troubled lake, stood out with startling distinctness. An intolerable smell of ozone filled the atmosphere, and under the electric brilliancy, reddish clouds of heavy vapour gathered slowly, twisting and curling in fanciful wreaths like smoke under the roof of a burning house.

'We shall be suffocated, captain!' I exclaimed during one of the lulls in this diabolical display of pyrotechny, and the commander seemed to understand me, for he led the way back over the boulders, his face muffled in the ample folds of his wet shawl.

Hardly had we started, when the storm broke out anew. Ned, drenched to the skin by his recent dip, hobbled along, cursing feebly, his hand, which was bleeding profusely from a cut, tightly enveloped in his muslin veil. As the flaming sheet of light again covered us, I noticed that the clouds had sunk lower. My lungs ached fearfully, and I pressed one hand to my chest in a vain attempt to quiet the gnawing pain.

A shock overthrew us. We rose fearfully bruised and dazzled under a rain of sparks. A great rock, a mass of iron weighing, perhaps, five hundred tons, displaced by the violence of the electric discharges, had fallen some thirty feet in front of us.

'This way!' shouted the captain, and from the summit of a boulder I saw his tiny lamp shining feebly.

As I scrambled up painfully, I became aware of a dull red light that seemed to be shining around us from on high, distinct and differing from the colour of the blue lightning as the light of red-hot metal differs in appearance from that of the electric arc.

'Look!' whispered Ned behind me hoarsely, his voice rising into a falsetto of fear, 'look! *the bridges are on fire!*'

I followed his gaze, and beheld a new and awful sight. The forked display of lightning had ceased, and the pent-up current was rushing across the narrow iron archways, which under its influence were changing from a dull red to a vivid orange-yellow colour. Even at this distance (and they were fully a thousand feet above our heads) we could feel the heat of that terrible furnace, and hear the joints of the metal cracking.

Over fifty of these glowing horrors were in sight, spanning the huge void like chains of solid fire, while long trails of sparks dropped with a hissing sound into the troubled waters below. Mute, almost paralysed with terror, we watched the awful spectacle. The shining bands above, their mirrored reflections below, formed a perfect avenue of fire on both sides, down which whirlwinds of inky dust poured, striking against the red-hot arches, to rebound in a rain of variegated sparks that settled on the tall iron pinnacles, covering the phantom city with a network of living jewels.

'Look!' whispered Ned again, 'I believe that one's going to melt!'

An ever-increasing glare made my eyes ache.

About a quarter-of-a-mile from us, a vast luminous band of an intense whiteness was beginning to curve slowly downwards, straining and crackling like any over-strained boiler-plate.   Then the end came.

With a loud explosion the causeway parted, and a cascade of white fire poured down into the water. I thought for a moment that we were lost.

Bathed from head to foot in a rosy cloud, we struggled on, while the vast masses of steam, condensing rapidly against the cooler cliffs, gushed down the rocks or poured down from overhead in the form of rain.

Everything has an end, however.   Was it the azure sun of Venus that awoke me on the following morning, as I slept the sleep of the just in my comfortable bunk on board the *Astrolabe*, or was it some new and inexplicable light, shining across the unpeopled spaces of this wild planet which had nearly made us living victims?

CHAPTER XXI

IMPRISONMENT AND—

No—this time it was no supernatural phenomenon I had to deal with.   The light of a bull's eye lantern was shining in my eyes, and I heard—yes, I heard these words spoken in French,—

'Will monsieur be so good as to dress himself at once?'

Three men, the French steward and two others, were standing by my bedside.   One of them held the lantern.   In the cabin all was darkness, and

not a solitary ray of light filtered through the thick
blue curtains. I stared about me wonderingly,
rubbing my eyes hard to make sure I was really
awake.

'Will monsieur please read this?'

This was a polite note, written on pink letter-
paper and surmounted by the crest of the *Astrolabe*.
Truly, on this vessel, wonders never ceased :—

'Professor Ralphcourt,

'SIR,—Circumstances which I cannot control,
combined with a desire to avoid the repetition of
certain disagreeable passages between myself and
your friend Mr Hatton, compel me to require your
imprisonment on board my vessel'—A shudder of
fear passed through me. So we were going to be
imprisoned? Well, it was what we might have
expected.—'together with Mr Hatton, till I shall
see fit to set you both at liberty again. As to the
safety of your lives, you need have no fear. You
will be carefully and kindly treated, but any attempt
at resistance will, of course, be duly visited by a
sufficiently stern retribution. In doing this, I take
all the responsibility. I cannot allow the ambi-
tions of either you or Mr Hatton to interfere with
the common safety.

'CAPTAIN CHLAMYL.

'*March 28th.*'

So the die was cast. This was the end of Ned's
plotting. And yet there was an atmosphere of
respectful civility about the letter which gave me
confidence. As the captain hinted, resistance of
any kind was out of the question. I rose and
dressed in a tremble. The men, unmoved as icicles,
offered to help me, but I refused their assistance
coldly.

Imprisonment! The word had an ugly sound.

There are political prisoners and prisoners of the law. The latter often get hung. To what category did we belong? The note promised consideration, even kindness; yet had not the commander promised the same thing to poor Andersen when he despatched him on his weary death-journey among the lunar volcanoes! For ought I knew, the captain might be in the act of despatching me to a horrible death. So overwhelmed had I been with wonders and terrors during the past week, however, that the prospect of death did not unnerve me quite as much as it might have done at any other time. I bundled on my clothes and followed the men without a word. A clean, plainly-furnished room in the neighbourhood of the engine-room was ready to receive me. Evidently my own luxurious cabin had not been considered a safe enough asylum. The walls of this apartment seemed more solid than usual, and the door was armed with a formidable array of complex steel hinges, leaving an unpleasant impression on the mind, and suggesting unlimited incarceration.

'Will monsieur breakfast?'

The French steward seemed all kindness and attention. The bare table was covered with a smooth white cloth, and the meal, consisting of coffee, wheaten bread, two kinds of strange vegetables (possibly Venusian), and a dish of preserved shell-fish resembling prawns, was served as tidily as the most fastidious epicure could have desired. The captain's notion of prison fare was evidently as original as his notions on all other subjects.

My attempts to discover Ned's whereabouts were unavailable. The steward could give me no enlightenment. His orders were too strict, he said. Would I like any books? Books? Why certainly. I detailed a list of my favourite volumes, which were duly brought from the library and de-

S

posited on my prison shelf. Then the discreet servitor withdrew, leaving me to my reflections.

The captain could, after all, only have my preservation in view. Had I not saved his life at the risk of my own on that dread morning when Ned's bullet had gashed my cheek? Had not the careful dressing of my wound and his subsequent kindness towards me proved that I could be no object of hatred to him? No—my imprisonment meant nothing more or less than my separation from Ned —that was all. The struggle between loyalty to the *Astrolabe's* commander and friendship towards my impetuous companion would be too bitter for any frail mortal. We must be separated from each other—the captain was right.

Though apparently correct in my reasoning, the thought still haunted me that there might be some trap concealed in my prison walls. Suppose carbonic acid were injected while I slept? Suppose the flooring were to give way, and I were to be hurled, an inanimate, flattened mass, through space.

I fell on my hands and knees, impatiently examining the planking for traces of an oubliette, a manhole that might bring me to death. In vain. The boards were regularly joined and cemented. Stamping with one's feet produced hardly a sound that would serve to indicate the existence of a hollow space beneath. The floor evidently overlaid the solider plates of aluminium composing the hull of the ship.

Death was not there, at all events.

The absurdity of my suspicions soon came forcibly home to me. We had been a whole year on board the *Astrolabe*. If the captain had wished to kill us, he would have done so ages ago. A few grains of strychnine or stramonium intermingled with our food, and we would both be as dead as the geological specimens in the Berlin museums.

Poison could have speedily removed us, yet we had partaken of no poison. An order given to the crew might have murdered us in our beds, yet no one had even offered to molest us—that is me. As to Ned—

Ned the revolutionary, Ned the mutineer, Ned the defiant champion of liberty, who had braved the lion to his face, what would become of him?

In fact, the two attempts (which the captain called coincidences) that had frightened us already wore an ugly look. Ned had practically endeavoured to kill the commander. Was it to be supposed that the captain would not now endeavour to be revenged on him—now that he was in his power?

I spent a miserable afternoon, reading desultory scraps here and there in the books Captain Chlamyl's thoughtfulness had provided for me, and pacing moodily up and down before the solitary circular window that illumined my prison, and which, much to my disgust, was covered with a thick fog of some kind, similiar to that collecting on a damp railway glass, thus rendering a view of any kind impossible. Not a sound was heard in the vast hull, and, for the life of me, I could not tell whether we had left Venus or not.

Towards 7 p.m., as far as I could guess at the time, the steward came in to lay the table for my evening meal, and while I was eating it the sun rose—that is, the *Astrolabe* revolved on her keel in such a way as to enable the solar rays to penetrate the circular window.

'Off again,' I said to myself, wearily.

On the following morning I was permitted to take some exercise on deck.

My walk was under strict supervision, it is true. The steersman's cabin, broken by the recent explosion, had been repaired, and through the glass

I was watched attentively by the tall helmsman and his assistant, a delicate-looking man of middle age, with a copper-coloured face, capable of all manner of evil passions.

Venus, twice the size of the terrestrial moon, was riding majestically in the zenith. The sun's rays, whenever they struck my face, burned so furiously that I was compelled to freeze in the shadow, and the reflection from the burnished aluminium covering was painfully dazzling.

April 1st.—No sign of the captain yet, though indeed there was not any particular reason why he should honour me with a visit. During the night I suffered somewhat from heat, and impatiently threw all the clothes off my couch. As a result, I awoke in the morning freezing, my limbs blue and my teeth chattering spasmodically. The *Astrolabe* had revolved during my sleep, and the intense cold of space had succeeded the sun's rays on my side of the vessel. The glass of my window was clear again, and I was able once more to contemplate the star-dust at leisure.

April 6th.—This morning brought an unexpected surprise. As I was eating my breakfast I found a tiny piece of paper imbedded in the crumb of one of the loaves. It was a note from Ned.

'DEAR OLD BOY,' it ran, 'I am confined in a small cell somewhere under the main stairway. I have no window, and they only leave the electric light on during six hours out of the twenty-four. I hope this'll reach you. If it reaches the captain instead, it'll be all up with me. My bed is comfortable, but I am being slowly baked alive, and the boredom of it is driving me mad. I tried to get the steward to take a message to you, but he wouldn't. Good-bye, dear old man. Keep up your spirits any-

how, and send me a line if you possibly can.—
Yours,   NED.

So he was alive! I shivered and hugged myself
with delight. As the door opened to admit the
steward, I crushed the note in my hand, and I
don't think he suspected anything.

To correspond with Ned is impossible. I must
content myself with waiting.

April 12th.—During the night I was awakened
by a loud, grinding sound, coming from the depths
of the ship. I raised myself on my elbow and
listened attentively.

First a rush, then a wheezing pant like the bursting open of an escape pipe ; then a long, trembling
spasm that seemed to shake the whole vessel.

Then came the clanking of iron tools, men's
voices raised in altercation, and silence. I think
I must have dozed off, in spite of my uneasiness,
for the first thing I remember is the snapping of
the steel locks in the door, and the sound of a well-
known voice saying,—

'Ah, professor! you are awake.'

It was the captain in person.

His head was bare, his hair was dishevelled, and
his face pale as that of a corpse.

I started up to a sitting posture.

'Has anything happened, sir ?' I asked.

'You are at liberty, professor,' was the answer,
delivered in a strange, husky voice.

'At liberty ?'

I was afraid I hardly caught his meaning.

'An accident has happened, professor—an unfortunate mistake—a fault in the working—we are
falling.'

'Back on to the planet, captain ?'

'No, sir—into the sun !'

CHAPTER XXII

A FALL OF TEN MILLION MILES

NEITHER of us spoke for a minute. The suspense was terrible.

'When I cast myself loose from the planet Venus fourteen days ago,' continued the captain, gloomily, 'I was ignorant, as it seems, of our true position in the universe, or rather in our own solar system. The explosion of hydrogen wrecked our astronomical instruments sufficiently to render all my attempts at reckoning our whereabouts inaccurate and futile. I landed on Venus, as you know, just in the nick of time to save us from destruction by suffocation. I left the planet, only to find, after a fourteen-day cruise, that we were on the wrong side of the sun !'

'The wrong side !' I cried, horrified, although for the moment I hardly understood the cause of my fright.

'Yes, sir. The translation movement only acts one way. Suppose, instead of carrying us away from the solar furnace, it should carry us right into its centre !'

My heart began to beat painfully. I was beginning to catch a glimpse of the truth.

'Then it is the sun that is falling on us !' I exclaimed.

'Exactly, sir. We are rushing into its embrace at the rate of half a million miles a day—impelled both by the power of its gigantic attraction and by the force of the translation movement.'

'But, captain,' I exclaimed, a ray of hope bursting upon my mind all of a sudden, 'can we not start the engines and maintain our position evenly in space, as we have done heretofore ?'

'No, professor. The engines are disabled. In fact, had it not been for the wreckage of the vacuum tunnel, that is the soul of my mechanical contrivance, last night, it is possible that I would not have discovered our course for some time to come. The stoppage of the discs and the consequent change in position of the sun, with regard to our centre of gravity, opened my eyes to the real facts of the case. To keep you and Mr Hatton imprisoned under such circumstances would be a useless piece of tyranny. In such a crisis it behoves us all to lend our labours for the safety of our vessel. You are free.'

In the saloon I found Ned, staring through the panel with his hands in his pockets.

'Hallo, old man. We're done for now, I reckon.'

'It seems so,' I replied simply.

'And we're to be burnt alive, burnt like rats in a trap!' exclaimed my companion, desperately, 'without even a chance of being saved. Well, after all, it serves us right!'

Ned's philosophy might be sound enough, in all conscience, but I could not help thinking that, in the present instance, it was somewhat unconsoling.

Speaking for myself, though my mind was fully awake to the awfulness of our fate, I felt, strange to say, a certain wild joy, when considering the peculiar grandeur of the prospect before me. Never had human being dreamed of such a death! To be absorbed in the central sun! Could the sage Empedocles have foreseen my strange destiny, he would doubtless have been envious. Would my moral courage hold out till the end, or would I awake from my gorgeous vision to become a shrinking, cowardly mortal? We would soon see.

Captain Chlamyl wasted no time in useless speechifying. By midday the engineers were hard at work, trying to repair the damaged machinery, unfortunately a sufficiently difficult task, owing to the nature of the injury. A vast rent had been made in one of the thin aluminium plates by a loose fragment of one of the revolving discs, which centrifugal force had served to detach from the main body. Assuming that we could manage to stop the rent, would our safety be assured? The odds were certainly against us. Even supposing that in three or four days we succeeded in closing the rent, would the efficiency of our patched-up machinery sufficiently counter-balance the ever-increasing attraction of the mighty sun?

Hardly likely. If Jupiter had been an object of distrust to our captain, when crossing its orbit some months back, was it not probable that we should be, under the influence of the sun's vigour, as impotent as a house-fly in the current of the Niagara River?

Added to this there was the impetus, which our delay with the engines must necessarily bring about. For three days or more we should be hurrying sun-wards at a speed of five hundred thousand miles in twenty-four hours, which by the time the reparations were completed would, perhaps, rise as high as a million. What hope had we of being able to check this mighty rush? Less than none.

The operations in the engine-room went on vigorously. The crew worked day and night. Ned, attired in a thin blue blouse, lent his aid with a will. Mechanical attainments had never been my *forte*. I could only grind my teeth and jealously watch the speeding hands of the electric chronometers, that ticked remorselessly in all the rooms, beating out, only too fast, the remaining seconds of our earthly career.

Strips of aluminium, torn from the inner partitions, were carefully welded together and laid across the gap. Then the vacuum engine began its panting labour, and with anxious eyes Captain Chlamyl and myself watched the needle of the pressure-gauge as the air was rapidly exhausted. Aluminium, most people know, is as brittle as glass, but capable nevertheless of resisting considerable pressure. On board the *Astrolabe*, owing to the rarefied nature of the atmosphere, the strain was not nearly so great as it would have been on the surface of one or other of the larger planets, where the atmospheric column was some hundreds of miles high. The new plates withstood the test—we were saved!

A lever connected the pyroxyline-engines with the revolving discs. The ponderous pistons moved, the speed accelerated, five hundred revolutions a minute—six hundred—seven hundred—the excitement was painful. At eight hundred and fifty revolutions there was a formidable explosion, followed by a sound like tearing paper. Dismay was written on all faces.

'One of the discs has flown to pieces,' said Captain Chamyl, as the engine stooped short with a series of jerks, like the convulsive spasms of a wounded bird. A fearful rent became visible in the tunnel. One of the men, his arm dripping with blood, tried to close the wound with a piece of waste, while a sympathetic group gathered about him. The captain, biting his lip in silence, watched the luminous rings thrown by the starboard windows travel slowly up from the floor to the ceiling, contract and vanish, as the vessel's centre of gravity, momentarily altered by the incipient effort of the engines, once more brought the sun under her keel.

'We must try again,' said he.

The reparative operations recommenced. This time it must be a lengthy piece of work. Not only had the rent in the tunnel to be closed, but the shattered disc had to be replaced—an affair of several days at least.

In the meanwhile the solar heat became inconvenient enough to tax our ingenuity.

The whole lower half of the *Astrolabe* was being boiled by degrees. The water in the cisterns grew lukewarm, the food became uneatable, a universal lassitude spread itself over all the men. Nothing daunted, Captain Chlamyl set the freezing-machines to work. Long draughts of air, compressed to sixteen atmospheres, were liberated about the below-deck portions of the ship. Day and night the machines kept at work, and on the morning of the 16th the thermometer had sunk to zero, and the water in the pipes was frozen hard. On deck, however, the tropical temperature still held good. Slices of bread, spiked on the end of a toasting-fork and held out over the taffrail, were roasted brown in less than a minute.

'What if the keel of our ship should melt?' suggested Ned, and the horrifying prospect fairly took my breath away.

On the following morning, the 17th, Captain Chlamyl entered the saloon, where I was sitting shivering in a cloak of sea-otter. His eyes were gleaming with a new excitement. He feverishly consulted the map. Then without further preamble,—

'The discs are repaired,' he said, 'we are going to start.'

'Ah!' I replied carelessly, and really the prospect of a near death had so utterly unstrung my nerves, that I hardly even felt grateful for our visionary chance of a respite.

He pressed a button. A well-known humming sound told me that the engines were in motion. I held my breath.

'Look out for yourself, sir!'

I understood, and sprang back as the flaming glare through the panels struck against my face like living fire. A glass of water. containing flowers half-frozen in a covering of thin frost, cracked with a loud report as the heat struck its side, and the silky fringe of the table-cloth began to smoke. It seemed to me that I could almost feel the heat-waves sweeping round our doomed vessel, and in spite of the intense cold, I felt the glow run along my limbs.

The *Astrolabe* accomplished a complete half-revolution, and the sun was now overhead, expending its strength on the metal covering that shielded the lower deck from stem to stern. A chorus of hurrahs broke out from the direction of the engine-room.

'We are saved !' I cried.

Captain Chlamyl did not seem to hear me. I touched his arm timidly. He shook me off with an impatient gesture.

'Ah !' he exclaimed, 'if my ship were only infusible enough to bear the heat of that pitiless furnace !'

'But captain—'

'Do you not understand, sir, do you not comprehend that, in spite of all efforts—oh, God !—in spite of all efforts, we must and will pass within little less than a million miles of the sun. The impetus we have acquired during the last four days is so powerful that nothing in the shape of mechanical energy can stay it ! Ah, could we only pass through the zone of the fire, we should be safe !'

I sank on the sofa, terrified into silence. Captain Chlamyl burst into a sort of sob.

'No metal can resist it, no cold can quench it,' he said desperately.

'Aluminium, captain, is—'

'However strong, however infusible the material of my vessel, professor, it will be melted like wax in that glowing ocean of fire ! You know it as well as I.'

He began to pace moodily up and down the

saloon. I knew him better than to interrupt his reverie. Presently he stopped before the map and followed with his finger an oval line that, passing within a few hundred thousand miles of the sun, lost itself in space at either side, after describing a vast parabola.

' A comet ! ' I cried.

' Yes, sir, a comet. A comet whose attraction, acting on our vessel before it had time to enter the fatal zone, might snatch it from the jaws of destruction—do you not see ? '

I was dumbfounded. Surely of all wild hopes this was the wildest. Once again a comet was to be our salvation, but how were we to make sure of meeting this celestial traveller ? Was it not a million chances to one that we should never cross its orbit at all ? And if we did cross it, who was to guarantee our crossing it at the right moment ? A faint hope is, however, better than no hope at all, and my faith in the captain was such that I clung helplessly to him as a drowning man is said to cling to a straw.

' Besides,' added the commander, ' there are other methods of working out our salvation, unless I am mistaken.'

Other methods ! I was indeed well-accustomed to the phrase by this, and for a moment I really and sincerely wondered whether this extraordinary being could be killed at all, or whether he were not some angel clad in a protecting raiment of intelligence, against whom death and the powers of darkness warred in vain.

' The intra-mercurial planets,' continued he, ' might each of them serve as a temporary asylum for us, in spite of their obvious inconveniences in the shape of boiling seas and rivers of molten metal, were it not for the fact that none of them are likely to be directly in our path—'

I laid my finger on the map.

'Which are the intra-mercurial planets, captain?'
I asked.

'These two,' he replied, pointing out a couple of
tiny black spots, one of which almost seemed merged
in the sun's disc, so near was it. 'Calliope and
Orestes I have named them. As for Mercury itself,
it is just possible it may help us. Have you not
thought of examining it through one of the glasses?'

'No, sir. Is it in sight?'

'Of course. Six million miles to leeward. See
there!'

He pointed through the panel. A large star,
half the size of the moon at her full, shone clearly
out against the misty background.

'I have no means of exactly calculating our distance,' observed the commander, nor can I exactly
tell at what moment I will cross that world's orbit.
The only way I can do, is by making test experiments at frequent intervals—by stopping the discs
to see whether the *Astrolabe* succumbs to its at-
tractive power. If it does, well and good, if not—'

He shrugged his shoulders.

'Look! We will make an experiment now.'

He touched the telegraph. Immediately the speed
of the discs diminished. With eager eyes and beating heart I watched the distant planet, my eye glued
to the long binocular. Presently the round disc,
with its bands of striated cloud slid boldly out of
the telescopic field. I followed it, and measured the
angle approximately.

'Five degrees, captain.'

In fact, the *Astrolabe* had revolved on her keel
through that small angle. The sun still had the
best of it.

Every two hours the experiment was repeated,
without our gaining more than two degrees. For
worlds I would not live that day over again.

Every chance missed was a dagger stroke. Ned, half-naked, was lounging about aimlessly, mopping his forehead with a large red handkerchief, for in spite of all the freezing operations the heat was beginning to be felt. The coldest place in the vessel was in the engine-room, and thither we adjourned at intervals. As fast as the artificial atmosphere was pumped through the iron reservoirs, so fast did the heat of that terrible sun re-heat it again to an unbearable temperature. To go on deck was impossible. Even in our cooler prison below deck, it was beginning to be a question of hours.

Next morning (it was the 18th), Captain Chlamyl knocked at my door.

'We have crossed the orbit of Mercury,' he said simply.

'And we cannot land?'

'No, sir.'

He sat down wearily, holding his head in his hands. In the midst of my own grief, I thought of his, and if ever I loved this strange solitary being, so far removed from the sphere of ordinary humanity, I loved him then. After all, what was the loss of my trivial life compared with the loss of this mighty vessel and the still mightier brain that conceived it.

'The comet is our only hope then?' I said desperately.

He nodded. Through the open door a gust of heated air came sweeping over my face, like the first blast of the African sirocco—withering, parching heat that dried my blood inside me and made my skin feel brittle like glass.

'When do we cross its orbit, captain?'

'On the morning of the 21st, at 11.30 a.m.

'We shall be dead first.'

'Perhaps so, professor.'

He rose and left me. The heat was terrific.

One of the stewards, passing down the corridor on some errand or other, fell prone on his face with a cry, his features swollen and distorted. He had been struck by heat-apoplexy.

'Cold water!' I cried. 'Water at any price!'

There was no such thing forthcoming. A tall negro brought me a dish of lukewarm fluid, and I bathed the features of the unfortunate man with it, as he lay stretched helplessly on the phormium matting outside my door. Captain Chlamyl appeared, the perspiration pouring down his pale face, his thin lips drawn tight in a convulsion of anguish. The stricken man, supported on either side by two stewards, lolled his head about like a captive animal, while large drops of moisture trickled from his protruding eyes.

Violent spasms succeeded. In the intervals of the sufferer's mute writhings, inarticulate cries escaped his lips. Terrified, we watched beside the couch where he lay, all day long, and far into the troubled night. Towards 1 a.m. Captain Chlamyl turned to me, his face looking ghostly and spectral under the electric light. It was all over. The man was dead.

I think I still see the scene. The sombre drapery of the cabin, the gloomy port-holes and the bowed heads of the men. All night the heat grew more unbearable. Denuded of our clothes, the perspiration baked out of us, we lay about in helpless inactivity, while the low humming of the engines echoed through our dizzy brains like a death-knell.

A distorted face with deep-sunk eyes and hollow cheeks bent over me. It was Ned.

'Morning,' he said.

Above the port-holes a thin streak of intense light broke out. The *Astrolabe* was beginning to revolve on her keel, and the dreadful 19th of April dawned.

CHAPTER XXIII

THE LAST OF CAPTAIN CHLAMYL

RUSHING, whirring, palpitating seconds of time, the ceaseless hum of the engines and the intense sufferings occasioned by the ever-increasing fires without—how adequately describe our impressions? How commit to pale paper the glowing horrors of that last day, the last day consciously passed on the *Astrolabe?* Even while the details remain fixed in my memory, it is difficult to find words to paint the sufferings we underwent.

The engine-room, the only place where the temperature was in any way bearable, was fairly besieged by the sweating, seething crew of men, on whose gaunt faces Death's angel already seemed to have left his fell mark.

We had, during our stay on the captain's vessel, slightly overestimated the number of sailors employed to manœuvre it. They only numbered sixteen in all now. A year back, the number must have been more considerable, for eight had been lost almost under our eyes at various times—in the tidal wave of Saturn, on the moon, thanks to the captain's treachery, in Ned Hatton's mutiny, without counting the steward who had lost his life that morning.

They had once been a sullen, dogged set of men, brave even to rashness, but now their bravery was fast oozing out of them. Some wept silently, and, faithful even in their last moments of despair, tried to kiss the fringes of their beloved commander's robe. Others gritted their teeth and sulked ominously—none spoke, the influence of the captain kept them in check, and the panting of the compressed air-engine was the only sound audible. From time

to time one of the engineers roused himself to tighten
a screw or pour oil into a brass oil-cup. The port-
holes had been closed to prevent the solar rays from
entering, and the rows of incandescent electric lamps
diffused a golden light.

At ten the captain touched me on the shoulder.

' I am going to attempt an observation,' he said.
' Will you lend your help ? '

I nodded.

' Then come into the saloon, sir.'

We passed out and along the passage. The long
drawing-room, deprived of the incessant draughts of
cold air during the whole of the preceding night,
resembled the hottest room of a Turkish bath. The
temperature must have exceeded that of boiling
water, for I noticed that the fluid in the vases had
all disappeared, and the beautiful orchids of unknown
planetary origin which till then had flourished in
the china pots, were brown and dried. Across the
polished back of the grand piano ran three great
cracks, and when I caught hold of a costly inlaid
chair it fell to pieces in my hands.

It was the end of the end, apparently.

' We must open the panels,' then said Captain
Chlamyl. ' We can see nothing in this metal prison.'

' We shall be roasted ! ' I gasped.

' There is no help for it, sir—we must risk that.
Besides, the sun is under our keel.'

The words gave me courage. I grasped the steel
handle that worked the shutters and screamed with
pain as I did so. It was nearly red-hot. Tearing
a pliant metal glove from one of the armed figures
in the corridor, the captain set to work, and presently the immense void was open to our eyes.
Through the binocular telescope, every minute
particle of star-dust seemed visible. Never had
astronomers scanned space with such eagerness.
Our lives, indeed, depended on the search. Would

T

this strange comet indeed appear? Would it be in time? Was it not utterly futile and ridiculous to count of such a slender chance of safety?

We relieved each other, straining our eyes out into the ocean of powdered diamonds, and hurrying to cool ourselves in the moderate temperature of the corridor. We were devoured by a ravaging thirst, but, fortunately, there was no lack of water now. Fresh from the cooling machines, large draughts of the miraculous fluid diffused new life through our throbbing systems, and unmercifully prolonged our misery.

Mute, gloomy, my head dazed, my eyes aching, I was sitting before the port panel, when Captain Chlamyl uttered a cry.

' Fools that we are ! ' he exclaimed. ' It is towards the sun that we must direct our gaze ! '

' Towards the sun ? ' I said.

' Yes, sir. The comet has swept round the solar disc, and must, at this instant, be hurrying towards us from beneath.'

He was right. In the excitement occasioned by our desperate sufferings, the reasonable probabilities of the strange phenomenon had been entirely over-looked and we were scanning the wrong side of space—had been doing so for the last hour in fact.

The captain touched a bell, and the *Astrolabe* commenced to revolve on her axis.

A glare, brighter and more intense than that of molten silver, struck on the ceiling above my head, and a bright sheet of flame told me that the curtains had caught.

I sprang aside in time to avoid the glow striking my face, and, at the same moment, Captain Chlamyl threw himself on the lever and closed the panels.

We battered out the flames with our hands, and stamped on the torn-down drapery. Suffocated, broiled, blinded by the stifling smoke, we sought refuge in the hall outside. Water was brought and in a few moments the danger was past.

'This will never do,' said the captain, desperately. 'We will be broiled alive like moths in the flame of a candle.'

Two sheets of glass, taken from an interior window, were smoked in the flame of burning paraffin oil, and set against the panels. Through this dense medium we scrutinised the burning focus, whose rays, tempered and softened by the refraction, no longer scorched us with their fierce heat.

At three the captain handed me the glass.

'The comet!' said he.

I breathlessly glued my eye to the binocular.

Yes. He was not mistaken. It was the comet, but how far off?

A pale strip of opacity, outlined feebly against the glowing furnace, with the shadowiest trace of a tail, bent into a semi-circle like an Oriental scimitar —how far was it off?

One day? Two days? If the latter, we should be dead first.

The engine-room was the only place in the vessel where the temperature was bearable. The men, converted into savages by their dire necessity, elbowed and pushed each other out of the way in order to get a breath of cool air at the mouth of the machines. The valves were beset by a pushing, struggling mass, which ere long would become wild beasts in real earnest. The captain, mute and impassive in spite of his great suffering, sought to reduce the poor fellows to order by his fortitude. Ned, seated in a corner, seemed to be sleeping stupidly.

In the early part of the afternoon I moved into the adjoining storeroom, using a private key, which the captain had lent me, to open the door. Here, thanks to the absence of all windows, save one small circular one on the starboard side, through which no light but the diffused light of space penetrated, was tolerable cool. It may have been nearly ninety deg. Fahrenheit or more. Here I reclined, my back against a bale of rugs, drowsily awaiting the end, while through the thin wall the wrangling of the crew came to me faintly.

The burning heat produced a deadly lassitude, through the medium of which, thanks be to a merciful Provdence, the more horrible details appeared softened and toned down, like images in a mirage.

Towards five in the afternoon two of the remaining crew succumbed, falling dead like logs across the smooth tiles of the passage-way. Captain Chlamyl vanished, and we were too sick to apprise him of the dreadful occurrences.

As I sat, moodily listening to the whirring of the engines, Ned touched me on the shoulder. I looked up. He held a revolver in his hand.

'I am going to make an end, Hal,' said he.

His face was awful. The bloodshot eyes seemed to start from their dark sockets, his cheeks were disfigured with dust and grime, and I thought he looked more like an avenging murderer than a suffering Christian.

'I am going to make an end, Hal,' he continued. 'This cannot last longer. We shall all be dead by nightfall. There is no use prolonging our misery. I shall die—but before I do so, there are some scores to settle between me and the captain. I am going to kill him—now, at once!'

He grinned hideously, and I saw the hammer of the revolver rise half-way under the nervous pressure of his fingers.

'No!' I cried, 'no! for God's sake, Ned! It will be a wicked crime—a dastardly return for his great hospitality. 'You will not do this?'

'I shall do it!' he answered doggedly. 'You may try to stop me if you like.'

His eyes were gleaming fiercely with a wild-beast look that sent a thrill of terror through my reeling brain. With a sudden movement I endeavoured to snatch the revolver.

In an instant I found myself lying on my back, bruised and sore, with Ned standing over me, laughing.

He was transfigured. His mouth gaped wide, as in a convulsive effort at breathing. His hair, long and matted from carelessness engendered by the easy life on board, hung wildly over his flashing eyes. Great sobs escaped him. He was going mad by degrees.

His fingers were playing nervously with the pistol. Twice I thought he was going to shoot me. Snarls like those of an angry dog came from his lips. He was irresolute, pausing apparently between murder and insanity.

'Ned!' I cried. 'Ned, old man!'

It was all I could do. I was helpless. The plates of aluminium covering the floor were burning hot and my hands were scalded by degrees, severely burnt in fact, though at the moment I noticed nothing.

Some vague recollection, awakened by me uttering his name, for a minute or two seemed to traverse the madman's brain, for he dropped the revolver and turned away, muttering absent-mindedly to himself.

As he did so a clamour arose outside. Fierce cries were heard. The door was burst open, and half-a-dozen horrible faces, distorted with pain and passion, appeared at the opening. One tall fellow, who had occupied the position of cook on board, rushed at me with an axe, yelling savagely. Was I to be butchered, then?

As he raised the weapon, I managed to pick up Ned's revolver, which went off with a crash, the bullet striking the man in the breast and killing him instantaneously. As his body fell heavily against me, I heard a tiger-like growl, and through the glowing atmosphere I saw Ned and another mutineer locked in mortal combat.

To and fro they swayed, gripping each other like bears. Ned's face, gashed in several places by his antagonist's long knife, was streaming with blood. Frozen with horror, I watched the savage struggle; I was helpless, powerless, dying almost, yet my eyes still held good, and I looked on doggedly. Ned, lithe and muscular as a leopard, tried to strangle his opponent by clutching his windpipe. I saw the man's face getting purple under his powerful grasp, the giant limbs relaxed, and the two fell to the ground together.

At that moment, whether the machines that fed the dynamos had stopped, or whether the conductors had been severed I know not, but suddenly the electric globes that lighted us went out, leaving a total darkness, only set off by the feeble starlight that filtered through the starboard panel. A strange phenomenon was taking place before my eyes. The star-dust, uniformly graded in density, appeared, through the thick refracting medium, to be split up into streaks and patches of pale iridescence, and a slight curvature was visible in the panes—the windows were melting! At the same time the noise of the engines ceased, and a thin vapour began to rise through the chinks and crevices of the floor. I closed my eyes. No, I was not to die yet. Panting, suffocating, burning in that pitiless furnace, I thought I heard an unaccustomed sound mingling with the roaring in my ears. It was the sound of footsteps falling on the iron floor. Nearer they came—nearer —nearer. The door opened and the spectre of Captain Chlamyl appeared—carrying a torch made of some resinous substance.

He bent, first over the two combatants, who were lying locked in each other's arms, dead apparently, then over me.

I could not speak. It was like a dream, an impotent, awful experience of the nightly hours—and as vague.

His hair was dishevelled, his eyes burning with fever, the whole beautiful face was disfigured by pain and mental suffering, but its indescribable charm remained, the charm that had worked so powerfully on me that morning when I awoke on board his marvellous craft, that mighty stamp of intelligence and power that had looked coldly on so many marvels, those dark lustrous eyes that seemed to bear the burden of the great brain that gave them light. Every terror, every detail, every supernatural occurrence that had brought colour into our life on the *Astrolabe*, flashed across my waning senses. The Icelandic crossing, the crevasse of Mount Archimedes, the lonely footprints on the lunar sea, the mist of life, the Saturnian girdle of fire, the flying wolves, the blue comet, our dreadful experience among the man-eating flowers of Venus, imprisonment, and the fearful fight among the perishing wretches who were even now dying or dead—it was a phantasmagoria of impossible wonders, reft from the jealous care of the Almighty by the brain of one lofty genius.

Lower bent the stately head, lower yet. Was it some sentiment of almost divine compassion that prompted this strange being to take an interest in a poor helpless mortal like myself, or had the cynical soul of this thinker, so far removed from ordinary sympathies, at length become illumined by the divine light of friendship. Tears could not glow in those eyes. The time was past for that, but the pity that shone from those dark orbs remains in my heart to this day.

Did his lips touch my forehead, or was it only the reflex of my own thoughts, speaking through the cloudy mist of a universe which was gradually fading from my view, dying, not as a lamp dies, in darkness, but in a glaring whirlwind of golden flame. . . .

———

CHAPTER XXIV

BETWEEN DAWN AND SUNSET

THERE is a certain state, between dreaming and waking, when the body is really unable to feel any outward impression, when the nerves, wrecked and shattered by some soul-shaking horror, refuse their agonising office, and the tortured fibres of the mind convey no impression to the brain save one of dreamy lassitude, similar in many respects to the indolence experienced by opium-smokers under the influence of their subtle narcotic, similar to the sensations of a mouse when seized by a cat, or a man when caught in the fell grip of a tiger.

The truth is, that an excess of terror, by paralysing the active nerves, at the same time deadens them to fresh impressions. A great shock, suddenly received, acts as a brake upon our later feelings, and every succeeding sensation is merely felt through the thickness of the first terror, so to speak. It is pale by comparison, and being such, loses its awfulness.

A canopy of solid darkness, analysed in the leisurely contemplation of a never-ending swoon, dwindled into the well-known ceiling of my cabin, crossed at intervals by cedar beams and marked with diamonds and crosses of gold. . . .

It was a vision, and faded as soon as realised.

At times, during the lulls of my fever, a face seemed to wander across my mental vision—a face, now assuming the familiar lineament's of Ned Hatton, now frowning forth out of the darkness in

the pale features and sunken eyes of Captain
Chlamyl. Had the philosopher deserted the
realms of space to become a mere human atom?
Was the distant, icy genius about to really descend
to my level, mingling himself with the throng of
greatness and smallness that peoples our far-off
little planet?

Far off? There it was nevertheless, its continents
and islands distinct under a ghostly radiance that
seemed to come from nowhere, save from the
misty land of dreams—and its satellite, the moon,
with its dead volcanoes sleeping in the light of a
phantom sun, lonely and desolate as when the
poor mortal atom perished in the sunny waste—
Andersen, Andersen. . . .

But I could not rest. A power stronger than
my better nature drove me on. I was falling, falling in immensity, past solitary, unknown planets,
bleak worlds of ice and fire lost in the voids of
space, dreaming in pathless eternity. . . .

Then I awoke with a bound, and hands, yes,
human hands, were clasping mine. Overhead was
the vaulted roof of a tent, and around me faces were
clustering, faces unknown to me, perhaps, but still
human, and therefore more loveable than the
phantoms that had pursued me in my dreams.
Was I among men? I struggled to speak, but
sank back senseless. . . .

'Hal! Hal!'

It was Ned—dear old Ned. Had I been a
billion of miles off, that voice might have recalled me. As it was, I woke and sat up stupidly,
mechanically feeling the woollen counterpane, and
wondering, after the manner of inter-stellar travellers, what planet I was on, and what sun it was that
was giving me so feeble a light.

'The *Astrolabe!*' I murmured. 'Where are we?'

'Just what I should like to know, old man,' was

the answer. 'Your geographical knowledge ought to be able to aid us. I think we have fallen back on Venus.'

'Venus!' I exclaimed, 'and who are these men?'

'Two sailors from the *Astrolabe*,' replied Ned, 'whom the captain has seen fit to abandon with us.'

'Abandon?'

Life felt as though it were forsaking my cheeks. The word had an awful meaning. I struggled to sit upright and stared about me, shivering with cold.

No! we were certainly no longer on the *Astrolabe*. A rude tent, supported by primitive-looking wooden poles, sheltered us from the blast of a wind which we could hear howling outside, and the frail walls quaked under the violence of an Arctic gale—so it seemed at least.

'We've piled all the available blankets on top of you,' continued Ned, 'so there is no excuse for your being cold.'

'But the sun,' I said confusedly, 'the sun? How did we escape?'

'How? Oh! in the usual way. The comet saved us. You've been senseless for nearly a month—raving mad with fever. We had to tie you down. The captain lost four men, the rest lived to tell the tale.'

'Where is the *Astrolabe* now?'

'Devil only knows! Roaming about space, I suppose. We were drugged during our sleep, and, on awakening, found ourselves in this shanty, which I suppose the captain has erected for our benefit. The only question is about the identity of the planet. At first I thought he had abandoned us on some floating aerolite, but the level plains stretch away in all directions, and the whole thing seems to be too big for a mere rock. We've not seen the sun for over a week. Nothing but thick mist and fog. There's a perfect network of lakes and rivers, crossing and inter-crossing one another like railway lines in a junction.'

'Mars?' I suggested.

'We haven't seen the slightest trace of a human habitation,' was the answer. 'Much more likely to be Saturn.'

'Impossible!' I said. 'Saturn is hundreds of millions of miles off. We could never have done the distance in a month. What do the men say about it?'

'They know as little as we do. The captain mistrusted them, as he mistrusts everyone, confound him! And he plunged us all into one common misfortune. I wish the deuce you were well, Hal, you might help us out of the difficulty.'

I was silent. Ned's confidence in my powers was, I felt, hardly justifiable. The two men, on scrutinising carefully, I recognised as two of the *Astrolabe's* sailors, a short, thick-set, bull-dog individual, and his companion, a tall, lanky Swede, whom I had many times noticed in the steersman's cabin and elsewhere. Their greeting was a mute one. The silent pressure of those horny hands said more than a volume of eloquence.

Abandoned! Was it the gloomy spectre of Jacob Andersen, risen from his cold grave, that hovered across my dreams that night? or, was it but another of those fleeting shapes, conjured from that far-off world that was to know me no more?

On the following morning I was able to leave my couch. Sickening internal convulsions made me writhe in agony, and my lungs seemed oppressed under a leaden atmospheric weight, beneath which it seemed almost impossible to move or breathe. Where were we? How could the mystery be solved?

Around us, as far as the eye could reach, stretched a cold, barren, undulating plain, covered with frozen lichens, and grey, inhospitable mosses. Not a tree, not a house was visible. The sky overhead was of that leaden, ashy hue, common to northern latitudes. Towards evening, as it grew darker, a strange light broke out in the heavens, a perfect pyramid of pale fire seemed to be floating in space. The stars were invisible, and there was not a trace of a moon to be seen anywhere.

During the night, my strange malady returned, a thousand tons were pressing my head flat, and it required all my resolution to prevent myself screaming out in presence of this painfully subtle torture, that defied even explanation.

It was evident that we had fallen on the surface of some planet where the atmospheric conditions were unlike those we had hitherto been accustomed to. Should we survive? It seemed unlikely.

The ironical kindness of Captain Chlamyl had left us provisions enough to last for a week or ten days. The store was gradually drawing to an end, and it became really urgent to set about delivering ourselves if possible.

'We must strike to the south,' was Ned's verdict, 'these mists make everything impossible. Do you think you are able to walk, Hal?'

'I think so,' I answered, with a forced air of gaiety, though, indeed, my spirits were at a very low ebb. 'Have we got any arms?'

'None—except our knives.'

'That's a bad look-out. We may be massacred, or attacked by wild beasts. Anyhow I suppose we are fated to go over to the majority within a day or two. Shall we take the tent with us?'

'Certainly. Where would we be without it?'

There was no answering this question. It only remained to complete the preparations for our journey. The poles were tied together in a bundle, and entrusted to the muscular Swede. Ned carried the canvas covering, and I shared the remaining provisions with the other sailor of the *Astrolabe*. Neither of these men could speak a word of English, so our conversation had to be conducted by signs, of all methods the most inconvenient.

By midday (at least what the Martians might have called midday) we reached the first of the famous canals.

A sheet of glassy water, with a faint current, nearly five miles wide, on whose banks huge bulrushes waved solemnly. Was this fluid actually water? In my over-excited state I believe I dreamt of all manner of untold marvels, as I bent wonderingly down to carry some of it to my parched lips.

Yes—water. Neither petroleum, nor molten metal, nor liquid carbonic acid, nor any other planetary marvel. Merely ordinary terrestrial water. I almost experienced a disappointment.

We travelled all that day without reaching a sign of human habitation. By nightfall the pillar of fire again shone resplendently in the sky, but the clouds were too thick to enable us to distinguish its form. Our provisions were reduced down to enough for one day only. Ned and the two sailors made fruitless efforts to lay some of the water-fowl low with stones, but the birds were wary and the attempts only resulted in disappointment and vexation. Evidently the Martian representatives of our feathered tribes feared the approach of man—a curious thought, that made the blood run riot in my veins, struck me as Ned called my attention to this fact, and I strained my eyes out across the dreary expense of fog, then up at the pyramidal column of fire, without saying a word.

Next morning the far-off horizon, opposite to the strange celestial display, began to glow with an unknown scarlet light. A fiery ball of flame (was

it the sun?) rose slightly above the dark rim
of the marshes, and travelled round in a semi-circle,
without ever seeming to rise an inch higher towards
the zenith. We struck boldly out across the level,
occasionally sinking up to our ankles in soft green
moss, now pausing to inhale the fresh breeze which
seemed to carry with it an odour of aromatics.
Towards 4 p.m. Ned uttered a cry and pointed
ahead.

'Another canal!' he said.

He was right. We had struck a second desert of
water, similar to the first. They were the celebrated
double canals of Schiaparelli, with which my early
studies had made me familiar. Could it be that
Mars was really a deserted planet, or were we—
Ned guessed my thought, and, as usual, dashed it
brutally to the ground.

'There is no moon here,' he said, 'and Mars
ought to have two.'

True. The celebrated twin sisterhood Deimos
and Phobos were totally wanting in the sky.

As for the yellow pyramid of flame, it had completely vanished.

'What's to be done now?' said Ned.

'Continue along the canal,' I answered; 'we can't
possibly think of crossing it. I'm not even sure
that we can really proceed. I feel completely done
up. If we were on Mars, our bodies couldn't
possibly manage to weigh so much. I don't understand it.'

Ned hastened in with an explanation that was
logical enough.

'It is merely by contrast with the *Astrolabe*' he
said, and I was forced to be content.

The men collected firewood while I sat shivering
and miserable in my wet boots, trying to solve the
mystery of our whereabouts and falling back helpless against a wall of unheard-of wonders.

We drank several cups of boiling coffee to warm ourselves and fell to unpacking the tent for the night. Two hours later a new surprise awaited us.

'Hallo!' said Ned, 'the sun isn't going to set!'

Such was the case indeed. The red disc showed not the slightest sinking tendency. We watched it, doubled in the glassy water, till we fell asleep, and awoke to find it still shining in our eyes with its persistent red glare.

I may have dozed off shortly after, for I was awakened by Ned shaking me.

'A boat! Hal,' he said.

I started up. The rhythmic sound of splashing oars struck my ear and guided my eye to a moving object that was slowly approaching from the direction of the sun, gliding across the burning red trail like a meteor across the disc of a star. The babel of voices also struck my ear.

'They are men!' cried Ned.

Men! My blood froze as I noted the swarthy features, overgrown with hair, it seemed to me, and the fierce dark eyes of the rowers, whose panting breathing came distinctly to our ears. They were muffled from head to foot in shaggy skins, and the oars hissed under the powerful impulse of their arms. Were we going to be attacked? I saw Ned's right hand steal towards his knife, while with the left he grasped mine in silence. The two sailors, rudely awakened from sleep, stared stupidly before them, as though they had hardly had time to grasp the situation.

We were soon to know.

With a shout, the boat crashed into the yielding rushes of the bank, and, quick as thought, a score of muscular giants threw themselves on us. The gleam of weapons passed before our eyes—there was no resistance. We were pinioned, gagged, and thrown helpless into the bottom of the boat.

One sentence, several times repeated, sent a flood of light across my understanding, and, even as I felt myself disabled, a cry of joy burst from my lips.

'Yield! In the name of the Czar!'

We were back on our own world, captives banished by the Russian autocrat to the wilds of Siberia.

CHAPTER XXV

CONCLUSION

DURING the confusion of the next few days I had little time in which to brood over my misfortunes and their extraordinary ending.

Our supernatural journey through the realms of space was ended. What we had taken to be Martian phenomena were simply the familiar curiosities of our own northern hemisphere. The pyramidal cone of fire was the aurora borealis, the twin-canals of Schiaparelli dwindled down into the estuary of a Siberian river—the Petchora, the very sun which had perplexed us by its singular movements was the burning orb that had so nearly proved our grave a month back, seen from high latitudes, where it remained above the horizon for a month at a time.

Ned—for a moment stunned by the shock of finding himself once more on his native planet, soon recovered and produced evidence that at a later date produced our liberation from the hands of the Russian police. The mistake was a sufficiently awkward one. Some days before a party of convicts had escaped from the neighbouring mines, and were roaming unbridled over the steppes— the forces had been ordered out, and everywhere the unfortunates were being pitilessly pursued. Our primitive encampment, our lonely little tent on the wind-swept bank of the Petchora, had attracted attention, and given rise to the brutal assault that was nevertheless the means of saving all our lifes.

The mistake, easily discovered, was soon rectified, and the apologies of the governor may be more easily imagined than described. One thing was puzzling—how to explain our presence in Siberia. For deliverance from this predicament we had to thank Ned's fluency in the art of lying.

For a short half-hour he was closeted with the plethoric little governor of the station. At the end of that time both emerged, beaming, from their hiding-place. And we dined in state with the head jailor (as Ned called him) that very evening.

I could never really discover what the nature of my companion's falsehood was, for the story he related to me was bald and unconvincing enough. According to him we had left Stockholm for Archangel some months back and had been driven out of our course by erratic winds. The name of our vessel he never seems to have hinted at. On the whole Ned was a most satisfactory fellow to have about when there was any talking to be done, and, indeed, when I consider his generally vast sphere of utility, I am inclined almost to forgive him that little mutiny on board the *Astrolabe*.

And now my story is done. Will it bear telling? Shall I be believed, or laughed at? Nothing but time can answer that weighty question.

What has become of Captain Chlamyl? Did he soar away sunwards after leaving us on the banks of the Petchora, or did he bury himself once again in that black abyss of night where together we roamed for one whole year? Will his daring genius carry him beyond the very confines of the solar system, among those strange suns whose very life is an inscrutable mystery?

Everything here is left to conjecture. Is not even the very miracle that saved us from that embrace of fire, covered by a veil of darkness and sleep? · What power guided the lone ship through those dread watches of the night that seemed so near eternity? Was it human, or divine? Be that as it may, nothing save death can dim or mar the admiration and love that both of us feel for him whom we know to be the wisest man that ever lived.

His fate is a strange one—no man born of woman ever had a stranger. Like the great German Wagner whom he adored, he has penetrated beyond the confines of the visible world into a land of shadow and gaunt mystery, where hardly anything is real, save the light of his own overwhelming genius.

What a destiny will be his! To be merged in the depths of immensity, perhaps chasing in the wake of one of those flying fires to which we owe our lives, perhaps halting to circle round some unknown moon, whose deserted mountains dream incessantly in the dark starlight or under the rays of a fading sun—some lost dead planet whose plains are still haunted by the spectres of a million ancient races—on, on, into the void of an endless night, the vessel and its dead crew, into the regions of forgetfulness and sleep, into a shadowless eternity.

THE END

LONDON : DIGBY, LONG & CO., Publishers,
18 Bouverie Street, Fleet Street, E.C.

SUPPLEMENTARY LIST

DIGBY, LONG & Co.'s
NEW NOVELS, STORIES, Etc.

IN ONE VOLUME, Price 6s.

By J. E. Muddock.

WITHOUT FAITH OR FEAR.

The Story of a Soul. By the Author of "Stripped of the Tinsel," etc. Crown 8vo, cloth, 6s.—_Just out._

By Mrs Alice M. Diehl.

A WOMAN'S CROSS.

By the Author of "The Garden of Eden," "Passion's Puppets," "A Modern Helen." Crown 8vo, cloth, 6s.—_Just out._

By the Princess de Bourg.

THE AMERICAN HEIRESS.

Crown 8vo, cloth, 6s.—_Now Ready._

*** _Published simultaneously in London and New York_

Much has been said and written about the matrimonial alliances of Trans-atlantic girls with British Peers, and most erroneous ideas have been circulated as to what the typical native American girl really is. In these vivid, bright and eloquent pages we have in Kitty Fauntleroy a picture of the native American girl at her best, and how very charming she is ! The reader follows the fortunes of the beautiful, charming and sweet-tempered Kitty to the very end with breathless expectancy and that true sympathy which is roused only in fiction that is really based on human nature.

By Mrs Florence Severne.

THE DOWAGER'S DETERMINATION.

By the Author of "The Pillar House," "In the Meshes," etc. Crown 8vo, cloth, 6s.—_Nearly ready._

By Bertha M. M. Miniken.

AN ENGLISH WIFE.

Crown 8vo, cloth, 6s.—*Shortly.*

> In the life story of Alice Grey we have a series of genuine idylls of English country life. The heroine and her husband are charming studies, and since "John Halifax, Gentleman," perhaps nothing more beautiful has been delineated in fiction.

By Albert Hardy.

A CROWN OF GOLD.

Crown 8vo, cloth, 6s. With a frontispiece by the Author.—*Ready.*

> The story takes a strong hold on the reader, and it has no lack of sentiment and humour. It is highly dramatic throughout, and always keeps on moving to the end.

By Kathleen Behenna.

SIDARTHA.

An Original and Powerful Novel. Crown 8vo, cloth, 6s.—*Ready.*

> Since the days of Edgar Allen Poe, the enigma and the puzzle story, the subtly-concealed plot have had an increasing charm for readers. In this extraordinary conception we have a heroine who is weighed down by a secret that the most experienced novel reader could never guess, and a hero who is a model of chivalric devotion. The interest intensifies with each successive chapter, and is finally wrought up to an overpowering climax. Doris, the heroine, wins on the reader's heart with each page; the sombre passages are finely contrasted by sunny gleams of life as it is down South. It is quite impossible, once begun to lay down this fascinating novel unfinished.

By May St Claire (Mrs Gannaway Atkins).

A STORMY PAST.

Crown 8vo, cloth, 6s.—*Shortly.*

> For all who love romance this story of the descendants of an ancient West-country family will prove fascinating. All the interest of the tale centres around the heroine Miriam and her faithful lover Jack. The scene is partly laid in France, and quite a number of well discriminated characters pass across the many stirring scenes of "A Stormy Past." The tone of the story is exceptionally pure.

By David Worthington.

EQUAL SHARES.

Crown 8vo, cloth 6s.—*In December.*

> This romance is laid among the steep, wild hills and lovely valleys of Derbyshire, and pivots on the keen quest by some half-dozen eager competitors for a certain mysterious cave. A tender love story is interwoven with the fascinating narrative, and the reader is drawn on page by page as the tragic *dénouement* approaches.

By Reginald St Barbe.

FRANCESCA HALSTEAD. A Tale of San Remo.

Crown 8vo, cloth, 6s.—*In December.*

By Alfred Smythe.

A NEW FAUST. Crown 8vo, cloth, 6s.—*Ready end November.*

By John Francis Temple.

THE DICE OF THE GODS.

Crown 8vo, cloth, 6s.—*Second Edition.*

> This a novel which is cleverly conceived and vigorously written. The main problem is whether it is possible for a man to be thoroughly and earnestly in love with his wife at the same time that he entertains feelings of affection for another woman.

By Evan May.

MUCH IN A NAME.

By the Author of "Wanted—an Heiress," "The Greatest of These," etc. Crown 8vo, cloth, 6s.—*Second Edition.*

> "The interest is well sustained and absorbing throughout. This story will undoubtedly place Miss Evan May in the front rank of present-day writers of fiction. A tale of unflagging interest."—*Aberdeen Journal.*

By G. Beresford Fitzgerald.

AN ODD CAREER.

By the Author of "Clare Strong," "Lilian," etc. Crown 8vo, cloth, 6s.—*Third Edition.*

> "An eminently readable book, written in a pleasant, brisk style. The hero is a fine fellow, and the minor characters are carefully sketched and thoroughly consistent."—*Pall Mall Gazette.*

By Julian Harvey.

A MODERN SIREN.

Crown 8vo, cloth, 6s.—*Second Edition.*

> Lilith, the heroine of this novel, is in her way a creation, and, as the central character, excites intense curiosity. The story is absorbing, thrilling and tragic.

By J. E. Muddock.

STRIPPED OF THE TINSEL.

A Story of Bohemia. By the Author of "Without Faith or Fear," "The Star of Fortune," "Basile the Jester," etc., etc. Crown 8vo, cloth, 6s.—*Fourth Edition.*

> "It gives us peeps behind the scenes in the lives of actors and actresses, of lawyers, barristers and judges, of press men, of clergymen, of members of the Savage Club, of military men, and of ladies married and ladies unmarried. . . . Mr Muddock possesses a powerful pen, and 'Stripped of the Tinsel' should prove as great a success as any of his previous books."—*Western Daily Mercury.*

By Mrs John Procter.

AN OAK OF CHIVALRY.

Crown 8vo, cloth, 6s.—*In December.*

> Both hero and heroine engross the reader's warm sympathy from the opening chapter. The reader follows with increasing interest the ramifications of the plot through a series of vivid scenes.

By Maria English.

AS THE SHADOW OF A GREAT ROCK.

Crown 8vo, cloth, 6s.—*Second Edition.*

> " One of the best and most common-sense stories that has come under our notice, and illustrates something which, unhappily, is happening almost every day."—*Western Daily Mercury.*

By Fergus Hume.

THE MASQUERADE MYSTERY.

By the Author of " The Mystery of a Hansom Cab," etc. Crown 8vo, cloth, 6s.—*Third Edition.*

> "Is as good as, if not better than, 'The Mystery of a Hansom Cab.' It is an excellent story, and the mystery is one which will puzzle most readers to solve. One of the most readable fictions of the month."—*The World.*
> "Mr Hume contrives to mystify us to the very end of his story. . . . His brisk and breathless narrative."—*Athenæum.*

By Annie Thomas (Mrs PENDER CUDLIP).

A LOVER OF THE DAY.

By the Author of " False Pretences," etc. Crown 8vo, cloth, 6s.—*Second Edition.*

> " Is an exceedingly interesting and well-written book. The studies of character are of excellent quality. Another item to the long list of her (the authoress) successes."—*Punch.*

By Jean Middlemass.

HUSH MONEY.

By the Author of " The Mystery of Clement Dunraven," etc. Crown 8vo, cloth, 6s.—*Third Edition.*

> "The character limning is bold, vivid and powerful, and the plot evidences deft constructive art."—*Aberdeen Press.*

By Dora Russell.

A MAN'S PRIVILEGE.

By the Author of "A Hidden Chain," "The Other Bond," etc. Crown 8vo, cloth, 6s.—*Third Edition.*

> "An eminently readable novel. The writer has constructed the story with conspicuous literary skill, and it may be read without the skipping of a page."—*Scotsman.*

By Arabella Kenealy.

THE HONOURABLE MRS SPOOR.

By the Author of "Some Men are such Gentlemen," "Dr Janet of Harley Street," etc. Crown 8vo, cloth, 6s.—*Fourth Edition.*

> "Her latest novel has advanced her to the front rank of lady novelists."
> —*Black and White.*

By B. W. Ward, M.A.

SIR GEOFFREY DE SKEFFINGTON.

A Romance of the Crusades. Crown 8vo, cloth, 6s.—*Second Edition.*

> "A splendid story of the Crusaders, so fascinating indeed that it is difficult to lay it aside unfinished. It deals mainly with the same theme as Sir Walter Scott's 'Talisman,' and, notwithstanding our high regard for Sir Walter, we feel bound to say that many will prefer the later novel."—*Aberdeen Journal.*

By Leda Law.

AND THE WORLD SAITH?

Crown 8vo, cloth, 6s.—*Second Edition.*

> "An exceptionally able novel. It is painful as 'Tess of the D'Urbervilles' was painful, but it is indubitably, just as much as Mr Hardy's work, the Picture of a 'Pure Woman.' Miss Leda Law is bound to make her mark."
> —*Glasgow Herald.*

By Henry Maurice Hardinge.

WHAT WE ARE COMING TO.

A Powerful Up-to-date Novel. Crown 8vo, cloth, 6s.—*Second Edition*

> 'It is so cleverly written that it deserves to be widely read.' —*The Daily Telegraph.*

By F. Thorold Dickson and Mary L. Pechell.

A RULER OF IND.

An Anglo-Indian Novel. Crown 8vo, cloth, 6s.—*Second Edition.*

> "So much excellent description and knowledge of European life. The Authors have plenty of quiet humour that serves them well. The heroine is not only well drawn, but thoroughly up to date. . . . She is not only possible and probable, but charming. 'A Ruler of Ind' is a good bit of Anglo-Indian fiction, and an amusing book."—*The Standard.*
> "A very ably written story. Its highly sensational *dénouement* is excellently told."—*The Daily Telegraph.*

By W. F. Alexander.
THE COURT ADJOURNS.
Crown 8vo, cloth, 6s.—*Second Edition.*
> "The book holds and fascinates the reader from the start. . . . A plot which keeps us continually interested in the characters."—*Daily Chronicle.*

By Walter Sweetman, B.A.
ROLAND KYAN.
An Irish Sketch. By the Author of "Libertas," "Schoolfellows' Stories," etc. Crown 8vo, cloth, 6s.—*Second Edition.*
> "'Roland Kyan' is a high-souled Irishman. The portraiture is powerfully depicted. The story is elevating."—*Aberdeen Press.*

IN ONE VOLUME, Price 3s. 6d.

By Mrs E. Lynn Linton.
'TWIXT CUP AND LIP.
By the Author of "Patricia Kemball," etc. Crown 8vo, cloth, 3s. 6d. —*Second Edition.*

By Fergus Hume.
A MARRIAGE MYSTERY.
By the Author of "The Masquerade Mystery," etc. Crown 8vo, pictorial cloth, 3s. 6d.—*Ready.*

By Dr Gordon Stables, M.D., R.N.
THE ROSE OF ALLANDALE.
By the Author of "289 R: the Story of a Double Life," "The Mystery of a Millionaire's Grave," etc., etc. Crown 8vo, cloth, 3s. 6d.—*Just out.*

By A. E. Aldington.
THE QUEEN'S PREFERMENT.
A Historical Romance. With original Drawings by H. A. PAYNE. Crown 8vo, cloth, 3s. 6d.—*Just out.*
> A vivid picture of the Elizabethan Age, portraying characteristic scenes with the great Queen and a love idyll in the romantic neighbourhood of Warwick and Kenilworth. The vigour of that full-blooded period, its poetry and passion, is displayed in many of the original and deeply interesting incidents with which the book abounds.

By the Hon. Ernest Pomeroy.

SKETCHES FOR SCAMPS.

Crown 8vo, pictorial cloth, 3s. 6d.—*Just out.*

From the days of "Gil Blas" down to Charles Reade's "Autobiography of a Thief," the scamp has been (let purists say what they will) a highly interesting figure whenever introduced into literature. In these light and airy sketches, the writer has struck out some rather novel sources of interest, and in his satire, irony and humour, he is often original. It is a volume that can be taken up at any point, and from cover to cover it is certainly, in an intense degree, level with the times.

By Norman R. Byers.

A DOUBTFUL LOSS.

Crown 8vo, cloth, 3s. 6d.—*Just out.*

The story of the heroine keeps the reader on the stretch as it is unfolded, and while every page is instinct with life, the interest ever intensifies to the very close. Rarely has a novelist succeeded so well in completely baffling all attempts to anticipate the end of what is a charming tale of contemporary English life.

By Edwin Pallander.

ACROSS THE ZODIAC.

A Story of Adventure. In pictorial cloth, with a Frontispiece, crown 8vo, 3s. 6d.—*Just out.*

The interest intensifies from page to page, and holds the reader spell-bound until the very last line. Incident succeeds incident with startling rapidity, each being more marvellous than its predecessor. The closing catastrophe is probably the most daring and splendid achievement yet made in fiction of this class.

By Edgar D. C. Bolland.

DOROTHY LUCAS.

Crown 8vo, cloth, 3s. 6d.—*Just out.*

Dorothy Lucas is the surpassingly lovely heroine of a very thrilling love story. She goes through a series of extraordinary trials and terrible temptations, simply through according an artist permission to sketch her fair face while travelling by railway. Some of the episodes keep the reader in breathless expectancy.

By Fred Holmes, M.A.

A MAN AMONGST MEN.

Dedicated to Human Society. Crown 8vo, cloth, 3s. 6d.—*Ready.*

Opening in the idyllic peace of a typical rural parsonage, the reader is introduced to the hero of this interesting story of clerical life, George Jinkinson. The work is remarkable for its many daring questionings.

By an Exponent.

CHRYSTAL, THE NEWEST OF WOMEN.

Crown 8vo, cloth, 3s. 6d.—*Third Edition.*

Chrystal, with her many questionings, her high courage, her candour, her truthfulness, and her quaint originality, is charming. Rarely, if ever, has such a close analysis of a child's character, and that child a girl, been given.

By Mrs Lodge.
THE MYSTERY OF BLOOMSBURY CRESCENT.
Crown 8vo, cloth, 3s. 6d.—*Second Edition.*

This is a cleverly-written and most entertaining book, full of incident, with just enough of mystery to rivet the reader's attention until the last page is reached. The author has depicted several phases of London life with the utmost truth and fidelity.

By Mrs Robert Jocelyn.
JUANITA CARRINGTON.
A Sporting Novel. By the Author of "Drawn Blank," etc., etc. Crown 8vo, cloth, 3s. 6d.—*Third Edition.*

"Mrs Robert Jocelyn is the pet novelist of the sporting person. Mrs Jocelyn is always bright and entertaining, and describes a run with the hounds better than any novelist we have had since Whyte Melville."—*The Star.*

Grant Allen's Successful Book.
THE DESIRE OF THE EYES.
By the Author of "The Woman Who Did," etc. Crown 8vo, cloth, 3s. 6d.—*Eighth Edition.*

By Robert Cromie.
THE CRACK OF DOOM.
By the Author of "A Plunge into Space," "The Next Crusade," etc. Crown 8vo, cloth, 3s. 6d.—*Fourth Edition.*

Mr GLADSTONE writes:—"I am reading the book with interest."
"It has a capital plot, which is admirably developed. The author has not only struck a vein of fiction rich and rare, but he has demonstrated his ability to work it."—*Black and White.*

By Henry Coxwell.
A KNIGHT OF THE AIR.
By the Author of "My Life and Balloon Experiences," etc. Crown 8vo, pictorial cloth, with Frontispiece, 3s. 6d.

"Full of bustle and activity of all kinds, and it is literally true that there is not a dull page from beginning to end."—*Academy.*

By "Mac."
THE LEADIN' ROAD TO DONEGAL.
Crown 8vo, cloth, 3s. 6d.—*Second Edition.*

"These are delightful examples of the Donegal peasants' unconscious humour. The wit and the brogue are admirably rendered. 'The Leadin' Road' is very good, and so too is 'Dinny Monaghan's Last Keg.' 'Barney Boddy's Penance' is one of the most amusing things we have read for a long time. We recommend these stories to the lovers of Irish humour."—*The Spectator.*

By Mary Anderson.
A SON OF NOAH.
By the Author of "Othello's Occupation." Crown 8vo, cloth, 3s. 6d.—*Fifth Edition.*

By Mrs George Martyn.

WORSE THAN A CRIME.

By the Author of "A Liberal Education." Crown 8vo, cloth, 3s. 6d.
—*Second Edition.*

"Mrs George Martyn's new novel is thoroughly good, and she tells her love story as charmingly as ever."—*Leeds Mercury.*

By Zero.

A GENTLEMAN OF THE NINETEENTH CENTURY.

Crown 8vo, cloth, 3s. 6d.

"Unfortunately for the reader there are but two stories in this book—the one giving the title to the volume, and the other 'An Anachronism.' Both are beautifully expressed, the latter being even better than the former. It is a long time since we have read such stories of pathos and real feeling."—*Pall Mall Gazette.*

IN ONE VOLUME, Price 2s. 6d.

By W. Carter Platts.

THE TUTTLEBURY TALES.

By the Angling Editor of the "Yorkshire Weekly Post." Crown 8vo, pictorial cloth, 2s. 6d.—*Just out.*

This book is highly creative of mirth, being decidedly nimble-witted, jocose, droll, ludicrous, funny, and irresistibly comic. Mr Tuttlebury and his good wife are intensely entertaining. Every page provokes mirth, and as good taste is never sacrificed for the sake of a joke, these sketches are sure to be universally welcome.

By Joseph Ashton.

INMATES OF THE MANSION.

Crown 8vo, cloth, 2s. 6d. Beautifully illustrated.—*Just out.*

This new conceived and carefully worked out allegory of human life, its trials, sorrows, temptations, together with its joys and triumphs, should charm all readers—young and old. It should rank high among the allegories of the century.

By Chieton Chalmers.

THE INSEPARABLES.

A Book for Boys. Crown 8vo, pictorial cloth, fully illustrated, 2s. 6d. —*Just out.*

By Nemo.

A MERE PUG. The Romance of a Dog. Crown 8vo, pictorial cloth, 2s. 6d.—*Just out.*

Since "Puck," by Ouida, nothing like this book has appeared. It is not, however, anything of an imitation, but an original variant, and the central idea of the dog-hero becoming the Toby of a "Punch and Judy" show is thoroughly well worked out. There is a charming child-heroine in little Nan, whose fortunes the readers follow with keen interest.

⤳ Digby's Popular Novel Series ⤳

In Crown 8vo, price 2s. 6d. per Vol. Each book contains about 320 pp., printed on superior paper, from new type, and bound in uniform handsome cloth, gilt lettered. These novels have met with marked success in the more expensive form.

Those marked with an * may be had in picture boards at 2s.

By Arabella Kenealy.

* SOME MEN ARE SUCH GENTLEMEN.—*Fifth Edition.*

"The story is so brightly written that our interest is never allowed to flag. The heroine, Lois Clinton, is sweet and womanly. . . . The tale is told with spirit and vivacity, and shows no little skill in its descriptive passages."—*Academy.*

* DR JANET OF HARLEY STREET.—*Seventh Edition.*

"It is a clever book, and well worth reading. Miss Kenealy has imagined an interesting character, and realised her vividly."—*Daily Chronicle.*

By Florence Marryat.

THE BEAUTIFUL SOUL.—*Second Edition.*

"We read the book with real pleasure and interest. . . . In Felicia Hetherington, Miss Marryat has drawn a really fine character, and has given her what she claims for her in the title—a beautiful soul."—*Guardian.*

By Dora Russell.

THE OTHER BOND.—*Second Edition.*

"Miss Russell writes easily and well, and she has the gift of making her characters describe themselves by their dialogue, which is bright and natural."—*Athenæum.*

* A HIDDEN CHAIN.—*Third Edition.*

"Intensely interesting, the excitement of the reader being sustained from start to finish."—*Sheffield Daily Telegraph.*

By L. T. Meade.

A LIFE FOR A LOVE.—*Second Edition.*

"This thrilling tale. The plot is worked out with remarkable ingenuity. The book abounds in clever and graphic characterisation."—*Daily Telegraph.*

By Jean Middlemass.

* THE MYSTERY OF CLEMENT DUNRAVEN.

"Distinctly good reading. Rivets all one's interests, as do very few of the plotless and slipshod novels of this generation."—*St James's Gazette.*

DIGBY'S POPULAR NOVEL SERIES—*continued.*

By Hume Nisbet.

THE JOLLY ROGER. Illustrated by Author.—*Fifth Edition.*

"Sorcery and the sea are deftly combined. Since Captain Marryat's impressive story of Vanderdecken and the fair Amine, these elements have never been handled as in Mr Nisbet's brilliant romance of Elizabethan times."—*Saturday Review.*

HER LOVING SLAVE.—*Second Edition.*

"Has abundance of go in it."—*The Times.*
"It is a good story well told."—*The Standard.*

By Annie Thomas.

FALSE PRETENCES.—*Second Edition*

"Miss Annie Thomas has rarely drawn a character so cleverly as that of the false and scheming Mrs Colraine."—*World.*

By Hilton Hill.

* **HIS EGYPTIAN WIFE.** Picture boards only.—*Seventh Edition.*

"The book is full of movement and episode, the attention never allowed to flag; while the introduction of an extremely funny female American journalist, Miss Nelly Shy, whose curiosity is insatiable, and whose enterprise is all-conquering . . . a thoroughly readable volume."—*Daily Telegraph.*

** *Other Works in the same Series in due course.*

IN ONE VOLUME, Price 1s. 6d.

By Hillary Deccan.

WHERE BILLOWS BREAK.

By the Author of " Light in the Offing." Crown 8vo, cloth, 1s. 6d.—
Just out.

By Aldyth Ingram.

SMIRCHED.

Crown 8vo, cloth, 1s. 6d.—*Just out.*

Mildred Grantham, the heroine, is in some respects rather a new study in
womanhood. The book contains much on the subject of Art and on the
struggle of artists, while in the heroine there is a pretty and charming study
of a wilful but lovable girl.

By F. H. Hudson.

THE VAGARIES OF LOVE.

Crown 8vo, cloth, 1s. 6d.—*Shortly.*

Dr Henry George, the young physician, is an interesting transcript from
contemporary medical life, and generally " The Vagaries of Love " carry the
reader far and fast into not a few thrilling scenes that are life-like in their
dramatic power and vivid colouring. One scene in particular is like an
excerpt from Sardou himself, and would not discredit that master of the
Comedy that is so close akin to Tragedy itself.

By Violet Tweedale.

UNSOLVED MYSTERIES.

By the Author of " In Lothian's Fields," etc. Crown 8vo, cloth,
1s. 6d.—*Second Edition.*

By Leonard Hawke.

WHERE THE WATERS EBB AND FLOW.

Crown 8vo, cloth, 1s. 6d.

" Excellent and thrilling. The book should find a large circle of readers. —
Aberdeen Journal.

By Gratiana Darrell.

THE HAUNTED LOOKING GLASS.

Crown 8vo, cloth, 1s. 6d.—*In December.*

Is in some respects a new study in the anatomy of horror. Interwoven
with the tale of the terrible is a charming idyll of love at first sight. Those
who begin this weird romance will not lay it down unfinished.

Roof Roofer's Sensational Novels

Price 1s. each; Post free, 1s. 2d.

LOVE ONLY LENT.
THE TWIN DIANAS.
TWO MOTHERS OF ONE.
PRETTYBAD ROGERS.

❧ Miscellaneous ❧

A BEAUTIFUL GIFT BOOK.

WIT, WISDOM AND FOLLY. Pen and Pencil Flashes. **By J. Villin Marmery.** Author of "Progress of Science," "Manual of the History of Art," etc. With 100 Original Illustrations by ALFRED TOUCHEMOLIN, Author of "Strasbourg Militaire." Demy 8vo, superior binding, 6s.

An *Edition de Luxe,* limited to 100 copies, will be issued, price 21s. net.—*Ready about mid November.*

New Work by Caroline Gearey.

TWO FRENCH QUEENS.

Elizabeth of Valois—Marguerite of Valois. By the Author of "In Other Lands," "Three Empresses." With Portraits, crown 8vo, cloth, 6s.—*Shortly.*

A BOOK FOR THE STUDENT.

IS NATURAL SELECTION THE CREATOR OF SPECIES? **By Duncan Graham.** Crown 8vo, cloth, 6s.—*Shortly.*

This work is a library of reference on the most controversial subjects of the day, and in it Darwin and his theories are analytically tested, and the whole of the teleological argument is set forth with much lucidity. The merit of this work is that it is a compendium of the subject of Evolution, and in itself a small theological encyclopædia made popular.

New Work by the Author of "Roland Kyan."

THE REIGN OF PERFECTION. Letters on a Liberal Catholic Philosophy. **By Walter Sweetman, B.A.** Crown 8vo, cloth 3s. 6d. net.—*Now ready.*

> "The book is ingenious and clever, the spirit of it is admirable, and its temper calm and sweet throughout. . . . The book is certainly significant, while, outside the region of contentious subjects, its intellectual and spiritual merits will command wide sympathy and appeciation."—*Bradford Observer.*

By G. A. Sekon.

A HISTORY OF THE GREAT WESTERN RAILWAY FROM ITS INCEPTION TO THE PRESENT TIME.

Revised by F. G. SAUNDERS, Chairman of the Great Western Railway. Demy 8vo, 390 pages, cloth, 7s. 6d. With numerous Illustrations.—*Second Edition.*

> "Mr Sekon's volume is full of interest, and constitutes an important chapter in the history of railway development in England."—*The Times.*

By Percy Russell.

THE AUTHOR'S MANUAL.

With Prefatory Remarks by Mr GLADSTONE. Crown 8vo, cloth, 3s. 6d. net. (*Eighth and Cheaper Edition.*) With Portrait.

> ". . . Mr Russell's book is a very complete manual and guide for journalist and author. It is not a merely practical work—it is literary and appreciative of literature in its best sense; . . . we have little else but praise for the volume."—*Westminster Review.*

By THE SAME.

A GUIDE TO BRITISH AND AMERICAN NOVELS.

From the Earliest Period to the end of 1894. By the Author of "The Author's Manual," etc. Crown 8vo, cloth, 3s. 6d. net.—*Second Edition carefully revised.*

> "Mr Russell's familiarity with every form of novel is amazing, and his summaries of plots and comments thereon are as brief and lucid as they are various."—*Spectator.*

By Robert Woolward ("Old Woolward").

IGH ON SIXTY YEARS AT SEA.

Crown 8vo, cloth, 6s. With Portrait.—*Second Edition.*

> "Very entertaining reading. Captain Woolward writes sensibly and straight-forwardly, and tells his story with the frankness of an old salt. He has a keen sense of humour, and his stories are endless and very entertaining."— *The Times.*

By John Bradshaw.

NORWAY, ITS FJORDS, FJELDS AND FOSSES.

Crown 8vo, pictorial cloth, 3s. 6d.

> "A book which every tourist may well buy.' —*Daily Chronicle.*
> "The work is much more than a guide book, and it is certainly that and an excellent one. It is a history as well of the country, and contains a series of admirably arranged tours."—*Leeds Mercury.*

By Josiah Crooklands.

THE ITALIANS OF TO-DAY.

Translated from the French of RENÉ BAZIN. Crown 8vo, cloth, 3s. 6d.

> "By those who would study more closely the political and social aspects of Italian life to-day, Mr Crooklands's translation should be accorded a hearty welcome and an attentive perusal.'—*Public Opinion.*
> "M. René Bazin is a writer whose style we have often praised."—*The Athenæum.*

By William F. Regan.

BOER AND UITLANDER.

The True History of Late Events in South Africa. Crown 8vo, cloth, 3s. 6d. With Copyright Portraits, Map, etc.—*Fourth Edition.*

> Mr GLADSTONE writes:—"I thank you very much for your work, and rejoice that by means of it public attention will be called to all the circumstances connected with the origin and history of the Transvaal, which possess so strong a claim upon our equitable consideration."
> "The writer should be able to speak with authority, for he is none other than Mr W. F. Regan, the well-known South African financier, whose name has been a good deal before the public in connection with the events following upon the 'Raid.'"—*Glasgow Herald.*

By Andrew Deir.

A MAN IN THE FJORDS.

By the Author of "When a Maiden Marries," "The Girl in White," etc. With Eight Illustrations. Crown 8vo, pictorial cloth, 3s. 6d. —*Fourth Edition.*

❧ Poetry and the Drama ❧

By Kathleen Behenna.

THE HISTORY OF A SOUL.
By the Author of "Sidartha." Demy 8vo, artistic cloth, gilt edges,
5s. net.—*Dec. 1st.*

By Cecilia Elizabeth Meetkerke.

**FRAGMENTS FROM VICTOR HUGO'S LEGENDS AND
LYRICS.**—Crown 8vo, cloth, 7s. 6d.
"The most admirable rendering of French poetry into English that has
come to our knowledge since Father Prout's translation of 'La Chant du
Cosaque.'"—*World.*

By C. Potter.

CANTOS FROM THE DIVINA COMMEDIA OF DANTE.
Translated into English Verse. Crown 8vo, cloth, 5s. net.

By Lily Overington.

RANDOM RHYMES AND CHRISTMAS CHIMES.
Crown 8vo, cloth, 5s net.
"Every page is readable."—*Scotsman.*
"A collection from which a reader may extract genuine pleasure. Several
items are marked by beauty, finish and thought.'—*Liverpool Post.*

By Henry Osborne, M.A.

THE PALACE OF DELIGHTS AND OTHER POEMS.
Crown 8vo, cloth, 3s. 6d. net.

By the late Ernest G. Henty and E. A. Starkey.

AUSTRALIAN IDYLLS AND BUSH RHYMES.
Crown 8vo, cloth, 3s. 6d. net.—*Shortly.*

By Leonard Williams.

BALLADS AND SONGS OF SPAIN.—Crown 8vo, cloth,
3s. 6d. net.—*Just out.*

By E. Derry.

**SOPHONISBA; OR, THE PRISONER OF ALBA AND
OTHER POEMS.**—By the Author of "Lays of the Scottish High-
lands." Crown 8vo, cloth, 3s. 6d. net.—*Just out.*

By Marinell.

THE MAID'S LAST MORN.—Foolscap 8vo, Art Linen, 1s. 6d. net
"The Maid is Joan of Arc, and the poem is one which can be read with
pleasure and praised with sincerity."—*Nottingham Guardian.*

** *A complete Catalogue of Novels, Travels, Biographies, Poems,
with a critical or descriptive notice of each, free by post on application.*

LONDON: DIGBY, LONG & CO., Publisher
18 Bouverie Street, Fleet Street,